The
Love Elixir
of
Augusta Stern

The
Love Elixir
of
Augusta Stern

A NOVEL

Lynda Cohen Loigman

ST. MARTIN'S PRESS
NEW YORK

First published in the United States by St. Martin's Press,
an imprint of St. Martin's Publishing Group

THE LOVE ELIXIR OF AUGUSTA STERN. Copyright © 2024 by Lynda Cohen Loigman. All rights reserved. Printed in the United States of America. For information, address St. Martin's Publishing Group, 120 Broadway, New York, NY 10271.

ISBN 978-1-250-27810-4

In loving memory of my father, Harris Cohen, and my father-in-law, Barry Loigman

When you are old and grey and full of sleep,
And nodding by the fire, take down this book,
And slowly read, and dream of the soft look
Your eyes had once, and of their shadows deep;

How many loved your moments of glad grace,
And loved your beauty with love false or true,
But one man loved the pilgrim soul in you,
And loved the sorrows of your changing face....

—William Butler Yeats, "When You Are Old"

ONE

JUNE 1987

Augusta Stern did not want to retire. She had no interest in learning to knit, studying a new language, or filling her plate at some overcrowded cruise ship buffet. She did not want to "slow down," take "time for herself," or surrender to any other nonsensical euphemism designed to make her feel better about being made to give up the work she'd been doing for most of her life.

The first mention of Augusta's retirement had come from the hospital administration five years ago; the second, two years after that. But this time, it was more than a mention. This time, Augusta had been summoned directly by the hospital's new director of human resources—a man far more competent and precise than his sluggish predecessor. Mr. Willard's office was small but tidy and smelled pleasantly of Lemon Pledge. After gesturing to the hulking device on his desk that Augusta recognized as a computer, he explained how he had been tasked by the head of the hospital's administration to modernize the workings of his department. "We're putting all employee records on a new network. Soon our paperwork will be entirely electronic."

Augusta stared at the computer between them, wondering what any of this had to do with her. "Fascinating," she replied.

"It is," the balding director agreed. "Though it requires a good deal of data entry work. Take, for example, the pharmacy department, of which you are an illustrious member. Even as we speak, the members of my staff are typing the personal information of every pharmacist into our new database."

When Augusta failed to respond, Mr. Willard continued. "Tedious stuff," he admitted. "Unfortunately, the process has necessitated a close review of the records—dates of licensure, birth dates, et cetera—for each and every employee. In cases where *irregularities* have been identified, my staff has been forced to make further inquiries to ensure accuracy going forward."

Augusta forced herself to look him in the eye. "How admirable," she said. She curved her lips into a smile, but she could feel her heart racing in the back of her throat.

"I'm glad you approve," Mr. Willard said. "Of course this transition marks a significant shift from our past way of doing things." He glanced at a folder on his desk that bore Augusta's first and last name. "I see from your records that you've worked at this hospital for a little over fifteen years."

"That's correct," Augusta said.

"And according to your employee questionnaire, you'll be turning seventy this fall?"

Augusta willed her cheeks not to redden. "Yes," she murmured. "Seventy years old. On October third."

"You have been a very valuable member of this institution, Ms. Stern. It's not my intention to coerce you in any way, but given your approaching milestone birthday, I was wondering whether you might be reconsidering retirement?"

For the briefest of moments, Augusta closed her eyes. The answer to the question came to her slowly, like a malted milk shake through a too-narrow straw. It pained her to say the words out loud, but she knew she did not have a choice. In the most respectful manner possible, Mr. Willard was telling her what she already knew: the dates in her paperwork did not add up.

With all the confidence she could muster, Augusta proffered her reply.

"In fact, I am," she announced. "I've decided to retire at the end of the month."

If Augusta was to face the end of her career, she was determined to do so with her dignity intact.

On Augusta's last day of work, she dressed with even more care than usual. Thanks to a lifetime of healthy eating, daily exercise, and the diligent application of Pond's Cold Cream, her skin was still a wholesome pink. Her hair had been freshly colored for the occasion. From her closet, she chose a timeless white blouse, a blue cashmere cardigan, and a pair of low pumps that her niece had selected. "Frumpy shoes really age a person," Jackie always said. "That and the wrong color lipstick."

At the pharmacy department's farewell party, Augusta accepted a piece of cake and a glass of cheap sparkling wine. Several of the pharmacists made heartfelt toasts, along with a few of the nurses. When they asked about her future plans, she told them she was moving to Florida in September. Her niece had found her a two-bedroom condo in a small retirement community called Rallentando Springs.

"That sounds wonderful," they told her. "All that sunshine—you're going to love it!" Augusta pretended to agree, but inside, she was not convinced.

At the end of the party, Mr. Willard asked for her forwarding address. Several people swore to keep in touch, but it was only the director who made good on his promise.

At the beginning of September, when Augusta got to Florida, a small bundle of mail was waiting for her, including a statement from her new bank and a greeting card postmarked from New York. The inside of the card was inscribed with a message penned neatly in navy ink. "Dear Ms. Stern," the inscription read. "I wish you the best of luck in Florida. Please also accept my warmest wishes for a very happy *eightieth* birthday."

Augusta tossed the card in the trash. Her birthday wasn't for a month yet. Did he really have to rub it in?

~⁊⊚⊃~

The first night she spent in her new condo, Augusta felt an unfamiliar flutter of nerves. The move had exhausted her physically, but her mind was restless, and when sleep would not come, she searched through the cardboard boxes in her living room until she found her father's battered copy of the *U.S. Pharmacopeia*. There were several more recent editions, of course, but she liked the way the old book felt—thick and heavy in her hands. It was the book she had used in pharmacy college, and though she had committed much of it to memory, it soothed her to see the catalogue of drugs, their effects, descriptions, and dosages in print. She whispered their names like the names of old friends, and they kept her loneliness at bay.

After a quick bowl of cereal the next morning, she dug out the first swimsuit she could find and walked to the Rallentando pool. A glossy photograph of this azure oasis had featured prominently in the Rallentando Springs brochure—the one Augusta's niece, Jackie, had foisted upon her several months ago.

In New York, Augusta swam three times a week at an indoor swimming pool run by the city's Department of Parks and Recreation. She did not much like the chemical smell, the chilly locker room, or the thin, scratchy towels provided by the sour-faced attendant. Still, she enjoyed the activity itself—the propelling of her arms and legs through the water, the peace that came to her when her body was busy and her mind was free to wander at will. It was good for her; it kept her strong. She reasoned that the towels and the stench of chlorine were a small price to pay for such obvious benefits.

Augusta's niece knew that her aunt always dreamed of having a swimming pool of her own. Of course the Rallentando pool wouldn't be *hers*—it was for all of the residents to enjoy. But it was only a brief walk from Augusta's apartment, and she could use it whenever she liked. She could swim or read or order her lunch from the cute little snack bar set off to the side. These were a few of the features her niece had used to argue for Rallentando's appeal. But when Augusta arrived at the pool that morning, she discovered what was perhaps the best feature of all: piles of neatly folded towels—thick, sweet-smelling, and marvelously soft.

Although the pool looked slightly smaller than in the photo, the water was clear, the patio well-kept, and the perimeter peppered with comfortable lounge chairs, wrought-iron café tables, and cheerfully striped yellow-and-white umbrellas.

There were only six people in the pool area when Augusta arrived—two men and a quartet of women playing canasta in the shade. When Augusta walked by, the men didn't bother to look up from the books they were reading. The women were too engrossed in their game to notice the new resident among them. Augusta did not mind in the least. After leaving her towel and her tote bag on one of the chairs, she tucked her hair up into her swim cap, pulled on her goggles, and slipped quietly into the water.

Back in New York, the pool teemed with swimmers, but here, she had every lane to herself. Here, there were no splashing toddlers, no shouting mothers, no other distractions. Lap by lap, Augusta swam forward, her heart pumping contentedly in her chest. Thirty minutes later, when she emerged, her face was flushed with satisfaction. She removed her goggles, pulled off her swim cap, and let the morning sun warm her skin. In the time it had taken to complete her workout, several of the empty lounge chairs had been filled. She walked the perimeter of the pool, trying to remember where she'd left her towel.

She had just spotted her sandals and bag on a chair when she heard a man calling to her from behind. "Goldie!" said the voice. "Is that you?"

Augusta froze solidly in place. Despite the heat and the sunshine, she shivered visibly in her swimsuit. *Goldie?* She hadn't allowed anyone to call her that for more than sixty years.

Impossible, she told herself.

When she didn't answer, the man spoke again. "Goldie? Goldie Stern?"

The voice was rough and much too loud, causing the other pool-goers to stare. Augusta felt all their eyes upon her as they looked up from their books and magazines. Even the women in the shade paused their card game to squint at the newcomer. There was nowhere now for Augusta to hide, nothing to do but turn around. Half-naked and on display, she felt like a cheap music box ballerina, forced into a clumsy spin.

"It *is* you, Goldie!" the man bellowed. "I'd know that *tuchus* anywhere!"

He stood in the same direction as the sun, so it took a moment for her eyes to adjust. Bit by bit, he came into focus: gray-haired and shirtless, still broad-shouldered, but now with a prominent potbelly that was slick with sunscreen and impossibly tan. .

Before she could protest, he embraced her, pressing his naked, oily torso against her thinly covered flesh. She tried to extricate herself, to put some physical distance between them, but his arms were stronger than she remembered. While keeping one hand around her waist, he removed his sunglasses with the other.

However much the rest of him had aged, his eyes, at least, were the same—heavy-lidded, naproxen blue, full of timeless boyish mischief.

"It's *me*," he said, as if she didn't know. "Irving Rivkin. Remember?"

The last time she'd seen him, she was eighteen years old—young and trusting and deeply in love. She was none of those things now. She removed his hand, took two steps back, and crossed her arms over her damp chest.

"Of course I remember," she snapped.

"I thought you said you'd never leave New York."

"And I thought you'd be dead by now."

He threw his head back and barked out a laugh. "Still as sharp as ever," he said. "What brings you to Rallentando Springs?"

"I moved here yesterday," said Augusta. The whisper of panic in her head grew louder. "Don't tell me you live here, too?"

The smile he gave transported her back to the first day they met in her father's drugstore—back to a time when her heart was still soft, like overripe fruit left out in the sun. Back to when lines were still blurry, hope was abundant, and love did not seem so far out of reach.

Irving Rivkin winked at her slyly. "You'd better believe it," he said.

TWO

JUNE 1922

Growing up in the apartment above her father's drugstore meant that Augusta Stern was bound from childhood to the world of the shop below. As a baby, she was mesmerized by the show globe in the window—an antique glass pendant filled with emerald-green liquid that hung from the ceiling on a shiny brass chain. Her favorite sound was the bell on the door that chimed whenever a customer entered. Not only did she take her very first steps in the aisle between the Listerine and the St. Joseph's Worm Syrup, but when, as a nearly mute eighteen-month-old, she slipped and fell headfirst into the display of McKesson & Robbins Cold and Grippe Tablets, family lore had it that the first word she spoke was not *Mama, Papa,* or *boo-boo,* but *aspirin.*

Every person within a half-mile radius of the corner of Sackman Street and Sutter Avenue knew Solomon Stern and Stern's Pharmacy. They sought his advice regarding every kind of ailment—from fevers, coughs, and constipation to insomnia and skin infections. They wandered into his shop from the delicatessen next door to ask what to take for their upset stomachs. They carried their screaming children to him directly from the playground down the block because he could disinfect a bloody knee with iodine faster than any doctor in town.

Not only was Augusta's father a skillful practitioner, he was also a thoughtful listener. To his customers, he was priest and rabbi, social worker and secret keeper. The precision with which he formulated his treatments—whether pills or powders, creams or tinctures—was lauded by everyone in the neighborhood. His medicines made everyone well.

Everyone except for Augusta's mother.

Irene Stern developed diabetes at the age of thirty-seven, when Augusta was only twelve years old. She saw all the specialists there were to see, but there was no medication available to help. When the doctor first made his diagnosis, Irene knew what lay ahead. She did not rail against her fate but set about making the two years she had left as pleasant as possible for her daughters. Even in her final weeks—starved to a bony, fragile shell—Irene was a calm and easy light, devoid of any bitterness. In the end, she simply floated away, like a blue balloon in a cloudless sky that, once set free, rises up, up, up until it vanishes entirely into the ether.

Augusta did not inherit her mother's patience or her predilection for acceptance. Her early upbringing among the boxes and bottles of her father's windowless prescription room had led her to believe that for every ailment, there was a certain cure. All it took was the proper formula and the right ingredients to concoct what was needed. In the wake of her mother's death, however, Augusta was forced for the first time to consider that medicine had its limitations. Her fourteen-year-old body vibrated with ceaseless outrage. How could she have been so misled?

And then, not long after Irene Stern passed, the first injection of a new diabetes medication called insulin was successfully administered to a boy in Canada. Before her mother was diagnosed, Augusta had never heard of diabetes. And now—now that her mother was lost—the newspapers were suddenly full of stories of people who had the same disease. Except that *those* people were being saved—not because they were smarter or more worthy, but simply because they had better timing. As it turned out, Augusta had not been misled. The scientists and doctors had simply been slow.

Augusta was happy the boy lived, of course, but as a motherless adolescent girl, she ached at the unfairness of it all. Irene Stern had been funny and kind. She had sung her daughters lullabies before bed every night. She had drawn them silly pictures and braided their hair. She had taken them to Coney Island to swim—instructing Bess, her elder daughter, to raise her arms high and reminding Augusta to lift her head and breathe. Irene continued to sing and braid and swim for as long as her body allowed, but in the end, she could not survive the storm her illness had become. Meanwhile, people like the Canadian boy skipped through the very same deluge as if it were barely a drizzle.

When Augusta fumed over the injustice, Bess reminded her of their mother's last moments. "Mama didn't want us to be angry," Bess said. "She would have been pleased that the drug was helping to make people well."

Augusta knew her sister was right, but that didn't make the articles any easier to read. Their father explained that insulin wasn't exactly a drug, but some sort of biological substance that their mother's body had failed to produce. Whatever it was, it was saving people's lives. Pharmacies like her father's did not stock it yet, but Solomon Stern assured his daughters that one day, very soon, they would.

His pronouncement was made with hope and awe, braided with a bitterness that Augusta recognized as identical to her own.

Most days, immediately after school, both Augusta and Bess reported for work at their father's store. They navigated the crowds on the avenues—past the stores selling men's suits and women's hats; past the banks and the cobblers and the stationery shops; past the carcasses that hung like so many trophies in the kosher butcher's windows. Wherever they walked, the sidewalks were packed. The Sterns had moved to Brownsville from the Lower East Side immediately after Bess was born—a move made by those who were lucky enough to afford bigger homes, brighter light, and better air. But every year Brownsville grew shabbier and more crowded, more like the place they had left behind.

When the girls got to Stern's Pharmacy on the corner, with its window displays of bottles and brushes and its red-and-white Coca-Cola sign, they remembered their mother's repeated instructions to neaten their hair and smooth their skirts before stepping even one foot inside. "Once you go through that door," she used to say, "the customers will look to you. I want them to know that your father and I raised polite, intelligent, and well-groomed young ladies."

Augusta was kept busy tidying shelves and dusting the displays in the storefront windows, while Bess was allowed to work behind the cosmetics counter, helping customers choose face powder and perfume. Augusta could not care less about makeup, but she resented the fact that Bess was given what was viewed as a more important task.

"I want more responsibility," Augusta told her father one night after they'd finished dinner. Dinners had become forgettable affairs—meat that Bess left in the oven too long or sandwiches they slapped together at the table. Gone were the days of their mother's roast chicken, with its golden-crisp skin, herbed carrots, and beans. Gone were the days of tangy meatloaf, whipped potatoes, and freshly baked rolls. Gone was the cheerful gathering at the table, their mother's laughter, their father's smiles. Meals were no longer something to be savored.

"A fourteen-year-old can't work behind the makeup counter," said Bess.

"I don't want to sell makeup," said Augusta. "But even if I did, age shouldn't matter. What *should* matter is intelligence and maturity." She turned to her father, who was busying himself with the evening newspaper. "Isn't that right, Papa?"

"Hmm?" said their father, his head buried deep within the pages, pretending he hadn't heard the question. Since their mother's death, Solomon Stern's jet-black hair had dulled to a wispy silver-gray, and the pillowy skin beneath his eyes sagged even more than the unstarched collar of his shirt or the pale green sofa on which the three of them sat. Since Augusta's mother's death, everything in the apartment drooped with grief.

Augusta knew that her father was still stuck in the quicksand of his sorrow. At the store, he managed to keep up with his duties. But at home, he had a more difficult time. There was a barrier between him and his daughters now, as if he were standing behind a screen—one sheer enough so that they could see him, but opaque enough to blur all his edges.

"No woman wants a child's opinion on lipstick," interrupted Bess, who had recently grown confident in both her retail skills and her burgeoning feminine charms.

If their father took up less space now, Bess seemed intent on making up the difference. She was uncomfortable in the quiet their mother's passing had created. If their father spoke less, she would speak more. If the shine on him dulled, Bess would become brighter.

"As if *you* know what looks best," said Augusta. "You barely pay attention to the customers anyway. You're too busy staring at the new soda jerk, batting your eyes, trying to get him to notice you."

The new soda jerk had been hired as an assistant to the full-time clerk who'd been there for a decade. Fred, the old-timer, was a no-nonsense fellow who ran the soda fountain like a soldier on patrol. He kept the zinc counter polished to a shine at all times, piling soda glasses, ice cream dishes, and sundae spoons in perfectly symmetrical, tidy stacks. The new assistant, George, was not quite as precise, but he was a step up from the last one, who was always having to mop up his own spills. George never overfilled the glasses; he was not sloppy with the walnuts. After a week, George had mastered the lingo. A glass of milk was a "baby." A scoop of vanilla ice cream was a "snowball." If someone wanted a Coke with no ice, George shouted, "Hold the hail!"

"I do *not* bat my eyes at George," Bess insisted. "Besides, even if I did, he's too busy to notice."

It was true that the soda fountain was packed every afternoon. Customers clamored for the red leather stools while calling out their orders for ice cream cones and egg creams. Since George's arrival, business was even busier—pretty girls in dresses sat sweetly at the counter, sipping their sodas more slowly than usual. In between sips, they smiled at George, who seemed completely immune to their charms. Augusta had seen him sneaking glances at Bess whenever he thought she wasn't looking.

"He notices," said Augusta, but she would not elaborate. At sixteen, Bess was already more concerned with men than Augusta considered necessary—she didn't need any additional encouragement. Augusta turned to her father again. "Papa, I want to learn more about your work. I want you to teach me about prescriptions." When Solomon Stern did not reply, Augusta spoke up again. "I refuse to take no for an answer."

This time her father looked up from his newspaper. He sat up a little straighter in his chair and blinked at Augusta from behind his glasses as if she'd suddenly appeared in the space before him. "You sound like your mother," he said before escaping back into his pages.

The next day, after the school bell rang and the girls made their way to the pharmacy, Augusta carried her books to the narrow back room where her father filled prescriptions. Shelves filled with carefully labeled bottles lined the neat, well-lit space. A locked cabinet held the most dangerous substances—medicines Augusta knew had to be handled with special care. Her father hadn't said she could be there, but he hadn't sent her away, either.

When her homework was done, Augusta watched as her father measured powders on a set of gleaming brass scales. As usual, he wore a white cotton coat over a knit sweater vest and a striped bow tie. After a while, he grew tired of her gawking and put her to work dusting bottles and shelves. This continued for weeks on end; in this way, she began to learn the names of the drugs. Whenever Augusta asked a question, her father pointed to the books sitting on his counter. Then she would skim the pages of the *U.S. Pharmacopeia* and the thickly bound copy of the *National Formulary* until she found the answer.

From where Augusta sat reading in the prescription room, she was certain to overhear at least a portion of many of her father's private consultations. Once Solomon Stern realized this fact, he gave his daughter an ultimatum. "In this store, people speak to me in confidence," he said. "They trust that whatever they disclose to me will not be revealed to anyone else. Whatever you hear, whatever you learn about a customer, is *never* ever to be repeated. If you break this rule, there will be no second chance." As he spoke the words, his eyes bore no trace of their usual softness.

"I understand," Augusta said.

"Being a pharmacist is more than powders and pills." Her father glanced toward the locked cabinet behind her. "Sometimes it means keeping other people's secrets."

For the first time, Augusta had an inkling that her father was more than the melancholy man she knew. He was not only a father and a widower, but a confidant to people she had never even met. She wondered whether that was what helped to keep him going after his heart had been hammered by loss: the part he'd pledged to play—both professional and personal—in the constantly evolving stories of strangers.

When Augusta grew bored of dusting bottles, she tried convincing her father to assign her more substantive tasks. Eventually he set her to work making simple suppositories. Her father mixed the ingredients first, using cocoa butter as a base. Only then was Augusta allowed to take over, placing the material in a cast-iron machine bolted to the wooden counter. As she turned the crank, the medicated paste was forced into bullet-shaped molds. It was a decidedly unglamorous job, but Augusta was determined to prove herself capable.

She was there, leaning over the heavy machine, her braids half unraveled, her forehead dripping with sweat, when her father came into the stuffy room accompanied by a boy she had never seen before. He was a few years older than she, at most, with an untamable cowlick and chalk-blue eyes. His pants, she noticed, were a bit too short, as were the cuffs on his shirt. He looked as if he could use a hot meal—even one of Bess's overcooked roasts would do.

"Augusta," said her father, "this is my new delivery boy. He'll be coming in on weekdays after school, like you. The two of you will be seeing a lot of each other."

The boy stepped forward to shake her hand. "Nice to meet you," he said. "Your pop's got a terrific store."

"Welcome," said Augusta. "What's your name?"

The boy ran one hand over the top of his head, but the spiky tuft of hair would not be subdued. "Irving," he said. "Irving Rivkin."

THREE

<hr/>

SEPTEMBER 1987

Of all the retirement communities in southern Florida, why did Irving Rivkin have to end up at hers?

He followed Augusta to her lounge chair and plopped himself down on the seat beside it. "You look terrific!" he said approvingly. "You've still got those long legs, like when we were kids."

"Well, now they're covered in varicose veins." Honestly, what could be more embarrassing than this damp, half-naked, forced reunion? Augusta wished she had worn one of her newer swimsuits—one that hadn't lost all its shape. Better yet, she wished she was wearing clothes. She'd never been prudish about her body, but now she wrapped the pool towel around her middle and covered as much of herself as possible.

"Not from where I'm sitting," Irving said. "Hey, how are Bess and George doing? Are they down in Florida, too?"

Augusta bit the inside of her cheek. She shook her head. "George died back in 1983, and we lost Bess six months ago."

"Shit, I'm sorry. Bess and George were the greatest."

Finally, something they could agree on. "She was the best friend I ever had."

"You must miss her."

"Every day. But her kids have been a huge comfort—especially her daughter, Jackie. Peter, the oldest, moved to Seattle, and Andy is a doctor in Connecticut. Jackie opened a boutique in the city, and since she stayed in New York, she's the one I see most. She has two wonderful kids." As Augusta talked, she grew more relaxed. *Keep going, keep going,* she told herself. *Answer his questions. Ask about his life. Get all of this over with and out of the way. Once the two of you are caught up with each other, there will be nothing left for him to say. He'll get bored and leave you alone.*

"What about you?" Augusta asked. "How is . . ." She paused, pretending that the name of Irving's wife wasn't permanently etched on her brain. "Lois? The last I heard, you had twin sons."

Irving smiled. "Bill and Michael, they're doing great. Bill is a math teacher back in Chicago and Michael's an anesthesiologist. They're both married, both got a couple of kids. Michael was in Florida with his family last month. They'll be back for Christmas break in December."

"And Lois? Is she still . . ."

Irving's smile disappeared. "Healthy as a horse, apparently. Lois left me back in '42. Ran off to Las Vegas with one of her *friends.* The boys were teenagers by then—we gave 'em a choice, and they stayed with me. She was happy enough with the arrangement—it wasn't like she wanted them with her anyway."

"I'm sorry to hear that."

Augusta wasn't the least bit sorry. But she was surprised by Irving's tone. He'd been so besotted with Lois once. So desperately in love with the young woman that he'd proposed to her and followed her to Chicago within the span of a single week.

"You probably don't remember much about Lois, but she wasn't exactly the maternal type."

Augusta remembered Lois perfectly, but she certainly wasn't going to say so. She could still see Lois's dark, wavy hair, her flawless skin, her pouty red lips.

"You were a single father in 1942? You couldn't have had much company."

Irving chuckled. "You got that right," he said. "But those boys were the light of my life. Still are, of course. Them and the grandkids.

"How about you?" Irving continued. "Tell me about your husband. How many kids do you have?"

Beneath her towel, Augusta's body stiffened. She wanted to punch Irving right then and there. How she loathed the cavalier way he spoke about marriage and motherhood! As if either or both were hers for the taking if only she'd chosen to partake. As if love was as common as breaking a nail.

"I have no children," she said sharply.

He stared at her blankly, as if the words pained him. "Really?" he said. "I thought I heard you had a daughter."

"Absolutely not," she snapped. "And, for the record, I've never been married." The response came out more forcefully than she'd intended, and Irving seemed slightly taken aback. He lowered his sunglasses to study her face, but she turned her head to read the sign that hung over the snack bar window. "How's the food over there, by the way?" she asked. "Are the sandwiches any good?"

"They got a nice turkey club. But whatever you do, *don't* get the tuna." Before she had time to contemplate the strange intensity of Irving's warning, he reached his hand out and patted her knee. "I hope life hasn't been too rough on you, kid."

The pity in his tone was more than she could bear—a slap in the face would have been more welcome. "It hasn't," she assured him, swatting his hand away. "I took over the pharmacy when my father died. I ran it myself for twenty years before I sold it. After that, I worked at a couple of hospitals. I only retired a few months ago."

"You've been working full-time all these years?"

Augusta shrugged. "Why not?" she said. She did not explain that work had been her salvation—her greatest escape from heartbreak and loneliness.

She did not tell him how she needed to keep her hands and mind busy so as not to dwell on the disappointments of her past. She did not tell him how she'd lied for years about her age because the idea of retiring had terrified her. "I love my work," she said instead. "Why would I want to give it up?" She gestured to the bowling ball of a stomach that swelled over the top of Irving's swim trunks. "It's better than sitting around, getting fat."

He patted his bump with both hands. "Watch it, kid," he said, amused. "I'll have you know that I'm proud of this belly. You remember how skinny I was when you met me? My mom could barely afford to put food on the table, which was why I was always so grateful to your dad for giving me that delivery job. I used to tell myself that when I got older, I'd eat as much as I wanted." He patted his belly again. "Life is for living and enjoying. I don't regret one inch of this beauty."

"Speaking of food," Augusta said, rising abruptly from her lounge chair, "I have to get back and unpack my kitchen. I have half a dozen boxes full of plates and glasses, and I need to figure out where to put them all." She tucked her sunscreen and goggles back into her canvas tote bag.

"You really gotta go so soon?" asked Irving. "You and me, we were just starting to catch up." There was a sweetness to his clumsy smile that Augusta remembered from her youth. *You fell for that smile once before,* she told herself. *You will not fall for it again.*

"I've told you everything there is to know," she answered.

"Impossible," Irving said. "You can't catch up sixty-two years in fifteen minutes. Come on, Goldie. I can't let you off that easy."

At the second mention of her childhood nickname, Augusta pursed her lips together. She murmured a hasty goodbye, walked through the pool gate, and headed quickly toward her condo. Five minutes later, she slammed her door shut, locked it, and lowered her blinds.

How on earth was she going to get rid of him?

FOUR

SEPTEMBER 1922

Six months after her mother died, Augusta's great-aunt came to stay. Esther would have come to Brooklyn sooner, but for reasons Augusta did not yet comprehend, her father was reluctant to welcome his mother's sister into his home. But one morning, after Bess burned the scrambled eggs and the dust on the mantel was half an inch thick, Solomon Stern finally admitted that their family needed help.

Esther had been living in America for years—first with a brother in Philadelphia, then with cousins outside of Boston, and most recently, with a different set of cousins in a tiny apartment in the Bronx. As a single woman with minimal funds, she'd gone wherever there was room and wherever she was needed.

The family gossip was that, though she was helpful, Esther was peculiar and old-fashioned. The dresses she kept in her brass-hinged trunk were more like potato sacks than clothes. Even worse was the black babushka on her head, which only accentuated her owl-like eyes and her heavy silver brows.

Solomon Stern explained to his daughters that Esther had stayed in Russia for decades, long after her sisters and brothers had left. Augusta wondered why the woman felt tied to a place with so few comforts and even fewer opportunities. Esther had no children to keep her there. Apparently, she had never married. When Augusta pressed her father on the matter, he said that Esther's letters to his mother were full of descriptions of her patients. "She was the self-proclaimed apothecary of her village," he said. "Though she never had any formal training."

Whatever initial goodwill Augusta felt when she was first told her great-aunt would be joining the household disappeared when she learned that the two of them would be sharing a bedroom. Both girls assumed that Esther would sleep in their mother's sewing room behind the kitchen. But when Esther peered inside, she told their father she couldn't stay in a room without a window. "I can't sleep if I can't see the sky," she said. Despite her accent, her English was decent enough. "Bess is old enough for her own room. She should have this for herself. I will move in with Augusta."

This development was like a dagger driven straight through Augusta's adolescent heart. She and Bess had always shared a bedroom, even after their mother was gone. Neither one of them had thought to move into the sewing room, preferring instead to keep their mother's belongings exactly where they had always been. Now, with the arrival of Aunt Esther, not only would Augusta be sharing a room with a stranger who smelled like tea bags and wet potatoes, but she would be losing the comfort of her closest confidante. It hurt even more when Bess seemed excited about the new living arrangement.

The main benefit to having Esther around was that she immediately took over the preparation of the family meals. Every morning, she slipped a long white apron over whatever hideous dress she had chosen. Both of the girls felt too guilty to admit it, but it was obvious that their great-aunt was a better cook even than their mother had been. Her brisket was tender, her vegetables were crisp, and her chicken soup was the most delicious concoction any of them had ever tasted. It brimmed with tiny homemade kreplach—meat-filled dumplings that melted on the tongue.

Despite the culinary benefits, however, the transition of welcoming

Esther into the household was full of unforeseen challenges—not only for Augusta and Bess, but for their father as well.

A few days after Esther's arrival, Augusta's father was late for dinner. Typically, he was late once or twice a week—sometimes due to last-minute prescriptions and sometimes because a new shipment of cigars begged to be sampled with his cohorts: three other shop owners who lived and worked on the same block.

If cigars were involved, there was likely to be whiskey (with Prohibition in force, Stern's Pharmacy was one of few places in the neighborhood legally allowed to sell liquor). Irene Stern had been used to this arrangement, and now Augusta and Bess were used to it, too. Neither of them minded their father's harmless bit of weekly recreation.

On that particular night, it was cigars and whiskey that kept Solomon Stern from his family. When he eventually got home, three hours later than usual, his aunt was waiting for him at the front door of his apartment. She stood with her arms crossed over her chest and a disapproving frown etched into her features. Augusta and Bess stood behind her.

"I had to work late," he said defensively. "The girls know my routine. They understand."

Esther sniffed the air in the doorway, her yellow-green eyes glinting under the lamplight. "In America, cigars and liquor are *work*?"

He stammered a string of lame excuses, but Esther was not deterred. "Next time," she said, "tell me first. That way, at least I won't worry."

After that came the matter of the night bell. The bell was meant to be used by pharmacy customers only in cases of genuine emergency after the store had closed for the evening. Still, there were several frivolous patrons who rang at all hours without crisis or need. In some instances, they rang the bell out of boredom; in others, the reason was impatience or a simple lack of consideration for others. Augusta's father had been awakened for talcum powder, Epsom salts, and other nonessentials, sometimes even after midnight. Once Esther arrived, however, she made it her business to put an end to such foolishness.

Against her nephew's wishes, she began accompanying him downstairs whenever the night bell roused him from slumber. If an after-hours customer was in real trouble, no one was kinder or more sympathetic than the stout and spirited aunt of the pharmacist. But if the late-night patron had rung the bell for a purchase that could have waited until morning, if he had woken the hardworking, dedicated druggist (and his family) without good cause, Esther made it clear that such behavior would not be tolerated going forward. She did not even have to open her mouth—the customers knew immediately what her steely scowl conveyed.

"Esther," said her nephew, "you have to stop making the customers uncomfortable."

"Uncomfortable?" Esther said. "I care about their comfort as much as they care about your sleep."

"Things are different in New York," said Augusta. "Customers want convenience here."

"How *convenient* will it be," Esther queried, "when the pharmacist drops dead from exhaustion?"

One customer who had rung the bell after midnight to purchase aspirin for a simple headache had been so shamed by Esther's withering glare that he returned the next afternoon, during proper hours, to request the woman's forgiveness. Augusta had heard all about him.

"I'm so sorry," said the middle-aged man. "I have insomnia, you see, and sometimes I forget how late it is." He glanced quickly around the well-stocked shelves for something to purchase as a gesture of goodwill. Eventually he chose a second box of aspirin, a tube of Huxley's Menthol & Wintergreen Cream, and a new hairbrush. Esther carried the items to the register, but only after adding a large bottle of the store's most expensive lily of the valley perfume. "That is for your wife," she told the man. "*Now*, you are forgiven."

Though it took time, eventually the customers grew to appreciate Esther's eccentricities. She was indulged not only because of her age, but because of her wide-ranging wisdom and talents. Esther could pluck a chicken faster than anyone in the neighborhood. She could get black ink stains out of white shirt cuffs and bloodstains out of almost anything. She could remove a cinder from a customer's eye with less pain and fuss than her nephew, who had been providing the service in his store for the better part of fifteen years.

Augusta's father was grateful for Esther's willingness to help and for her dedication to his customers. What he could not abide or condone, however, was when she encouraged pharmacy patrons to bypass *his* treatments in favor of her own.

The first time Esther offered personal advice regarding a pharmaceutical matter, the recipient was Mrs. Fanny Lowenstein. Mrs. Lowenstein was the mother of twin seven-year-old boys, both of whom had been complaining of stomach pains every evening after dinner. When Augusta's father asked what the boys had been eating, Mrs. Lowenstein swore that she prepared only the healthiest of foods—fish and an assortment of leafy greens. Despite her vigilance, however, the children seemed to be in agony. Recently, the pains had gotten so bad that the boys complained even *before* the meal. Neither the patented Stuart's Dyspepsia Tablets she'd purchased, nor Solomon Stern's store-made tonic, seemed to alleviate her sons' discomfort. Not wanting to put her boys through further torture, she gave up feeding them a proper dinner and began giving them toast and jam instead. Now she was back in the store a third time, picking up some capsules the pharmacist had suggested.

Before Mrs. Lowenstein made her purchase, Augusta saw her great-aunt pull the woman aside. "I have an idea, Mrs. Lowenstein," Esther said. "Come upstairs with me, will you?" Augusta and her father watched together as the two women left the store.

That night at dinner, Augusta's father questioned Esther about what had happened.

"The boys don't like her cooking," Esther said. "They'd rather have toast than the *dreck* she serves. They're pretending to be sick so they don't have to eat."

"It sounds to me like she's been taking great care to serve her sons nutritious meals. If they don't like her cooking, why don't they say so?"

Esther gave him a look. "Seven-year-old boys are shifty," she said. "Maybe they don't want to hurt her feelings; maybe they just like toast and jam."

"But they can't eat toast for dinner forever," said Bess.

"That's why I gave Mrs. Lowenstein a little something."

Augusta's father let out a sigh. "What exactly did you give her?"

"I gave her a jar of my chicken soup and told her to give it to her boys. Watch—they won't have any stomach pains tonight."

"And what happens when she makes fish for them again?"

Esther avoided his stare and busied herself with her napkin. "I told her to stop with the fish and the spinach. *It's possible fish doesn't agree with them,* I said. *Spinach can be difficult to digest. Stick to meat and potatoes for a while,* I said. Boys like meat and potatoes."

"You can't diagnose digestive issues without any evidence!"

"Who needs evidence?" Esther said. "Besides, better the woman should think her children have bad stomachs than find out she's killing them with her own cooking!"

"Esther," Augusta's father said sternly, "I have a reputation to uphold. If people find out you're giving fake medical advice, that undermines *my* authority."

"Who's giving medical advice?" Esther scoffed. "All I did was give the woman a jar of soup."

Eventually, Augusta's father forgave Esther for meddling with his customers. Augusta, however, was less forbearing, not only because she found herself frustrated by the steady stream of her great-aunt's flippant comments, but because she did not like the way Esther spoke to her father. Since spending so much time in the prescription room, Augusta's admiration for her father had multiplied. The more she watched her father at work, the more she understood why he was so well respected. Despite constant bouts of debilitating headaches, Solomon Stern maintained a strict schedule. No matter how bad his own pain was, he refused to slack off on his responsibilities to his customers.

For her part, Augusta tried to learn what she could about headache treatments. She scanned the advertisements in *American Druggist* magazine and read about the benefits of caffeine. When she noticed her father rubbing his temples, she brought him a cup of steaming hot coffee or a Coca-Cola from the soda fountain. Sometimes she turned off the lights in the prescription room and made her father sit quietly in the dark. Once, when she'd brought him a compress for his forehead, Esther walked in looking for a bottle of white pine syrup for a customer's cough. After finding what she needed, the old woman patted Augusta's shoulder and murmured a few words of praise. "You do a good job taking care of him," she said.

Esther didn't dole out compliments often, however—she was far more likely to scold than to flatter. Her presence posed other problems, too. When she cleaned the kitchen drawers and reorganized the cabinets, it made Augusta feel as if the memory of her mother was somehow being scrubbed away. Her great-aunt ran the household differently from the way her mother had. Intellectually, Augusta knew she and her family had been struggling before Esther arrived. Even so, she couldn't help being upset when small things were altered—when the cloth on the kitchen table was changed, or when an extra lamp was purchased for the living room. It didn't matter that the space became physically brighter—for Augusta, the light only illuminated the fact that the person who'd loved her most was missing.

The last straw was when Bess came to breakfast wearing one of their mother's old dresses. "Who said you could wear Mama's clothes?" asked Augusta, sucking in her breath at the ghostly sight.

But Bess didn't seem bothered in the slightest. "Aunt Esther," she said. "My dresses are all too short and she said it made no sense to let Mama's go to waste. I might as well get some use out of them."

The words spilled out before Augusta could stop them. She turned to her great-aunt, who was boiling eggs. "You can't just come in here and change things!" she shouted.

Immediately, Bess reached for Augusta's hand. "Shh," she said softly, "it's going to be all right." Tears spilled down Augusta's cheeks and all her breath left her, as if she'd been punched. Only Bess's whispers had the power to calm her. "Mama wanted us to have her things. She told us so before she died, remember? I'm sorry, Augusta. I don't want to upset you."

When Augusta stopped crying, Esther set a bowl of warm oatmeal in front of her. She patted Augusta on the shoulder, as if to communicate that she was forgiven for her outburst. She stroked Augusta's flaxen braids with a rough and wrinkled hand. "Such pretty hair," Esther murmured. "Little Goldie, with the beautiful braids. You have hair like my sister."

"Don't call me Goldie," Augusta said, pushing her oatmeal away. Augusta's father, watching the exchange, released a brief, beleaguered sigh into his morning cup of coffee, as if he had a feeling the conversation between the two would not end well.

Esther raised a silver eyebrow, but Augusta would not be intimidated. "I don't like nicknames," she said sharply. "I prefer the name my mother gave me."

"We called your grandmother, my sister, Goldie," said Esther. "With that hair, Goldie is a perfect name for you, too."

"That's ridiculous," said Augusta. "That's like saying I should call you Hazel because you have hazel eyes."

Her great-aunt shrugged and lifted her chin with a practiced nonchalance. "Go ahead," she said. "I've been called far worse." She squared her shoulders like a boxer in the ring. "It makes no difference what anyone calls me. I know exactly who I am."

To Augusta, the reply was the worst kind of challenge—meant to put her in her place. "I know who I am, too," she insisted, but without any of the confidence of Esther's assertion. She wished she sounded less like a child and more like the adult she wanted to be. Even as the words left her lips, she was certain that Esther knew she was lying.

FIVE

SEPTEMBER 1987

Retirement was every bit as awful as Augusta knew it would be. Without her work to fill up the hours, Augusta was purposeless. Adrift. She had been in Florida for less than a week, and already she was losing track of the days. She missed having a place to go every morning. She missed the intellectual stimulation. She missed being the first to know about new medications before they hit the market.

It didn't help that her eightieth birthday loomed on the horizon like a sinking ship.

"It will get easier," her niece Jackie told her when she called from New York. "I'm sure you'll make plenty of new friends soon. You'll probably meet a bunch of transplanted New Yorkers. Isn't half the population of Florida from Brooklyn?"

"I don't know about that," Augusta responded. She hadn't mentioned Irving to her niece yet, and she didn't feel like relaying the whole sordid story. Jackie was a detail-oriented person. She wouldn't be satisfied with a passing reference or a brief description of her old . . . acquaintance. Jackie would want to know the specifics. She would have questions and she would want answers.

"Is the pool as nice as the pictures, at least? And the condo? How is the space?"

"The pool is nice," Augusta told her. "And the condo is even bigger than the pictures. There's plenty of room for when you come."

"I can't wait," Jackie told her. "Believe me, I've already started packing."

"I know I've told you this before, but you can bring the whole family, you know. Philip, the kids. The couch pulls out . . ."

"Trust me, Phil's completely on board with me taking a weekend for myself to celebrate my favorite aunt's eightieth birthday!"

"I'm glad you're coming," said Augusta. "It will be nice to see a familiar face."

"See you in three weeks," said Jackie.

Augusta ended the call without mentioning the other familiar face she had seen. The face that popped up, unsolicited, wherever she seemed to turn.

On her second morning at Rallentando Springs, Irving waited by the swimming pool steps as Augusta emerged from the water. In his hands, he held up a towel like some kind of geriatric matador. Did he honestly think she was going to stand there and allow him to wrap the towel around her? Did he think she was going to encourage this intimate and wildly presumptuous gesture? "No thank you," she said as she breezed right past him, in a voice loud enough so that not only Irving but everyone at the pool would hear.

"New suit?" asked Irving. "Looks nice on you, by the way."

She'd put on one of her best bathing suits that morning. *I'm not wearing it for him,* she told herself when she checked the straps in the mirror. It was only that she didn't want the canasta-playing biddies to think she didn't own anything decent. She had promised Jackie that she'd try to make friends, and she wanted to make a good impression.

"I don't appreciate comments on my appearance," said Augusta, reaching for the towel she'd left on her chair.

"No problem," said Irving, not the least bit offended. "I feel the same way myself, of course, but I didn't want to say anything to you yesterday."

"Yesterday?"

"Uh-huh. When you called me fat, I said to myself, *Forgive her, Irving. She doesn't mean it. You've known each other too long to hold a grudge.*"

It took a moment for Augusta to recover from the shock of Irving's verbal agility, but eventually she managed to speak. "I apologize," she said. "It won't happen again."

Augusta was determined not to let Irving's presence interfere with her exercise routine. She would not allow his lurking to get in the way of her cardiovascular wellness. The third morning at the pool passed without incident. Irving waved to her from his lounge chair, but he did not attempt to get any closer.

On the fourth morning, when Augusta got out of the pool, Irving was nowhere in sight. Delighted, she swam a few extra laps. Even after she toweled off, there was still no sign of the menace from her past. Leaning back against her lounge chair, she allowed herself to enjoy the stillness. She closed her eyes and felt the sunshine warming her clammy skin. Soon two Rallentando employees unlocked the charming little snack shack and opened the takeout window for business. At twelve o'clock, she wandered over and read the list of lunchtime specials. A veggie burger might be nice for a change. Or maybe a chef's salad.

What had Irving told her again? *They got a nice turkey club. But whatever you do, don't get the tuna.* Augusta never ate anything with mayonnaise unless she was certain about the refrigeration. Leave it out a minute too long and ... well, she didn't like to think about it. She was choosing between the turkey club and the veggie burger special when she remembered the rest of what Irving had said. *I hope life hasn't been too rough on you, kid.* The nerve of him, saying such a thing. As if the path her life had taken had nothing whatsoever to do with him. As if he didn't remember what had happened all those years ago in Brooklyn. Despite the sunshine and the idyllic setting, rage bubbled up in Augusta's chest. She would be damned if Irving Rivkin was going to dictate her life choices.

"I'll have the tuna," she told the young man taking orders at the window. He was in his early twenties—tall, gangly, and quick, with a slightly lopsided smile. His pinned-on name tag read PAUL.

Twenty minutes later, she was finishing her sandwich when she spotted Irving approaching her table. "You got the tuna?" he asked, incredulous. A line of worry stretched across his forehead.

"So what if I did?" Augusta shot back. "Why are you so concerned with my lunch order anyway?"

Irving looked as if she'd struck him. "I'm sorry," he mumbled. "I'm not judging, but Paul has a habit of leaving out the mayonnaise jar. Of course, you should have whatever you like."

While he stood in line to place his order, Augusta wolfed down the last few bites of her tuna sandwich. She heard Irving ask for a turkey club with no mayo, a side of chips, and a Diet Pepsi before she left the pool and headed home.

An hour later, she began to feel queasy. Her temples throbbed on and off like some kind of defective light bulb. Unable to concentrate, she put down her book, clutched her abdomen, and closed her eyes. *No*, she told herself. *No, no, no. Please don't let that man be right.* But an hour later, she was sick to her stomach. She spent the rest of the day and early evening vomiting until she fell asleep.

The next morning, she was weak and dehydrated. When she opened her front door to pick up her newspaper, someone had left a brown paper bag filled with Pepto-Bismol, a box of saltines, and a small green bottle of Schweppes ginger ale. She carried the paper bag inside and filled a glass with soda and ice. When she removed the groceries, she saw a handwritten note scrawled on the outside of the bag. *I hope you don't need this, but I left it, in case. Irving.* As Augusta sipped the sweet, bubbly liquid, she wondered how Irving had figured out which of the condominiums was hers. She took two tablespoons of Pepto-Bismol, ate a few crackers, and got back into bed. Before long, she was asleep again.

The telephone woke her a few hours later. In her dreams, she was back in Brooklyn, and the phone was the night bell from her father's drugstore. When she finally remembered where she was, the telephone was still ringing. Other than Jackie, she hadn't given anyone her new number.

"Hello?"

"It's Irving. Everything okay over there?"

"Irving. How did you get my number?"

"The receptionist over at the clubhouse gave it to me. You're not in the resident directory yet—they don't print the new one until December."

"Oh," said Augusta, vaguely remembering a booklet or two in her welcome packet.

"When I didn't see you at the pool today, I figured maybe the tuna didn't sit so well. If you were somebody else, I might not have worried. But if you don't mind my saying, you seem a little bit on the obsessive side when it comes to your exercise. The type of person who likes to adhere to a specific routine. *If she's not swimming,* I said to myself, *something has to be wrong.*"

She was too exhausted to argue with him. Too weak to tell him to mind his own business. "Oh," she said, "that's an interesting observation."

"You need me to bring over anything else? Did you get the Pepto? The saltines?"

"I did, yes. That was very . . . thoughtful. I'm fine now, though. I'll be fine."

"If you think of anything, gimme a call. I'm in the directory. R for Rivkin."

"Duly noted," Augusta said.

"You should be all right tomorrow. If you're not, lemme know and I'll pick you up some soup. There's a little deli over on Jog Road that makes the best chicken soup around." He paused for a moment, his voice turning quiet. "Not as good as your aunt Esther's, of course. I still dream about her kreplach."

When Augusta didn't answer, Irving kept talking. He spoke like someone weaving a spell he desperately didn't want her to break. "You remember how good that soup was, Goldie?"

For a moment, she could taste it on her tongue—the salt, the schmaltz, the dash of parsley. So rich and flavorful, it was almost otherworldly. A single spoonful could make you swoon; a bowl was as heady as the first day of spring. Esther was happy to give the recipe to anyone who asked, but no one else's soup ever tasted like hers. She was always tinkering with the broth, always adjusting the ingredients. *I never make my soup the same way twice,* she used to say. Augusta had buried the memories, but now Irving had brought all of them back.

"I don't care for soup anymore," she said brusquely. "I've been burned too many times."

SIX

OCTOBER 1922

After word got around about the Lowenstein twins, everyone in the neighborhood wanted some of Esther's soup. Mrs. Lowenstein told anyone who would listen about its miraculous digestive powers. "I never saw my boys eat anything so quickly. Their appetites are back. Their stomach pains have disappeared!"

Customers asked Augusta's father for the soup when they came into the store. At first he found the requests amusing, but as they multiplied, he grew annoyed. "It's only *soup*," Augusta heard him say to a mother who spoke as if it were liquid gold.

"That's not what Fanny Lowenstein says. She says that Esther's soup *healed* her boys. Now they eat everything—except for fish and spinach. Their stomachs can't handle those foods, apparently. They're very difficult to digest."

Solomon Stern let out a groan. When the customer left, he told Augusta, "Your great-aunt is going to put me in an early grave. At the very least, she's going to give me an ulcer."

"Should I tell her to make extra soup for the customers?"

Her father sighed. "I suppose it couldn't hurt."

On Friday mornings, Esther always went shopping. She was the first one at the kosher butcher in the morning, where she picked out the plumpest, most succulent chickens. She gave the butcher a sweet yellow onion, which he ground into a pound of fresh red meat, to be used for her kreplach filling.

Esther made her soup in the giant stockpot that had once belonged to Augusta's mother. She added carrots, onions, and celery to the chicken, and filled the pot three-quarters of the way full with water. After the whole thing came to a boil, she threw in a pinch of salt and pepper and a handful of parsley, garlic, and dill. She added other herbs and spices, too, some of which Augusta didn't recognize. These, Esther macerated herself with a heavy brass mortar and pestle she'd brought to New York in the bottom of her trunk. As she worked, she hummed and swayed. Sometimes she sang the strands of a tune that Augusta did not know.

On the outside, the bowl-like mortar was plain, measuring about four inches across. Inside, faded words were carved into the metal—beginning at the bottom and swirling upward in a single spiral toward the rim. Augusta thought that the letters looked like Hebrew, though she had no idea what they actually meant. Like most American-born girls in her neighborhood, Augusta could understand some spoken Hebrew and Yiddish, but she did not know enough to read or translate. The mortar looked rough and not particularly clean. Certainly it did not seem to be valuable, but it must have been meaningful to her great-aunt, or she wouldn't have taken such care to transport it from one end of the world to the other.

"My father has mortars in his prescription room, but I've never seen one decorated like that. What does the inscription mean?"

"Hmm?" said Aunt Esther, as if she hadn't heard.

Augusta wanted to press the matter, but her aunt began rolling out the dough for the meat dumplings—the kreplach. As she stood hunched over their wooden table, a different tune, livelier this time, flowed from her lips. She cut the dough into perfect squares and placed tiny dollops of seasoned ground meat into the center of each square. As the old woman folded and pinched and crimped, Augusta could have sworn that she was singing to the dumplings, cooing to them as if they were babies gently being put to bed. Augusta waited until Esther was finished before asking her question again. "What does the inscription mean?"

This time Augusta knew Esther had heard. But instead of answering her great-niece properly, the old woman shrugged and looked away.

"Only words," Esther said.

On the first Friday that Esther sold soup at the store, Augusta helped to carry the jars downstairs. She placed six jars on the cosmetics counter, but Bess was miffed that they broke up her display. The disruption did not last long, however. Esther charged thirty cents per jar, and, within minutes, the six jars were gone.

On the Monday that followed, Augusta overheard more customers asking her father for the soup. This time, it wasn't only young mothers asking for their picky children. Mr. Kaufman, a retired teacher in his seventies, wondered whether the soup might help his wife get over a mild bout of bronchitis. The pharmacist replied that all warm liquids were soothing in such situations. "Any tea or broth will be useful," he said. He gave Mr. Kaufman capsules for the cough and a box of lozenges.

On Tuesday, there were more inquiries. Gertie Feldman cornered Esther and asked whether the soup might be good for her granddaughter's chicken pox. "The fever is down," Gertie said, "but the poor thing can't stop scratching. I suppose the soup can't help with itching?"

Aunt Esther shook her head. "I have something else for that," she said. "Why don't you come upstairs with me?"

When the pharmacist saw his aunt leave with Mrs. Feldman, his face turned an angry, mottled red. "You stay here," he said to Augusta. "Help the customers if you can. If someone needs me, tell them to wait. I'll be back in ten minutes." He stopped Irving on his way out the door. "Wait with Augusta, please. In case she needs help."

Once her father was gone, Augusta reassured Irving. "It's okay, you can make your deliveries. You don't have to stay here with me."

"I don't mind," Irving told her. "Besides, your pop wants me to."

It was the most the two of them had said to each other since Irving had begun working at the store. For a talkative young man, Irving was surprisingly quiet when Augusta was nearby. He seemed to have no problem talking to her father, to George at the soda counter, or even to Bess. But when it came to Augusta, Irving Rivkin was uncharacteristically tongue-tied.

"I think he likes you," Bess said one evening when the girls were brushing their teeth in the tiny bathroom.

"That's ridiculous," Augusta answered, but Bess raised both eyebrows in mock surprise.

"Is it?" she said. "I don't think so. Mama always said you were going to be a beauty. Irving has eyes, doesn't he?"

"He's two years older than me," Augusta said.

"So what? Papa was six years older than Mama. And George is three years older than me." Lately, Bess seemed to be making headway in her quest to get George to notice her.

"Stop teasing," said Augusta, pretending to be more embarrassed than she was. Meanwhile, that night, for the first time in her life, Augusta dreamed she was dancing with someone. In the dream, she could not make out the young man's face, but his eyes were the palest shade of blue and his hair stuck up in front like Irving Rivkin's.

While Augusta's father was out of the store, two customers came to the prescription counter. Both were picking up medications that her father had already prepared. Augusta answered a few simple questions, handed over their orders, and gave them change.

Irving watched her during both encounters with a look of admiration on his face. "You're a natural," he told her.

"Talking to customers or making change?"

"Both," said Irving. "Everything. You could practically run this whole place."

Augusta laughed. It turned out that Irving was much easier to talk to than she had thought he would be. "Hardly," she said. "I want to go to pharmaceutical college one day, though."

"Aren't you afraid of all the reading? All the studying you'll have to do?"

Augusta shook her head and smiled. "I like reading," she said. "And studying."

"Not me," Irving said, lowering his gaze so that he didn't seem quite as confident as before. "I promised my mom I'd finish high school, but I don't think I'm smart enough to go to college."

"I'm sure that's not true," Augusta said.

"My mom says I got all the street smarts in the family, and my older brother got all the book smarts. She said it's lucky we each got one, because according to her, my dad had neither."

Irving had never mentioned his father before. "What does your father do?" she asked.

"Dunno," Irving said. "He left when I was three. Went out one night and never came back. Nobody's heard from him since." From the way his eyes dimmed, Augusta knew it wasn't something he liked to talk about. "I don't remember him at all. I don't even have a picture."

"I'm so sorry," Augusta whispered.

"What about you? Your pop and your sister are always around, but how come I never see your mother?"

"She died last year," Augusta told him. She rarely spoke about her mother's death, but somehow, with Irving, she didn't mind.

"That's awful," he said. "It's good you were old enough to remember her, though. What's your favorite memory of her?"

Augusta stared at the rough, skinny boy. No one had ever asked her such a question. Sometimes at night, back when they shared a bedroom, she and Bess discussed what they missed most about their mother. It was always a melancholy conversation, always spoken in the harrowing language of their communal loss. But now Irving had somehow reframed the discussion. His question was not about her grief, but about the lingering joys.

Augusta took a moment to consider her answer. "When she used to take us to the beach. My father usually had to stay back at the store, but she would take me and Bess to Coney Island. She's the one who taught us to swim. Bess preferred lying in the sun, but I always wanted to be in the water. Sometimes I'd just float on my back. Sometimes we'd race to the shore. Swimming in the ocean made me feel like I was part of something bigger. It made me feel strong. It made me feel . . ."

"Brave?" offered Irving.

Augusta smiled. "That's it exactly. With my mother gone, I don't feel as brave as I used to." She bit her lip to keep her tears at bay. "I don't go to the beach anymore." She had never spoken this way about her mother before. Even with Bess, she couldn't always explain her grief in a way that the older girl appreciated. But there was something about Irving—his easy manner, his open expression, his willingness to listen—that made her feel as if he wanted to understand. In that moment, she felt as if she could tell him anything.

When Augusta's father returned to the store, he looked even angrier than when he'd left.

"What happened, Papa?" Augusta asked, afraid of what he might say.

"Your great-aunt is up to her old tricks again."

"What do you mean? What old tricks?"

He dismissed her question with a wave of his hand. "Some stories my mother used to tell me. It isn't important right now." He took a deep breath before he continued. "The point is that I made it clear to Esther that she is no longer allowed to work at the store or converse with my customers."

"Is she allowed to keep selling soup?" Augusta asked.

"Not in the store," her father said. "If Esther wants to make some extra money, that's entirely up to her. But I will not have my pharmacy business affiliated with any of that woman's nonsense! It's one thing to give my mother's sister a home—a place to stay, a roof over her head. But I will *not* have my reputation sullied because some old woman lures away my customers with superstitions and old wives' tales!" Augusta's father punctuated this statement with a bang of his fist on the pharmacy counter.

"Of course, Papa," Augusta whispered. Irving, sensing it was a good time to leave, scooped up the bags that had been left out for him. "I'll make those deliveries now," he said.

When Irving was gone, Augusta followed her father to the stock room, where he pulled a pint bottle of whiskey from the shelves and took a small, careful swallow. When she glanced pointedly at the bottle, her father said only, "It helps me to think."

Augusta wished that she, too, had something to help process her thoughts. What had her father meant when he said that Aunt Esther lured his customers with superstitions and old wives' tales? What had he meant when he said that she was up to her old tricks again? Augusta's father had plenty of creams, plenty of fancy ointments and salves— surely there was one in the store that might have helped Mrs. Feldman's granddaughter. Certainly Aunt Esther didn't know more about such remedies—or *any* remedies for that matter—than Augusta's own father.

She wished she could ask Aunt Esther her questions, but she wasn't on the best of terms with her. Besides, although Esther's command of the English language had been good from the moment she arrived in Brooklyn, she had a way of pretending she didn't understand whenever she didn't feel like talking.

In moments like these, Augusta felt her mother's loss more deeply than ever. What would Irene Stern think of Aunt Esther and the tensions brewing with her father? What would her mother think of Irving— would she have judged him by his rough exterior, or would she have been charmed by his thoughtful observations? As it turned out, the delivery boy had something in common with her great-aunt: both were multifaceted and complex—much more so than they first appeared. *Like the ocean,* Augusta thought.

Irene Stern had always been a good swimmer—a skill she was determined to pass on to her girls. During one of their afternoon excursions to the beach, the water was particularly calm. Augusta floated on her back, without a single care in her head. Aside from the fact that they were outside, it was almost like floating in the bath. Augusta stared at the peaceful blue of the sky and felt the sun warming her wet skin. In her contentment, she forgot about everything else.

A minute later, a wave broke over her, catching her entirely by surprise. The force of the water flipped her upside down and she found herself flailing and gasping for air. Her mother had been swimming nearby at the time, but although Irene Stern had seen the wave coming, she hadn't warned her daughter of its approach.

"Why didn't you tell me?" Augusta shouted, rubbing salt water from her eyes and picking clumps of seaweed out of her hair. "At least then I could have braced myself for it!"

"My job isn't always to keep you safe," said her mother. "My job is to teach you to *keep yourself* safe. The ocean can be beautiful and serene, but it's so much more than that, Augusta. It can be overwhelming. Sometimes it can be dangerous. Its complexity is what makes it so special. There is always another wave forming in the distance. Some turn out to be only ripples, but some may head toward you at full speed."

Augusta felt like she wanted to cry. She could feel the water she had swallowed sloshing around in her empty stomach. "Maybe I shouldn't swim anymore. I'm scared of getting knocked over again."

Her mother's smile was as bright as the afternoon sun in the summer sky. "You can't give up something that brings you joy just because it is difficult. Or because there may be a risk. I know how much you love swimming, Augusta. You must promise me that you will never stop. There will always be waves in the distance. With practice, you'll learn to swim around them."

Augusta had avoided the ocean ever since her mother's funeral. Instead, she kept her childhood promise by swimming twice a month at an indoor pool a few subway stops from her apartment. Still, she missed the sunshine and the sea. She missed her mother's voice in her ear. Inside the hideous, squat brick building, the air smelled like chemicals and sweat. There were no waves, but there was no blue sky, either.

Coney Island was a million miles away.

SEVEN

SEPTEMBER 1987

Two days after the tuna incident, Augusta hadn't entirely recovered. She thought about skipping another day of swimming, but the last thing she wanted was a second phone call from Irving, or—God forbid—another unannounced visit.

Before she got out of the pool that morning, she spotted him sitting in the shade, chatting with a few other men. Despite the fact that it was only ten, Irving was nursing a can of Diet Pepsi. Didn't he know how bad that stuff was for him? She must have stared a bit too long in his direction, because the next thing she knew, a buxom woman in a lavender bathing cap swam up beside her and tapped her gently on the shoulder. "I hear the two of you grew up together," she said.

"Excuse me?"

"You and Irving, back in Brooklyn. You were kids together, he told me. I'm a Bronx girl myself." She stuck out her hand. "Shirley Polushuk." The polish on Shirley's nails matched her bathing cap.

Augusta shook Shirley's water-pruned fingers. "Augusta Stern. Nice to meet you."

Shirley tilted her head as if she'd heard incorrectly. "I could have sworn he called you Goldie."

"That . . . well, that's a *very* old nickname. No one calls me Goldie anymore."

"Anybody ever call you Gussie?"

Augusta forced herself to smile. "Just Augusta," she said.

"Got it. No nicknames," Shirley said. "You know, I just lost a wonderful friend of mine—she was Margaret-Anne, but we all called her Honey. That may be why I have nicknames on the brain."

"I'm sorry about Honey," Augusta said, softening. "I lost my sister six months ago. She was my best friend in the world."

Shirley took Augusta's hand again, but this time she gave it a sympathetic squeeze. "The two of us understand each other then. Will I see you at Book Club this afternoon?"

"I didn't know there was a book club."

"Didn't you look at the club directory? Book Club takes up the whole first page. It used to come second, after the Astronomy Club. But when the man who owned the telescope died, people stopped going, and the club dissolved. That's when the Book Club got bumped to page one."

"I guess there's no Art Club?" Augusta joked.

Shirley, not recognizing the sarcasm, lowered her voice to a whisper. "Marlene, the president of the Art Club, was sleeping with Dora Shapiro's husband. Dora is in charge of printing the directory, and when she found out about the affair, she changed the name of the Art Club to the *Visual* Art Club so she could stick Marlene's group on the last page." Shirley glanced around the pool to make sure no one else was listening. "It was quite the scandal."

Augusta wasn't sure how to respond.

"Anyway, Book Club is wonderful," said Shirley. "Last month, we read *The Cider House Rules*."

"What about this month?"

"In September, we always choose a classic. This month, it's *Sense and Sensibility*. Have you ever read it?"

Augusta nodded. She didn't say so, but *Sense and Sensibility* was one of her favorites. To be honest, she was surprised by the choice—she imagined they'd be reading the new Tom Clancy book or perhaps a mystery by Agatha Christie. Of course, Augusta read those authors, too. In fact, she read everything she could get her hands on. "When is the meeting?"

"Three o'clock, at the clubhouse. We meet in the library, which is right past the cardroom. Go to the front desk and take a left." Shirley glanced up at the clock that hung above the sandwich shack window. "I have to run, but I hope you'll come." She paddled over to the steps, grabbed the railing, and pulled herself slowly out of the water. Once both feet were planted on the patio, Shirley pulled off her lavender swim cap to reveal a head of bright red hair cut in a chin-length bob.

As Shirley dried herself off, Augusta watched as the men around her sat up in their seats to watch. "Hi there, Shirley!" one called out. The others elbowed him and laughed.

It doesn't matter how old we get, Augusta thought. *Some things never seem to change.*

She went home for lunch—no tuna this time—then showered and dug out her battered copy of Jane Austen's *Sense and Sensibility*. At two-thirty, she made her way to the clubhouse, a white stucco extravaganza flanked on all sides with swaying palm trees and giant red hibiscus plants. In the middle of the building's circular driveway was a sculpted fountain that ran continually. Augusta greeted the receptionist and made her way to the library.

The "library"—if you could call it that—was a brightly lit room with floor-to-ceiling bookshelves lining three of the four walls. Hardcovers and paperbacks were jammed onto the shelves in no particular order; they were borrowed and returned in haphazard fashion with little oversight by the Rallentando Springs staff. A long wooden table stood in the center, surrounded by a dozen hardback chairs. There were tufted chairs, too, sprinkled around the room—chairs to curl up in, if one's body still curled.

Shirley, who was already seated at the table, waved to Augusta when she came in. Shirley sat with her book propped open in front of her, surrounded by half a dozen other women. Augusta was surprised to see three men as well, all of whom she recognized from the pool that morning. She took a chair, pulled her book out of her bag, and tried to follow the bit of whispered conversation that popped up here and there around the table. For the most part, however, the members of the club seemed to be a quiet bunch.

The woman across the table from Augusta noticed her puzzled expression. "We're waiting for the moderator," she explained. "We all take turns leading the discussion, and we never start until the moderator arrives."

At 2:59, when the moderator entered, Augusta was grateful that she was sitting down. Irving sauntered into the room, carrying a dog-eared copy of the Jane Austen novel as if he'd actually read the damn thing. Augusta felt like ripping the reading glasses off of his tanned, wrinkled face. *This is your moderator?* she wanted to say. *For god's sake, he doesn't even read!* Augusta would have bet her entire life savings that Irving hadn't read a book for the past sixty years.

Apparently, she would have lost the bet.

Not only had Irving read the book, but it appeared as if he'd taken notes. He sat down at the head of the table, opened his book, and pulled out a few folded sheets of paper on which he'd typed a bullet-point list of questions. "Welcome, everyone," he said. "Thanks for letting me lead this month's discussion. For any new members who might be with us, why don't we introduce ourselves. My name is Irving Rivkin."

They went around the table, one by one. When it was Augusta's turn, she told everyone that she had recently moved to Rallentando Springs.

The tall, balding man to the left of Irving—he'd introduced himself as Harold Glantz from Flatbush—pointed his thumb at Irving and smiled. "We hear you grew up with *this* guy," he said in a raspy smoker's voice.

"Yes, I did," Augusta admitted.

"I bet you've got some good stories, then."

A few of the others around the table chuckled softly in agreement.

"Not really," said Augusta. "Sorry to disappoint you."

"Come on," said Harold. "You gotta give us something."

My mom says I got all the street smarts in the family, and my older brother got all the book smarts.

"Well, it's certainly a surprise to find him at a book club. He wasn't much of a reader back when I knew him."

From across the table, Irving shrugged. "She's not wrong," he said. "But people can change."

For the next twenty minutes, the group discussed whether sense or sensibility was the more admirable trait. Was it better to be stoic, like Elinor Dashwood, or sentimental and romantic, like her sister, Marianne?

"Best to be a little of both," said Shirley. "Everything in moderation."

"Well, I felt bad for Marianne," said the woman sitting across from Augusta. "That terrible Willoughby broke her heart. What a liar he was!"

"It's not that simple," argued Harold. "Willoughby loved her. His apology was sincere."

"Apologies don't excuse what he did!"

"I feel worse for Elinor," said Shirley. "She had to keep Lucy's secret, and it isolated her from everyone."

Harold shrugged. "I didn't care much for Elinor. She was too resigned, too indifferent."

Augusta couldn't help herself from chiming in. "Elinor isn't *indifferent,*" she argued. "She's trapped in a no-win situation. What is she supposed to do? Cry herself sick like Marianne?" Before Harold could answer, Augusta continued, her voice rising both in pitch and volume. "Elinor doesn't have that luxury. The only man she ever loved is going to marry someone else, and she has to *live* with that heartache. She has no choice but to suffer in silence to protect everyone else around her. How can you call that *indifferent?*"

Harold held up both hands in mock surrender. "Listen, I don't wanna argue. All I'm saying is, she wasn't my favorite."

Augusta felt the others staring. It wasn't like her to reveal such emotion in a room full of people she barely knew. "Sorry," she mumbled. "I shouldn't have raised my voice."

From the other end of the table, Shirley smiled. "Don't apologize," she said. "I agree one hundred percent."

"Everyone's entitled to their opinion," said Harold. He turned to his right and gave Irving a nudge. "What does our moderator have to say?"

Irving put down his notes and strummed his fingers on the cover of his book. "At first I thought Elinor was cold," he admitted. "She seemed so unmoved by what was happening, you know? But by the end of the story, I changed my mind."

"Yeah?" said Harold. "What'd you think at the end?"

"I realized how hard it was for her." He paused a moment, took off his glasses, and laid them carefully on the table. When he looked up, he was looking directly at Augusta. "By the time the story was over, I admired the hell out of her."

EIGHT

DECEMBER 1922

Whatever ointment Aunt Esther gave Gertie Feldman, it worked wonders on Gertie's granddaughter. The child's itching ceased, the pox dried up, and Esther's reputation expanded from digestive advisor to skin remedy expert. Because she no longer worked at the store, the customers called on Esther at the apartment, but only after Augusta's father had left and gone downstairs for the day.

In the evenings, when the family ate dinner together, Augusta's father didn't ask about Esther's side business and she did not ask him about the pharmacy. But although the adults had reached an affable truce, Augusta remained confused.

A few times, when customers asked for Esther, Augusta saw her father point to the ceiling. "She's right upstairs," he told them.

"Papa," Augusta said, "I don't understand. I thought you were still angry with Aunt Esther."

But Solomon Stern didn't seem angry. Instead, he seemed resigned. "Your aunt and I had a long discussion, and I decided to let it go," he said.

"I don't want her interfering with my customers, but if she sticks to soup and skin rash ointments, I won't have any problems with her."

Augusta was almost afraid to ask. "But what if . . . what if she doesn't stick to those things?"

Her father's lips flattened into a frown. "I don't want to think about it."

Following her father's lead, Augusta tried to forget the rift that had occurred. As a show of support for her father, she challenged herself to learn even more about the ingredients on his shelves. She wanted to please him, to bring back his smile, to pierce the screen of his grief so that he might return to her.

Meanwhile, Augusta and Irving got to know each other better. Augusta told herself that the reason she was always at the store was because she wanted to be there for her father. But the truth was that she also wanted to spend as much time as possible with the delivery boy.

Irving never sat still for long. He was constantly in and out of the store, picking up prescriptions and setting off on his bicycle to distribute them all over the neighborhood. When he wasn't making his rounds, he was dusting the shelves, sweeping the stock room, or helping to unload the trucks that pulled up in the alley behind the pharmacy. Every once in a while, there were afternoon lulls, quiet moments when nothing else needed his attention. These were the moments Augusta savored—when Irving would sit on the stool beside her and wait for her to finish an English essay or one of her geometry problems.

Augusta didn't mind having an audience for such tasks. Other girls might have preferred to be observed when they were at their most beautiful or beguiling—all dressed up for a weekend dance or performing onstage in the school play.

Not Augusta.

She may have been young, but she knew herself well enough to understand her own particular strengths. She was always most poised with a pencil in her hand, most confident with a book spread beneath her long fingers. She had turned fifteen years old in October and she did not know the first thing about seduction. All she knew was that she had never felt more admired than when Irving Rivkin watched her do her schoolwork.

"You barely have to think," he would whisper, awestruck, as she sped through the problems in her math book. "How can you possibly keep track of so many numbers all at once?"

The veneration in his voice, the way that he stared—no one had ever looked at her that way before.

A few times, he brought homework to do alongside her, but he did not focus on it for long. After a few minutes of leafing through pages, he would push his books aside. When Augusta offered to help, Irving would shake his head and grin.

"I'd rather watch *you* study," he'd say, winking an impish eye. And even though Augusta knew that she should encourage him to review for the science test or history quiz he had the next day, his response stirred something in the center of her chest—an innocent thrill that pumped its way through her heart and made her feel like the most beautiful girl in the world.

In December, Augusta noticed that her sister and George had graduated from sneaking glances at each other to smiling openly at each other from across the store. She wasn't surprised when Bess asked their father if she could invite George for dinner.

Given that they were having company, their father requested that both girls help Aunt Esther after school. Augusta, who was less than accomplished in the kitchen, was put to work polishing the candlesticks and setting the table. Meanwhile, Bess braided the challah, washed the vegetables, and peeled the potatoes. Aunt Esther had made her famous soup that morning and a whole chicken was already in the oven, roasting. The smell of yeast, lemons, and dill filled the overheated kitchen. At six o'clock, Augusta's father arrived—not only with George, but with Irving as well.

Suddenly Augusta was aware of every defect in her appearance. Why

hadn't she bothered to brush her hair? Or to change out of her wrinkled dress? As she eyed her sister's immaculately rouged lips, she tried
to remember how old Bess was when she was allowed to begin wearing
makeup.

"Hi, Augusta," Irving said, raising his hand in an awkward wave. She
returned the gesture, just as clumsily, and immediately wished that she
hadn't. Downstairs, it was easy to talk to Irving. But he had never come up
the stairs before, and seeing him now in her family home left her tongue-
tied and uneasy.

For the first few minutes of the meal there was almost no conversation—
only the steady scrape of spoons on bowls. George had a healthy appetite,
but Augusta had never seen anyone eat like Irving. Three bowls of soup,
thick with kreplach, disappeared as if they were bowls of air.

"Slow down, *boychik*," Aunt Esther advised. "There's plenty more. No
one should choke at my table, please."

Irving looked up from his bowl. "Sorry," he said. "But I've never tasted
anything so delicious in my life." After the soup, at least half a challah
found its way into his bottomless stomach. Chicken, potatoes, piles of green
beans. It was as if he had never eaten before. As if he might never eat again.

Meanwhile, George was less focused on the food than he was on Augusta's sister. For her part, Bess seemed equally smitten. Augusta watched
as the two of them stared at each other from across the wooden table.
Bess, already a senior in high school, told her father that George was
finishing his degree at Brooklyn College in between his shifts at the store.

"Tell us about your classes, George," Augusta's father said. "Any plans
for the future?"

"I'll be starting law school next year. My uncle wants me to join his firm."

Augusta wondered whether she was imagining the twinge of disappointment in her father's features. "No interest in pharmacy school, then?"

George shook his head. "I'm afraid not, sir. I only got through chem-
istry by the skin of my teeth."

"I suppose a career in pharmacy isn't for everyone," Augusta's father
admitted.

Irving put down his fork. "Augusta's gonna make a *great* pharmacist one day."

Augusta felt her cheeks grow warm. It wasn't that her family didn't know of her interest. She'd been watching her father compound prescriptions for months—asking him questions, poring over his books. But hearing Irving declare her intentions so plainly in front of everyone at the table made Augusta feel strangely exposed.

Her father smiled and wiped his lips with the corner of his napkin. "You think so, do you? You seem to have a lot of confidence in my daughter."

"'Course I do," Irving said. "Augusta's smarter than anyone I know." He helped himself to another serving of potatoes before sheepishly adding, "No offense to you, sir."

Augusta's father chuckled softly while Bess kicked Augusta under the table. Aunt Esther, meanwhile, looked at Irving with newfound appreciation. "He isn't wrong," Esther said. "There's nothing our brilliant Goldie can't learn if she puts her mind to it."

Irving put down his fork again. "Goldie?" he said, sounding confused.

Augusta glared at her aunt from across the table. She'd already told Esther countless times that she had no interest in the nickname. "My aunt calls me that sometimes," she admitted. "But I prefer to go by Augusta."

Irving failed to notice the embarrassment that had crept into Augusta's voice. "Goldie is a pretty name," he said. "I think it's perfect for you."

For the rest of the meal, Augusta's heart thumped so loudly that it threatened to burst. The compliment was painfully oblique, but Augusta followed it to its logical conclusion. If the name was pretty *and* it suited her, that could only mean one thing.

Irving Rivkin thought she was pretty.

A few weeks after their dinner, Brooklyn had its first snowfall of the season. It buried the streets in soft, hopeful white, concealing the grimy rubbish beneath before the inevitable thaw. Days later, the cycle started anew: snow slowly replaced with sludge; anticipation replaced with desolation.

At the pharmacy, customers requested deliveries, but given the condition of the roads, they took more time for Irving to complete. Late one afternoon, he returned to the store, still shivering in his thin wool coat. No amount of pedaling on his bike was enough to keep him warm. Augusta went to get him a cup of coffee poured hastily by George at the soda counter, but by the time she reached him with the mug, he'd turned whiter than the freshly fallen layer outside. She touched his forehead with the back of her hand and felt the heat radiate off his skin. "You have a fever," Augusta told him. "You need to go home and get some rest."

He shook his head. "Your pop has a few more deliveries for me. I gotta get out and finish those first."

His fingers trembled as he raised the cup of steaming liquid to his lips. His eyes had dulled to a stormy blue—the color of icy, churning waves instead of a sunny cobalt sea.

"You're not going anywhere," she said firmly. "Papa! Come take a look at Irving!"

A moment later her father was beside them, pressing his hand to Irving's cheeks. "Go home, son," Mr. Stern insisted. "Augusta, I want you to go with him. He looks like he's about to fall over."

"I'll be fine, Mr. Stern. I can go by myself—"

"Augusta, get your coat on, please. Irving, this isn't up for debate."

Irving's building was only two blocks from the store, but he had to keep stopping to catch his breath. Eventually, Augusta looped her arm through his to help propel him toward home. When they were only a few feet away, Irving pulled his arm away and vomited loudly into the snow. He didn't want her to come inside, but she insisted on accompanying him up the three flights of stairs. When he opened the door to his tiny apartment, his mother leapt up from her chair, took one look at his face, and helped him inside. Both of them thanked Augusta repeatedly, but it was clear that they didn't want her to stay.

"I'll stop by tomorrow," Augusta promised, but her father insisted on going instead. He brought aspirin, Vicks VapoRub, and Dr. Birnbaum—his longtime friend—to the Rivkin home. It didn't take long for Dr.

Birnbaum to diagnose Irving with the flu. Warm liquids and plenty of rest were prescribed. Irving was young and healthy, the doctor said, and certain to make a full recovery.

But as the days passed, nothing seemed "certain" at all. Irving's fever refused to break, and his cough clung stubbornly to his lungs. His mother, after leaving him in the care of a neighbor, appeared at the pharmacy, distraught. Dr. Birnbaum was consulted again, and Augusta's father made up some capsules.

On the sixth day, when Augusta insisted on visiting, Irving's mother stopped her at the door. "I'm not sure you should come in," she said. "I don't want you getting sick, too."

Augusta didn't even try to wipe the tears from her cheeks. "Please let me see him, Mrs. Rivkin. I promise I won't get too close." In the few days since Irving had been absent, a terrible emptiness had filled her. Augusta hadn't known how much Irving's presence meant to her until he was no longer there. She did not know what she would say next if Mrs. Rivkin refused her entreaty. But dark circles bloomed beneath the woman's brown eyes, and Augusta could see that she was too worn out to put up much of a fight for long.

Augusta asked again, begging this time. *"Please?"*

Mrs. Rivkin stepped aside, waving the young girl into the apartment. "Irving is in the bedroom," she said. "Usually, he sleeps out here, but I wanted to make him comfortable."

Augusta was wholly unprepared for how ill Irving had become. He looked so much smaller than she remembered, and she'd seen him only a few days ago. His eyes were closed, but his skin was flushed, and his damp hair was plastered to his head. Even his cowlick drooped.

"Irving?" his mother said. "Your friend is here."

"It's me," Augusta said brightly, forcing a smile into her voice.

For a moment, Irving's eyelids fluttered, but he could not manage to open them. When he lifted one arm, as if reaching for her, she forgot the promise to keep her distance. She perched herself on the edge of his bed and took his clammy hand in hers. "Everyone misses you at the store," she said. "So you have to try and get better soon. George said that when you get back, he'll give you all the ice cream you want."

Augusta squeezed Irving's fingers, but when he didn't respond, she kept on talking. "As soon as you're out of bed, you'll come over for dinner again. I'll ask Aunt Esther to make her brisket next time. It's the best I've ever had—better even than my mother's. Bess thinks so, too, but we made a pact to never let Esther know. It's a little mean of us, I guess. Maybe one day we'll tell Esther the truth."

Augusta turned to Irving's mother. "Has he been awake at all?"

"No—last night he was tossing and turning like he was having some kind of nightmare. I gave him some of your father's capsules. And the other medicine, too. But his fever keeps getting higher . . ."

Augusta did her best to hold back her tears. It was one thing to cry in front of Mrs. Rivkin, but she didn't want to cry in front of Irving. It didn't matter that his eyes were closed or that he might not be listening. She didn't want him to know how worried she was. She didn't want him to know how much she missed him. Not the way she missed her mother, but still. She remembered the question Irving had asked: *What's your favorite memory of her?*

Mrs. Rivkin excused herself for a few minutes, and Augusta gripped Irving's hand even tighter. "You know what my favorite thing about *you* is? You say you're not smart, but that isn't true. You're smart about people. You know how to ask the right questions and say the right things to make people feel good."

When his mother returned, Augusta could sense that she'd begun to overstay her welcome. Reluctantly she let go of Irving's hand and promised to return soon. Irving's eyes did not open, but his lips moved slightly to release one word.

"Goldie . . ." he muttered, in a voice so soft that Augusta questioned whether he had actually spoken.

For the first time since she'd heard her aunt say it, Augusta didn't mind the name at all.

As soon as they gathered for dinner that night, Augusta began quizzing her father. "Did you talk to Dr. Birnbaum? What does he say about Irving?"

Aunt Esther set a heavy platter of stuffed cabbage on the table. "The delivery boy is sick?" she asked. "Such a nice boy, such a good appetite." She raised her eyebrows at Augusta's father. "Now that I'm not in the store anymore, you must remember to tell me these things."

"Forgive me," Augusta's father said, sighing. "Yes, Irving Rivkin has the flu. Dr. Birnbaum saw him again today. Unfortunately, the boy's condition has taken a serious turn."

"But there's something you can give him, isn't there, Papa? Another medicine you can try?"

Solomon Stern did not answer. He busied himself with his napkin in order to avoid his daughter's gaze. During the Spanish flu outbreak, he'd lost over a dozen customers, some even younger than Irving. There was no cure for influenza, and no one could predict the twists and turns that the illness might take. "I have nothing left to try," he finally admitted. "We will have to pray that his fever breaks."

Augusta could not believe what she was hearing. "But you have a whole *room* full of medicine downstairs. You have over a hundred bottles and jars. And all of your books—there must be something in one of those books that can give you the answer." Augusta's voice rose in both pitch and ferocity until she finally broke down in a torrent of tears. "There has to be *something* to make Irving better!"

Bess rose up from her chair and knelt down beside her sister. "Shh," Bess whispered. "It will be all right."

Their father was accustomed to emotional displays, but they usually came from Bess, not Augusta. "I'm sorry, Augusta," he said, "but I don't want to lie to you. I was honest with you about your mother, and I want to be honest with you now. Irving is very, very ill."

But Augusta didn't need to hear him say it—she had already seen the fear in his eyes, had already heard the doubt in his voice. Solomon Stern was a brilliant druggist, as educated and capable as a pharmacist could be. But there were limits to his skill and limits to the drugs at his disposal.

This should not have been surprising to her. She had been through it before, with her mother. But now, more than anything else, Augusta wanted to believe that medicine had the power to heal. She wanted to believe that scientists and doctors and pharmacists could consult their books, study their formulas, measure their ingredients, and make things right for anyone in need. She wanted to believe in this so much that she'd been planning to make it her whole life's work.

But this time, she could see that it wasn't so simple. There were no guarantees. The books she had relied on were deficient, the formulas inchoate, the explanations incomplete. Neither science nor scholarship offered the assurances Augusta so urgently desired. She could not depend on them.

As Augusta sat in worried silence, Aunt Esther went about filling their plates. Her stuffed cabbage was a study in contrasts—both delicate and filling, savory and sweet. Like all of her specialties, it was delicious. And yet no one at the table could manage to eat. They were all too concerned about Irving Rivkin, too worried and heartsick to take even one bite.

Aunt Esther glanced wordlessly at Augusta, absorbing the full measure of her grand-niece's sorrow. She murmured something the others could not hear before patting her lap with a palpable thud as if to signal that some sort of decision had been made.

"Did you say something?" Augusta's father asked.

Aunt Esther ignored the pharmacist's question and pointed her fork in Augusta's direction. "Tomorrow," she said, "we will go see the delivery boy."

Augusta stared back at her aunt, trying to make sense of the announcement. "You want to come with me to see Irving?"

"Yes," Esther said, "we will visit him together." She shrugged and tilted her head to one side as if there was nothing surprising about what she had said.

"We will bring the boy some of my soup."

NINE

SEPTEMBER 1987

After the book club meeting was over, Augusta couldn't stop thinking about what Irving said. Was he implying that he admired *her*? If so, she refused to care. His admiration—if that's what it was—was like one of those cheap plastic trophies presented to children when their team comes in last: performative, meaningless, and hollow.

That evening, she called to order a new bathing suit from the Eddie Bauer catalogue. When she chose the racerback one-piece in poppy red, the saleswoman whistled into the phone. "That color will get you *noticed*," she said. Augusta concentrated on reading out her credit card number and banished the comment to the back of her mind. Did she want Irving to notice her? It made her uncomfortable to think about.

A few mornings later, when Irving wasn't at the pool, she hated herself for noting his absence. Eventually, when she looked up from her book, she realized that it wasn't only Irving who was missing. The pool was completely deserted. "Where is everybody?" she asked the snack bar attendant.

"There's a big tennis tournament today," Paul said. "I left my car in the clubhouse parking lot earlier, and there was already a crowd over at the courts."

"I didn't know about it," said Augusta, feeling a little bit left out.

Paul shrugged and pointed to the flyer taped up next to the sandwich menu. THE ANNUAL RALLENTANDO OPEN it said, with a hand-drawn cartoon of a smiling tennis racket. "They do it every year, as soon as the U.S. Open is over. Do you play?" the young man asked.

"No," said Augusta. "It's not my sport. But I might go over and watch for a bit."

"Tuna sandwich for the road?" he asked, gesturing toward the jar of mayonnaise sitting on the snack bar counter.

"Absolutely not," she said. "And for god's sake, Paul, keep that in the fridge. It's ninety-five degrees outside! One of these days, you're going to kill someone."

There were six tennis courts at Rallentando—far fewer than at some of the bigger Florida developments, where there were separate tennis centers, clubhouses, and pro shops. Rallentando had none of those accoutrements, but it did have Bob, the beloved tennis pro, a group of die-hard doubles players, and—as Augusta was about to find out—an enthusiastic cadre of spectators.

She stopped at her apartment first, to change out of her wet bathing suit, and then walked around the back of the clubhouse, following the noise of the crowd. The organizers of the tournament had set up portable bleachers with room for two dozen alongside one of the courts. The benches were packed, so some extra café chairs had been set out by the court as well. It was almost twelve o'clock and there wasn't even a hint of a breeze.

When she spotted Shirley at the end of the bleachers, Augusta wandered over to say hello. "How can they play in this heat?" she asked. Shirley scooted over to make room. "They're used to it, I guess," she said.

Augusta nodded, clapping with the others as the set they were watching came to an end. A few minutes later, the match was over—Milton

Krugel and Al Koestler narrowly beating Sam Feinerman and Arnold Zilkha. The next match, Bob the pro announced, would be Isaac Zinn and Morris Prober against Harold Glantz and Irving Rivkin.

Irving sauntered onto the court wearing dark sunglasses, a white FILA shirt, and a pristine pair of white cotton shorts. Despite the somewhat showy outfit, Augusta found his confident smile alarmingly appealing. The other players wore mismatched shirts, baggy shorts, and droopy socks. Only Irving had dressed for the occasion.

"Hey, Rivkin," shouted Isaac Zinn. "Whaddya think this is? Wimbledon?"

A few of the people in the bleachers chuckled, but Irving didn't bat an eye. "I can't help it if I happen to look good in white," he said.

"You're no Boris Becker," shouted Shirley, causing Irving to turn in her direction. When he spotted Augusta, he removed his sunglasses and waved. Shirley nudged Augusta's shoulder. "Somebody's happy to see you here," she whispered.

"Shh," Augusta snapped. "Don't be ridiculous."

After a few perfunctory stretches, the men took their positions on the court. When Harold's second serve fell into the net, Isaac Zinn let out a snort. "Ignore him, Harold," Irving shouted. "Don't get too comfortable out there, Zinn. You're gonna be flat on your ass before long!"

For the next forty-five minutes, the quartet of seniors ran and lunged as if they were teenagers. As the two sides traded winning shots, the games stretched on interminably.

"Deuce," called Morris for the third time in one game. Meanwhile, the sun pounded down on the court like a heavy metal drummer showing off on a solo. When the score finally reached five all, the men began to move more slowly. Harold stopped for a drink of water, Morris retied the laces of his sneakers, and Irving leaned his body forward to rest both hands on top of his knees. Despite the heat, his face looked pale.

"You okay there, Irv?" Isaac Zinn called.

"Sure, sure," Irving wheezed. But even from her seat on the bleachers, Augusta could see that he didn't look well. His face had turned a sickly white, and he wobbled unsteadily on his feet. A moment later, his knees gave way and he fell over onto the service line.

Without thinking, Augusta leapt up from the bench and ran to where Irving lay on the court. His eyes were closed, but he was still vaguely conscious, mumbling something about volleys and serves. Augusta shouted at the pro to call for an ambulance while she patted Irving's cheeks. "Irving! Irving! Can you hear me?"

She turned to his doubles partner. "Get him some water!" By the time Harold was back with a cup from the drinking fountain, she had managed to get Irving to open his eyes. Together with Morris, she sat him up and forced him to take a few sips.

"Do you remember where you are?" she asked.

He blinked his eyes until they rested on her face. "Hi there, Goldie," he whispered.

"Irving, do you know where you are?"

He took another sip from the cup and flashed her a woozy smile. "You look beautiful," he said.

"Don't be an idiot," Augusta said. "Answer my question or I'll tell the paramedics you had a stroke."

"I'm sitting on the tennis court. This concrete is burning a hole in my *tuchus*."

Augusta released a sigh of relief. "Good. And can you tell me your name?"

"Irving Rivkin. Are you happy now?"

"Of course I'm not happy!" Augusta blurted out. "For god's sake, Irving, you scared me half to death!"

His smile grew broader and all of the color flooded back into his sweaty cheeks. "You were worried about me," he said, obviously pleased with the idea.

Augusta gestured to the people on the bleachers and to all the men still standing on the court. "*Everyone* was worried," she said. "Eighty-year-old men shouldn't play tennis."

"I'm eighty-two."

"I know that, Irving. I was making a point. But I'm glad that you still remember your age. I guess you didn't have a stroke after all."

"You know," he said, taking another sip of water, "I don't think I was down for more than half a minute. You must have run over here pretty quick."

"You *collapsed*," Augusta said. "Of course I came quickly."

"Sure," he said. "But it's not like *everybody* rushed over to help me."

"I wanted to make sure you were still breathing."

"What if I wasn't?"

"Why would you say that?"

He winked at her slyly. "If I wasn't breathing, you might have done CPR. Maybe even mouth-to-mouth resuscitation."

Augusta took the paper cup of water from his hand and dumped what was left of it over his head.

"What'd you do that for?" He grinned.

"You looked like you needed cooling off."

When the paramedics arrived, they took Irving's blood pressure, helped him up off the ground, and told him they wanted to take him to the hospital for some intravenous fluids. At first he tried to brush them off, but Augusta insisted that he go. "You're completely dehydrated," she said. "I think you should listen to them."

"I'll follow behind the ambulance in my car," said Harold. "And I'll give you a ride home when you're done."

As she watched the ambulance drive away, Augusta's eyes filled with tears. Seeing Irving that way—so pale and so weak—had produced a terrible surge of memories: she pictured him lying in his mother's bed, barely able to open his eyes. She heard his pained, shallow breathing. She felt the fever pouring off his skin. She remembered the fear that threatened to choke her—fear she might lose her best friend, fear that she would never hear him laugh again.

Augusta concentrated on steadying her nerves. Irving had recovered then, and he was well on his way to recovering now. *Stop it*, she told herself. There was no need for histrionics.

So what if she'd jumped from her seat and run to his side to check his breathing? She told herself it was a perfectly normal reaction to a stressful situation. All it proved was that she was a good human being who cared about the health of others. She told herself that if it had been Harold or Morris who had fallen so abruptly to the ground, she would have behaved exactly the same way.

If Irving teased her about it later, she would be sure to tell him as much.

TEN

DECEMBER 1922

That night, Augusta tossed and turned in her sleep. At three in the morning, she woke with a start from an awful nightmare that she couldn't remember. She tried to slow her breathing by silently reciting the elements from the periodic table. When her muscles relaxed, she went to the kitchen for a glass of water.

She was surprised to find Esther there, working by candlelight, rummaging through a wooden apothecary case that she had set out on the table. As Augusta got closer, she saw that the case was a remarkable contraption: Over a foot high and a foot wide, it opened almost like a miniature wardrobe. Inside the doors were dozens of shelves and compartments, filled with stoppered glass bottles and square tins. Tiny knobs were screwed on to small drawers, filled with all kinds of herbs, leaves, and seeds.

Augusta watched as Esther opened a tin, pulled out a single raspberry leaf, and dropped it into the brass mortar. From a stoppered glass bottle, she chose what looked to be a piece of dried gingerroot and did the same. Over and over, she foraged in her case, until a small pile of items had been collected. A beam of moonlight shone in from the window, illuminating Esther's long silver hair. Augusta rarely saw Esther without her headscarf, and the vision was almost otherworldly. Wrapped over her plain white nightdress was a robe Augusta did not recognize. It was long and silky, a deep sapphire blue, unlike anything she'd seen her aunt wear before. There was a haunting and powerful beauty about the woman that Augusta had previously failed to notice.

When Augusta first walked into the room, Esther seemed neither surprised nor startled. She placed a single finger over her lips in a motion that signaled absolute silence. Then she gestured to one of the kitchen chairs for Augusta to take a seat. The air in the room crackled with expectancy.

Esther's brass mortar and pestle sat in the center of the table. As she worked, she murmured the softest of songs. Augusta did not recognize the Yiddish words, but she felt the full force of them deep in her chest. She forgot about her nightmare. She forgot about the glass of water she'd come for. She forgot about everything but Esther's words and the rhythm of her voice.

A multitude of scents swirled around them—ginger and garlic, rosemary and yarrow, cinnamon and horehound, lemon and hyssop. There were other scents, too, for things she could not think to name. Augusta shut her eyes, and when she opened them, the scents in the room shifted yet again, smelling now of solace, of something wholesome and strong. A vision of Irving—healthy once more—filled her mind, as if Esther had conjured it out of the moonlight.

Esther emptied the contents of the mortar onto a waiting square of plain white muslin. The powder on the fabric sparkled like sunshine reflecting off a pile of freshly fallen snow. It shimmered like the wings of a firefly on a hot summer night. As Esther tied the pouch shut with a piece of string, Augusta swore she could see the light melt away.

Once Esther was finished, she blew out the candles and pulled her hair back up into her scarf. The silver patch of moonlight in the kitchen dulled to gray. The electric charge that had filled the room sputtered out.

Augusta felt as if she had been swimming underwater and had suddenly come to the surface for air. She took a deep breath and pointed to the bundle. "What is that for?"

Tilting her head this way and that, Esther weighed what and how much to say. "For the soup," she finally answered. "The soup for your friend, the delivery boy."

"I've seen you make dozens of batches of soup. You've never gone to all this trouble before."

"That's true," said Esther, taking a seat. "But this boy is your special friend, yes? For him, I will make a special batch."

When tears welled in the corners of Augusta's eyes, Aunt Esther patted her niece's hand. "Save your tears, Goldie," she said. "In the morning, I will go to the butcher and get the best chicken in the store. I will make my soup—only the broth—and I will add my special herbs. Then when you come home from school, we will take the soup to your friend."

"And you think that the soup will make Irving better?"

"It will." Esther spoke with a quiet confidence, but she refused to say anything more.

"Aunt Esther, what were the words you were chanting? Were they the words that are carved into your mortar? The ones in the center of the bowl?"

Aunt Esther shrugged. "We'll talk about it another time. It's late and you should be in bed."

In school, Augusta couldn't concentrate on a single word her teachers said. She rushed home after class to find Esther by the stove, humming over a pot of soup. The room smelled of dill and garlic and broth and the fainter scents of the evening before. Augusta watched as her aunt ladled the soup into a clean clear-glass jar. Before she screwed on the lid, Esther pulled the muslin pouch from her apron pocket, untied the string, and sprinkled the herbs into the steaming liquid. She mumbled some words only she could hear. "Now, let us go to your friend," she said.

Augusta had a thousand questions, but she didn't want to delay their departure, so she decided to keep them to herself. They walked the two blocks to Irving's building, climbed the narrow, dimly lit stairs, and knocked on Mrs. Rivkin's door.

Irving's mother looked as if she had been crying—her eyes were swollen bloodshot hollows, her lips a dry and mottled pink.

"Mrs. Rivkin, this is my great-aunt Esther. We've brought some of her soup for Irving."

Mrs. Rivkin blinked back tears. "It's kind of you both to come," she said. "But he hasn't been able to keep anything down." She held her hands out for the jar. "You can leave that with me, and I'll try to give him some of it later."

Aunt Esther had no time for niceties. "He must have the soup now," she said brusquely. "Where is the boy? I will give it to him."

Even in her exhausted state, Mrs. Rivkin was taken aback. She was used to the soft-spoken Dr. Birnbaum, and to Solomon Stern's reassuring ways. "But Irving is sleeping now," she said. "I'm sure a bowl of soup can wait."

"No," said Esther. "He must eat it now."

Augusta stepped in to explain. "She means that Irving should have the soup while it's hot. She took it off the stove right before we came. I'm sure we can get him to have a spoonful or two. Please, Mrs. Rivkin? Will you let us try?"

Mrs. Rivkin twisted the corners of her apron in her hands. "Yes," she finally said, relenting. She nodded to Esther. "Augusta can show you into the bedroom. I'll get you a spoon from the kitchen."

Augusta led her aunt into the bedroom, where the air was dark and slightly fetid. Irving lay under a heap of blankets so that only his face and one arm were visible—both thinner and paler than they should have been. Immediately, Esther pulled up the window shades to let in some of the afternoon light. She rested the jar of soup on the nightstand and used both hands to push open the windows. Then she peeled back a layer of blankets so that Irving's neck and chest were exposed. As a blast of icy air filled the room, Irving began to stir.

Esther sat on the edge of his bed and took one of his hands in both of hers. She rubbed it as if it were a twig in the forest, as if she were trying to summon a flame. "Wake up, *tateleh*," she said. "I brought you something good to eat. Remember when you came for dinner?" A short laugh bubbled up from her throat. "I never saw someone so skinny eat so much." She laid his hand gently on top of the blanket and patted it. "You'll be back for dinner soon, I think."

Mrs. Rivkin returned with the spoon and frowned. "Why are the windows open?" she said. "He still has a fever; he's going to freeze!"

Esther took the spoon from Mrs. Rivkin. "The fresh air is good for him," she said. "It will wake him up. I will shut the windows after he eats the soup."

Mrs. Rivkin's frown turned to a grimace. "I told you, he can't keep anything down. I couldn't even get him to take a sip of tea—"

But Esther was no longer listening. As she hummed the tune from the night before she motioned to her niece to help move some pillows so that Irving's head was better supported. "Sit up, *tateleh*," Esther said. "There we go, very good."

Carefully, Esther twisted the lid to open the jar of still-warm soup. Tiny green specks sparkled in golden liquid like flakes of glitter inside a snow globe. Esther held the jar closer to Irving to tempt him with the savory smell. As his nostrils began to twitch, Augusta thought she saw his eyelids flutter. He parted his chapped and colorless lips the tiniest fraction of an inch.

"Taste this now," Esther whispered, gently spooning the soup into his mouth.

Augusta had hoped that Irving might eat one or two spoonfuls of the broth. She thought that after the first or second, her friend would most likely fall back asleep. But instead of rejecting the offering, Irving opened his mouth wider. Both Augusta and Mrs. Rivkin watched in amazement as, spoonful by spoonful, he consumed half the jar. He did so without once opening his eyes, without speaking or uttering a sound. After he had taken his fill, he nestled his head back against the pillow. The expression on his face was peaceful, like a satisfied infant, half intoxicated from the abundance of his mother's milk.

"I can't believe it," Mrs. Rivkin murmured.

Esther nodded at her and smiled. She sealed the lid back onto the jar.

"Take this," she said, passing it to Irving's mother. "Give the rest of it to him when he wakes."

Dr. Birnbaum stopped by the next morning, before Augusta left for school. Bess ushered him into the kitchen, where the rest of the family was having breakfast. The sight of him sent Augusta's heart sinking. Why was he visiting them so early? Was Irving worse?

"Good news!" the doctor said, smiling broadly as he dropped his black bag onto the floor. "The Rivkin boy's fever broke last night. I called on his mother this morning, and he was already up and alert. Only the faintest hint of a cough."

Augusta's father put down his newspaper. "That's wonderful," he said. "Come and sit. Would you like to have some breakfast?"

Augusta leapt up from her chair and poured the doctor a cup of coffee. "What happened?" she asked.

"What do you mean? He's a healthy young man—almost the same age as my Nathaniel. Irving got better, that's all." Dr. Birnbaum answered her inquiry with a dismissive wave of his hand.

"But Papa said it was very serious. None of the medicines were working."

The doctor took a sip of coffee. "That *is* true," he admitted. "But influenza is an unpredictable illness. We don't know enough about the virus to say why some people recover and some don't."

"Esther and I brought him soup yesterday. Did Irving's mother tell you that?"

"She did, yes. That was very kind."

"Do you think the soup could have helped? Esther added some special herbs . . ."

Her aunt gave Augusta a warning glance while Solomon Stern looked up from his paper. When he turned his head to stare at Esther, she busied herself making a plate of toast.

"A little garlic and dill," she clarified. "For flavor only." She passed the doctor the plate and pushed a jar of preserves across the table.

"Thank you," said the doctor, slathering his toast with the homemade sweet-smelling jam. "There's nothing magical about soup, Augusta. The illness simply ran its course."

"Dr. Birnbaum is right," said Esther, her voice as firm as unripe fruit. "Soup is only soup."

ELEVEN

SEPTEMBER 1987

The ER doctor told Irving to take it easy. "Stay inside and avoid the sun," he said. "At least for the next few days."

Harold gave Augusta the full report when he called her on the phone the next morning.

"Thanks for the update," she said. "I'm glad Irving has such a thoughtful friend."

"I'm sure he'd do the same for me. Irving is a *mensch*, you know. He's the best friend I have."

Harold spoke gently, in a voice that sounded as if he wanted to say more. "He puts on a good show, but don't be fooled—Irving has had some hard times in his life. He's been through a lot of heartache."

What exactly was Harold trying to say? Had Irving told him to speak to her? She knew a few things about heartache herself, but she didn't go around advertising that to strangers. Frustration gathered in her chest and she decided it was best to end the call. "I have to go, Harold," she said abruptly. "I have some errands I need to run." She hung up the phone, determined to avoid thinking about Irving for the rest of the day.

Then she remembered how he'd left her the bag of saltines and the ginger ale when she was sick. If he went to all that trouble for her, how could she do nothing for him now? She decided that it would be mean-spirited to ignore him after his trip to the hospital. She would pick up a small get-well gift—she didn't know what—in the course of her daily errands.

But as she made her way from the post office to the strip mall, she struggled to come up with an appropriate token. Flowers felt too intimate, but wasn't a potted plant impersonal? She thought about buying a simple get-well card, but she had no idea what to write inside it. Then later, at the supermarket checkout line, a pile of yellow-wrapped Oh Henry! candy bars caught her eye. Before Augusta finished paying for her groceries, she threw two of the candy bars on the conveyor belt.

The first time any of them had seen an Oh Henry! bar was when a shipment arrived at her father's drugstore. The chocolate peanut bars were such a hit in the neighborhood that all of them were gone before the morning was over. Unsure of what all the fuss was about, Augusta's father saved one for her. Later, when Irving got to work, Augusta cut the bar in two and passed half to her friend.

Irving didn't have much of a sweet tooth, but he never turned down food. When he bit into the Oh Henry! bar, his expression went from curious to ecstatic. In the years to come, the two friends tried dozens of other kinds of candy. But Irving never found another to rival the confection that was his first love.

Augusta went over to Irving's in the late afternoon with the two candy bars tucked inside her purse. She'd tied them together with a scrap of red ribbon she'd saved from a present her niece Jackie had given her.

When he opened the door to his condo, a flicker of surprise flashed across Irving's features. "Goldie!" he said. "I wasn't expecting you! Why didn't you tell me you were coming?" If he hadn't looked so much paler than usual, she would have reminded him not to use her nickname. But this time, she let the matter slide. When he leaned forward to kiss her cheek, she pulled back clumsily so the peck landed on her chin. She tried to ignore the strange knot in her stomach and the unfamiliar sensation in her knees.

"How are you feeling?" she asked.

"A little tired, but otherwise fine. That was some crazy tennis yesterday."

"It certainly was," she agreed. *I was worried about you.*

A voice like squealing brakes on pavement interrupted their conversation. "Irving! Who are you talking to?" Irving pulled the door open farther to reveal a woman in a black sequined blouse standing in his foyer. She wore heavy black eyeliner and the longest false eyelashes that Augusta had ever seen.

"Vera, this is Goldie. Goldie, Vera." Was it Augusta's imagination, or did Irving seem suddenly sheepish? *Who is this woman?*

"Vera is my neighbor. She's a snowbird," Irving said. "She got here last night from New Jersey."

Is it normal for people from New Jersey to wear sequins at four o'clock on a weekday? "Welcome back," said Augusta, wondering whether Vera could hear the insincerity in her voice.

Vera didn't seem to notice. "It's a good thing I got here when I did," she said. "I go away for a few months, and this one ends up in the hospital. Sunstroke at a tennis match! Can you imagine such a thing?"

"I can," said Augusta, trying not to notice how close Vera was standing next to Irving. "I was there yesterday. I saw the whole thing."

"Oh?" said Vera, eyelashes fluttering like miniature bat wings beneath her brows. "What were you doing at the tournament?"

"Goldie just moved to Rallentando," said Irving. "But—here's the crazy part—we grew up together! I used to work at her father's drugstore. I was the delivery boy." He shook his head and smiled at them both. "It sure is a small world, isn't it?"

"Uh-huh," said Vera, placing one hand on Irving's shoulder and pulling him ever so slightly toward her. "It's awfully sweet of you to come by, Goldie, but the doctors said Irving is supposed to take it easy. He's going to have a nap before dinner. I'm making his favorite—my famous turkey meatloaf."

Who makes meatloaf in this heat? Augusta wondered. She flashed Vera her most saccharine smile. "Of course," she said. "I'll get out of your hair." She pulled the Oh Henry! bars out of her purse and practically threw them at Irving.

She'd been planning to say, *I remembered how you loved these.* Or maybe *I know these used to be your favorite.* But she was too irritated now to say anything of the sort—anything that would serve as an admission of how much she used to care about him.

When Irving looked down and saw the candy, his eyes grew wide with delight. "Would you look at that," he said dreamily. "I can't believe you remembered." He smiled at her then, the way that he used to, back when the two of them were still young, back when a candy bar still had the power to turn a crummy day around.

The next moment, Vera reached for the bars and tugged them out of Irving's hands. "I'll put those in the kitchen," she said. "Irving, you really need to rest. Goodbye now, Goldie. See you around."

"Thanks so much for coming over," said Irving. "This heat wave is supposed to break tomorrow. I'll be back at the pool in a couple of days."

As she made her way home, a seething Augusta suppressed the sudden urge to scream. She never should have bought that candy. She never should have knocked on Irving's door. How could she have let down her guard again? Had sixty-two years taught her nothing?

The next morning, in an effort to boost her mood, Augusta put on her new swimsuit. In the mirror, she admired the wide red straps, which showed off the elegant line of her shoulders. Not that she expected anyone to notice.

Rage propelled her through the pool, fueling her strokes with an intensity that translated into the speed and strength of a woman half her age. With every stroke, her mind raced ahead. Was Irving still with Vera now? Why hadn't he mentioned her before?

As Augusta's arms cut through the water, she was aware of another body beside her. There were three lap lanes on one side of the pool, but usually Augusta was the only one in them. Now, however, someone was matching her, stroke for stroke and kick for kick. Not racing against her exactly but doing his darndest to keep up. It was a man, but no one she recognized, especially not when all she could see was the blur of his forearms and fluttering feet.

She swam a few more laps than usual, and when she finally stopped, he stopped, too, pulling the goggles from his face and the swim cap from his head. In her experience, men who wore swim caps were usually covering up a bald spot. But this man shook out a copious mane of slightly tousled, thick white hair. Her first thought was that his face was familiar, like someone she had seen before. Powerful features; rough, tanned skin. Who did he remind her of?

"You have an excellent breaststroke," the stranger said.

"I bet you say that to all the girls."

He barked out a short, embarrassed laugh. "I apologize. That didn't come out the way I had hoped. I meant to say that you're a very strong swimmer. I'm usually the only one doing laps around here."

"We must be on different schedules, then—this is the first time I've seen you."

"Until yesterday, I was still up north. September is when the great migration begins—all of us snowbirds heading down south."

"So I've noticed," Augusta murmured.

"What's that?"

"Oh, nothing. Yesterday I met another one—a returned snowbird, that's all."

"Ah, I see." He held out his hand. "I'm Nathaniel," he said. "Nice to meet a fellow swimmer."

Something clicked in Augusta's brain. When she squinted, she could see the stranger not as he was, but with darker hair, leaner cheeks, and all the sharpness and flash of youth. "Oh, my goodness. Nathaniel Birnbaum? I haven't seen you for sixty years!"

"Augusta?" he said, incredulous. "Augusta Stern . . . I can't believe it!"

She turned her head to scan the crowd. "Is Evie here? How is she?"

His face was already wet from the pool, but Augusta saw the tears well up in his eyes. "We lost her twelve years ago. Ovarian cancer. It happened fast."

"I'm so sorry. I have such vivid memories of the two of you on the floor at all those dances. You were a beautiful couple."

"You know, Evie never stopped talking about you, even after we moved to Boston. She admired you so much. She used to say you were the smartest woman she had ever met."

"I'm sure that isn't true, but it's nice to hear." She paused for a moment, her head spinning. "You know, you're the *second* person from our neighborhood I've run into since I moved here. What are the odds that three of us would all end up in the same place?"

Nathaniel's lips twisted into a grimace. "You've already seen Irving then? Ah, well . . ."

Augusta frowned. "What do you mean?"

"Oh, nothing, nothing. It isn't important." He followed her to the swimming pool steps and pulled himself up out of the water. "It was such a nice surprise to see you, Augusta. I'm sure we'll see quite a bit of each other now."

"I hope so, Nathaniel. Enjoy your morning."

When she got to her lounge chair, Shirley was waiting with a bottle of sunscreen and a mischievous grin. "I see you met Nathaniel," she said.

"Why are you looking at me like that?"

"Because Dr. Nathaniel Birnbaum is far and away the most eligible bachelor at Rallentando Springs. Half the women here are in love with him, but he never seems to take any interest. The two of you looked *very* cozy, though."

"Don't get so excited," Augusta said. "I knew Nathaniel back in

Brooklyn. His father was a doctor, too, and a good friend of my father's. He married one of my closest friends."

Shirley slapped one hand against her thigh. "Of course!" she squealed. "Irving knows him, too. I should have put that together." She tapped one finger against her scalp. "I'm not as sharp as I used to be."

"Nathaniel seemed uncomfortable talking about Irving. Is something going on there I should know about?"

Shirley nodded slowly, for dramatic effect. "No one knows how that feud started, but Nathaniel and Irving are definitely *not* friends."

"Well, I met one of Irving's *friends* yesterday," said Augusta, "and I wasn't exactly impressed." Her voice boiled over with irritation.

"You must mean Vera," said Shirley. "That woman has had her sights set on Irving for at least the past two years. Ever since she moved here."

"I'd say her patience finally paid off. She was at his apartment, nursing him back to health and making him turkey meatloaf for dinner. Apparently, it's her *signature* dish."

"Who makes meatloaf in this heat?"

"That's exactly what I was thinking!"

"Anyway, that doesn't mean the two of them are together."

"I don't know. They seemed *very* close." Augusta rubbed some lotion onto her arms. "In any event, I'm putting it out of my head. I don't care. I couldn't care less."

"That's not what it sounds like to me."

"Irving and I grew up together. We have a shared history, that's all."

"History, huh?" Shirley lowered her voice. "I'd love to hear more, but it looks like Nathaniel is on his way over."

Sure enough, when Augusta looked up, there was Nathaniel, at the foot of her chair. He'd dried off a bit, and thrown on a polo shirt—a nice crisp white one, Augusta noticed.

After he and Shirley exchanged pleasantries on how they'd spent their respective summers (Shirley had been stuck in the Florida heat, while Nathaniel escaped to his cottage in Maine), Nathaniel focused his gaze on Augusta. "I know this is awfully last minute," he said. "But I have two tickets for the Palm Beach Symphony tonight, over at the Royal Poinciana Playhouse. Any chance you'd like to join me? We can catch up a little more."

Augusta had little interest in classical music, but an evening out was an enticing prospect. The truth was that she could barely remember the last time she'd gone anywhere with a man. At some point, it stopped being worth the trouble. The men who asked were either too frail, too hunched, too forgetful, or too needy. Her thoughts turned to the scene at Irving's apartment—Vera, telling Irving it was time for his nap. Vera, cooking dinner in Irving's kitchen. The more she went over it, the more she realized that she had most likely dodged a bullet. Who wanted to be stuck playing nurse? *Let Vera take care of him*, Augusta thought.

Nathaniel, on the other hand, seemed like a man who took care of himself. Why shouldn't she go to the symphony with him? Maybe an evening with an old friend was exactly what she needed.

"Thank you, Nathaniel. I'd love to."

TWELVE

MAY 1923

The harsh Brooklyn winter turned to spring. The dogwoods exploded on Pitkin Avenue, and everything everywhere was in bloom.

After Irving's full recovery, everyone forgot about the soup. Augusta's father didn't discuss it. Esther never brought it up again. Irving couldn't even remember Esther feeding him from the jar. Only Augusta had lingering questions—questions that her great-aunt pretended not to understand.

It was true that Irving had gotten well. But neither the doctor's care nor her father's pills had brought about her friend's recovery. That, she sensed, had been the work of Esther, by means of a process Augusta still did not entirely understand.

When she tried to discuss it with her sister, Bess told her not to be ridiculous. "So Aunt Esther put some extra herbs in the soup. That's where medicine comes from, right? From plants and herbs and flowers and things? I don't see why you're so confused. I thought you knew all of that already."

Augusta struggled to explain. "That's not the confusing part," she said. "It was the way Esther looked with all her hair down, the moonlight streaming in through the window. The air in the room felt *different*, Bess. It felt electric somehow, like it was plugged into something. And the song she was singing—the tune and the words—it wasn't anything I'd ever heard."

Bess rolled her eyes. "So what are you saying? You think it was some kind of *magic*? You think Aunt Esther is a witch?"

Stated out loud, it sounded absurd. "Of course not," Augusta protested. "But I've watched her make soup a hundred times, and I've never seen her do what she did that night. And the way she behaved at Irving's house . . . so insistent that he eat it right away. I thought his mother was going to throw us out."

"Look, it doesn't matter *what* made Irving better. The important thing is that he's well."

"I know. But, Bess, I keep on wondering . . . what if there was something else that Mama could have taken? Something that would have made her better, too?"

Bess glared at Augusta with a feral intensity, as if she had crossed some invisible line. It was one thing to contemplate Irving's illness and their great-aunt's role in his recovery. But to suggest that their mother could have been saved so easily—to imply that her suffering might have been avoided if only they'd had the right powders or prayers—was an affront that Bess could not bear.

"The only medicine that could have saved our mother was discovered *after* she died. *Nothing* but insulin could have made her well."

Augusta knew better than to contradict her sister, so she kept her thoughts to herself. *Nothing that we know of, at least.*

Meanwhile, it wasn't just the dogwood trees that were blooming along their block. A neighbor a few doors down had triplets. The eggs in the nest on the firehouse roof hatched all at once in the first week of May, filling the slowly warming air with the trill of early morning birdsong. Dandelions pushed up through cracks in the sidewalk, and even the cat in the alley had kittens.

For one loyal customer—Harriet Dornbush—the kittens were the final straw.

It began one rainy Saturday morning when Augusta found the mother cat scratching at the store's back door. Augusta brought her in from out of the wet and arranged the five kittens in a shallow cardboard box on top of a threadbare yellow towel. She left the box behind the register, where the customers could see them.

When Mrs. Dornbush arrived at the pharmacy, she purchased a bottle of Dr. Platt's Cal-Rinex capsules, two cakes of soap, a bottle of talcum powder, and a box of twelve Kotex from the new store display.

Augusta estimated that the soft-spoken Mrs. Dornbush was somewhere between her late twenties and early thirties. There was nothing particularly unique about her, except for one specific detail: Mr. Dornbush, her husband, was a traveling shoe salesman, and while he was often on the road, leaving his wife alone and lonely, she reaped the benefits of his occupation with a collection of the most stylish footwear anyone in the neighborhood had ever seen. On that spring day, neither Bess nor Augusta could pry their curious eyes away from the two-tone, one-strap, brown kid shoes currently clacking across the pharmacy floor. The shoes were pointed at the toe, with a sleek Louis heel and a striking blond patent leather trim. Both girls were so busy admiring them that neither of them noticed the tears that had formed in the corners of Mrs. Dornbush's eyes.

It was when Bess rang up the box of Kotex that Harriet Dornbush broke down entirely. She pointed to the cardboard box. "Even the cat is a mother," she cried, sobbing. Augusta's father came out from the prescription room to see what the fuss was at the register. When he saw how upset Mrs. Dornbush was, he guided her gently into the quiet back room. "Please, have a seat, Mrs. Dornbush," he said, pointing to the chair in which Augusta usually sat to do her homework. "Augusta, go ask George for a glass of seltzer water and bring it back here, will you, please?"

When she returned to give Mrs. Dornbush the seltzer, Augusta understood from the bits she overheard that the woman was explaining her struggle to have a child. It seemed an awfully personal thing to discuss, but then again, Augusta knew that customers trusted her father with their secrets. And it wasn't as if this was a secret exactly. Everyone knew the Dornbushes had no children.

"We've been married for seven years now," said Harriet. "We've seen all the specialists in the city, but nothing we try seems to work."

Augusta's father nodded sympathetically. He didn't seem the slightest bit squeamish or uncomfortable with the conversation. Most men would have steered away from the subject as quickly as courtesy would allow, but Solomon Stern spoke as easily to Harriet as if they were discussing a rash on her elbow. When he remembered that Augusta was still in the room, he told her to return to the front of the store. Eventually, both he and Mrs. Dornbush emerged from the prescription room. On the way out, Mrs. Dornbush asked Augusta what she was planning to do with the kittens.

"You can have one if you like," Augusta told her. "They should be weaned by the end of June. My friend Evie is taking one, but the rest are all available."

Mrs. Dornbush gave her a tender smile. "I'll think about it," she said.

Later, when Augusta asked her father whether any of his medicines could help the woman, he shook his head and frowned. "The doctors haven't found anything wrong with her. There's nothing left for me to recommend."

A month later, Mrs. Dornbush came in again for another bottle of Cal-Rinex pills and another box of Kotex. This time, her shoes were a front-strap model in black patent leather, ornately trimmed with rose-blush patent on the vamp and the back of the heel. In contrast to her colorful footwear, Mrs. Dornbush's complexion was a waxy gray. Dark circles bloomed beneath her eyes, and she looked as if she hadn't slept in weeks. When she asked to speak with Augusta's father privately, he led her to the prescription room and motioned for Augusta not to follow. When Mrs. Dornbush emerged a few minutes later, tears streamed down her ashen face. She bolted out of the store so quickly that she forgot to take her purchases with her.

Augusta went looking for her father in the back room. She held up Mrs. Dornbush's bag. "She left these behind. Should I go after her?"

"No, Augusta. Leave her be for now. I'll have Irving deliver them to her apartment tomorrow."

"What happened, Papa? Why was she so upset?"

"She asked me for arsenic," said her father, raising a single eyebrow. "To lighten her complexion."

Augusta was familiar with arsenic, but she knew her father rarely sold it. "But Mrs. Dornbush is so pale already. Why does she want—" The truth struck Augusta in the middle of her sentence. "Oh," she said softly. "And you wouldn't give it to her."

Her father nodded solemnly. "You're old enough to understand these things now. It's no use pretending about it. Dispensing drugs is a complicated business, but arsenic is particularly tricky. The drug itself is useful, of course—for syphilis and other ailments. Good for killing rats, too, come to think of it. But if a person takes too much, the results could be . . . tragic."

Augusta tried not to think about what Mrs. Dornbush might have done with the arsenic. She tried to wipe the image from her brain, of Mr. Dornbush returning from his business trip and finding his wife on the bed or the floor, her body still, her eyes shut tight . . .

Her father knew what she was thinking. "Being a pharmacist is more than filling prescriptions," he said. "I told you once that sometimes it means keeping other people's secrets. But it can also mean protecting people from themselves. We have to know our customers as well as we know our family. We have to know when they aren't being honest with us."

"How can you be sure that Mrs. Dornbush was lying?"

"No one can ever know for sure. But I've learned to trust my instincts."

"What if she tries to get arsenic somewhere else? From another pharmacy, where they don't know her as well?"

Augusta's father shook his head. "She won't," he said adamantly. "She was too embarrassed when I confronted her. Also, I made sure to tell her that no one else in the neighborhood would sell it to her."

"Is that true?"

"Probably not. But for now, at least, she believes it is. I'll talk to her husband when he's back from his trip."

"And there's really nothing you can prescribe that might help the two of them have a baby?"

"The doctors and I have done all we can."

Augusta nodded solemnly, but she couldn't help wondering whether it was true. After all, both her father and Dr. Birnbaum had said the exact same thing about Irving.

That night, after everyone was in bed, Augusta lay awake thinking about Mrs. Dornbush. The words her father spoke when he first explained his work echoed loudly inside her head. *Whatever you hear, whatever you learn about a customer, is never, ever to be repeated. If you break this rule, there will be no second chance.*

Augusta had promised him she would comply. She knew Mrs. Dornbush's condition was sensitive, and she would never want to betray the woman's trust. But this was a far more complex case than any Augusta could have contemplated. What was Augusta's duty to Mrs. Dornbush, or to anyone, in such a situation?

By now Augusta had grown accustomed to sharing her small bedroom with Aunt Esther. She was used to the sound of her great-aunt's breathing, used to the snores from that side of the room after her aunt had fallen asleep. Now she could tell from the silence that Esther was still awake.

"Aunt Esther?" said Augusta, into the darkness.

When there was no answer, she tried again. "I know you're up," Augusta said. "Please, I have something I want to ask you."

From a few feet away, there was a rustle of blankets, but still no acknowledgment that Esther was listening.

"Fine," Augusta said. "Pretend if you want, but I *know* you can hear me."

When her aunt still did not answer, Augusta took a deep breath and began.

"Mrs. Dornbush came into the store today. Do you remember who she is? She's the quiet woman with the beautiful shoes. Anyway, last month, Papa spoke to her privately for a bit after she started crying at the register. She told him she's been trying to have a baby ever since she got married, which means they've been trying for seven years. The doctors say there's nothing wrong so there's nothing to be done." Augusta paused to listen for a response, but she couldn't hear anything in the darkness, not even a change in the old woman's breathing.

"I'm sure some people don't get sad about not having children," Augusta continued. "Some people don't want any. I mean, you don't have any and it doesn't seem to bother you at all. But Mrs. Dornbush isn't like that. She cried when she saw the alley cat's kittens. And today, something much worse happened. Today, she asked Papa for arsenic, only she didn't want it for her complexion." Augusta stopped herself again, but there was still no answer from Aunt Esther.

"Papa says she won't ask another pharmacist for the powder. He says he's going to have a talk with her husband. But I'm worried that won't be enough. I'm worried she's going to try again." Augusta choked back a sob. "When she left today, she seemed so desperate. Aunt Esther, she looked like a ghost."

Aside from the echo of her own words, the room was painfully silent. Was it possible that Esther really was asleep? Darkness enveloped Augusta on every side. She rolled over onto her stomach and closed her eyes.

At some point, she must have fallen asleep, because the next thing she knew, Aunt Esther's voice woke her, rousing her from a bottomless dream. In the dark, the voice was more substantial—it had a weight and a heft that it lacked in daylight.

"Goldie," she whispered. "Little Goldie . . . I see how you tend to your father's headaches. I hear how you share the pain of this stranger. You have the heart of a healer. Together, we will try to help this woman. Together, let us see what we can do."

THIRTEEN

SEPTEMBER 1987

The concert was a nice change of pace, but if Augusta had any doubts before, by the time the musicians took their bows, she was certain: classical music was not for her. She knew what she was *supposed* to feel when the cellos hummed and the timpani rumbled—she was supposed to be moved to a place beyond words, transported by the sound, swept away. But all she felt was mild irritation at being confined to her seat for so long. It was pleasant enough for the first half hour, but then her calves began to cramp. At intermission, she stared longingly at the door, then trudged back to her seat like a child being punished. Her turquoise beads felt heavy on her neck, and the patent leather slingbacks she'd chosen were giving her the beginnings of a blister.

Afterward, they stopped for frozen yogurt at one of the strip malls on Palmetto Park Road. They filled paper cups from the self-serve machines and waited in line to have them weighed. Since Nathaniel had treated for the tickets, Augusta insisted on paying for dessert. They were overdressed, but Augusta didn't mind. She was happier in the shop's pink plastic chairs than she had been in the velvet auditorium seats.

"So fill me in," said Nathaniel. "It's been at least sixty years. What have you been doing with yourself all this time?"

"Working mostly," said Augusta. "You remember my father? I went to work for him when I graduated pharmacy school, and when he died, I took over the store. Ran it myself for twenty years. After that, I worked in a couple of hospitals. I only retired a few months ago, and that's how I ended up in Florida."

"Wow," said Nathaniel. "You've certainly been busy! I bet you kept your husband on his toes."

Augusta shook her head. "Not exactly. I never got married."

Nathaniel's mouth fell open in disbelief. "I thought . . . I assumed . . . that you were widowed. Like me."

Augusta stirred her cup of yogurt. "I suppose I never found the right person," she said. "But enough about me—tell me about you. How many kids did you and Evie have?"

"Three," said Nathaniel. "Two girls and a boy. My son is in L.A. and the girls are in New York, but we all get together up in Maine every summer. One of my daughters is a doctor, too—a cardiologist, like me. I've got seven grandkids, if you can believe it."

"Seven! Goodness! That house must be bursting at the seams!"

"It's what Evie always wanted," said Nathaniel. "That's why we got the house in the first place—so everyone could be together." His eyebrows drooped. "It's a shame she isn't here to enjoy it."

"I'm so sorry, Nathaniel," Augusta said. "I know how much you loved her. In fact, I still remember the night you got engaged."

Nathaniel's eyes brightened. "You remember that, huh?"

"Who could forget it? We were all at Arcadia Gardens, eating and dancing the night away, and then you pulled Evie to the center of the floor, got down on one knee, and proposed. The band stopped playing and everyone clapped. It was like a scene from a Hollywood movie—the most romantic thing I ever saw."

He was practically beaming now. "That's exactly how Evie used to describe it."

"Isn't that how you remember it?"

"To be honest, that night has always been blurry. I'd been thinking about asking Evie to marry me, but a public proposal wasn't my style. If I hadn't had so much to drink, I probably would have waited until we were alone."

"You never seemed like a big drinker to me."

"I'm not. I wasn't. It was only that night. I must have been nervous."

Augusta smiled. "I understand." She pointed to her cup of frozen yogurt. "When I get nervous, I eat."

"Evie used to polish off an entire bag of pretzels every time one of the kids was traveling," Nathaniel said. He looked so forlorn that Augusta decided it was best to change the subject.

"So how do you keep yourself busy down here? Golf? Tennis? What else do you do?"

"A bit of everything," Nathaniel said. "The beach is gorgeous, by the way. I go a couple of times a week. I have a group I meet on Tuesdays— open-water swimming for us old folks. You should come—you're in great shape. I'm sure the others would love to meet you."

She shook her head. "Thanks, but I stick to swimming pools. I haven't swum in the ocean for years. I don't like the way the bottom keeps shifting, the way your feet get sucked into the wet sand. And don't get me started on the waves—at my age, the last thing I need is to get tossed around."

Nathaniel shrugged. "Suit yourself. As for me, I like the sand. I even like getting tossed around a bit." He thumped one fist against his chest. "Helps me remember I'm still alive."

FOURTEEN

JUNE 1923

At breakfast the next morning, Augusta told her father that she would gladly deliver Mrs. Dornbush's purchases. The Dornbushes lived near the library and Augusta had some books she needed to return. School was out for the summer, so aside from helping out at the store, she had no other place she needed to be. "It will save Irving a trip," she said.

"Fine," her father agreed. "Let me know how she's doing."

Augusta did not mention that, in addition to the pills and the Kotex, she would be delivering something special to their valued customer.

The Dornbushes lived on Glenmore Avenue, on a wide, tree-lined block filled with wooden row houses. The block was cleaner and brighter than most, filled with schoolgirls playing jacks and young boys riding bicycles. As they approached the door, Augusta held her breath. What if Mrs. Dornbush wasn't at home? What if she was home, but refused to answer? Augusta tried not to dwell on all the unlucky possibilities.

Fortunately, Harriet Dornbush opened the door, wearing a crisp day dress in brown-and-white gingham and the same pair of two-tone, brown kid shoes she had worn last month when she'd first seen the kittens.

"Good morning," Augusta said. "I'm Solomon Stern's daughter, from the pharmacy." She held up the plain white paper bag and waved it slightly in the air. "You left your purchase at the register yesterday."

Despite her stylish appearance, Harriet Dornbush was bleary-eyed and pale. Her dress hung limply on her frame, and she looked as if she hadn't slept in days.

"Oh," she said, staring blankly at Augusta. "How nice of you to come. Thank you, dear."

Augusta held out the bag. "It's no problem," she said. "It isn't far from the store."

From behind her, Esther cleared her throat. "Not far for young legs," she clarified. "A little farther for old ones, like mine."

Augusta stepped to the side to make room for Esther in the doorway. "This is my great-aunt," she said. "We were walking to the library and your house was on the way."

The young woman tilted her head and stared. Despite the summer heat, Aunt Esther was dressed in her usual attire: a baggy black dress, thick black stockings, and old-fashioned boots up to her ankles. Her silver hair was hidden by a scarf, and she smelled earthy and wet, like the herbs from her kitchen.

"Oh," said Mrs. Dornbush. "Well, thank you again. I hope you both enjoy the library." As she moved to push her front door shut, Augusta jumped forward. "One more thing!" she said, motioning to Esther, who pulled a jar from inside her bag and thrust it into Harriet Dornbush's hands. "We brought you some homemade soup."

Mrs. Dornbush looked at the jar and blinked. "How thoughtful," she said. "What a nice surprise. But isn't it a bit warm for soup?" She held the jar a little higher so that she could make out what was inside. "Is that kreplach?" she asked, brightening a bit. "My mother used to make kreplach for me. I haven't had it in years."

"*My* kreplach melts in your mouth," said Esther. "You should only enjoy it in good health."

Augusta elbowed her aunt. The night before, she'd made it clear that Esther was *not* to bring up Mrs. Dornbush's condition. "She spoke to my father in confidence," Augusta had said. "She doesn't know that I overheard."

"How can I help if I can't talk to her?"

"Can't you just put some herbs in her soup?"

Esther had glared at her niece. "This isn't like adding a pinch of salt. Listen to me now, Goldie, and remember what I tell you. You must *never* treat anyone without permission. Don't you dare speak such foolishness to me again."

"You didn't ask Irving for permission."

"Irving was *ill*. It was an emergency. That was a different situation. I need to know more about Mrs. Dornbush's condition, from her own lips, in her own words. She will have to tell me what she wants."

Augusta had let out an exasperated sigh. "How are we going to get her to do that? She's too embarrassed to come to the pharmacy. What if she never comes back again?"

"We'll drop off some soup as a gift," Esther said. "Whenever anyone tastes my soup, they always come back for more."

Two days after they delivered the soup, Mrs. Dornbush returned to the store on Sutter Avenue. She was still too pale and much too thin, but her eyes were brighter than they'd been before. She carried the clean, empty soup jar and held it out to Augusta. "I brought this back for your aunt," she said. "I was wondering if I might ask her for another jar?"

Augusta glanced around the store to make sure her father wasn't watching. "I'll take you upstairs," she said quietly. "You can talk to her there."

She scooted far enough ahead so that anyone watching wouldn't notice that Mrs. Dornbush was following her. They went out the shop entrance and to the building's side door, where Augusta led the young woman up the stairs. When they got to her apartment, Aunt Esther was in the kitchen, rolling out dough for her kreplach. A pot was bubbling on the stove, and the room smelled of onions and browning meat. The windows were open so that a breeze blew in from the street, ruffling the edges of the curtains. Aunt Esther did not look up when they entered, but on her lips, Augusta saw a satisfied smile.

Augusta cleared her throat. "Remember Mrs. Dornbush?"

"Of course," said Aunt Esther. "You liked the soup?"

"Very much," said Mrs. Dornbush. "It was exactly as you said. The kreplach melted on my tongue."

Aunt Esther nodded and wiped her hands on her apron.

"I'd been feeling poorly," Mrs. Dornbush confessed. "But I'm feeling a bit better now."

"Soup makes everyone feel better," said Esther. Her tone was cool and noncommittal, as if she were daring the woman to say more.

Mrs. Dornbush tugged at the skirt of her dress with obviously trembling fingers. "That's true," she said. "But I've heard that *your* soup is special."

Aunt Esther kept her eyes on her dough while Mrs. Dornbush continued to fidget.

"One of my neighbors saw you leaving our building. She said people say your soup cures indigestion. They also say you make a cream that gets rid of blemishes."

"You have no blemishes," Aunt Esther observed.

"No. But I do have a different problem."

Esther gestured to the chairs around the kitchen table. She wiped her hands on her apron. "Sit," she said. "Start from the beginning."

As soon as she began to tell her story, Harriet's face became a map of her grief. Sorrow poured through her lips like rivulets breaking off from a swollen stream: seven years of frustration, untold visits to doctors and specialists, daily mortifying encounters with pregnant women and children on the street. She described it all in painful detail.

"I wonder whether you can give me something," she said. "Some kind of advice or medicine or . . . *anything*."

Esther bit her lower lip. Augusta sensed that her aunt was more moved by Harriet's story than she'd expected to be. "I may have some advice," Esther said cautiously. "Perhaps a few remedies as well. But if I agree to help you, you must do everything I say."

A flash of skepticism crossed the young woman's face, but she quickly remembered herself. She folded her hands on the top of her lap and nodded at Esther, the picture of obedience. For the next fifteen minutes, Esther was in motion, gathering items from around the apartment: a jar of castor oil, a soft white cloth, an old hot water bottle from the trunk by her bed. All these she placed on the kitchen table in front of Mrs. Dornbush.

Next came a list of strict instructions. "Rub the castor oil onto your stomach, cover it with the cloth and then the hot water bottle. This you should do for one hour every day, after you eat your breakfast."

"I don't eat breakfast."

"Humph," Esther grunted. "From now on, you will have two eggs every morning. Then use the castor oil. You understand?"

Mrs. Dornbush bowed her head in agreement and tucked the items carefully inside her purse. But when she tried to get up from the table to leave, Esther motioned for her to stay put.

"Tomorrow, I will prepare some special soup—a plain broth for you to eat. Augusta will deliver it."

"All right," said Mrs. Dornbush. "Is there anything else?"

"Your husband," said Aunt Esther. "He travels for work?"

"He does. But I don't see how that matters—"

"You must ask him to stay home for two months."

Mrs. Dornbush's hopeful expression crumpled. "I'm not sure I can convince him of that. Jerry has accounts all over. He's very serious about his work."

"Is he serious about having a child? If you want a baby, you need your husband at home. A man and a woman . . . it requires time and frequency. I don't have to explain this to you, do I?"

"Of course not!" The young woman blushed. "We don't need to get into that in front of your niece. I'll convince him not to travel for a couple of months. At least I promise to do my best." Mrs. Dornbush rose from her chair, looking utterly exhausted. "I assume that's everything then?"

"No," said Esther, pointing one finger at Mrs. Dornbush's feet. Harriet was wearing the black-and-rose patent leather shoes that Augusta had so recently admired. "Your shoes," Esther said. "Take them off."

Mrs. Dornbush blinked repeatedly. "You want me to walk home barefoot? Are you joking?"

Aunt Esther wasn't laughing. "What is your shoe size?"

"Seven. But I don't understand . . ."

Esther exited the kitchen and began rummaging in the front hall closet. A few moments later, she returned carrying a pair of plain brown boots that had once belonged to Augusta's mother. Augusta bit her lower lip. She didn't want Mrs. Dornbush to take her mother's boots, but she swallowed down her protests.

"Put them on," Esther said. "From now on, *kinehora*, you will wear only these."

Augusta knew what *kinehora* meant—it was the phrase the old women in the neighborhood spoke when they wanted to ward off the Evil Eye.

Esther murmured an explanation, but Mrs. Dornbush still looked confused.

"Jealousy tempts the Evil Eye," Esther clarified. "Even in those who are unaware of it." She pointed to the patent leather shoes on Harriet's feet. "The shoes you wear—so beautiful, so elegant. No one in the neighborhood has anything like them. Everyone sees them, everyone notices. People want what they don't have."

"Are you saying that I can't get pregnant because people are jealous of my *shoes*?"

Aunt Esther shrugged. "Who can know?"

"Let me make sure I understand. You think if I wear these old boots, it will help me to conceive a child?"

Esther shrugged a second time. "Seven years you've suffered without a baby. Seven years of fancy shoes and seven years of an empty womb. What's the harm now if you follow my advice?"

Mrs. Dornbush stared at the boots in Esther's hands. With a resigned expression on her face, she sat back down and unbuckled her pumps. Once the boots were on her feet, she tested them by walking around the table. "Not bad," she said. "At least they're comfortable."

As Esther's newest client circled the table a second time and then a third, Augusta knew exactly what her aunt was thinking. *Your comfort is the least of my concerns. I would have told you to wear those boots even if they gave you blisters.*

But all Esther said was "*Kinehora.*"

The night following Harriet Dornbush's visit, Augusta slept with one eye open. Long after midnight, when she heard her aunt stir, Augusta followed her into the kitchen. Esther knew that Augusta was trailing her, but she didn't say a word as she moved down the hall, carrying the wooden apothecary case that she had taken from inside her trunk. Her long silver hair hung loose down her back, and the bottom of her silky blue robe skimmed over the wooden floor.

This time—for Augusta's benefit—she whispered the names of her ingredients: pomegranate seeds, black cohosh, stinging nettle, raspberry leaves, viburnum. The spicy aroma of licorice root hit the back of Augusta's nostrils.

The moon showed itself as if Esther had summoned it, peering in through the window like a dutiful friend, illuminating the mortar until the brass seemed to glow. As she ground the ingredients, she hummed her strange song. An entreaty. A wish. An incantation. A prayer. The pestle blazed bright from between her long fingers, until the room smelled of potency, abundance, and hope.

When she was finished grinding the herbs, she deposited the powder in another square of clean white muslin and tied it with string. This time, she handed the mortar to Augusta and asked her to wipe it clean. It was heavier than Augusta expected, and felt rougher to the touch. "How long have you had this?" Augusta asked.

"It belonged to my mother, her mother before her, and her mother before that. One day, perhaps, it will belong to you."

Augusta felt her pulse quicken in her veins. "Do you really think so?"

Esther nodded. "I told you that you had the heart of a healer, and I believe it to be true. Of course, the path will not be easy. There is a great deal to learn and you will have to work very hard."

"I'll work harder than anyone," Augusta insisted. "But if I want to learn from you, does that mean I shouldn't go to pharmacy college?"

"Of course you should go to college!" Aunt Esther snapped. "When I was young, I had no such opportunity. My brothers were sent to study in Lviv, but my sisters and I were not allowed to go. I was as bright as you are now—equally curious, equally ambitious. But because I wasn't born a man, I was forced to stay at home. I learned everything I know of plants and potions from my mother and my grandmother. But if I'd had the chance to go to university, who knows how much more knowledge I might have collected? You *must* go to college, Goldie. You must do what I could not."

"Did your mother and grandmother teach your sisters, too?"

Aunt Esther shook her head. "Neither of my sisters wanted to learn. One married a farmer and one a stonemason. When I grew older, they were ashamed of me—ashamed of their strange spinster sister. What was more, they did not like that I advertised my knowledge. My mother and grandmother had kept their skills private, but I chose to share mine with others. Many in my village were grateful to me, especially when my powders cured them of illness. But others accused me of being a witch, a Baba Yaga of the forest. They said I flew above the trees at night, sitting inside a wooden mortar, like a witch on a broom. They said I steered with an enchanted pestle, inflicting disease on whoever wronged me. They blamed me whenever they had a cough, or if they sneezed or had a toothache."

"That's ridiculous," Augusta said. But she didn't feel entirely convinced.

Esther raised her silver eyebrows. "I wanted to study medicine and healing. If I had been born a man, they would have called me an apothecary. Perhaps even a doctor, if I'd had the training. But because I was born a woman, they called me a witch instead. To ignorant men, every gifted woman is a witch."

"But you know things my father doesn't know," said Augusta. "You're able to help people in ways that he can't. How?"

"If a person is denied a formal education," said Esther, "she must be inventive in her quest for knowledge. She must study the folktales and the old stories. She must learn however she can. She must use every tool at her disposal."

"Like your mortar?"

"Like my mortar."

"Will you tell me about the words inside it? The words you are always repeating? Please, will you explain what they mean?"

"The words themselves could not be simpler. They state the mortar's purpose, that is all." She held up the mortar and pointed inside it as she recited the words in English.

To ease the pain of those who suffer
To repair the bodies of those who are ill
To restore the minds of those in need

"But if the words are so simple," Augusta pressed, "why are they so important?"

"Must words be complicated or unusual for us to believe in them?"

"Maybe not, but you still haven't explained why the words are necessary at all. Words can't simply *make* someone better. Words don't have that kind of power."

Esther put all of her tins and bottles back in the proper places in her case. She stared at Augusta for a good long while. "Words can do *anything*," she said. "A kind word can fix a person's spirit. A cruel one can break a person's heart. Wicked words have caused wars, and honest words have made peace. Why shouldn't they be able to heal?"

FIFTEEN

SEPTEMBER 1987

Y ou wanna tell me why you went on a date with that *schmuck?*"
Augusta had fallen asleep by the pool, but at the sound of
Irving's voice, she opened her eyes. When she pulled off her
sunglasses, there was Irving beside her, frowning.

"Excuse me?" she said. "What are you talking about?" Augusta raised
the back of her lounge chair to a sitting position. She never napped in the
afternoon, but the sun was strong and the air was heavy with a somnolent
humidity.

"You and *Dr. Birnbaum.* At the yogurt shop. Drooling over each other
like teenagers." As usual, his voice was a notch too loud. People were
turning their heads to see what the commotion was about.

"Shh," she hissed. "Have you lost your mind? Or did you finally have
the stroke we joked about?"

"Don't be cute," Irving said. "I'm asking you a serious question."

"More like making a serious accusation. Yes, I got frozen yogurt with
Nathaniel, but we certainly weren't *drooling* over each other. Not that
frozen yogurt could even make me drool—I prefer real ice cream, in case
you're wondering."

"That's not what I heard." Irving pouted.

"What do you mean, *what you heard*?"

He shrugged. "Harold picked up a pint of yogurt last night. He was in and out quick, but he spotted the two of you."

"He spotted us, huh? And he reported this to you?" Augusta sat up a little straighter. "So now you have people spying on me?"

Irving swiped his hand in the air as if to say it was no big deal. "No one's spying. Don't be so dramatic."

"Me, dramatic? You're the one accusing me of drooling in public, over a man I haven't seen for six decades."

"Harold said you were all dressed up."

Augusta sighed. "*That's* what's bothering you? Yes, I admit it. I was overdressed for frozen yogurt."

When Irving continued to pout, she continued. "Fine. You want to know all the details? Yesterday morning I was swimming my laps and Nathaniel was in the pool swimming his. He looked familiar and then we figured out that we knew each other back in Brooklyn. I asked about Evie, his wife—you remember her? She used to be one of my closest friends."

Irving nodded.

"So then we talked about his grandkids and the house he goes to in Maine. Turned out he had an extra ticket for the symphony, and he asked me if I wanted to go. It was in Palm Beach, so I figured I'd better wear something decent. After the concert, we went for yogurt. And that's the whole story. Are you happy now?"

"I don't like you dating him. He's a snob, is what he is. With his fancy degrees and his summer house." Irving motioned to the chairs around the pool and the dozing men that occupied them. "You wanna date? Pick someone else."

Augusta sucked in an angry breath. Her blood was boiling in her veins. "I don't even know where to begin with that statement. First," she said, through tightly clenched teeth, "last night was *not* a date. I'm not dating Nathaniel. Second, even if it had been a date, whether you like it or not makes no difference to me. You have no say in who I choose to date, just as you have no say in what I choose to eat for lunch."

"Yeah, look how well *that* turned out." Irving snorted. "I told you not to get the tuna!"

"This isn't about a tuna sandwich! What's your problem with Nathaniel Birnbaum anyway? What did he ever do to you?"

Irving winced as if he'd been punched. "He ... took something from me. I don't wanna talk about it."

"He *took something* from you? What, like money? Are you telling me that Nathaniel swiped your wallet or something? Because he doesn't seem like that kind of guy to me."

"He didn't take money."

"What was it then? Whiskey from your bootlegging father-in-law?"

"Lower your voice with that, okay?" Irving whispered. "People here don't know who my father-in-law was."

"So you're allowed to shout at the top of your lungs that I was throwing myself at some man, but I'm supposed to protect *your* reputation?" At that moment, Augusta wished she were anywhere but Florida. Anywhere but sitting beside Irving Rivkin. She wished she were back home in New York, in her apartment. Alone. She lowered her voice. "Fine," she whispered. "Whatever you say. But tell me what Nathaniel took that was so terrible."

"It wasn't a *thing*. It was more like ... a moment."

Augusta stared at him. "What is that supposed to mean?"

"It means ..." He paused. "Dammit. Look. All you need to know is that if it hadn't been for Birnbaum, my life would have turned out the way it was supposed to."

There was something heartbreaking about the way Irving said it—a hitch in his voice that caught her by surprise. *What in the world is he talking about?*

If she hadn't been so annoyed, she might have reached for his hand. But Augusta kept her hands and her thoughts to herself. "Seems to me your life didn't turn out so badly," she said.

He opened his mouth as if he wanted to say more, before shutting it abruptly and turning his head. From the side, he looked like the Irving she once knew—the sweet, funny young man from so long ago. When he finally turned his face back toward hers, the wrinkles and age spots faded away. All that was left were two sad blue eyes staring at her as if time had reversed. As if he were still her father's delivery boy, still her dance partner, still her best friend.

The Florida sunshine beat down on her chest, but Augusta found herself shivering in the heat. Her body and brain stiffened and froze, as if she'd swallowed a mouthful of ice cream too quickly. She waited for Irving to take his eyes off her, but he refused to look away.

"It wasn't supposed to be like this," he said.

That night, Augusta called her niece. "Are you making new friends?" Jackie asked.

"More like old ones."

"Come on, Aunt Augusta. We talked about this," Jackie insisted. "You shouldn't call people your age *old.*"

"I don't mean old as in age," said Augusta. "I mean old as in I know them from my youth. Old as in I knew them before you were born."

Jackie sounded excited now. "Really? Anybody I've heard of? Anyone my parents knew?"

Augusta hesitated for a moment. She still hadn't told her niece about Irving. It hadn't occurred to her before that he'd known Bess and George as well. She took a deep breath.

"Your parents knew *both* of them, actually. One was Nathaniel Birnbaum, a guy from the neighborhood. He married Evie Sussman, one of my girlfriends, and they moved to Boston when he started medical school. Nathaniel's father was a doctor, too—he filled all his prescriptions at our pharmacy. Everyone we knew went to Dr. Birnbaum."

"And the other old friend?"

"The other used to work at the pharmacy. He was your grandfather's delivery boy."

"Wait a minute," Jackie said. "Are you talking about Irving Rivkin?"

"How do you know that name?"

"My mom used to tell me about him sometimes. She said . . . now don't get mad, but she said that the two of you had quite a thing for each other."

"Your mother was a hopeless romantic, Jackie."

"Maybe, but—"

"She was always exaggerating."

"She liked to *embellish*, maybe, but overall—"

"Trust me, whatever she said about me and Irving was definitely an exaggeration. Did she tell you he married Lois Diamond? Love at first sight, or so people said. It's a nice idea, if you believe in all that."

"Which, of course, you do not."

"Bingo," said Augusta. "Anyway, Irving and I were friends as kids, and then, when we got older . . . well, there's not much to say. We were dating, and I thought it was serious. I even thought we were in love. But he must have been seeing Lois behind my back, because after one of our dates, he disappeared. He didn't show up for work at the store, and then a week later, he and Lois were engaged. Lois's family moved out to Chicago, and Irving went with them to work for her father. I never heard from him again."

"Lois was Zip Diamond's daughter, right?"

"Exactly. I guess your parents told you about him?"

"A couple of times," Jackie said. "Zip sounded like a scary man."

"He was, but we were used to him. The neighborhood was *full* of guys like that. *Everything* back then was a racket: kosher chicken, chocolate syrup. Everywhere you looked, someone was on the take, someone was paying someone else off. I was oblivious when I was young—I didn't realize how dangerous some of those men were. But as I got older, I started paying attention. Those guys would poison someone's horse to send a message, or shoot up a truck if you crossed them. They put honest people out of business. Sometimes, they killed people who wouldn't cooperate."

Augusta remembered the delicate line her father had been forced to walk during Prohibition. "Your grandfather had to be especially careful: Pharmacies were catnip for men like Zip Diamond. Doctors were allowed to write prescriptions for whiskey, and guys like Diamond would get doctors to write fakes. But if the pharmacists refused to go along, their stores would be robbed or vandalized or worse. My father knew a pharmacist in Williamsburg whose store was burned down—his wife and son almost died in the fire. After that, my father was terrified. It was only after Zip moved his family to Chicago that my father finally felt safe."

"That's terrible," Jackie said. "But Irving never got involved in any of that, right?"

Augusta hesitated. She thought about the way Irving stared at her earlier, the way his voice broke when he talked about his past. There was so much she didn't know about him. She never asked what his work in Chicago was like; she didn't know how or where to begin.

"I don't think so," she said.

"What was it like seeing him again?"

Augusta wasn't sure how to answer. She wished she could forget her conversation with Irving, forget his expression, forget his sad eyes.

"It was fine," Augusta said when she finally spoke. "Nothing to write home about."

SIXTEEN

SEPTEMBER 1923

Irving Rivkin had a problem.

Thomas Jefferson High School had just opened in Brownsville—a pristine building made of fresh red brick on Pennsylvania Avenue, between Blake and Dumont. The building itself was not the problem, but the new route Irving took to school was. It was on the first day of that new route that Irving made his first real enemy.

Unlike many of the boys in the neighborhood—especially those without fathers—Irving had never joined a gang. His job at the pharmacy kept him too busy, and after his bout with the flu, his mother kept too close an eye on him. He did not pay attention to who ran with which crowd, and without any of that unsavory wisdom, he had no way of knowing that the block on Snediker Avenue between Sutter and Blake had been declared the territory of Freddie Schechter and his crew.

On the first crisp morning of the new school year, Irving said goodbye to his mother and pedaled off on the secondhand bicycle he had bought for himself two summers before. The bicycle made his deliveries easier, especially when the store was busy. He'd gotten it cheap, but he was proud of the purchase; other than the clothes on his scrawny back, it was the one thing Irving could truly call his own. Which was why, when half a dozen boys surrounded him on Snediker Avenue, he held tight to his handlebars and refused to hand it over.

"Give us the bike," Freddie ordered. Between Freddie's height and his pocked complexion, he seemed older than his sixteen years. He crossed his arms indignantly over his chest while his buddies blocked Irving's path.

Irving tried his best to sound confident. "Get one of your own," he said.

"Very funny," Freddie said. He uncrossed his arms, threw back his shoulders, and moved toward Irving with a nasty grin. "I said, get off. Or you'll regret it."

The other boys echoed the message. "You'd better do what Freddie says. Nobody says no to him on this block."

Before they had the chance to come any closer, the squeak of a window sash struggling against a frame cut through the noise of their threats. Across the street, an elderly woman popped her head out of a second-story window. Irving recognized her immediately—Mrs. Levinson was a regular at Stern's Pharmacy. From her perch, she pointed an angry finger at the mob. "You leave that boy alone!" she shouted. "I haven't had a moment of peace from you since you started hanging around. Get out of here now, or I'll call the police! I know all your names, so don't think I won't!"

In the confusion that followed, Irving sped away, but in his haste to make the best of the opportunity, he accidentally ran over Freddie's toes. The last thing Irving saw as he pedaled away was Freddie Schechter hopping up and down on one foot, shouting a string of curses into the wind.

For all the next week and several more that followed, Irving avoided Freddie's block. He managed to elude Freddie at school, mostly because the boy never came to class. But a month into the new school year, as Irving passed by that treacherous corner, he saw something from a few yards away that caused him to come to a stop on the sidewalk.

Freddie and his goons were teasing a boy, a kid no more than ten years old. They'd snatched the cap off his head and were tossing it to each other, out of the boy's reach. While they played catch with the cap, they jeered at the boy and called him names.

"Look at him, Freddie, I think he's gonna cry."

"Are you gonna cry, *baby*?"

"Why doncha go home and cry to your mother?"

"I bet the baby still wears diapers. Should we see if I'm right?"

Irving watched silently from the corner as the talk turned increasingly menacing. Eventually, however, Freddie spotted him and pointed him out to the others.

"Look who's back!" Freddie shouted. "Where ya been, Irv? Doncha wanna be sociable? See the new friend we made here? *He* ain't afraid of us, are ya, kid?"

The little boy's eyes filled with tears, but he shook his head and kept his chin high.

"See that?" said Freddie. "Ain't the baby brave?"

Irving couldn't help himself. "Stop it," he said. "Why don't you leave the kid alone?"

Freddie's grin was as wide as Pitkin Avenue. "Come and make me," he said.

Irving rode shakily to the middle of the block, where two of Freddie's cronies pulled him off his bike and held him by his arms as he struggled against them. The assault unfolded so quickly that he barely knew what was happening, until he felt Freddie's fist in his stomach.

"That's for running over my foot," said Freddie. He delivered a second blow to Irving's face. "And that's for being such a wiseass."

Blood erupted from Irving's nose, gushing over his lips and chin. The little boy began to cry in earnest then, and a dark spot bloomed at the front of his breeches. Next he crumpled to the ground as if he'd been punched in the nose himself.

One of Freddie's friends let out a whistle. "I guess he ain't wearing diapers after all." He chuckled.

Disgust flashed over Freddie's features. "Ugh," he said. "Did you *piss* yourself, kid?"

"Let him go," Irving muttered, still trying to pull out of his enemies' grip.

"Suppose I do? What'll you give me?" Irving could tell that Freddie's satisfaction at teasing the child had dissipated. Freddie was beginning to get bored, and Irving was smart enough to know that he might use that boredom to his advantage. No matter what Irving said next, he was sure to lose his bike, but if he offered Freddie a quick resolution in the guise of a negotiation, the nasty incident could come to an end without any damage to Freddie's reputation.

"If you let us both go, you can have the bike."

Freddie pretended to consider the offer, but Irving knew what his answer would be.

"Fine," said Freddie. "But you'd better scram. Get outta here, both of you, before I change my mind."

Irving motioned to the child to get up from the ground. "Come on, kid," he said gently. "Didn't you hear? We gotta go."

The little boy remained on the sidewalk, crying into his sleeve.

"Please?" said Irving, trying again. It was the *please* that finally broke the boy's trance. He rose from the ground and made a beeline for Irving, who practically carried him to the end of the street. Once they were safely on a different block, Irving asked the boy for his address. "Don't worry, I'll walk you home," Irving said.

The little boy nodded and—before Irving could object—grabbed and held tightly to his left hand. They walked slowly and companionably along together until the boy was calm enough to speak. "My name is Sammy. What's yours?"

"I'm Irving," said Irving. "How old are you?"

"Eight and a half. How old are you?"

"Seventeen," said Irving, using his free hand to wipe the drying blood from his chin. "How come you were on that block, anyway? It's nowhere near the elementary school."

"I got lost," Sammy said. "Usually, my sister Lois walks me, but she's home sick with a cold today."

Sammy lived in a brownstone, up on Glenmore Avenue. The steps were freshly swept and painted, and the round brass handle of the door had been polished to a shine. When Sammy's mother—at least that's who Irving assumed she was—opened the heavy paneled door, her eyes narrowed at the sight of them. "Sammy, why are you home from school? And why are your clothes such a mess?" The woman in the fine silk dress looked from Sammy's breeches to Irving's bruised and bloody face. "What happened to your friend?"

"This is Irving," Sammy said. "He rescued me and brought me home."

"Rescued you from *what*?" the woman asked, pulling the boy firmly toward her and pressing him against the folds of her skirt. She was calmer than most mothers would have been, thought Irving. Calmer, cooler, and surprisingly indifferent about the possibility of ruining her expensive clothes. As she bent down to check Sammy's body for bruises, he told her about the gang that had harassed him, and how Irving's bravery in the face of such danger had resulted in the loss of his beloved bicycle. The woman turned her attention to Irving's nose. "If it's any consolation, your nose isn't broken."

"How do you know?"

She smiled knowingly. "I've seen my fair share of broken noses. Your face certainly is a mess, though. Would you like to come in and use the washroom?"

Irving could see over the woman's shoulder to the cozy living room behind her. The tangy scent of braising beef (was there a brisket in the oven?) permeated the spotless foyer. To his embarrassment, Irving could not squelch the anxious grumbling of his stomach. "I'm fine, ma'am," he said. "I don't want to spill blood on your floor or anything. I'll go wash up at home."

"Blood has never bothered me, young man, but I understand you wanting to get home. Thank you for being so good to our Sammy. His father will want to thank you, I'm sure." She tilted her head. "What's your last name?"

"Rivkin," said Irving. "And it was no big deal. Sammy is a real sweet kid." He leaned over and ruffled the little boy's hair. "See you around, Sammy," he said. "Promise me you'll stay off that block, okay?"

Sammy nodded solemnly. "I promise," he said.

The next day Irving walked to school, wondering along the way if he'd ever see the boy again. When he got to the pharmacy, around four o'clock, Solomon Stern was waiting with a concerned look on his face. "I had a visitor a few hours ago," he said. "He left something here, with strict instructions to make sure you got it as soon as you arrived."

Now it was Irving's turn to be concerned. "Who was it?" he asked. "What did he leave?"

Mr. Stern relaxed his shoulders, reassured by Irving's obvious confusion. He jerked his thumb toward the stock room and motioned for the boy to follow him inside. There, parked in front of a tower of boxes, was a new Schwinn Excelsior bicycle in shiny red, white, and chrome. Irving let out a gasp. "Is that . . . someone left that for *me*? I don't understand. Who was it, Mr. Stern?"

Mr. Stern shut the stock-room door and lowered his voice so that the customers wouldn't hear. "Do you know who Zip Diamond is?"

Irving frowned. "Wasn't he involved with the World Series scandal? He's one of the guys they say helped Arnold Rothstein fix it?"

Mr. Stern nodded. "Exactly. Rothstein and the other big shots wanted him out of Manhattan after that, told him to lay low for a while. They sent him to Chicago for a couple of years, but I guess he's back in Brownsville now."

"What's that got to do with me?"

"He was my visitor," said Mr. Stern.

The realization dawned on the boy slowly, like the sun poking through the clouds. "But why would Zip Diamond want to give me a bicycle? And how does he know I work for you?"

"A man like Mr. Diamond can find out anything. He has plenty of

friends who can get him information. He found out you work here, for
me, and he thought it might be better to leave the bike here so as not to
trouble your mother with it. As for why he got it for you, it seems you
helped his son yesterday. The boy told his father what you did for him and
that you lost your bicycle because of it."

"Freddie Schechter was bullying him, so I gave Freddie my bike to let
the kid go. You're saying Sammy is Zip Diamond's son?"

Mr. Stern nodded and clapped one hand on Irving's bony shoulder.
"You're a good boy, Irving, with a good heart. Mr. Diamond was very
grateful. He bought a few items for his wife and asked that you deliver
them to his house this afternoon. Do you remember where it is?"

"Of course."

"All right, then, I'll give you the package and you can take it over now.
I think it's best not to keep a man like Mr. Diamond waiting for too long."

Before the two of them left the stock room, Irving couldn't help noticing that Solomon Stern's face was blanketed with worry.

"Is there anything wrong, Mr. Stern?"

"I want you to be careful," the pharmacist told him. "Zip Diamond is
a good man to have in your corner, and right now he is in your debt. But
a man like that is dangerous, Irving—not only to his enemies but to his
friends, too. Be polite. Thank him for the gift, of course, but whatever you
do, don't get too close. With someone like Diamond, it's best to keep your
distance. Be respectful, but not too friendly. Don't offer to do him any
favors. You're a smart young man with a bright future ahead of you. If he
gets his hooks into you, he won't want to let go."

Though Irving understood what Mr. Stern was trying to say, the little
speech left him with more questions than answers. Still, something deep
in the center of his gut told him the pharmacist was right.

Back at the house on Glenmore Avenue, Mrs. Diamond was expecting
him. "Irving Rivkin," she said smoothly. "You clean up nicely, young man."
She took the package from him without asking and led him into the living
room.

"Look who's here, sweetheart," she said to the slender, hard-looking man in a chair by the window. Zip Diamond looked up from his newspaper and shot Irving a crooked smile. A cloud of confidence surrounded the man, wafting off his skin like expensive cologne. His suit was immaculately tailored, and his tiepin was made of solid gold. In a nod to his surname, he wore a large diamond pinkie ring that sparkled fiercely in the fading afternoon light. The grip of his handshake was so ferocious that Irving lost all the sensation in his fingers.

Zip looked Irving up and down. "You hungry? Thirsty?"

Irving shook his head. "No, sir. Thank you."

"Have a seat. Did ya get the bicycle? How does it ride?"

"It's terrific, sir. Thank you very much."

"That was my wife's idea," Zip said. "Listen, Irving. It's Irving, isn't it? What you did for my Sammy was a real nice thing. When he told me about those other punks . . . well, let's just say that Schechter kid and his friends won't be bothering anyone anymore."

Irving blinked a few times at his host. "Did you talk to their parents?"

Zip Diamond chuckled. "Nah," he said. "I *talked* to those kids myself. They won't go near Sammy or you again."

Irving didn't know how to respond, so he thanked Mr. Diamond again.

"How old are you, kid?" Zip Diamond asked.

"Seventeen, sir."

"Seventeen, huh?" Zip looked thoughtful. "I had a nice talk with your boss this morning. He said you were a real good worker. Responsible, intelligent. You show up on time and you work hard, he said. Only you and your mom at home, I heard?"

"Yes, sir. That's right. My older brother goes to college in Albany. My father left when I was three."

"And do you like school as much as your brother?"

Irving gave the man a sheepish smile. "My mother says my brother got the book smarts and I got the street smarts. I had to repeat a couple of grades. But I promised her I'd get my high school diploma."

Zip's laugh was warm and cold at the same time. "Well, Irving, I'm real appreciative of what you did for my Sammy, and I'm happy you came to see me today. If you ever need anything, you let me know. Don't hesitate to come to me. I hope to see you again real soon."

"Thank you, sir. It was nice to meet you."

As Zip went back to his newspaper, Mrs. Diamond walked Irving to the door. "Your mother sounds like a smart woman," she said. "Listen to her and stay in school. You'll have plenty of time after that."

"Time for what, ma'am?" Irving asked.

Mrs. Diamond's tone was cryptic. "We'll just have to see," she said.

As he rode back to the store on the new bicycle, Irving was certain that everyone he passed could hear the uneasy pounding of his heart. He could not say exactly what he'd expected, but his meeting with Zip Diamond felt significant and strange. What had the man meant when he mentioned that Freddie wouldn't bother him again? What exactly had Zip Diamond said to bring boys like Freddie and his friends to heel?

Then there was the matter of Zip's goodbye. *Don't hesitate to come to me. I hope to see you again real soon.* It was as if Solomon Stern knew exactly what would happen, exactly what a man like Zip Diamond would say. Having grown up without a father, Irving didn't have much experience with paternal-sounding advice, but he was certain of at least one thing: if he had to choose one of those men to trust, he'd pick Solomon Stern any day of the week.

Irving was so flustered by Mr. Diamond that he gave no further thought to his wife's parting words.

———————

SEVENTEEN

SEPTEMBER 1987

G oldie Stern was driving Irving crazy.

Her sudden appearance at Rallentando Springs had un-leashed an avalanche of memories. Even from behind, with her hair in a swim cap, he had been certain it was her. And when she turned around, it had taken all his self-control not to blurt out that he'd thought about her almost every day for the past sixty-two years.

To him, she still looked fantastic. She should, with all that swimming she did. But it was more than staying in good shape. Goldie looked exactly like herself, with every expression he remembered intact. When she pulled away from him, he wasn't insulted. It was exactly the reaction he knew she *would* have—annoyed, stunned, exasperated. By eighty, most people had lost their mettle. But Goldie still had plenty to spare. It was like the line from that Shakespeare play he'd read in his continuing education class at Florida Atlantic University last year: "Age cannot wither her, nor custom stale her infinite variety."

He almost recited the line right then, almost started quoting Shakespeare at the goddamned pool! Back in Brooklyn, he'd hardly heard of Shakespeare. But now he understood what all the fuss was about. Those words might have been written about the queen of Egypt, but they applied to Goldie Stern as well. In his eyes, she would never be boring; her unpredictability was part of her charm. Still, he didn't want her to think he'd gotten pretentious in his old age. The Irving she knew barely made it through high school. She wouldn't expect him to be a reader.

One day, maybe he would explain to Goldie the influence she'd had on him, how it was that he'd finally come to appreciate the power of the written word. He doubted she remembered the gift she'd given him for his high school graduation—a book of poems by Robert Frost. Irving took the volume with him to Chicago (at the time, it was the only book he owned), but he didn't open it up until his twins were three years old.

Lois wasn't one for cuddling or reading, so as soon as the boys were a little older, Irving took over their bedtime routine. One evening, when the two of them grew bored of the picture books in their limited collection, Irving pulled out the book of poems and read them to his sons out loud.

The boys couldn't grasp the meanings, of course, but the words and the rhythm held their attention. Irving read a few poems every night, and when he finished the collection, he started over from the beginning. Between the boys' third and fourth birthdays, he read Frost's book at least a dozen times. Certain poems made him more emotional than others, but every time he read "Nothing Gold Can Stay," he could not stop his eyes from tearing.

The collection of poems was just the beginning. Though he was eight hundred miles away from Goldie by then, he still remembered the way she used to talk about books, the way she'd called them her best friends. He remembered her telling him that when she was sad about her mother, reading helped to make her feel better. And so, as his marriage grew increasingly painful, he began turning to books as a source of comfort. After Lois left him, he joined a book club at the local community center. When he retired to Florida, he decided to take literature classes at the nearby college. It was there that he read Dickens and Austen and all the other classics he'd skipped in high school.

More than anything, he wanted to tell Goldie how much her graduation gift meant to him.

Unfortunately, he wasn't sure she'd ever sit still long enough for him to explain. Goldie had made it very clear that she did not want to spend time with him. Of course, after all that had happened, he supposed he couldn't exactly blame her.

He sure as hell could blame Nathaniel Birnbaum, though.

Dr. Birnbaum just had to be tall and handsome, didn't he? With season tickets to the Palm Beach Symphony and a fancy "cottage" up in Maine. Birnbaum went to college *and* to medical school. He probably knew every Shakespeare sonnet by heart. And somehow, he still had a full head of hair. How was Irving supposed to compete with *that*?

At least he'd had a few days alone with Goldie before the competition showed up. Jesus, he'd go straight back to the hospital tomorrow if only she would look at him the same way she had after he'd fainted on the tennis court—like if he croaked, it might break her heart.

Those Oh Henry! bars she bought meant something, too. She hadn't forgotten that they were his favorite. It was a less-than-ideal way for her to meet Vera, but when the time was right, he would explain. There was nothing romantic between him and Vera—they were dinner companions, nothing more. One day Vera had moved to Rallentando, and the next day, she was making Irving dinner. He'd never had the heart to tell her to stop. He asked his son Bill a few times if he should put an end to it, but Bill said he thought it made Vera feel useful. "As long as you don't lead her on," Bill insisted, "I don't think there's anything wrong with eating the woman's food."

But from the way Goldie and Vera had glared at each other, Irving knew he'd made a mistake. He never should have listened to Bill. Now he could see the situation more clearly: Vera wasn't cooking him dinners for fun. If that woman cooked, it was because she meant business.

Ever since that unfortunate encounter, things had been going in the wrong direction. Goldie was traipsing around with Birnbaum and patently ignoring Irving. Vera was calling him every five minutes and had already made him promise to accompany her to the Rallentando barbecue.

Every spring, dozens of Rallentando Springs residents left behind the blistering summer heat for their family and friends up north. And every September, the Social Committee held a cookout to welcome everyone back. The cookout marked the official start of the Rallentando Springs social season.

The barbecue was nothing fancy—it was always held around the pool, and some people even came in their bathing suits. The men who ran the snack bar brought in extra grills to cook hamburgers and hot dogs for the crowd. A long folding table bowed from the weight of the smorgasbord of sides: coleslaw, potato salad, corn on the cob, baked beans, sauerkraut, and platters of pickles. A second table was placed on the other side of the pool, piled high with an array of homemade desserts supplied by the many residents: Shirley always brought her strawberry cheesecake and Dora made her famous lemon meringue pie. Harold's wife, Gail, made Black Forest cake every year, and Marlene usually made apple or cherry strudel.

An hour before the barbecue, Irving showered and searched his closet for the unworn polo shirt his daughter-in-law had given him a few years back. He usually favored crew-neck T-shirts—the collared polos were stiff and itchy. But he'd noticed that Birnbaum always wore them, so he decided to wear one, too. He walked to Vera's, but she kept him waiting, fussing first with her outfit, then her makeup, and finally with the dessert she was bringing—an enormous lime-green Jell-O mold, which wobbled precariously on the plate. By the time they got to the barbecue, it was half an hour after the appointed time. The two of them made quite an entrance—Vera, in a shiny leopard-print blouse and oversize coral beads at her throat, and Irving, carrying the quivering green mound as if it were a ticking bomb.

When he spotted Goldie out of the corner of his eye, talking with Shirley, Birnbaum, and some others, he felt his pulse begin to race. He'd made up his mind to play nice with Birnbaum, to keep the conversation light and upbeat. He was going to show Goldie that he could be civil. He could be as gracious as anyone else.

Unfortunately, Vera wouldn't let him out of her sight. When he got a hot dog, so did she. When he sat down, she sat beside him. After he'd polished off two hot dogs and a Diet Pepsi, he brushed off his shirt and rose to his feet.

"I'm gonna go say hello to some people."

"I'll come with you. Let me fix my lipstick."

He gritted his teeth, but what could he say? Vera followed him over to the table where Goldie, Birnbaum, and Shirley were sitting. When Irving saw Goldie's empty plate, he couldn't help making a joke. "Tell me you didn't eat the potato salad."

"What's wrong with the potato salad?" said Shirley.

Goldie covered her smile with one hand and tried to comfort her friend. "He's only being funny, Shirley," she said. "Remember I told you how sick I got from the tuna? Anything with mayonnaise in this heat doesn't sit well in my stomach, that's all."

But Vera's face was abloom with concern. "I ate the potato salad, Irving. Why didn't you say anything to *me*?"

He did his best to reassure her. "It's a joke, Vera. The potato salad is fine."

While Vera was pouting, the Rallentando staff were clearing away the dinner buffet to make more room for dancing. Music began flowing through the outdoor loudspeakers, and a few of the residents got to their feet. Birnbaum danced with Shirley first, while the others looked on quietly. After a few songs, the couple returned.

"Augusta," said Birnbaum, extending his hand, "would you do me the honor?"

Vera's lashes were like windshield wipers doing double time in a downpour. "Augusta?" she repeated, confused. "I thought you said her name was *Goldie*?"

"It's Augusta," Goldie clarified. "Goldie is a childhood nickname. I haven't let anyone call me that for the past sixty-two years. No one except Irving calls me that now."

Vera frowned. "He doesn't have any nicknames for *me*." But before Irving could address her grievance, Birnbaum and Goldie left the table. Irving cursed under his breath as he watched the two of them go. That Birnbaum was a smooth operator. He'd always been a good dancer, too.

The combination of the music, the lights, and the image of Goldie in Birnbaum's arms transported Irving back to that evening at the Arcadia Gardens restaurant in Brooklyn. The night when Birnbaum had proposed to his wife. The night when everything had gone wrong. As he watched Birnbaum lead Goldie in a waltz around the pool, a spark of anger ignited in Irving's throat. And when Birnbaum spun Goldie around and she smiled, the anger exploded in his chest. Before he knew it, he was heading toward them, on a furious collision course.

"I'm cutting in," Irving said roughly after tapping Birnbaum on the shoulder.

"What are you talking about?" said Goldie. "People don't do that anymore."

"Well, I'm doing it," Irving insisted, elbowing Birnbaum out of the way.

"Listen, Irving," Birnbaum said. "Please try to calm down."

"Don't tell me what to do!" shouted Irving, stepping between the graceful pair.

"Irving, shh. People are staring." Goldie was trying to reason with him now, but he was having none of it. He didn't care if he embarrassed himself. He didn't care if he caused a scene. He felt as if he'd been struck by lightning—desperation surged through his eighty-two-year-old body, burning him from the inside out.

"You already ruined things once!" he said to Birnbaum. "I won't let you do it again!" The next thing he knew, his hands were on Birnbaum's shoulders and he was pushing him out of the way. Birnbaum tried to steady himself, but it was no use—one moment he was standing next to Goldie, and the next, he'd fallen onto the dessert table, landing on top of Shirley's strawberry cheesecake. The plastic folding table gave way, Birnbaum crashed to the ground, and the rest of the desserts slid on top of him in a spectacularly hideous mess.

Dora yelped for her lemon meringue pie, and Harold's wife cursed for the Black Forest cake she'd spent the better part of the day baking. Vera's Jell-O mold had melted slightly in the heat, and puddles of the greenish goo splashed all over Birnbaum's polo.

Irving was instantly overcome with remorse. He hadn't meant to go that far. He moved toward Birnbaum to apologize, to help the man up, to offer a napkin, but Goldie managed to get there first. "Nathaniel!" she shouted, "are you all right?"

She darted to him, knelt down on the cement, and checked to make sure that he wasn't injured. Shirley handed her some napkins, and Goldie began scooping melted Jell-O and chocolate frosting off of Birnbaum's neck. The care with which she did so made Irving's heart ache. It seemed to him that Goldie had sprinted to Birnbaum even more quickly than she'd run to him when he'd collapsed on the tennis court. Had he read that incident incorrectly? Was Goldie simply the kind of woman who ran toward others in a crisis? Irving's head began to spin, and he felt as dizzy as if he'd fallen himself.

Once she was satisfied that Birnbaum wasn't hurt, Goldie stood up and scoured the crowd for Irving. Eventually she spotted him, sitting on a folding chair with his head in his hands. He didn't need to look up to know that she was standing beside him.

"I don't know what game you think you're playing," she whispered. "Coming here with Vera and then flirting with *me*, causing a scene while your *girlfriend* is waiting."

When Irving finally lifted his head, all he could see was the white-hot resentment flashing in Goldie's gray eyes.

"Vera isn't my girlfriend," he murmured, but he knew she wasn't listening.

Her tone was as dark and bitter as a pot of overbrewed coffee. "Do you really think I'd fall for the same stunt twice?"

"Look, can we go somewhere and talk? Please, Goldie? There's a lotta things I want to explain."

"Save your explanations for Vera," she hissed. "And for the very *last* goddamned time: My. Name. Is. Augusta."

EIGHTEEN

JANUARY 1924

The happy news of Harriet Dornbush's condition was revealed on a Friday in early January. Augusta was home from school with a cold when Harriet came to the house for more of Aunt Esther's soup. As soon as their guest removed her coat, Esther made a clucking sound. "Ah," she said. *"B'sha'ah tovah."*

Augusta knew what the words meant. It was customary, when wishing a pregnant woman well, to refrain from congratulatory language. *Mazel tov,* Augusta had been taught, was appropriate only when referring to something that had already occurred. Pregnancy, on the other hand, was the expectation of something yet to come, a potential yet to be fulfilled. Esther had chosen the more prudent phrase, which, translated loosely, meant "all in good time." It was a wish for the future, rather than a blessing for the past—a wish that the pregnancy should be smooth, the baby healthy, and the birth without complication.

Harriet stared at Aunt Esther. "Are you certain?" she whispered. "I suspected, but I didn't let myself hope. How do you—how can you know so soon? Even the doctor won't give me assurances."

"There is a fullness to your figure that I haven't seen before," said Aunt

Esther. "But I knew even before you took off your coat—your hair is thicker and your skin glows with the joy of what is to come."

"Will it be a boy or a girl, do you think?"

"It should only be healthy," Aunt Esther insisted.

Once Harriet left the apartment, Augusta was eager for answers. "She's been trying for *seven* years," said Augusta. "Please, Aunt Esther, tell me the truth. She's pregnant now because of *you*, isn't she?"

Esther tossed her head back and laughed. "I didn't realize that my great-niece had so little knowledge of conception." The two of them were alone in the kitchen, preparing for the *Shabbos* meal. Augusta was slower on her feet than usual—her head was still achy from her cold.

"You know exactly what I mean. Was it the herbs you put in her soup? Was it the boots you made her wear?" Augusta lowered her voice. "Was it the words carved inside of your mortar?"

Esther did not rush to answer. Instead, she opened the door to the oven and pulled out the two challahs she had baked. She gestured to the braided loaves—glossy, warm, fresh, and fragrant. "You see the strands we weave together every Friday for our bread? Why do we not make a simple loaf? Why burden ourselves with complications when there is always so much else to be done?"

Augusta did not understand the change of subject, but she attempted to answer the question. "Mama used to say that the three strands of the challah are meant for truth, peace, and justice."

"A lovely explanation," said Esther. "But why not past, present, and future? Braiding is associated with strength, is it not? Why not beauty, honor, and strength? And what of a loaf with more than three strands? Six strands may be the six days of the week, leading up to the day of rest. Eight strands may mean new beginnings, as in the way we circumcise a child on the eighth day after birth. My mother used to make a twelve-stranded loaf, to represent the twelve tribes of Israel."

When Augusta didn't answer, Aunt Esther continued. "It is not so simple, is it? I could offer many more interpretations, but the point is, there isn't *one* explanation. Things are never as straightforward as we want them to be, Goldie. Why must I choose a single solution when the truth lies somewhere in between them all?"

Augusta's head reeled from the possibilities. Unable to think of a proper response, she nodded and pretended to agree. It was only later on, as she was drifting off to sleep, that she realized how cleverly her aunt had avoided the question.

Four months later, in early spring, Mrs. Dornbush was back in their kitchen. This time, instead of her slim-fitting dress, she wore a billowy blouse and a long, loose skirt. In place of the rose patent leather pumps were a pair of stiff, nondescript boots, identical to the borrowed pair that had belonged to Augusta's mother.

Harriet's face was flushed and full, and there was an unmistakable swelling around her middle. She was nearly six months along in her pregnancy, but aside from her husband and her parents, Esther and Augusta were the only people she'd told. March and early April had been cold that year, and whenever Harriet left her apartment, she'd worn a heavy woolen coat that covered her body, all the way down to her plain brown boots. Because of this, almost no one else knew of or suspected her condition.

"Let me see you," Esther said, smiling, after Harriet took off her coat. "You're growing nicely, *kinehora*. Tell me, how do you feel?"

"Other than the heartburn, I feel good." Along with the baby in her womb, a quiet confidence had blossomed inside her.

"Honey in warm milk will help," said Esther, and Harriet nodded obediently.

"Are you tired?" asked Augusta, offering the pregnant woman a chair. "You didn't have to walk here, you know. I'm happy to bring you whatever you need." Ever since Harriet found out she was expecting, she had painstakingly avoided the icy sidewalks and slippery steps of her local stores. She ventured outside only when necessary, and she never got very far. Augusta had been bringing her soup every week, along with anything she ordered from the pharmacy.

"Thank you, but after all this time at home, I need some exercise. For months, all I've done is rest and eat. It was a wonderful way to pass the winter, but now I want to stretch my legs, feel the breeze, and join the world again." She placed both hands on top of her stomach. "I haven't told anyone else, but I'm sure my neighbors suspect. No one wants to ask me plainly."

"Good," said Aunt Esther. "Let them wonder. When they hear the baby crying this summer, then they will have their answer."

The next week, on the first sunny day of April, Mrs. Dornbush came into the pharmacy. She had replaced her heavy woolen coat with a light spring jacket that did nothing to hide her expanding middle. Augusta's father was in the prescription room, but when he heard Mrs. Dornbush's voice, he came out front to say hello. He hadn't laid eyes on her since that awful day when she'd asked him for the arsenic. Now, when he saw that she was expecting, the back of his neck turned a blotchy crimson, and from behind his wire-rimmed spectacles, his eyes grew wide with amazement.

"I see there has been a happy development," said the always proper Mr. Stern. Although he was not as superstitious as his aunt, he knew better than to say more.

"Yes," said Mrs. Dornbush. "A wonderful development, indeed."

"I'm so glad that the doctors were able to help you and your husband at last," he said.

"Oh," demurred a slightly embarrassed Mrs. Dornbush. "It wasn't the doctors at all." She placed both hands protectively on her stomach, cradling the gift that was yet to come. "No, Mr. Stern, I am certain that I have your aunt to thank for this."

That evening, at dinner, Augusta's father was furious.

"I thought I'd made myself clear! It's one thing to sell your soup to soothe stomachs or to offer your creams for children's rashes. But you promised me you would not intervene in the legitimate medical concerns of my customers! I am a highly trained pharmacist, Esther. Doctors rely on me. Customers trust me. Do you know how it looks to have a member of my *own family* interfering in this way? Peddling nonsense to anyone who is dissatisfied or doesn't agree with my opinion?"

Aunt Esther slammed the pot of stew she was carrying down onto the kitchen table. Potatoes and carrots quaked in tandem. "I don't peddle nonsense!" she said. "How dare you disparage my knowledge? I studied for years, the same as you. I worked hard, the same as you. You and your *doctors* had no answers, so I stepped in to do what you could not. Where I come from, they call that a kindness!"

"Maybe in the old country," he said coldly. "But here, pharmaceutical study is a *science*. We follow formulas. We use precise instruments. Our work relies on accuracy and scholarship, not the recipes and spells of superstitious old women."

"And yet, with all your formulas and equipment, none of you could manage to help her."

Solomon Stern gritted his teeth. "The doctors said there was *nothing* they could do!"

Esther rolled her eyes at her nephew. "You put too much faith in doctors."

"And you should mind your own business."

"How can I mind my own business when a deserving woman is abandoned? She was desperate, Solomon. You *know* this. Goldie told me what she wanted to buy at the store."

Augusta sank into her seat and braced herself for her father's wrath. She had not forgotten what he said when he first agreed to teach her. *Whatever you hear, whatever you learn about a customer, is never, ever to be repeated. If you break this rule, there will be no second chance.*

Although Augusta kept her head down, she felt her father's eyes upon her. Bess gave her hand a sympathetic squeeze under the heavy wooden table, but the weight of Solomon Stern's disappointment was like a fog that settled on them all.

The rest of the meal was spent in strained silence. Bess tried once or twice to lighten the mood, to offer an observation about a book she was reading or to praise the tenderness of Esther's stew. But the only contribution the others made was the scraping of silverware on porcelain plates. When the meal was over, Solomon Stern stood up, tossed his napkin onto the table, and left the apartment without another word.

It was long past midnight when he finally returned, smelling faintly of whiskey and cigars. Augusta had waited up for him, and he did not seem surprised to see her there, holding vigil on the sagging sofa in the dark.

"I know you're angry with me," she began.

"I'm not angry anymore."

Relief, like a blanket, warmed her skin. "You're not?"

"No." He sat down beside her. "In fact, I owe you an apology. I forgot how young you are, Augusta. I forgot how frightening a situation like Mrs. Dornbush's can be for someone without the proper experience. I should have realized how much it would upset you."

"I was so afraid of what she might do. It's all right now, though, isn't it, Papa?" Augusta released a shaky breath and leaned closer to embrace her father. "I'm so glad that Aunt Esther was able to help her."

Solomon Stern stiffened and pulled away. As his anger flared back to life, his lower lip quivered, and his voice grew cold. "Harriet Dornbush's good fortune has *nothing* to do with your aunt," he said. "No one conceives because of old wives' tales, Augusta. You must never confuse your aunt's charms and concoctions with real pharmaceutical knowledge."

Augusta answered in a whisper. "She didn't use charms . . ."

"Then tell me, what did she do? What exactly was your aunt's *prescription*?"

Augusta rubbed the back of her head in an effort to remember. "She said the most important thing was for Mr. Dornbush to stop traveling so much. She told Mrs. Dornbush to be sure to eat breakfast, and to rub castor oil onto her belly every day."

Augusta's father rolled his eyes.

"There were special herbs for Mrs. Dornbush's soup—I remember some of the names. Oh, and then there was the matter of the shoes."

"What do you mean, the matter of the shoes?"

Augusta could tell from her father's reaction that the topic was one she shouldn't have raised. Still, it was too late now. "You know Mrs. Dornbush has beautiful shoes, on account of her husband's job?"

"I suppose I do, yes. Go on."

"Well, Aunt Esther felt it would be best if Mrs. Dornbush wore plain boots from now on. She thought . . . well, she said that some people in the neighborhood might be jealous of her, and that perhaps, even without knowing it, they may have unleashed the Evil Eye."

Solomon Stern's hands curled into fists. "I knew it!" he said, almost shouting. "The Evil Eye? This is *exactly* what I was afraid of!"

"But, Papa, Aunt Esther's way worked, didn't it? What's the harm if it actually *worked*?" She wanted so much to make her father understand; she wanted him to see all the good that her aunt was capable of.

"The harm, young lady, is that Esther's rubbish is not only an insult to my profession but a threat to my reputation!" Suddenly his breathing grew ragged; his cheeks turned a bright and furious red. "Listen to me now, Augusta. I can excuse you involving your aunt this time, but I will not be able to forgive it twice."

Tears filled the corners of Augusta's eyes. How could her father ask her to choose between the enigmatic splendor of Esther's work and the solid satisfaction of his own? Between the thrill of a patch of kitchen moonlight and the security of the prescription room? Why couldn't he see that they were equally powerful? Why couldn't he appreciate the beauty in *both*?

Augusta thought back to Irving's illness—to his dark, stuffy bedroom and his mother's strained expression. Could it really be only a coincidence that his fever broke the morning after Esther's visit?

She contemplated the once-hopeless Mrs. Dornbush and the bottomless well of her despair. Was Augusta really supposed to believe that Esther's intervention had no effect? That her advice and midnight ministrations had not altered the course of Harriet's life?

Finally, Augusta considered her mother. What a cruel end she'd been forced to endure, all because the doctors and the scientists couldn't give her the help she needed in time.

Of the three, only one of them had been lost—the one Aunt Esther had not helped.

What, then, was Augusta supposed to believe?

NINETEEN

SEPTEMBER 1987

The next morning, Augusta couldn't shake the image of Nathaniel covered in frosting and melted green Jell-O. As horrifying as the evening had turned out, and as angry as she still was at Irving, she couldn't keep herself from laughing. She snickered while her coffee brewed; she chortled while putting on her bathing suit. During her walk to the swimming pool, she replayed the scene so many times in her mind that she fell into a fit of hysterics and had to stop to catch her breath. She had only just managed to regain her composure when she walked through the swimming pool gate, saw the green Jell-O stains on the pavers, and began cracking up all over again.

"What's so funny?" said Shirley, looking up from her magazine.

Augusta tried to suppress a snort. "Nothing . . ." she said.

"That was quite a scene, last night. I have to say, there's been a lot more excitement at this place since you arrived. It's not every day that we have a fight break out—and over a *love triangle*, no less."

"It wasn't a fight," Augusta protested. "And it certainly wasn't over me."

Shirley lowered her sunglasses and fixed an amused gaze on her friend. "That's *exactly* what it was, and it was most *certainly* over you. Irving Rivkin is so in love that I'm surprised the man can still see straight. I suspected as much a while back, but after last night, I know for sure. Hell, after last night, *everyone* knows. Including Vera, I'm afraid."

"Oh no. Did she say anything to you?"

"What was there for her to say? The man she clearly thought was her boyfriend followed you onto the dance floor, tried to cut in, and when that didn't work, he shoved your dance partner into her Jell-O mold."

Another chortle escaped Augusta's lips and her shoulders began to shake. "That Jell-O," she said. "It was so messy and so . . . *green*."

Shirley began giggling, too. "Did you know that some of the old biddies here insisted on eating the crushed bits of my cheesecake, even after Nathaniel sat on it? They said they didn't want it to go to waste."

The image sent Augusta into fresh peals of laughter.

After both women recovered, Shirley cleared her throat and took Augusta's hand. "I want to tell you something," she said. "And I want you to give me your honest opinion."

"Of course," said Augusta. "Should I be worried? You're very serious all of a sudden."

"Nothing to worry about," said Shirley. "But dancing with Nathaniel last night made me realize something." Before she could finish her thought, Nathaniel himself appeared at the pool gate.

"Nathaniel!" Shirley said, waving him over. "The two of us were just talking about you. Are you all in one piece? Any bruises?" She was looking at Nathaniel with a brightness that Augusta hadn't noticed before.

Nathaniel flashed a sheepish smile. "A little twinge in my shoulder, but other than that, everything's fine. I'm sorry about your cheesecake, Shirley, though I do think it helped to break my fall."

Augusta apologized for the umpteenth time, but Nathaniel cut her off. "No more apologies necessary," he said. "There was absolutely no harm done, except to the desserts, I'm afraid. Anyway, ladies, I'm off to do my laps. Enjoy the sunshine."

Once Nathaniel was safely out of earshot, Augusta asked Shirley what she'd been planning to tell her. "Oh, nothing important," Shirley murmured. "I'll tell you another time."

Augusta did not want to press, so she waited for Shirley to steer the conversation. Eventually, the topic returned to the strange events of the previous evening. "What do you think Irving meant last night when he said that Nathaniel had ruined things for him?"

Augusta shrugged. "I have no idea. From everything that I remember, the two of them used to be friends. Nathaniel used to date my girlfriend Evie, and eventually he married her. The four of us went on some double dates."

Shirley clapped her hands together like an overexcited schoolgirl. "You and Irving *were* an item, then? I knew it! Why didn't you tell me before? And Nathaniel eventually married Evie. So what was all that nonsense Irv was saying? Do you think *he* had a thing for Evie, too?"

Augusta shook her head. "Definitely not. And I didn't tell you about me and Irving because . . . honestly, it's embarrassing."

"Why should you be embarrassed?"

Augusta winced and lowered her head. "I was only eighteen years old, but you know how it was back then. A lot of us got married at that age. Anyway, Irving was a few years older. He worked at my father's pharmacy, as a delivery boy. He was never much of a student, but he was good at his job.

"The two of us were best friends for years, until things turned romantic between us. At least I *thought* they were romantic. I thought he and I were meant to be, but I misread the signs. I really thought he might propose . . . I was young and *very* naive." Augusta briefly closed her eyes at the memory.

"Anyway, a week after Nathaniel proposed to Evie, I found out that Irving had proposed to someone else—a girl from the neighborhood named Lois. I hadn't even known they were dating! There were a lot of rumors then. The next thing I knew, her whole family moved to Chicago and they took the two lovebirds with them. Irving never said goodbye, and I never saw him again."

When Augusta finished telling the story, Shirley looked as if she were about to cry. "Oh, Augusta," she said. "What an *awful* story. No wonder you're so prickly with him. Irving was your first love, and then he went and broke your heart!"

"Shh," said Augusta. "Not so loud, please. And you don't need to be sorry for me. It's been sixty-two years. Trust me, I'm over it."

Shirley reached for Augusta's hand. "I'm not so sure about that," she said. "At our age, we're so set in our ways that we can be afraid to admit our feelings." Shirley glanced over at Nathaniel, who was busily finishing up his laps. "Trust me, I know what I'm talking about."

Later, at home, Augusta continued to ponder the real reason for Irving's ill will toward Nathaniel. Nothing about it made any sense. According to everyone at Rallentando—including Nathaniel Birnbaum himself—Irving's resentment toward Nathaniel had been obvious long before Augusta arrived. So even if the attention Nathaniel paid her exacerbated the grudge, that certainly hadn't been how it started.

Could Shirley's theory possibly be right? Had Irving been in love with Evie? Was that what he meant when he told Augusta that Nathaniel had taken something from him?

Augusta let her mind return to the night Nathaniel proposed to his wife. The four of them had gone to Arcadia Gardens, the fanciest restaurant in Brooklyn. It had started out as a perfect evening. Augusta had never been to such an elegant place, and she'd been mesmerized by the lights and the people, by the swell of the music and the buzz in the air. One moment, Augusta was passing Irving the flask she'd filled with her father's whiskey, and the next thing she knew, she and Irving were watching Nathaniel slide down to one knee in the middle of the dance floor. In all the excitement and chaos that had followed, Augusta lost Irving in the crowd. He never came to find her later, and she'd gotten a ride home with Nathaniel and Evie.

Of course, when Augusta told Shirley about that time, she'd revealed only the bare minimum. She'd said nothing about who Lois's father was or his dangerous reputation. She hadn't mentioned the name Zip Diamond, or the role he had played in their neighborhood. She'd spent the better part of her life blocking out every memory of him and his daughter.

There were other details of those early days that she'd forced herself to block out as well—memories she never spoke about, memories she *never* allowed to resurface: her great-aunt Esther, bathed in moonlight, sharing her knowledge during late-night lessons; the lonely nights Augusta had tried and failed to apply those lessons on her own. For sixty-two years, she had managed to keep all that unpleasantness out of her mind. And now here she was, being forced to relive it.

All because of Irving Rivkin.

TWENTY

JUNE 1924

Jeremiah Ezekiel Dornbush was born healthy and well at the end of June, weighing in at a robust seven pounds. A few days after the baby's birth, a package arrived at the Stern household containing two pairs of women's shoes—a soft black leather pair for Aunt Esther with a one-inch heel and a two-eyelet tie, and a second tan calfskin pair in a similar style for Augusta. The shoes were nowhere near as extravagant or eye-catching as those Mrs. Dornbush used to wear, but they were relatively stylish and sturdy. Esther, though appreciative of the gift, insisted that no good could come of putting fashionable shoes on old-fashioned feet. But Augusta wore hers happily, despite her father's disapproval.

Augusta had been planning to spend the bulk of her summer helping her father in his prescription room. It soon became clear, however, that he no longer trusted her to keep the secret concerns of his customers. She was still expected to work the cash register, ring up purchases, and rearrange shelves, but the back room, with its vials and its mysteries, was no longer part of her domain.

One morning, when Augusta was restocking shampoo, Bess asked her to take over at the cosmetics counter. "I need to use the ladies' room," Bess whispered, keeping her voice low so the customers couldn't hear. Beads of sweat dampened her forehead.

Ever since her high school graduation that spring, Augusta's sister had not been herself. She'd had almost no appetite at dinner, and she was constantly alluding to stomach pains and headaches. Her complexion, normally so rosy and bright, had turned a pasty, ashen gray. Whenever Augusta asked what was wrong, Bess's answers were unsatisfyingly vague.

After Bess left, George waved Augusta over. It was still early for the lunchtime rush and the stools at the soda counter were empty.

"Bess will be back soon, so I only have a minute." George spoke in a nervous whisper. "There's no time to beat around the bush. The fact is, I want to propose to your sister, and I was hoping you could help me pick out the ring."

George's words were thrilling, but they did not surprise her. All of Bess's friends were getting engaged—almost every week brought another announcement.

"Of course," she whispered. "Let me know when and I'll meet you wherever you like."

A wave of relief washed over George's features. "Thanks, Augusta. I can't tell you how much better that makes me feel. To tell you the truth, I've been a wreck all week."

"You don't need to be nervous," Augusta assured him. "You and Bess are perfect for each other." Before she had the chance to say more, a group of customers took seats at the counter and began vying for George's attention. "I'll let you get back to work," said Augusta. "Besides, if my father sees me slacking off, he'll be even less happy with me than usual."

Back at the cosmetics counter, Augusta rearranged the display of perfumes. She took short sniffs from the ornate glass bottles and moved her favorites up to the front. When Bess still did not return, Augusta decided to explore the other items. She had never been interested in makeup before, but now, the shiny golden compacts and bright silver cases held a surprising allure.

If Bess was old enough to get engaged to George, surely *she* was old enough to start wearing lipstick. Augusta ran her eyes over the myriad of choices—pinks and plums, crimsons and corals—wondering what color might suit her best. In the end, she chose a medium shade of pink—not so bright as to be vulgar, but not pale enough to go unnoticed. She was studying the effect in the countertop mirror when she heard her sister's voice.

"Hallelujah!" said Bess, smiling the kind of carefree smile that made her look like herself again. "I never thought this day would come!"

Augusta smiled back, embarrassed, not knowing quite how to respond.

"Can I offer some suggestions?" Bess asked. And when Augusta nodded in agreement, Bess let out a squeal and squeezed her shoulder. She pulled a few lipsticks from beneath the counter and picked a slightly different shade to apply over the first. "This will be better with your complexion—the color is deeper, and it won't wash you out."

Next, Bess chose a shiny gold compact and dusted Augusta's baby-smooth cheeks with a touch of powdered rouge. Finally, she worked on Augusta's eyes—pressing ivory shadow onto the eyelids, wetting the dark brown cake mascara and using the applicator to sweep the paste ever so lightly over her younger sister's lashes. When she was done, Bess held up the silver hand mirror so that Augusta could view the results.

When Augusta looked into the mirror, she forced herself to suppress a gasp. Bess had always been the beautiful sister—the one that made schoolboys turn their heads and strangers smile in the streets. Bess had been the one young men fell in love with, and now she would be the one getting married. Augusta had never thought to be jealous—it was simply the way things had always been. But now her reflection made her wonder whether one day someone might fall in love with her, too.

"Augusta!" Her father's voice broke through her reverie. "I need you back at the register. Now!"

She tore herself away from the mirror and hurried to the rear of the

store. A line of customers had formed at the counter while her father
had been making up some pills. Augusta sprang quickly into action. She
wanted to keep the customers happy and keep her father happy, too. It
had been weeks since he'd smiled at her. Weeks since he'd offered her
any kind words. As the line receded and the customers exited, Solomon
Stern emerged from the prescription room. "Are you wearing *makeup*?"
he asked.

"Yes," Augusta admitted. "Do you like it?"

Her father stared and then lowered his head. Eventually, when he was
able to speak, he swallowed to clear the lump in his throat. "You look like
your mother," he murmured.

The comment left Augusta shaken. Whenever the subject of her mother
came up, she noticed how quickly her father retreated to a familiar place
of despair. Although it had been almost three years, grief had not loosened
its grip on him. She wished he'd said that her mother would be proud of
her. She wished he'd told her that it warmed his heart to see the resem-
blance between two people he loved. But Solomon Stern said neither of
those things, and Augusta was left feeling the loss of her mother even more
deeply because of his silence.

The next several hours passed quickly, until Irving returned from his
morning deliveries. He called out to Augusta from the stock room as she
was making change for a customer. When she turned, she saw the soft
pretzel he was waving in the air like a prize. "I passed the cart on the way
back," he said, "and I got this beauty for us to share."

Augusta's mouth began to water. Irving knew pretzels were her
favorite—the spongy dough, the pebbles of salt. As he got closer, he
ripped the pretzel in two and was about to hand her the bigger half when
suddenly his expression changed, and he froze in place.

"Don't tease me, Irving," she said. "Hand over the pretzel, okay?"

When he didn't respond, she spoke again. "Irving," she said. "The pretzel? Please?"

The tips of his ears had turned bright red. "Here," he said, holding out her portion. "What did you . . . what did you do to your face?"

Augusta had forgotten about the makeup. She patted at her lower lip, wondering whether the color had worn off. "Bess put some makeup on me. Why?"

He shoved a chunk of pretzel into his mouth. As he chewed, he mumbled something incoherent, a gobbled mess of meaningless words. "Ew ook iffent," he said.

"What? Don't talk with your mouth full."

Irving's entire face was red now. Carefully he chewed and swallowed the pretzel. "You look different," he said softly. "I mean, not *that* different, but still . . ."

"I knew I shouldn't have let Bess put on so much. It looks terrible, doesn't it?" She rubbed at her cheeks with one hand while holding the pretzel in the other.

"No! Goldie, Jesus, I'm such a *putz*." Irving shook his head back and forth like a dog shaking water from his fur. Then, slowly, he tried again. "You look pretty," he said. "Not that you didn't look pretty before! But . . . I can't say anything right. You look nice, Goldie, that's all."

Her initial reaction was confusion. She broke her pretzel into bite-size pieces and ate them methodically, one by one. Rip, chew, swallow. Rip, chew, swallow, until the pretzel was gone.

"Are you all right?" Irving asked. "You're not mad at me, are you?"

She could not explain the strange sensation coursing its way through her limbs. The way Irving had stared at her then, the timbre of his voice when he said she looked pretty—nothing could have prepared Augusta for the effect these things had on her. If her father's comment made her feel alone, Irving's made her feel the opposite. His nearness was a palpable comfort, his admiration a balm that soothed her fractured, lonely heart.

She cleared her throat and tried to smile. "Of course I'm not mad at you," she said.

A moment later, Solomon Stern emerged from his prescription room.

When he saw the manner in which his youngest daughter was staring at his delivery boy and the way Irving was staring back, he raised his eyebrows in dismay. Augusta felt strangely exposed—as if he could sense what they both had been thinking. "Augusta," her father said brusquely, "you're done here for the day. Go home and help your aunt with dinner."

But upstairs, there was only more confusion. It turned out that Aunt Esther wasn't alone; the sound of raised female voices was coming from the back of the apartment.

Augusta followed the commotion and stood motionless outside the kitchen doorway.

"I'm sorry," she heard Esther say. "What you ask for is not possible."

"But you *have* to help me," a young woman whined. From her spot in the hallway, Augusta couldn't see who was speaking. Still, she thought she recognized the voice as belonging to the older sister of one of Bess's classmates. At twenty, Talia Friedman was still unmarried, living with her family a few blocks away.

Next, she heard Mrs. Friedman's voice, calmer and more cajoling. "Miss Minkin, please. We're willing to pay. I'm certain that for the right price—"

From the hallway, Augusta felt the reverberation of Esther's palm slapping the kitchen table. "Do not insult me," she said. "I am not some greedy witch from the forest. I am an apothecary, Mrs. Friedman."

"Apothecary, witch—what's the difference? Harriet Dornbush was barren for seven years, but after meeting you, somehow she got pregnant. If that's not witchcraft, I don't know what is."

"I'd like you to leave now," Esther said coldly. "I'm afraid I can't help you."

"Can't or won't?" sneered Mrs. Friedman. "You know, if you want to keep your reputation, you should really reconsider . . ."

"I don't think so," snapped Aunt Esther. "People in this neighborhood know exactly who and what I am. On the other hand, if they were to find out what *your daughter* has asked of me, *her* reputation might suffer greatly. I'm not sure if *anyone* would marry her then ..."

"Mama!" shrieked Talia, her voice rising in fear. "It's time for us to say goodbye. *Now!*"

Augusta ducked around the corner and watched as the pair headed for the door. Aunt Esther did not bother escorting them out but stayed in the kitchen until they were gone.

"You can come out of hiding now," she said. "How much did you hear?"

Augusta knew there was no point in pretending. "I'm not sure," she admitted. "When I came in, you were saying that what they wanted wasn't possible." She paused, considering what to say next. "What were they asking for exactly?"

Aunt Esther didn't answer right away. Slowly she shuffled to the stove and put the kettle on to boil. She filled two mugs with scoops of loose tea, waited for the water to be ready, and poured it into the cups. "Sit," she said, gesturing to the spot where she had placed one of the mugs. The air in the kitchen was warm and fragrant with lemon, currant, and ginger.

Augusta sat down and waited.

After a few moments of silence, Esther began to speak. "Talia is in love with a man," she began. "Or at least she says she is—it sounds more like infatuation. In any event, the girl has embarrassed herself."

"Did they ... she isn't pregnant, is she?"

"No, no," said Aunt Esther. "Thank goodness, no. Luckily, the young man rebuffed her advances, but the mother is afraid that her daughter will try again and that he won't be such a gentleman the second time. Mrs. Friedman wants them to be married."

"Married? But it sounds like the man isn't interested in Talia! Why would he want to *marry* her?"

"Ah," said Aunt Esther, blowing on her tea. "That is where Mrs. Friedman thinks I can help."

Augusta frowned. "I don't understand. Talia isn't sick, is she? What could you possibly do for her?"

"They want me to *convince* the young man."

"Convince him how?" Augusta took a sip of tea and savored the ginger on her tongue.

"They asked me to make a love potion for him."

The answer was so absurd that Augusta spit her tea out onto the table. "A—a *love potion*?" she stammered, coughing into her sleeve.

"She wouldn't be the first to ask."

Augusta sat up straighter now, mopping the spilled tea with a dishrag. "Can you . . . do you . . . do you know how to do that? Is that something you can teach me?"

Esther frowned. "Stop talking nonsense. And finish your tea before it gets cold." The conversation was officially over.

Once again, Aunt Esther had managed to avoid a particularly complicated question. Once again, she had provided a response that offered no real answer at all.

TWENTY-ONE

SEPTEMBER 1987

The next morning, Augusta woke before sunrise. When she could not manage to fall back asleep, she decided to go to the pool. It was too early for any of the regulars to be there, but one person was already swimming laps in the water. When she got closer, Augusta saw Irving Rivkin moving through the cool, clear liquid. She watched, incredulous, as he propelled himself forward, his crawl stroke steady and shockingly smooth. She was sorry to say that his form was excellent.

The last thing Augusta wanted to do was to join that man in the pool, so she decided to wait until he was finished. She was sure it wouldn't be long.

He did twenty-five more laps before stopping—not bad considering the shape he was in. There was the matter of his age as well, but Augusta didn't accept that as an excuse. She was almost as old as he was, wasn't she?

She planted herself at the shallow end and stood, looking down at him with her hands on her hips. "What do you think you're doing?" she said.

It shouldn't have bothered her so much—the fact that he was swimming laps in the pool. It wasn't *her* pool, after all. And she'd seen him in it before. But all the other times, he was merely cooling off—not engaging in the one activity that had kept her sane for all these years; the one activity that, if she were being honest, had helped her most to forget about *him*. She didn't want to share swimming with Irving. It felt like a violation.

"Swimming," he said. "You're here early. Don't worry—I'll get out of your way."

"Listen, Irving," she said. "I don't know what kind of game you're playing, but whatever *this* is"—she made a circular motion with her hand—"I'm telling you now, it isn't going to work on me."

He stared at her blankly as if he didn't understand. "I apologize," he said. "If I had known you'd be starting so early, I would have skipped today. Usually my timing is better." He pulled the swim cap off his head and walked up the steps and out of the water. After he dried himself off, he slipped on his T-shirt and his sandals. "I'll leave you to it, Augusta," he said, before he opened the pool gate to leave.

He didn't protest, he didn't make jokes. He didn't flirt or even say goodbye.

Have I finally lost my mind, or did that man actually call me Augusta?

The water felt cooler than usual, probably because it was still so early. Normally, when Augusta swam a set of laps, she felt the tension leave her limbs. There was something about the regularity of the movement—the lifting of each arm over her head, the flutter of her feet, the rhythm of her exhale—that stripped the stress and strain away. And oh, how she relished the fatigue when she was finished! The tiredness that signaled to her overworked brain that it could finally relax.

But today, there was no relief for her. There was no break from her anxious thoughts. There was no respite from the curiosity that hammered her head from the inside out.

Augusta wished she could talk to Shirley, but it was far too early for the sunbathers. She should have gone home and back to bed, but once she emerged from the water, she planted herself in a chair and didn't move. At nine o'clock, the canasta group showed up, and at ten Shirley finally arrived. She waltzed through the Rallentando pool gate wearing a one-piece ruffled yellow bathing suit with a Zabar's tote bag slung over her arm. Augusta waited for her to adjust her umbrella, apply her sunscreen, and get comfortable in her chair.

"Something strange happened this morning," said Augusta, once Shirley was finally settled.

Shirley set down her magazine. "What?"

"I couldn't sleep last night," said Augusta. "So I decided to get my workout in early. I got over here around seven and Irving was already in the pool. At first I thought he was swimming laps just to spite me, but I swear he was a natural in the water. It looked like he swims laps every day."

"He *does*," said Shirley. "He always has, at least since I've been living here. I assumed you already knew."

"How would I know? And how do *you* know?"

Shirley shrugged. "Chester is up with the sun every morning, and we always take a walk first thing. It gets too warm in the afternoon and the hot pavement isn't good for his paws. Most of the time we pass by the pool. Irving is out here every morning."

Chester was Shirley's miniature poodle, and like most dogs, he was an early riser.

Augusta drummed her fingers on her lounge chair, tapping out a nervous beat. "Why didn't he tell me about this before?"

Shirley let out a long, low whistle. "No offense, but it seems like you're making a giant fuss over nothing. Why do you care if he swims in the mornings? He doesn't get in your way, does he? Other than today, I mean. Plenty of people swim, Augusta—it's the perfect activity for people our age. Low impact, good for the heart . . . Besides, it's not like we give each other notice of our daily workout schedules. I did my Richard Simmons video yesterday, but I didn't go around telling people. For all we know, after his laps, Irving goes home and does a bunch of sit-ups."

"Not with that bowling ball belly of his."

"Wow," said Shirley, shaking her head. "That man has *really* gotten under your skin."

Augusta scowled. "No one is under my skin, okay? But don't you find it odd that he *never* said anything? If someone has something in common with you, isn't it typical for them to mention it?"

"You're an awfully suspicious person—you know that?" Shirley said. Before Augusta could respond, Shirley held up a hand to silence her. "Look. Ever since you and I met, you haven't been shy about the fact that you want Irving to leave you alone. He may be flirtatious, and he may tell stupid jokes, but Irving isn't an idiot. I'm sure that even before the barbecue, even *before* you publicly scorned him, he knew exactly how you felt about him. Maybe he didn't mention the swimming because he didn't want to invade your space. It's kind of thoughtful if you think about it."

Augusta wasn't sure she appreciated this kind of honesty from her new friend. "I didn't publicly *scorn* him," she said, failing to keep the defensive tone from creeping into her reply.

"Oh no? What would you call it then?"

Augusta had no good answers. Had she been too harsh with Irving? Ever since she'd first run into him, she *had* been consistently up front about the fact that she wanted to be left alone. Was that what Irving was doing? Trying to give her some space? Was Shirley right?

"Why does he swim so early?" said Augusta. "He doesn't strike me as a morning person."

Shirley shrugged. "Maybe you don't know him as well as you think. There's also the matter of Nathaniel—he swims here, too, same as you. If I hated Nathaniel as much as Irving seems to, I'd probably come early to avoid confrontation. Who wants to share the pool with your nemesis?" Shirley rubbed more sunscreen on her shoulders. "It's simple when you think about it. Irving doesn't want to swim with Nathaniel, and you don't want to swim with Irving."

Augusta hated the way Shirley made it sound. "Irving isn't my nemesis," she protested. "I never said I didn't want to swim with him." But even as she spoke the words, a slippery wave of self-loathing threatened to drag Augusta under.

⤙⤚

When Jackie called her that evening, her niece asked point-blank about Irving.

"So what's going on with you two?" asked Jackie. "Have you guys been hanging out?"

Augusta snorted. "Not exactly. There was a barbecue the other night, and Irving came with his girlfriend, Vera. I was sitting with Nathaniel, but then Irving waltzed over and started flirting with me. Right in front of the girlfriend!"

"Maybe she isn't his girlfriend," said Jackie.

"Well, she certainly *thinks* she is. Or at least she did before the barbecue. I'm not sure what she thinks she is now."

"That sounds juicy! What happened?"

"They were playing music—piping it through speakers—and Nathaniel asked if I wanted to dance. He's always been a wonderful dancer. Anyway, the next thing I know, Irving is trying to cut in. When Nathaniel refused, Irving tried to push him out of the way. Then Nathaniel lost his balance and ended up falling onto the dessert table. The whole thing went crashing down to the floor and Nathaniel ended up covered in cake and frosting. Shirley's cheesecake got ruined."

"Oh my god! Was he okay?"

"Luckily, no one was hurt. Except for Vera's green Jell-O mold. Unfortunately, Nathaniel was covered in it." Augusta giggled into the phone. "That part was funny, actually. You should have seen it—what a mess!"

"Vera must have been furious!"

"Oh, she was angry, that's for sure. And I can't say that I blame her. It isn't fun when your date causes a scene and everyone at the party is staring."

"Plus, her date started a fight *over you*."

"Don't be ridiculous," said Augusta. "No one was fighting over me.

Irving had a grudge against Nathaniel long before I ever showed up. I just can't seem to figure out why. I asked Irving about it a few days ago, but he was strangely cryptic about it."

"Hmm," said Jackie. "That sounds weird. You should ask him about it again. Try to get the truth from him."

"Maybe," said Augusta. "By the way, I checked the calendar. Only ten days until you come to Florida!"

"I know! I can't wait to see you! Also, I was thinking about your birthday. I would love to meet some of your new friends. What if I take you and a group—whoever you want—out to dinner to celebrate? You tell me who and how many and I'll make a reservation."

"I suppose I could invite my friend Shirley," said Augusta. "And Nathaniel would love to meet you. After all, he knew your mom and dad."

"What about Irving?" Jackie asked. "The more I hear about that man, the more I'm dying to meet him, too."

The idea of inviting both Nathaniel and Irving out to dinner seemed unwise. What if the two of them argued again and caused a scene in the restaurant? What if Nathaniel decided to pay Irving back for the dessert debacle? Still, if she got them in the same room with Jackie, maybe her niece could help uncover what their feud was really about.

"We'll see," said Augusta. "I'll think about it."

TWENTY-TWO

JULY 1924

Augusta could not stop thinking about her aunt's reaction to Talia Friedman's visit. Esther may have been irritated by Talia's request, but she certainly did not seem surprised. It was this lack of incredulity that sent Augusta's mind racing. Did such a "love potion" really exist? And if so, what was the formula? Were the ingredients and the dosage fixed, or did they vary depending upon the person for whom the elixir was intended? The only way for Augusta to know was to ask her aunt.

Over the past several months, Esther had been educating Augusta on a variety of basic home remedies: the proper herbal pastes for soothing bee-stings, reducing pimples, and treating rashes; a helpful tincture for calming coughs; a powder for alleviating congestion. Because of Esther's willingness to teach, Augusta was hopeful that if she could approach her aunt at the proper time and in the proper manner, she could convince her to reveal more details about the potion in question.

And so Solomon Stern's younger daughter spent the next weeks practicing how to ask without sounding too nosy or too eager. She didn't want to seem like a wide-eyed teenager or a gullible romantic. It was important, she thought, to be appropriately inquisitive and to emphasize that her interest was driven only by scientific curiosity and a thirst for knowledge.

As it turned out, all her preparation was for nothing: one week after denying Talia Friedman, Aunt Esther offered to make a similar potion for none other than Augusta's sister.

The subject presented itself on a Tuesday morning, after Solomon Stern had left for the store. Augusta was finishing up her toast, but Bess was still lolling around in bed in the windowless room off the kitchen. Before Augusta left for the pharmacy, she opened the door to check on her sister. "Bess? It's late. Don't you want some breakfast?"

Augusta expected to find her sister asleep, but Bess was very much awake, sitting up and hugging her chest to her knees. Her head was down, her face was hidden, and her fragile body was shaking with sobs.

"Bess? What's wrong? Why are you crying?" Augusta scurried to her sister's side and laid a soft hand on her back. "Oh, Bess, what is it?"

Instead of comforting her sister, Augusta's words had the opposite effect. Bess's weeping grew exponentially louder and her body shook even more fiercely.

"What is it?" Augusta asked again, gently wrapping her arms around Bess's neck.

Suddenly Aunt Esther appeared in the doorway. "It is her young man, I think," she said.

A startled Bess lifted her head and stared at their aunt through a shroud of tears. "How do you know that?" she said. "I haven't said any-thing to anyone."

Esther smoothed her kitchen apron over the front of her shapeless black dress. Her lips curved into a small, knowing smile. "I'm not as old as you think I am. I still remember having such feelings."

"I don't know *what* I'm feeling," said Bess. "That's why I've been so miserable. I haven't been able to sleep for weeks. And every time I try to eat, the food gets stuck in my throat. I can't keep anything down—I end up feeling sick to my stomach."

Esther nodded as if she already knew, but Augusta was thoroughly confused. "I don't understand," she said. "Everyone knows how much George loves you. He didn't do anything awful, did he? You don't think he has another girl?"

Bess shook her head. "It isn't that. George is wonderful. He's absolutely perfect."

"Then why are you so upset?"

"She does not know if she wants to marry him," said Aunt Esther, in a tone as cursory as if she were ordering a cut of beef from the butcher.

Augusta looked from Esther to Bess. She didn't have to ask if the assessment was true—from Bess's face, it was obvious. "George asked me to look at engagement rings for you," Augusta confessed. "He wanted to know what I thought you would like. I would have told you earlier, but he swore me to secrecy."

Despite the heat, Bess was shivering. "I know. He let it slip a while ago."

"Can you talk to him about it?" Augusta suggested. "Explain that you need more time to think?"

"I'm not sure time is going to help. I love George, Augusta. I really do. But how do I know I won't change my mind? How can I be sure that he's the man I'm supposed to be with *forever*? How does *anybody* know?"

Augusta had no answers for her sister. How could she hope to have opinions on a subject she knew absolutely nothing about? Augusta had never been in love. She had never even been kissed.

"I don't know what to do," Bess said, swallowing down a fresh batch of sobs. "What if I say yes to the proposal and then, later, I change my mind? If only I could be sure that I'm making the right decision."

Aunt Esther paced the narrow room and clucked her tongue against the roof of her mouth. "You want to know your true feelings for the man? Is that what you want?"

Bess wiped her eyes with the hem of her nightgown. "Yes," she said. "That's what I want."

"Very well, then," said Aunt Esther. "I will help."

Bess suppressed a frustrated groan. "Please don't tell me you can solve my problems with another bowl of soup."

Aunt Esther chuckled. "No soup, no. What you need is my mother's recipe—perfect for matters of the heart such as this."

Augusta couldn't believe what she was hearing. "But when Talia Friedman asked for a love potion, I heard you refuse with my own two ears! And when I asked you about it after, you told me I was talking *nonsense!*"

"Talia Friedman and her mother are fools! What they want is not possible—and even if it was, it would be wicked. Only a charlatan would make such promises. Love is not something that can be forced."

"Then I don't understand," Augusta said. "What does your love potion do?"

"There is no *love potion,*" Esther snapped. "My elixir only helps the mind to see and to feel more clearly."

For the first time in weeks, Bess looked almost hopeful. She had consistently rejected Augusta's suggestions that there was something uncanny about Esther's remedies. But now, suddenly, she seemed to accept that Esther knew more than just how to make kreplach. "How exactly does it work? Will it make me fall in love with George?"

Aunt Esther shook her head. "It can't make you feel what you do not. *If* it works, all it can do is help to illuminate your true emotions."

"What do you mean, *if it works?*"

"It is difficult to explain. The recipe helps to unlock the mind. Some people have minds that are more closed than others. If a person's mind is shut too tightly, the recipe may not work at all. But if a person's mind is open enough, the elixir may help them to decide whether what they feel is lasting love or a passing infatuation."

"How soon can I take it?" said Bess. "Can you make it for me now?"

"I do not have all the necessary ingredients. I will give it to you on Friday, when George comes for dinner. That will be the best time—when the two of you are together."

Once the whole business was decided, Bess braided her hair and got dressed. For the first time in weeks, she ate a real breakfast—a hard-boiled egg and two slices of rye bread, slathered thickly with butter. As she drank her second cup of tea, the color came back into her cheeks and the worry lines disappeared from her face.

One way or another, Augusta knew now, her sister would finally have an answer. The air in the kitchen was sweet with relief, shimmering with propitious resolve. Neither of the sisters had any doubt that their great-aunt's recipe would do what was promised.

All that was left was to make sure their father didn't find out.

TWENTY-THREE

SEPTEMBER 1987

Augusta set her alarm for six forty-five the next morning.

This time, she didn't stand on the pool deck, staring down at Irving while he swam back and forth. This time, Augusta was all business—securing her swim cap neatly on her head, stretching out her arms and legs to avoid cramps, and then slipping silently into the water. She could almost hear her mother's voice. *You can't give up something that brings you joy just because it is difficult.* She would not let Irving Rivkin's presence or her own mixed feelings dissuade her from doing what she loved.

She kept a respectful distance from Irving, who was so ensconced in his routine that at first he didn't notice her. Still, there was no way for him not to feel the delicate ripples her presence triggered or the slight undulation of the current that the rise and fall of her body caused. She could not say when he became aware of her, but at some point, she knew that he knew she was there. For a dozen laps afterward, they swam side by side, mirroring each other's movements.

As her workout came to a close, a welcome fatigue set in. Augusta followed Irving up the pool steps, and each of them dried off without a word to the other. Then Irving pulled a T-shirt over his head and slipped his sandals on his feet. "Have a nice day, Augusta," he said before walking through the gate and heading for home.

The encounter left Augusta slightly confused and strangely at peace, all at the same time. Irving had not questioned her presence in the pool at such an ungodly hour. He had not commented on her departure from her notoriously strict routine. He had not ogled or flirted or joked or mentioned her *tuchus* or her swimsuit. When he left, he had addressed her politely. He had used her preferred name to say goodbye.

That night, she set her alarm clock again.

Three days later, Vera came looking for Augusta in the cardroom. Augusta was finishing a game of mah-jongg when Vera tapped her on the shoulder. Vera's perfume was a cloying mixture of sweet vanilla and burnt rose petals. "I want to talk to you," she said.

Shirley gave Augusta an encouraging nod. "Go ahead. The rest of us will clean up the tiles."

In the brightly lit hallway of the clubhouse, the resentment on Vera's face was clear. It poured out of every exaggerated feature—from her heavily lined eyes to her brightly coated lips.

"What do you think you're doing?" Vera hissed.

"Excuse me?"

"Don't play dumb with me, Augusta. Or Goldie. Or whatever your *real* name is. You know exactly what I'm talking about!"

"I'm sorry, Vera, but I swear I don't."

"You've been throwing yourself at Irving!"

Augusta covered her mouth with her hand in an effort to suppress her laughter. "Throwing myself? At Irving Rivkin?"

"Is this some kind of joke to you? You've been meeting him every morning for the past three days in a row."

The specificity of the accusation caught Augusta's attention. "How do you know that?"

"Because people talk. People have eyes around here, you know. We're not as stupid as you think we are." Vera rummaged through her purse for a tissue and dabbed the corners of her eyes.

"Look, Vera, I'm sorry if you're upset, but trust me, Irving and I barely speak. We've hardly said more than two words to each other. I've been getting up early to swim, that's all."

"Why?"

"Why what?"

"Why get up so early? You never used to. When you first moved here, you got to the pool every day at nine o'clock. I know because that's when I play canasta. Every day it was always the same. Until Irving tried to dance with you . . ."

"I understand that the night of the barbecue was embarrassing for everyone, but that was a misunderstanding. Irving didn't mean to push Nathaniel, and I'm sure it had nothing to do with me—"

"Yes, it did," Vera insisted. "Don't try to lie about something so obvious!" Her voice grew louder as she struggled to contain her burgeoning rage.

A group of women on their way to the cardroom tried their best not to stare. When the group was out of earshot, Augusta continued her explanation.

"Vera," she whispered. "Vera, I'm sorry. But I swear to you. I absolutely *swear* that nothing is going on between me and Irving." Augusta tried to place a hand on Vera's shoulder, but Vera stepped backward, out of her reach.

Vera pulled a fresh tissue from her purse and wiped the mascara from her cheeks. Her rage had melted as quickly as her makeup, and all that was left of it now was a cloud of melancholy and bad perfume. "You know," Vera said, "I can't decide." Her quivering voice had become so pitiful that Augusta was suddenly filled with shame.

"Can't decide what?" Augusta said softly.

The spark of anger in Vera's eyes was gone, and most of her mascara with it. Without her armor, she looked lighter and more vulnerable than before.

"Whether you're lying to me or to yourself."

Augusta swam with Irving again the next morning.

Before they got into the water, neither said anything to the other. After they completed their laps, Augusta dried herself off in silence and Irving went to the other side of the pool to do the same. They did not linger or socialize, except for Irving's now-familiar goodbye. "Have a nice day, Augusta," he said.

She responded, "Same to you."

Only when they were in the pool did the barrier between them fade and the awkwardness subside. In the water, Augusta's mind played tricks on her. Place was irrelevant, time turned backward. In the water, she was back at Coney Island, laughing and swimming with her sister. She could hear her mother during their lessons. *Don't forget to stop and breathe.* When Augusta was swimming and her body was occupied, her mind expanded in unforeseeable ways. She was meeting Irving for the first time. She was in the kitchen with Aunt Esther.

In the water, Augusta could remember the subtle magic of her youth.

In the water, Augusta could remember what it felt like to be brave.

In the water, Augusta could finally forgive.

TWENTY-FOUR

JULY 1924

For the next several nights, Augusta tried her very best to stay awake. She wanted to be ready to follow Esther into the kitchen at any hour.

But try as she might to keep her eyes open, sleep kept a powerful hold on her. No matter what sounds Esther made, Augusta slumbered on and on. Sleep found her early every evening, and she didn't stir or open her eyes until the morning light came through her window.

On Friday morning, when she entered the kitchen, Augusta thought she smelled maple syrup and apples. But when she asked Esther if there were pancakes for breakfast, her aunt laughed and shook her head. "No pancakes today," she said. "That maple smell is fenugreek seeds. And the apple scent is mandrake root."

Aside from the smells, the only other evidence of Esther's late-night kitchen activities was the puffiness beneath her eyes.

Augusta's lips formed a frustrated pout. "I thought you were going to teach me."

"Not this time," Esther said. "This is a difficult and dangerous recipe. Too many things can go wrong."

⁓⊙

Later, the maple and apple smells were replaced by the rich scents of braising brisket and a casserole of sweet potatoes and prunes that Esther had been baking in the oven. When Esther cooked, she swayed and hummed. Her face lit up, her hazel eyes sparkled. There was something in the alchemy of the endeavor that transported her to a joyful place.

Bess frowned as she set the table. "George was a wreck at the store today—he spilled the cherries, knocked over the straws, and gave a little boy the wrong flavor ice cream. He's never broken a glass before, and then today he broke *two*!"

"Maybe he's going to propose tonight," Augusta said.

Bess's face turned a bilious green. "I think I'm going to be sick."

Outside, the summer sun was retreating in the slowly darkening sky. "Sit down and rest," Esther told her. "It's almost sundown. Your father and George will be here soon."

From the cabinet over the sink, Esther took a bottle of dark purple wine. Despite the law of the land, wine was allowed for religious purposes, and every month, Augusta's family received a bottle from their synagogue. There were rumors that the rabbi exaggerated the size of his congregation in order to obtain a larger allocation. In this way, he was able to sell the extra bottles in order to supplement his paltry income. Like so much of the gossip she overheard from the whispering pharmacy patrons, Augusta was never sure what she should and should not believe.

Esther poured a cupful of wine, but before she handed it to Bess, she took a familiar white pouch from her apron pocket and emptied the contents into the liquid. Again the distinctive maple smell, the scent of ripe apples, leather, and hay. Esther mumbled a few words under her breath. "Drink," she said, handing the cup to Bess. "All of it."

Bess poured the wine down her throat. When she set the cup back down on the table, Augusta peered into the bottom. She studied the leftover drops, wondering what it might be like to drink them. What would they taste like? What would she feel? She was about to lift the cup to her lips when Esther yanked it away. "That *isn't* for you," she said firmly.

Esther rinsed the cup carefully in the sink, and slowly Augusta came back to her senses. She glanced at Bess and wondered whether their great-aunt's promise would come to fruition.

"Do you feel any different?" Augusta whispered.

"I don't think so," Bess whispered back.

But when the men returned to the apartment, Bess stared admiringly at George as if she were meeting him for the first time. When she lit the *Shabbos* candles, she was almost too flustered to say the prayer.

As the meal was coming to a close, Solomon Stern cleared his throat and gave George a noteworthy nod. George tapped his spoon against his water glass. "May I have everyone's attention, please?" he said. "There is something I would like to say."

He turned his chair until he was facing Bess and took both of her hands in his. "Bess," he said, "from the first day I saw you, I knew that you were special. I know I don't have much to offer you yet, but I promise that I will work as hard as I can to give you everything you ever dreamed of. If you let me, I will spend the rest of my life trying to make you happy." George pulled a ring from his pocket and knelt down on the floor beside her. "Bess, I love you. Will you marry me?"

From under the table, Augusta reached for Aunt Esther's calloused hand. Her heart thumped wildly in her chest; perspiration soaked her skin. Would Esther's powder have any effect? What answer would Bess be prompted to give? What would the rest of them say to George if Bess decided to refuse?

Augusta studied her sister's face. For weeks now—perhaps even months—Bess had been anxious and unwell. But now her expression was serene. When she spoke, her voice was vibrant and certain, as unwavering as the mourning dove's song when the first streak of sunlight brightens the sky.

"Yes, George," she said. "I will marry you."

～◌～

Later, when Augusta asked her sister what had been going through her mind, Bess said that from the minute George entered the apartment, she knew, without question, that she wanted to marry him. "I've never been more certain of anything," she said.

"So you think Aunt Esther's powder worked?"

The girls were in Bess's tiny bedroom, whispering together into the night and looking through stacks of old magazines for sketches of bridal gowns and veils.

"I don't know," Bess admitted. "It could have been the powder, I guess, or maybe the wine she put it in. Or maybe it was the excitement of seeing George standing with Papa and smiling at me. All I know is that finally I didn't have any more doubts."

"That must be nice," said Augusta wistfully. "I used to know exactly what I wanted, but the older I get, the more uncertain I become."

"About Irving, you mean?"

Augusta shook her head. "No. Well, yes, but not only Irving. I used to be *positive* about going to pharmacy school, but the more time I spend with Esther, the more I wonder whether I should be studying something different."

"One day you'll figure it out," Bess told her. "One day, either with or without Aunt Esther's recipes, you'll decide what you want and who you're meant to be."

TWENTY-FIVE

‹———————❦———————›

SEPTEMBER 1987

Irving Rivkin was perplexed.

He'd been trying—he really had—to get on Goldie's good side again. He'd even stopped calling her Goldie, which, in his opinion, was a terrible waste of the perfect name.

He still remembered the first time he had heard her great-aunt call her that. It was a common enough nickname in those days, but Irving had never met another girl or woman who was better suited to it. From the first day he had met Augusta, everything about her was exceptional. She was as golden as her name.

She hadn't liked it, however. Or at least, not at first. Eventually she'd let him use it. But he heard that after he left for Chicago, she never let anyone call her that again.

Irving wasn't a fool. He knew that he had hurt her terribly. He knew what she must have thought of him then, when their whole neighborhood was swirling with rumors about him and Lois Diamond. And yet, despite his mother's urgings, he hadn't had the courage to tell Goldie the truth. Even after Lois left him and his boys were fully grown, he never tried to get in touch. Irving let sixty-two years go by, certain he'd never see Goldie again.

But then, when she showed up at Rallentando Springs, it was like the line from the old Humphrey Bogart movie. Of all the retirement communities, she had walked into his. Miraculously, she was single— she'd never married, not in all those years. His heart had leapt when he'd learned that fact, but after the elation came overwhelming guilt.

From the minute he spotted her, he had let himself hope that fate had brought them together again, that they would finally have their second chance. At least until Nathaniel Birnbaum showed up and everything fell apart again. Irving knew he shouldn't have gotten so carried away at the barbecue, but when he saw the two of them on the dance floor, something in him had snapped. After the fiasco with the dessert table, Irving tried his best to explain. But Goldie had looked at him with such disgust that he knew it was too late. *Do you really think I'd fall for the same stunt twice?*

The resentment in her voice, the anger and hurt—none of it was about the strawberry cheesecake clinging to the backside of Birnbaum's trousers. It was a heartache sixty-two years in the making. A heartache that *he* had caused her to suffer. It would be selfish to risk hurting her a second time. So in the hours that followed the incident, Irving made up his mind to let Goldie go. He would not seek her out again.

Only now, she was the one who was seeking *him* out!

Irving knew that Goldie thought he was the same man—the same foolish man she had loved back in Brooklyn. In large part, he supposed that this was true. But there were different facets to him now. He chuckled to himself as he recalled her expression when he showed up at the book club meeting. But even better was the look on her face when he pulled himself out of the pool that first morning.

What do you think you're doing? she'd said. As if it hadn't been obvious. He'd never told her that he'd become a swimmer, too; never explained how, after his marriage fell apart, he tried searching for solace doing what *she* loved. She'd told him once that swimming made her feel brave, so he decided to give it a try. When he was in the water, the world seemed lighter and he could almost forgive himself for all the ways he had failed her.

The next day, despite his presence at the pool—or perhaps *because* of it—Goldie had shown up early again. She got there a little after seven and swam alongside him for half an hour. At first he hadn't known she was there—he felt her movement in the water before he spotted her. When he finished, she followed him out of the pool and dried off on the opposite side of the patio. He thought it wisest not to ask why she had again come so much earlier than usual. He made a point of not lingering long, not getting too close, not saying too much.

In his mind, she was still a matchless being—rare, exotic, wary, exceptional. The last thing he wanted to do was spook her into running away again.

The next morning, he convinced himself that the day before had been a fluke. There was no way she would show up a third time; it was foolish to allow himself to hope. When he felt her presence beside him again, his eager heart hammered against his chest. And when he finally pulled himself out of the pool, he was grateful she could not differentiate his tears from the chlorinated water that clung to his skin.

Vera was yet another complication. He'd tried to apologize to her the day after the barbecue, but she hadn't let him finish his sentence. "It's fine," Vera said, dropping off a casserole. "I don't want to talk about it."

"Please, Vera, let me explain. Let me apologize."

"I'm too old for explanations and apologies."

"Then how can we have a conversation?"

"Enjoy the casserole. I've got to go."

Irving knew he had to end things with Vera. No more letting her make him dinner. No more accepting the meals she delivered. It was time to be brutally honest, no matter how difficult that might be.

In the end, though, he didn't need to say anything. One day Harold told him that Vera and Goldie had been seen arguing in the clubhouse hallway, and the next, Vera showed up at his door, holding another Jell-O mold. This time the Jell-O was electric red—cherry or raspberry, if he had to guess. In any event, it wasn't quite set, which, he realized later, was intentional.

"Hello, Vera," Irving said.

Vera didn't greet him back. She lifted the ring-shaped aluminum pan over his balding head, flipped it over, and watched in silence as the crimson concoction oozed onto his scalp, slid down his face, and fell in clumps around his shoulders. After Vera left, Irving took off his T-shirt, wiped his head with it, and tossed it in the trash. There was no way those stains would come out in the wash.

On the fifth day when Goldie showed up to swim, Irving had to work harder to keep his distance. Was this what their future was going to look like? A bit of nodding, a modicum of eye contact, and little to no conversation? Only in the water did he feel connected to the woman he had once known so well. This was a torture all its own, but one he was willing to suffer through—swimming beside her, the synchronicity of motion, knowing her skin was close enough to touch, even if he wasn't allowed to touch it.

This time, when both of them finished their laps, neither moved toward the stairs right away. Goldie spread her arms on the surface of the water, as if smoothing the wrinkles from a bedsheet. She kept her head down like a child searching for something shiny at the bottom of the pool.

"My birthday is in a week," said Goldie, still gazing into the water.

"How could I forget?" said Irving. "October the third. You'll be eighty years young."

Goldie looked up and nearly smiled. "My niece, Jackie—Bess's daughter—is coming from New York to celebrate. She wants to have a little party for me, take me to dinner with some of my friends."

"That will be nice for you," said Irving, trying his best not to sound too hopeful. It would be a mistake, he thought, to let her know how much he yearned for an invitation.

"Honestly, I don't know many people yet."

"You and Shirley seem friendly," Irving offered. "I'm sure she would love to come."

"Yes, I've asked her," Goldie said, lowering her head again. "I'm going to ask Nathaniel, too. He knew her parents . . . I was hoping he would share some memories of them with her."

Irving peeled off his swim cap—his head was suddenly boiling hot. "Good idea," he said, swallowing down the lump in his throat. Slowly he headed toward the steps to pull himself up and out of the pool.

"Jackie thinks you should come, too," said Goldie, calling out after him.

He turned around on the bottom step and forced himself not to look too excited. "Is that an invitation?"

"Yes," said Goldie, "it is. But you have to promise—you have to swear—that you'll get along with Nathaniel. No arguing, no yelling. No pushing."

Irving held one hand up in the air, like a Boy Scout taking a solemn oath. "I swear," he said. "I'll be good as gold."

"And try to think of some stories for Jackie. That's why she suggested you come along—she'd love to hear more about what life was like in Brooklyn when her parents were young."

Irving couldn't help it—he winked. "Oh, I've got some stories," he said.

TWENTY-SIX

JULY 1924

Irving's mother had been wearing the same winter coat for as long as Irving had been alive. It was a mud-brown, threadbare, wretched thing, and Irving knew that at the end of every winter, his mother's enthusiasm for the coming of spring was more about the putting away of the coat than about the pale green buds forming on the trees, the daffodils blooming in the park, or the extra hours of daylight the new season promised.

It was for this reason that Irving had ventured east out of Brownsville for a few hours. It was a rare afternoon outing for him—one he had made for the specific purpose of purchasing a new coat for his mother's birthday. The day before, in the drugstore, Irving had overheard a pair of women discussing a winter coat sale. Summer—he'd learned from his recent eavesdropping—was apparently the best time to buy winter clothing. The sale today was at Oppenheim Collins, a large department store on the corner of Bridge and Fulton Streets in downtown Brooklyn.

Because he so rarely left his neighborhood, Irving had no familiarity with what shopping was like outside of Brownsville. He was used to the crowded mom-and-pop stores, the local men's shops filled with stale cigar smoke, and the brash saleswomen on every corner trying to lure him inside for "a deal."

Nothing he'd experienced in his gritty neighborhood had prepared him for what it would be like inside the sweet-smelling, grand, and airy stone palace that was known as Oppenheim Collins. The sheer enormity of the store—its marble pillars, sparkling floors, and labyrinth of glass display cases—set Irving's nerves on edge. He felt as out of place inside as if he'd somehow wandered into a church confessional. And yet, although he knew he did not belong, he was determined to stay until he found the gift that he had given up his day to buy. He followed the signs to the second floor, where the women's winter coats were supposedly waiting.

Irving wove his way through a maze of rooms—full of bathrobes, handbags, and velvet shawls. He'd expected to fight off the salesmen, but here, unlike on Pitkin Avenue, none of them pushed Irving to buy. In fact, they acted as if he did not exist, which only frustrated him further. After several attempts to get someone's attention, he was directed to the back of another room, where a single rack of woolen coats was marked with a discreet ON SALE placard.

"That's all?" he asked, his shoulders tensing. The salesman nodded curtly and turned away, leaving Irving alone to pore over the limited selection. Irving's frustration turned to despair when he began checking the price tags on the sleeves. The *sale* prices were three times as much as the *regular* prices in Brownsville! The money he'd been saving would not pay for half of one of the coats on the rack.

He had made up his mind to leave the store when he felt a vigorous tap on his shoulder. A familiar-looking woman in a sleek dove-gray suit was grinning at him when he turned. At her feet were two enormous bags bearing the Oppenheim Collins logo.

"It *is* you," the woman said gleefully. "You certainly got tall, young man." She called out to her husband, who was enjoying the attention of not just one, but two of the salespeople. "Zip, dear! Look, I told you it was him."

Almost a full year had passed since Irving had last seen Mr. and Mrs.

Diamond. If people with *that* kind of money shopped here, he thought, it had certainly been a mistake to come. And to think he had wasted his afternoon off searching for bargains at a place like this!

"You're the kid who helped our Sammy?" Zip Diamond shook Irving's hand with less ferocity than the first time they'd met.

"Yes, sir. Irving Rivkin. Nice to see you both again. How is Sammy doing?"

"Aren't you sweet for asking?" said Mrs. Diamond. "Sammy is doing fine."

"This place is far from the neighborhood," said Zip. "What brings you all the way downtown?"

An embarrassed blush crept into Irving's cheeks. "I heard there was a sale on winter coats. It's my mother's birthday and I wanted to buy one for her."

"Well, aren't you a wonderful son," said Mrs. Diamond. "I'm sure she's going to be delighted."

"I don't think so, ma'am," said Irving. "I had no idea how fancy this store was."

Mr. Diamond flashed Irving an oblivious smile. "There's gotta be *something* you can get her. The clerks here are all top-notch."

"I'm sure they are, but I don't think I'm the kind of customer they're used to."

Mrs. Diamond understood immediately. She snapped her fingers at the waiting salespeople and beckoned them to come closer. She addressed her comments to the taller of the two—a blank-faced man in a neat black suit whose gold-embossed name tag read ALBERT.

"Albert," said Mrs. Diamond loudly, "this young man is my good friend, Irving. Irving wants to buy a coat for his mother, for her birthday. Isn't that right?"

"Yes, it is, but I don't think—"

"Albert, I'm wondering if you can help us. Irving came all this way because he was under the impression that your winter coats were on sale."

"Yes, ma'am," said Albert smoothly. He gestured to the rack a few feet away. "These are our women's wool coats, all discounted from last season."

"But there are so few of them," complained Mrs. Diamond. "Don't you have any more?"

"I'm afraid not, ma'am," Albert apologized. "We did receive a shipment of coats for this winter, but we haven't put any of them on display yet. It's only July, after all."

"But you have the shipment in the store?"

"Yes, ma'am," Albert said. "In the back."

Mrs. Diamond turned to Irving. "What is your mother's favorite color?"

"Oh, I don't know," said Irving nervously. "Besides, I don't think I can afford—"

"What size is she?" Mrs. Diamond asked.

Irving hadn't thought to check his mother's size. Besides, the coat she had was so old, he doubted the label was still attached. "She's about your size, Mrs. Diamond, ma'am. A few inches shorter, I think."

Mrs. Diamond patted him on the shoulder. "You leave this to me," she said. She looped her arm through Albert's elbow. "Albert is going to show me a few of the new coats and I'll bring back the one I think your mother will like best."

Before Irving or Albert had a chance to protest, Mrs. Diamond led the salesman away, leaving Irving alone with Mr. Diamond and a second, shorter salesman, who pointed them to a cluster of chairs and a matching sofa on which to wait. Irving stood until Mr. Diamond had made himself comfortable.

"Brooklyn plays Cincinnati tonight," said Irving, searching for a topic of conversation. "Are you a Brooklyn fan, Mr. Diamond?"

Zip pulled a pack of cigarettes from his pocket and lit one. "Not me," he said. "I'm for the Giants. Now *that's* a team."

"You think they'll win the pennant again?"

"That's the beauty of baseball, kid. You can never tell who's going to win." As Zip flashed an enigmatic smile, Irving suddenly remembered the World Series rumors. Of all the topics he could have chosen, why had he stupidly brought up baseball? A trickle of sweat dripped down Irving's neck. He gritted his teeth and stopped talking.

"How's school going?" Zip asked next. "You keeping that promise to your mother?"

"Yes, sir. I'm starting my senior year this fall. I'll be graduating next June."

"Look what we found!" Mrs. Diamond called out, returning from wherever the new coats were kept. In her hands, she held up a black wool coat trimmed with fur on the cuffs and collar. She took a few steps closer to Irving and dangled the coat in front of him. "Isn't it perfect? It's wool velour with a raccoon collar and a silk crepe lining. I thought black was best—it's the most versatile." Albert, the salesman, stood a few feet behind her, frowning and fidgeting with his bow tie.

"It's a real nice coat," Irving told them, "but I can't afford—"

"That's the best part!" Mrs. Diamond trilled. "As it turns out, the store is offering a special promotion. Isn't that right, Albert?"

Albert gritted his teeth and nodded. "Buy one, get one free," he murmured. Behind him, another salesman appeared, holding a long black sable coat.

"I'm getting *that* one," Mrs. Diamond said cheerfully, pointing to the shimmering fur. She continued before her husband could object: "Thank goodness we ran into Irving today! Otherwise, I would have waited until October to look for the new sable you promised me, and by then they would have been all picked over. This way, I got my first choice. In any event, since I'm buying the sable, that means the second coat is *free*."

Irving tried to protest, but Zip Diamond shook his head. For the first time since they'd sat down together, Irving noticed the dark circles blooming beneath the man's eyes. "Do me a favor, don't argue with her. It took me years, but I finally caught on. As a matter of fact, that's how I got my nickname. When Mitzi says how something is supposed to go, I just nod and zip my lip."

Mrs. Diamond pretended to laugh, but her eyes were as hard as the shiny black buttons sewn to the front of the "free" wool coat. "Don't fill the boy's head with stories, Zip," she snapped. "Albert, I'd like you to wrap Irving's coat and box it up for him to take home."

"Certainly, madam," Albert said.

The trickle of sweat on the back of Irving's neck suddenly turned cold. What was he doing on this couch, in this store, with these people? As Zip exhaled a puff of smoke, Irving found it difficult to breathe. In the wake of Mrs. Diamond's laughter, a foreboding silence filled the air. He felt her staring at him now, quietly appraising him—but for what future purpose, he did not know.

Irving turned back to Mr. Diamond, who suddenly looked exhausted. "You're lucky my wife likes you, kid," Zip said. "If you know what's good for you, you'll keep it that way."

TWENTY-SEVEN

SEPTEMBER 1987

Once Augusta had asked Irving to her birthday dinner, Nathaniel was the only person left to invite. She still felt uncomfortable about putting them in a room together, but Irving had promised to be on his best behavior, and Augusta wanted to believe him.

She ran into Nathaniel after mah-jongg the next day, in the clubhouse hallway, outside of the library. It was silly, she knew, to compare him to Irving, but sometimes the contrast was too pronounced to ignore. While Irving was short and teapot-stout, Nathaniel stood tall, straight, and slim. He wore his clothes like a Brooks Brothers model—crisp polo shirts with pleated khaki shorts or neatly ironed trousers with spotless button-downs. No matter what time of day she encountered him, Nathaniel's thick head of wavy hair was painstakingly coiffed. He even brought a comb to the pool to tame his hair after swimming.

Irving, on the other hand, preferred a rotation of well-worn T-shirts from his grandchildren's schools and extracurricular activities. As far as Augusta could tell, his favorites were from the New Trier Drama Club and the Boston University Baseball Team. His barely there hair had a mind of its own, and he paid it very little attention. Irving's bathing suits were too loud, his sandals were scuffed, and she did not think he owned a belt.

"Good morning, Augusta," Nathaniel said, smiling. "I haven't seen you in the pool the past few days. Don't tell me you've been slacking off?"

"Absolutely not," she said. "I've just been getting my laps in early. Without a job to report to, I've been at loose ends in the mornings. I don't like feeling so unproductive."

Nathaniel smiled. "I understand. When I left my cardiology practice, it was hard for me to adjust. I missed seeing patients. I missed puzzling their treatment out in my head."

"Absolutely." Augusta sighed. "I'm always happier when my mind is active. To be honest, I was terrified of retiring. I loved my work. I loved being the first to know about every new treatment and medication. It's terrible being so out of the loop."

"I know exactly how you feel! A few years ago, I missed out on the first tissue-type plasminogen activators. Let me tell you, that was a blow."

Augusta nodded sympathetically before remembering the dinner. "I almost forgot. I'd like to invite you to a little birthday dinner my niece is having for me next week. She's coming down from New York and she wanted to meet some of my new friends." She lowered her voice. "I'm turning eighty."

"Wonderful!" Nathaniel said.

"I invited Shirley, too."

"Nothing could keep me away," he said, his cheeks glowing with pleasure.

"And Irving Rivkin as well."

The pink in Nathaniel's cheeks deepened to scarlet.

"I hope that isn't a problem?"

"No, no. Of course not. I'm more than happy to break bread with Irving."

"Jackie, my niece, is excited to meet both of you. Especially because you both knew her parents. I think she's hoping for a little trip down memory lane."

"That will be nice." Nathaniel nodded. "Evie would have turned eighty this past August. She always loved having a summer birthday. We celebrated in Maine every year, with lobsters and whoopie pies for dessert." He checked the gold watch on his wrist. "So sorry, Augusta, but I've got to run. I have an afternoon tee time today and I don't want to be late."

It was only after Nathaniel was out of earshot that Irving emerged from the library doorway.

"I didn't realize you were in there," said Augusta. "I was just telling Nathaniel about the dinner."

Irving scowled. "I could hear you both, as clear as day." He began mimicking Nathaniel, making his voice low and ridiculous. "I missed the first tissue-type plasminogen activators. Look at what a brilliant cardiologist I am!"

"Irving, please. You promised to get along with him. Stop acting like a five-year-old."

"Better a five-year-old than a pompous ass."

"Nathaniel wasn't being pompous. He was being sincere. That medication he mentioned was a big development in his field."

"Well, some of us didn't have a *field*! Some of us didn't have fathers who were doctors and paid for us to go to medical school. Some of us had crummy jobs, and when it was time to retire, we were happy it was over."

Augusta was confused by the hurt in his voice. She'd always assumed that Irving's working years in Chicago had been glamorous and exciting. He'd moved there on a whim with a woman he loved—the daughter of a rich and powerful man. Regardless of what happened with his marriage, the idea that he hadn't been happy professionally had never once occurred to her.

"For what it's worth," she said, "my father always admired you. He used to say you were his favorite employee, the most responsible young man he knew. He was hoping you would manage the pharmacy one day."

Irving's eyes softened. "Your father was always good to me."

Augusta thought about saying more, but she was hesitant to steer the conversation into even more personal territory. She worried that if Irving revealed too much, he might expect her to do the same. Still, something compelled her to keep talking, to learn more about the man she'd once known so well.

"I never asked what you did in Chicago," she said. "Did you work for your father-in-law?"

"In a way," he said, stiffening. "I didn't do anything illegal, if that's what you're wondering."

"I wasn't implying that at all. But it's hard to believe that your work was boring. You were Zip Diamond's son-in-law. You must have had your pick of jobs."

"Not exactly. Once we got to Chicago, Zip began slowing down quite a bit. Nobody knew, but he hadn't been well, and he'd started handing off a lot of the decisions to his wife, Mitzi. By the time the twins were born, my mother-in-law was the one really in charge. She delegated all the work—she actually handpicked me for my job."

"Well, whatever job it was, it had to be better than delivering aspirin."

"Trust me," Irving said, frowning, "it wasn't."

TWENTY-EIGHT

AUGUST 1924

After Bess and George were engaged, Augusta saw much less of her sister. If Bess wasn't working at the pharmacy, she was spending time with her fiancé or planning their upcoming wedding with the help of George's mother. It would have been different, Augusta knew, if their own mother were still alive or if their father was remotely interested in planning his older daughter's nuptials. But Solomon Stern could not seem to muster the joyous energy that was required. It was not that he disapproved of the groom or of the upcoming wedding. It was simply that, for the melancholy druggist, happiness was something reserved for the past.

In Bess's absence, Augusta spent more time with her friend Evie Sussman. If Augusta was being 100 percent honest, she might confess to being bored around Evie, but she mostly found the girl's even temper and blithe personality to be soothing. Evie was fair-haired and pale, with a melodic voice and an expensive wardrobe of demurely cut pastel dresses. She was the friend that mothers wanted for their children, the type of girl who never made demands or got into trouble of any kind.

It was because there was nothing at all objectionable about Evie that the girl was so universally liked. And so when Evie's mother sent the invitations for her daughter's seventeenth birthday party, everyone who was asked said yes, including Lois Diamond.

Until two days before the party, neither Augusta nor Evie nor anyone else was aware that Lois would be in attendance. Though all three girls went to Thomas Jefferson High School, Augusta and Evie ran in very different circles from the eldest daughter of the racketeer. They were responsible, bookish girls, both spending the bulk of their summer days working in their fathers' stores—Augusta at Stern's Pharmacy and Evie at Sussman's Corner Bakery, which was only a few blocks away. Lois, on the other hand, spent the summer keeping company with a mostly older, mostly male crowd. Augusta and Evie spotted her sometimes, smoking cigarettes on the sidewalks of Brownsville, surrounded by a gaggle of gape-mouthed boys. Next to Evie's muted exterior, Lois's ruby lipstick and jet-black hair stood out like a fly in a glass of milk.

Evie's party was scheduled for noon on a Sunday, and would include sandwiches, board games, and a frosted cake made with painstaking care by Evie's baker father. It was because of the cake, as a matter of fact, that Lois was invited to join the festivities. On the Friday before the party, Mitzi Diamond made her weekly trip to Sussman's to purchase two challahs and a dozen of Zip's favorite cookies. When Mitzi entered, Mr. Sussman was arguing with his wife about whether their daughter's birthday cake should be decorated with pink or yellow roses.

Mitzi Diamond was familiar with Evie Sussman and her saccharine reputation. The girl was everything her own daughter was not, and though she would never go so far as to say that she wished Lois could be more like Evie, she did think that her daughter might benefit from such a safe and steadying friendship. She did not like the rumors she'd been hearing about Lois and the reckless crowd she was part of. Mrs. Diamond was neither a prude nor a fool—she knew what kind of trouble her daughter could get into and she was hoping to steer her in a different direction.

"Is it Evie's birthday?" Mrs. Diamond asked, in a voice so sweet that Mrs. Sussman barely recognized it.

"Mrs. Diamond?" Mrs. Sussman blinked to confirm the identity of the speaker. "We have your challahs and cookies ready. Let me get them from the back."

While Mrs. Sussman retrieved the order, Mrs. Diamond questioned the baker. "Evie is the same age as my Lois, you know."

"Is that right?" Mr. Sussman said. "Yes, Evie's birthday is on Sunday. Mrs. Sussman has invited some girls over to celebrate. Lunch, board games, that sort of thing."

"How lovely," Mrs. Diamond cooed. "I'm sure my daughter would love to come. Lois can't get enough of board games."

Mr. Sussman stared blankly at his customer, uncertain of how to respond. When his wife returned with the challahs and cookies, Mrs. Diamond took it upon herself to explain the situation. "Mrs. Sussman," she said smoothly, "I was just telling your husband how grateful I would be if you included my daughter in the festivities you've planned for Evie's birthday."

Mrs. Sussman resumed her blinking. "Lois wants to come to Evie's party?"

"Yes, she'd love to attend." Mrs. Diamond pretended not to notice Mrs. Sussman's confusion. Given her husband's reputation, she was certain the Sussmans would not refuse her. "What time on Sunday should she arrive?"

"The others are coming at twelve o'clock . . ."

"Perfect! Thank you so much, Mr. and Mrs. Sussman." Mrs. Diamond took a step closer to the counter. "I'll be sure to tell my husband about your kindness. I know how much he will appreciate this. Zip *never* forgets a favor." She tucked the box of cookies under her arm. "I never forget one, either."

Lois was as surprised to be at the party as everyone else was to see her there. Mrs. Sussman—mindful of the danger that might ensue should Lois report being snubbed—asked the girls to introduce themselves so that Lois would feel welcome. At first the atmosphere was awkward, but after sandwiches and lemonade, the other girls grew less self-conscious. When Mrs. Sussman left the room, the conversation began in earnest. All the girls, except for Evie and Augusta, began questioning Lois.

"Are you carrying a torch for David Bloom?"

Lois laughed. "Absolutely not."

"But I saw you with him the other day. He couldn't take his eyes off you."

Lois shrugged. "That's not *my* fault. Anyhow, I prefer older men."

As the gossip continued, Augusta watched Evie to make sure that her friend did not feel slighted. But Evie didn't seem to care how much attention Lois received. She was staring at the grandfather clock that stood in the corner of her living room.

"What's going on?" Augusta whispered. "Are you expecting someone else?"

Evie nodded. "Do you remember Nathaniel Birnbaum? Dr. Birnbaum's son?"

"Of course," said Augusta. "Our fathers are friends. He's been away at college, hasn't he?"

"Yes, but he's home now, for the rest of the summer. He came into the bakery a few days ago. We got to talking, and he said he'd stop by this afternoon to wish me a happy birthday. He's so polite, Augusta, and so handsome. He's going to be a doctor, just like his father."

"Evie Sussman! I can't believe what I'm hearing! I've never heard you talk this way about anyone!"

Evie giggled. "I know," she said. "But I feel so ... *happy* when I'm around him."

Augusta couldn't remember a time when Evie was ever *un*happy, but she knew it would be rude to say so.

Sure enough, twenty minutes later, there was a knock on the Sussmans' door. Nathaniel entered, wearing a smart summer suit and holding an enormous bouquet of flowers. The other girls murmured and giggled shyly—all except for Lois Diamond, who stood from her seat, marched over to Nathaniel, and flashed him a confident, ruby-lipped smile. "I'm Lois Diamond," she said. "Who are you?"

Though Evie was dismayed at first, Augusta thought Nathaniel did a perfect job of handling the situation. After shaking Lois's hand politely, Nathaniel turned his full attention to Evie. Before offering her the bouquet, he lifted her hand to his lips. "Happy birthday, Evie," he said, so resolutely that even Lois Diamond had no choice but to back away.

While Nathaniel chatted with Evie's parents, the other girls whispered their approval. "You and Evie are so lucky," Dottie Schwartz told Augusta. "I'll probably never have a beau."

Lois looked at Augusta with renewed interest. "Who are *you* dating, Miss Smarty-Pants?"

"No one," said Augusta. "Dottie is just teasing."

"I am not," Dottie insisted. "Every time I turn around, I see you with Irving Rivkin."

"Irving and I are just friends. He's the delivery boy at my father's pharmacy."

Lois nodded dramatically. "He's probably just being nice to you because he works for your father. Trust me, I know *all* about that."

Augusta bristled at the suggestion that Irving wasn't a real friend. She was sick to death of Lois Diamond. Sick of her hair, sick of her makeup, and sick of her know-it-all attitude. Suddenly she couldn't help herself. Augusta wasn't unflappable like Evie. She couldn't pretend to be sweet and calm. "No one asked for your opinion," she snapped. "You don't know the first thing about Irving!"

Lois Diamond clearly didn't appreciate being put in her place. She flashed Augusta a menacing glance. "I might not know him *yet*," Lois said. "But I can always get an introduction. If I decide that he's worth meeting, I'll be sure to let you know."

TWENTY-NINE

SEPTEMBER 1987

What are you wearing to your party?" asked Shirley. She and Augusta were sharing a turkey club with an extra side of pickles from the snack bar. The weather had cooled overnight and both women wore sweatshirts over their swimsuits. Augusta let Shirley have the last potato chip.

"It isn't a party," Augusta told her. "We're going out to dinner, that's all."

"Dinner to *celebrate* your eightieth birthday. Sounds a lot like a party to me."

"What does it matter what I wear? Who's going to be looking at me?"

Shirley almost choked on her chip. "Who's going to be—Jesus, Augusta, you invited two men who have literally been *fighting* over you for weeks! I'd say both of them are going to be looking. Besides, at our age, we have to dress for *ourselves*."

"I'll probably wear my black pants," said Augusta.

Shirley pursed her lips together as if that were the saddest thing she'd ever heard. "Absolutely not," she said.

"But why? They're comfortable. And black is chic!"

"Tell the truth—are they your funeral pants? How many funerals have you worn them to?"

Augusta frowned. "Why does that matter?"

"It matters because it's your birthday party! You should be wearing something to celebrate life!"

"Like what?"

"With those legs? How about a dress?"

"I don't have any dresses."

"Then it looks like the two of us are going shopping."

It wasn't strictly true that Augusta had no dresses. Of course she had a few hanging in her closet: the one she'd worn to a cousin's wedding, the one Jackie helped her choose for her daughter's bat mitzvah, a beaded shift that her niece had given her for a New Year's Eve party a few years earlier. But she didn't want to wear any of those dresses again. None of them felt like the right thing to wear on her eightieth birthday.

The next day, Augusta let Shirley drag her to department stores and boutiques all over Boca Raton. She hid her irritation and did her best to stay positive while Shirley held her hostage in various dressing rooms. But everything her friend picked out was too short, too tight, or too low-cut.

"You're no fun, you know that?" Shirley lamented, after passing half a dozen rejected dresses back to yet another scowling saleswoman. "I don't see what the problem is—you look great in everything!"

They were at the fifth store of the day when the latest saleswoman tapped on the dressing room door. "How about this?" she asked politely, holding up a soft pink sleeveless sheath with a flowy deconstructed jacket. It was long and loose and modest enough, without a single bead or sequin. Shirley sucked in a breath. "It's perfect!" she gasped.

Augusta felt her pulse begin to race. "No pink," she said briskly. "I never wear pink." She did not say that the last time she'd worn pink, it had been the worst night of her life. She did not say that the thought of wearing it now made her feel as if she couldn't breathe. "Actually, Shirley, I'm getting tired. I think I'm done looking for today."

"Don't you want to try this one first? Pink would look beautiful on you. Or maybe it comes in another color?"

Augusta leaned back against the wall and placed one hand over her chest.

"Augusta, are you feeling all right? You look like you're about to faint."

"I'm fine . . . a little dizzy, that's all."

The saleswoman frowned and left the dressing room. "I'll get you a glass of water," she called out from the other side of the door.

But Augusta didn't stay long enough to drink the water. Once she'd gotten her shoes back on, she fled from the dressing room to the parking lot, where Shirley had to race to keep up with her.

In the car, Shirley searched for answers as she drove them back to Rallentando Springs. "Maybe your blood sugar got low," she said. "That happens to me sometimes when I don't eat enough. Or maybe it was those dressing room lights. Sometimes overhead lighting gives me a migraine."

"Maybe," said Augusta. "Next time I'll bring a granola bar. And a pair of sunglasses. I'm feeling much better now, actually. Thank you for taking me today."

"Of course," Shirley said. "That's what friends do."

They rode in silence for a few miles before Shirley spoke again. "Augusta, if I ask you something, will you promise you won't be upset with me?"

"I could never be upset with you."

"You know I was married once, and that my husband died too young. But you . . . you've got so much going for you. You're smart and beautiful. How is it that you never married?"

Augusta stared out the car window. She'd heard this question so many times, from so many people over the course of her life. When she was younger, the question made her angry. Sometimes it had driven her to despair. But now, at almost eighty years old, she had made her peace with it. "Do you really want to know?" she asked.

Shirley nodded. "I do."

Augusta leaned back in her seat. "I'll begin at the beginning then. When my mother died, I was fourteen years old."

"Oh, Augusta, I'm so sorry."

"My father never got over her death. He became more and more distant with me and my sister. At home, he hid away in his bedroom or behind the pages of his newspaper. The drugstore was the only place that he still seemed to be himself—for the most part, at least. So he threw himself into his work. He stayed at the store until all hours, day after day, year after year. He never took a vacation—he couldn't bear to be away from the pharmacy.

"The thing was, my mother didn't die in a car crash or in an accident or anything like that. She died of diabetes less than a year before insulin became available. Imagine what that did to my father—he had a room full of medicines that couldn't help my mother; a room full of medicines that were essentially useless to save the one person he loved the most in this world."

"I never would have thought of it that way—how awful."

"I was as bitter as he was at first. But once I got over the unfairness of it all, it made me realize how much I wanted to be a pharmacist. I wanted to learn about all those medicines. I wanted to help all our customers. You remember what it was like back then—pharmacists were almost like doctors. I wanted that kind of responsibility. I didn't know any women pharmacists, but I knew that I could do the job. Fordham's pharmacy college had been open for a decade by then, and I knew they were accepting women."

"Isn't that a Catholic school?" Shirley asked.

Augusta nodded. "Yes, but the pharmacy students were mostly Jewish, so they were exempt from the theology classes. When my mother died, that became my goal—to go to that school and follow in my father's footsteps. That was all I wanted to do.

"But six months later, my aunt Esther—my grandmother's sister—came to stay with us. Esther was sort of a . . . homeopath, I suppose we'd call her today. She and my father didn't get along, but she was a wonderful teacher. She made me believe in another way of healing, and, for a while, I thought I might share her talent."

"You've never mentioned Esther before," said Shirley.

Augusta thought back to those terrible months immediately after Esther had died: the silent meals in their barren kitchen where her great-aunt had once reigned over the stove; the empty bed beside her own where Esther had slept and feigned exhaustion to avoid Augusta's most prying questions; the hollow air in the darkened living room that would never bear the scent of chicken soup again.

"I don't like to talk about her," Augusta said quickly. "Anyway, Esther passed away not long after I started at Fordham. By that point, Irving had left for Chicago with his new fiancée and her family, and I was completely distraught. I'd suffered too many losses all at once. So I did exactly what my father had done: I threw myself into my work. My father encouraged it—probably because it was the only coping mechanism he knew."

Shirley's face was quizzical. "You didn't date *anyone* after Irving left? Not for all those years?"

"Oh, I dated, but it never worked out. Men didn't appreciate career women back then—they didn't like that I was so devoted to the pharmacy, and to working with my father. They wanted me to promise that I'd give up my job once I got married and gave them children. But why would I ever want to give up my work? Work was the one thing I could depend on!"

Shirley smiled. "Which explains why you never wanted to retire."

"I came close to quitting a few times. Once, during my second year of college. I worked at my father's store for school credit at least two days a week back then. A customer I'd known since I was a child told my father he didn't want me making up his pills because I was a woman."

Shirley's mouth fell open, but she kept her eyes on the road. "What did your father say to him?"

"My father defended me. He told the customer that if he didn't like it, he could get his pills someplace else."

"Wow."

Augusta's eyes filled with tears at the memory. "It was the nicest thing he ever did for me. After that day, something mended between us. We'd been so disconnected from each other for so long, but after that, we were finally a family again." Augusta wiped a tear from her cheek. "We worked side by side for ten wonderful years until he had a heart attack. After that, I ran the store on my own."

They had finally reached the entrance to Rallentando Springs. As they slowed down to drive through the mechanized gate, past the rows of flowering bushes and trees, Shirley took one hand off the wheel to pat her friend on the shoulder. The guard at the gate recognized them and waved to both women as they drove past. In a few minutes they would be at Augusta's apartment, but Shirley wasn't ready to end the conversation.

"Did marriage ever come up again?"

Augusta paused. "There were a few men I knew who probably would have asked—but I never felt like any of them truly saw me. Mostly, they just wanted to take over my store."

"What convinced you to finally sell?"

"The neighborhood kept getting worse. In the thirties and forties, it was all the gangsters—Brownsville had *a lot* of those. By the late fifties, though, everything changed. All the people I knew were gone. There were so many new housing projects being built, but not enough jobs for all the newcomers. That's when the store started getting robbed. The third time it happened, in 1962, Bess and George sat me down and told me it was time to sell."

"It must have been difficult to let it go."

"It was, but I knew that it was time. I was fifty-five years old by then. Bess had moved to the Upper West Side, so I followed her there and got an apartment nearby."

"Did you think about retiring then?"

"Not even a little bit. Trouble was, no one wanted to hire me. Outside of Brooklyn, no one knew Stern's. The fact that I had run my own store for decades meant absolutely nothing to the managers at big chains. All they saw was a middle-aged woman who they assumed was past her prime. And the family-owned stores didn't want to hire me, either—they were planning for their sons and sons-in-law to take over. So I started working at a hospital—it was the only job I could get. At first I was stuck filling prescriptions, but eventually I was given a more clinical role—interfacing with the nurses, advising on adverse drug reactions. It wasn't like having my own store, but it was better than nothing. I managed to keep that position for a while, but when I turned sixty, they wanted me to retire. That was when Jackie had the idea of doctoring my paperwork before my next job."

"To make you seem younger?"

"Exactly."

"But what happened when you reached sixty the second time? And the third?"

"I moved hospitals and Jackie changed the paperwork again. Eventually, I found a hospital that let me stay until I turned seventy. Of course, I was actually almost eighty."

Shirley looked shocked. "Augusta! You're a regular Bonnie and Clyde!"

Augusta smiled. "Without the bank robbing or the killing. Mine is a purely victimless crime."

"So that's the story, then? That's why you never married?"

"That's the story," Augusta said. "But I accomplished what I set out to do. I followed in my father's footsteps."

By now, they had reached Augusta's apartment. Shirley pulled her car into the driveway, put it in park, and turned to her friend. "Not exactly," she said gently.

"What do you mean? I ran my father's store. I carried on the Stern legacy." Augusta crossed her arms over her chest. "I did everything my father did and more."

"Except that he had your mother," said Shirley gently. "It might not have lasted forever. It might not have been perfect. But your father was able to experience that joy—those special years with the woman he loved." Shirley reached for Augusta's hand. "Now that your working days are behind you, don't you think you deserve the same?"

THIRTY

JANUARY 1925

Three years after her arrival in Brownsville, Esther was still pursuing her vocation. The unpleasantness with Talia Friedman did not slow her down in the slightest—in fact, it only solidified her reputation.

Meanwhile, after countless squabbles with her nephew, she had settled on an area of practice that interfered as little as possible with his trade. Of course there were sometimes exceptions, but Esther's bread and butter became advising her neighbors on a myriad of "women's problems": fertility, pregnancy, the illnesses of young children, and treatments for women as they drifted slowly toward the perilous Charybdis known as the "change of life."

It was for this last reason that Zip Diamond's wife appeared one day at Esther's door.

As it happened, the Diamonds lived on the same street as one of Esther's most loyal customers—Mrs. Harriet Dornbush. It was one of the cleaner and quieter streets in the neighborhood, and even more so since Zip

Diamond had moved there. No one would dare to cause a disturbance or drop a single piece of litter on the sidewalk where the notorious racketeer made his home. The trees stood taller on Zip Diamond's block, and the flowers knew better than to droop in the heat. Even in the winter, the snow wouldn't dream of turning to slush on his stoop.

Mrs. Dornbush paid little attention to the rumors and knew very little about the family. She had greeted Mrs. Diamond only in passing and had never spoken with her before. She was a bit surprised, therefore, when Mrs. Diamond stopped her one morning to admire her son as he slept in his stroller. "What a beautiful baby," Mrs. Diamond sighed, rubbing her thumb against Jeremiah's cheek. The next thing Harriet knew, Mrs. Diamond was in tears.

As the elegant lady cried into the collar of her lavish sable coat, she reminded Harriet of herself, back when the sight of the drugstore kittens had brought about a similar rush of emotions. Harriet felt a surge of pity for this woman she did not even know.

"I miss this age," Mrs. Diamond sniffed. "My son and daughter are getting so big. They hardly need me anymore."

"I've seen you walking with them," Mrs. Dornbush admitted. "They both seem like lovely children."

"That's just it—they won't be children for much longer." Mrs. Diamond took a handkerchief from her purse and dabbed at the corners of her eyes.

Harriet couldn't say exactly what came over her, but something about Mrs. Diamond's tears made her feel as if she knew her. "Have you ever thought about having more?" As soon as she asked the question, however, she felt sure that she had gone too far. "Oh goodness," she said. "I'm so sorry. I don't even know you . . . I shouldn't have asked . . ."

"Don't apologize. I wish I could. I'm much too old for all that now. Too old, too withered, too muddled, too weak . . ." Mrs. Diamond began to cry again.

"Oh dear," Harriet Dornbush whispered, patting the stranger on the shoulder. "Is there anything I can do?"

"No, no. Oh, how embarrassing this is. For the past few months, I've been an absolute mess. It's ... well ... it's what happens to us all at my age, I'm afraid. But I've honestly never felt worse. My heart keeps racing, and I can't sleep at night. I wake up drowned in perspiration. I have cramps and headaches and terrible pains. I've been to all kinds of doctors, but they don't seem to have any real answers."

"Doctors!" Harriet scoffed. "I listened to *doctors* for seven years, but none of them did anything to help me have Jeremiah."

Mrs. Diamond parted her lips in surprise. "I don't understand. If the doctors didn't help you, then who did?"

Harriet Dornbush lowered her gaze and let it rest on her precious son, the child she thought she would never have. "The most brilliant woman I've ever met. I'd be happy to give you her name ..."

The next morning, after Augusta's father left for the pharmacy, there was a sharp knock at their door. Augusta put down her piece of toast. "Were you expecting anyone?" she asked. But Esther shook her head and took another sip of tea.

The woman waiting in the hallway didn't look like one of Esther's typical customers. With her shining fur coat and styled hair, she was far more glamorous than the Brownsville housewives who usually visited to ask for advice. Augusta guessed she was in her late forties—older than Augusta's mother would have been, and yet not so very far off. Her beauty was like the ocean in winter—cold and splendid in its austerity.

"Can I help you?" Augusta asked politely.

"Thank you, yes. I'm looking for Esther. Harriet Dornbush recommended her. I am Mrs. Mitzi Diamond."

From inside the kitchen, Esther was listening. "Augusta, show our visitor in."

Augusta led Mrs. Diamond to the back of the apartment, where Esther was waiting by the sink. She'd tidied up their breakfast dishes and put a clean apron on over her clothes. As always, her dress was black and shapeless, her hair tucked away under a scarf, her face completely unadorned. She looked as different from Mitzi Diamond as another woman could.

Esther gestured for Mrs. Diamond to remove her coat and take a seat. Without her fur, Mrs. Diamond was less intimidating. It was then that Augusta saw the dark circles that clung to the skin beneath her eyes. Her dress may have been expensive silk, but the body beneath was stooped over slightly, as if she were holding some kind of pain.

"Would you like tea?" Augusta offered, but Mrs. Diamond declined.

"How can I help you?" Esther asked, though Augusta was certain that her aunt already had some idea. She never stopped being surprised by Esther's diagnostic abilities.

"Harriet Dornbush is my neighbor," said Mrs. Diamond. "She told me that you were able to help her when none of her doctors could. She made it sound like you worked a miracle."

Esther chuckled and smoothed her apron. "Do I look like a woman who can work miracles? No, what I do is very simple: I look, I listen, and I try to understand what it is that my customers need. Sometimes I make them a nice bowl of soup. Then I help them if I can."

Mrs. Diamond tilted her head. "Do you think you can help me?"

"That depends," said Esther. "Why don't you tell me what is wrong?"

After a moment of hesitation, Mrs. Diamond's story poured from her lips: the listlessness, the feverish episodes, the backaches, the cramps, the palpitations. Like almost every other woman her age, she'd been taking Lydia E. Pinkham's Vegetable Compound for assorted female complaints, but the medicine had not helped to alleviate her symptoms. Augusta knew that her father had labeled Mrs. Pinkham a "quack" and that he refused to sell her tonic in his store.

Augusta saw the pity in Esther's eyes. The two women may have been from different worlds, but there was an unmistakable bond between them—the type of bond that sometimes surfaces between those who have shared the same kind of suffering.

Esther stretched out a single calloused hand and placed it on top of Mrs. Diamond's smooth one. "I will help you," she said. "Come back tomorrow."

⚘

That night, Augusta followed Esther to the kitchen, with the apothecary case in hand, but this time, Esther motioned for her niece to gather the ingredients herself. Augusta had seen her aunt make powders for women like Mrs. Diamond before. With her gift for following formulas, she already knew the recipe by heart. Having memorized the contents of Esther's case, Augusta was able to pull and pluck all the ingredients with relative ease.

The fernlike leaves were mimosa, the dried yellow flowers were St. John's wort, and the sand-colored root was ginseng. Augusta found black cohosh and sage, sesame seeds, and the dried pink petals that she recognized as red clover.

Outside the kitchen window, the Brownsville sky was bright with January stars. Patches of light from the flickering streetlamps fell across the back of Esther's robe, turning the fabric from sapphire to lapis until it finally resolved in a rich indigo. As was her custom during such work, Esther let her hair hang loose over her shoulders. The strands were silver and pearl, and every shade in between. They heightened the splendor of her weathered face like thunder exaggerates a summer storm.

Esther handed the mortar and pestle carefully to Augusta. "You should say the words now," Esther told her.

"Can I say them in English?" Augusta asked. "The Yiddish never sounds right when I say it."

"As long as you feel the words in your heart, the language you say them in should not matter."

"Why didn't you tell me that before?"

Esther shrugged. "You never asked."

Augusta took a steadying breath, shut her eyes, and tried to focus.

To ease the pain of those who suffer
To repair the bodies of those who are ill
To restore the minds of those in need

Although Augusta recited the words correctly, something in the room felt wrong. The candles flickered in their holders; the electric charge in the air had weakened.

"Say them again," Esther told her.

To ease the pain of those who suffer
To repair the bodies of those who are ill
To restore the minds of those in need

The starlight remained on the outside of the windows. The room felt sterile and cold.

"Again," Esther encouraged. She thumped the left side of her chest with her fist. "You must *feel* the words, Goldie, in here."

This time Esther joined in her chant, transforming the words into a kind of song. Over and over, the two of them sang, until the words became a wish. The air filled suddenly with the scent of citrus—sour and sweet like lemons and honey. The candle flames swelled and swayed and brightened; starlight pushed its way into the room.

To ease the pain of those who suffer
To repair the bodies of those who are ill
To restore the minds of those in need

After the energy in the room settled, Esther flashed Augusta an enigmatic smile. She took the mortar from her niece's hands, emptied the powder onto another muslin square, tied the bit of fabric with string, and tucked it into the pocket of her robe. Her hazel eyes sparkled in the candlelight. "You did well," she said.

But Augusta was not convinced. "Why did it take so long to work? Did I say the words wrong?"

Esther pressed one hand against her niece's cheek. When she spoke, her voice was low and warm. "You said them perfectly," she said. "But the words are not like the formulas in your books or the bottles on your father's shelves. You cannot memorize and repeat them. You must feel them in your bones."

"But I want to be able to do this on my own. I can't have you helping me all the time!" Augusta's voice betrayed her frustration.

Esther tried to reassure her. "I believe you are gifted," she said. "That is why I agreed to teach you. But you are young, and you must learn patience. I do not doubt that you will work hard, but you are still searching for the easiest answers. You still think illness can be cured with a pill or a powder and a few old words. You still think that the outcome is something you can control."

"But isn't that true? You *do* control it! I've seen what you do—things the doctors couldn't, things no one can explain. You saved Irving! You gave a barren woman a child! You made Bess know she wanted to marry George!" Augusta's eyes grew wide and wild. "Maybe . . . maybe if you had treated my mother, you would have been able to save her, too!" She sank down on one of the kitchen chairs and buried her face in her hands.

Esther took a step closer to her niece and placed a hand on Augusta's shoulder. "Sometimes," she whispered, "I am able to help. But other times, I cannot. There were many people back in my village for whom I could offer no cure. There were times when my powders and my elixirs did more harm than good. You and I have not known each other long. You have seen only my most fortunate outcomes. But do not mistake a few successes for an unblemished past."

Augusta's tears fell freely now. "But *could* you have healed my mother, Aunt Esther? Please, tell me the truth."

Esther shook her head. "No," she said sadly. "I tell you this honestly. Her illness was nothing I could have cured. There was a man in my village who died of the same sickness. A child died, too, and I could not help her. The world we inhabit is not always kind."

"But you said . . . you *told* me that words could heal!"

"Sometimes yes, sometimes no. Sometimes, no matter the powders or words, a person's time on this earth must end. There is no magic any of us have that can make someone live forever."

"Then what is the point? Why do this at all?"

"Because there is still good that we can do. Because sometimes our remedies can cure. Because we can bear witness to a woman who suffers when her doctors refuse to see her pain. Because even when we cannot heal, a bowl of chicken soup can offer comfort."

Augusta wiped the tears from her eyes. She was still too young to understand all the subtleties of her great-aunt's message, but she could comprehend enough to know what she still wanted for her future. "I want to learn from you," she told Esther. "I want to learn everything you can teach me."

Esther nodded. "I will teach you, but we must progress slowly and with the greatest care. I do not want you to make my mistakes. You have opportunities that I did not have, Goldie. You must make the most of them."

THIRTY-ONE

OCTOBER 1987

On the morning of Jackie's arrival, Augusta swam her laps even faster than usual.

"You got a shark behind you or something?" asked Irving. He'd stopped in the shallow part of the pool and motioned for her to stop as well. On any other day, Augusta would have been annoyed that he'd interrupted her routine.

"Jackie is coming today," said Augusta, in an almost giddy voice. "I'm picking her up at the airport at eleven."

"Fort Lauderdale or West Palm?"

"West Palm," said Augusta. "It's closer."

"Will you bring her over to the pool for lunch?"

"We'll see," said Augusta. "I'll let her decide."

"I can't wait to meet her," Irving said, readjusting his goggles. "Imagine . . . Bess and George's daughter." He shook his head as if he couldn't believe it. "George was such a *mensch*. He always looked out for me, you know. He gave me advice about how to handle the customers; he even used to slip me extra food from the soda counter when your dad wasn't looking."

"My father knew," said Augusta.

"'Course he did." A grin spread over Irving's face. "I didn't say he didn't *know*, only that he looked the other way."

Later, as she showered and got ready for the airport, Augusta remembered all the times George swore that a particularly difficult customer had changed his mind after placing an order. *I made the guy a grilled cheese, but now he says he wants egg salad. The sandwich is already made,* George would say. *Either you eat it, Irv, or it will go to waste.* She remembered her father overhearing one such conversation, catching her eye, and winking at her. Solomon Stern could always tell when his soda jerk was fibbing. For all Augusta knew, he encouraged it.

That was the nice thing about spending time with a person you'd known for almost all of your life—the memories you shared grew even more vivid when you remembered them together.

Later, Augusta waited at the gate for Jackie to get off the plane. As passengers poured through the gateway door, Augusta watched half a dozen couples embracing their children and grandchildren—scenes that made Augusta long for a family she could never hope to have. The yearning was certainly nothing new, but now, at this stage of her life, it took on a different kind of permanence. She hadn't mentioned it to Shirley when the two of them talked about marriage; she hadn't mentioned how tempted she'd been by some of the men she had dated. When she was younger—in her twenties, thirties, and forties—she'd imagined a hundred diverse pathways offering a hundred different life choices. She could marry another pharmacist and share the store; she could marry the widowed professor and help him to raise his three young children; she could marry the wealthy childless banker and live a life full of travel and romance. But with each passing year, as she grew older, the number of Augusta's opportunities dwindled; her choices—both real and imagined—fell from a hundred to fifty, from twenty to ten, and finally to one. Now, on the cusp of her eightieth birthday, Augusta's *what if?* days were gone.

Only when Jackie's face appeared did Augusta's melancholy fade.

Having Bess for her sister had been a blessing, but it was Jackie who had always been the balm for the worst of Augusta's loneliness. Jackie was Bess's "change of life" baby, born when her brothers were ten and twelve. Augusta was thirty-four at the time—an unmarried pharmacist who worked too hard. When the whispers and pitying glances of her customers became too much for her to bear, Augusta would leave the pharmacy early, head to Bess's apartment, and scoop the baby onto her lap. There was something about the softness of Jackie's skin and the scent of the wispy hairs on her head that slowed Augusta's racing pulse and calmed her overexcited brain.

When Jackie got older, there were trips to the library, movies, plays, and countless sleepovers at Augusta's tiny apartment. When Augusta finally sold the Brooklyn store, her niece was already in her early twenties. It was Jackie who collected the newspaper ads for rental apartments on the Upper West Side. And when Augusta was forced out of her first hospital job, it was Jackie who purchased the Liquid Paper to change the date on her pharmacy license. (*With all that hospital bureaucracy,* Jackie said, *no one will have time to question your age.*)

And it was Jackie who found Rallentando Springs and suggested the two-bedroom layout, so there would be an extra bed whenever she came for a visit.

"I can't believe you're finally here!" said Augusta, kissing her niece on the cheek.

"I can't believe how *tan* you are! The Florida weather agrees with you!"

When they reached the exit door to the terminal, the humidity hit them both like a slap. Jackie pulled off her oversize blazer. "I can't wait to get out of these jeans and into my bathing suit!"

Augusta eyed her niece's two suitcases—one large checked bag and one carry-on. "Are you sure you're only coming for the weekend?" she asked. "It looks like you packed for a month!"

Jackie's smile was enigmatic. "I wanted to be prepared."

"Should we stop for lunch along the way or eat when we get home, by the pool?"

"Let's wait until we get to your place."

At the pool, Shirley was already saving them seats. "I feel like I'm meeting a celebrity," she said, wrapping Jackie in a hug. "Your aunt hasn't stopped talking about you all week!" To Augusta, she said, "Thank god the plane was on time. Edna Gerstein tried to take one of these chairs. You should have seen the look she gave me when I told her I needed two."

"I'm so happy to meet you," Jackie said. "Thanks for being such a wonderful friend to my aunt."

"No need to thank me. I love Augusta!" Shirley leaned in conspiratorially. "She's really spiced things up around here!"

"You don't say? Do tell."

"She told you about the barbecue, didn't she? How she had *two* men fighting over her?"

"I heard!"

"Did she tell you how the dessert table got tipped over? And how Nathaniel sat on my strawberry cheesecake?"

"Oh, she painted *quite* a picture—I almost felt like I was there. I've heard an awful lot about Nathaniel. Not as much about Irving, though."

Shirley nodded. "It's complicated. But Irving's crazy about her. I don't suppose she mentioned that?"

"Stop talking as if I'm not here," said Augusta. "And can the two of you lower your voices, *please*? People are starting to stare!"

Jackie ignored Augusta's protests. "No, but she didn't need to," said Jackie. "The fact that he pushed a man into a cheesecake is a pretty clear indication." She popped her sunglasses on top of her head, narrowed her eyes, and scanned the crowd. "Where *are* your suitors, Aunt Augusta? Are either of them around?"

Shirley shook her head. "They both play cards on Friday afternoons— not together, of course. Augusta told you that they don't get along?"

"She did," said Jackie.

"It isn't only about your aunt, though. Irving had some sort of grudge against Nathaniel before she moved here."

"That's what Aunt Augusta said. I wish I knew how that feud started, don't you?"

Augusta rolled her eyes and groaned. "I *never* should have introduced the two of you."

Shirley squeezed Augusta's hand. "You can't blame us for being curious." To Jackie, she said, "I don't have any idea. But maybe we can get some answers at Augusta's birthday party tomorrow."

"It's *not* a party," Augusta said.

"Of course it's a party," Jackie insisted. "We're celebrating your eightieth birthday! Speaking of which, I brought you the perfect birthday outfit from my store." She turned to Shirley to explain. "My mother had a real eye for clothing. I inherited that gene, which is why I opened my own boutique. Anyway, Aunt Augusta, it's a beautiful dress, sapphire-blue silk, with a touch of silver piping. It'll be wonderful on you. Not too short, not too tight, a nice A-line fit—you'll look like a dream!"

"*I* tried to take her shopping for a dress," said Shirley. "But she didn't like anything I suggested."

"She's very particular," Jackie said. "But I've been helping her pick out clothes for years, so I know exactly what she likes."

"As long as she doesn't wear her funeral pants," said Shirley.

Augusta frowned. "Don't get started on that again," she said.

"I don't know about the funeral pants," said Jackie. "But I promise you're both going to love the dress." She pointed her thumb over at the snack bar. "All this gossip is making me hungry. I'm going to get something to eat." Jackie got in line behind Harold Glantz and made small talk while they waited. Augusta couldn't hear their conversation, but from the wide smile on Harold's face, it seemed to be going well.

"Look at her—she can talk to *anyone*," said Shirley. "You must be so proud of her."

"I certainly am," Augusta said. From her seat she waved her arms wildly at Jackie until she finally caught her niece's attention. "Don't get the tuna, sweetheart!" she said.

THIRTY-TWO

FEBRUARY 1925

Augusta knew her father would worry when he learned that Esther was treating Mitzi Diamond. She still remembered how shaken he'd been when Zip bought the bicycle for Irving. "I wish that man had never set foot in my store," said her father bitterly.

"What does that mean?" Augusta asked.

"It means that men like Zip Diamond are dangerous."

"But why would he be dangerous for you? I thought he was mostly involved in gambling—horses and baseball and the neighborhood card parlors."

Solomon Stern shook his head. "Men like that don't stop at one vice," he said. "Where there's gambling, liquor always follows. And liquor now is big, big business. When Prohibition started, the government took all the alcohol off the market. Pharmacists can sell it for medicinal purposes, but only when a customer has a prescription."

Augusta had seen the special forms. Customers were allowed one pint every ten days, as long as they brought in a new prescription each time. "What does that have to do with Zip Diamond?"

"Speakeasies are selling *dreck*—bathtub gin and watered-down spirits, dyed and cut with wood alcohol. Half of it will make you sick, and some of it might even kill you. But pharmacies can still get quality whiskey—bottled-in-bond at 100 proof, aged, and stamped by the U.S. government. Which means that everyone wants what we're selling." Solomon paused, as if the next part pained him to say. "A few years ago, some of Zip's associates paid huge bribes for drug licenses. They set up fake pharmacies so their bookkeepers could make everything look good on paper. They paid off the distributors and the warehouse operators and got their hands on the alcohol withdrawal permits to make sure everything ran smoothly. But the government started cracking down on the permits. So now the racketeers have been forcing pharmacy owners to go into business with them."

Augusta had no idea all this illegal activity was happening in drug-stores like Stern's. She could not hide her shock. "Have any of those men approached you?"

"Once or twice, but I got lucky. There was some pharmacist with a little store in the Bronx who tried to poison one of the bootleggers with fake pills. After that, the men around here decided they needed a druggist they could actually trust. I'm more valuable to them as a *real* pharmacist than as some kind of fake business partner."

"Then you don't have anything to worry about."

Augusta's father scratched his head. "Maybe," he said. "But it's not that simple. Every time somebody new comes along, they want to change the status quo. Now that Zip Diamond knows where to find me, I just hope he won't make trouble."

But that had been a year and a half ago now, and so far Solomon Stern had heard nothing else. Zip had never returned to his store. Either the man and his family were never sick or they were getting their medicine somewhere else.

After a month of taking Esther's remedy, Mitzi Diamond was a changed woman. Finally, she could sleep at night without sweating through her nightgown. Her aches and pains and palpitations disappeared. Her energy and zest for life were back.

Like many of the women in the neighborhood, she began visiting Esther every other week. At first she came on the days Esther requested, but as she settled into her former vigor, the humility and patience that had accompanied her symptoms waned. She began showing up whenever she liked, and if other people had appointments, she was not content to wait her turn. Instead, she decided to come early in the morning in order to make sure that she was the first person seen.

Esther was quite firm with all her patrons about the hours that they were welcome in her home. She preferred to make appointments if possible, but whether people were new or repeat customers, it was common knowledge that Esther *never* saw customers before nine o'clock in the morning. This was to ensure that her nephew would not have to encounter any of them coming or going. Solomon knew about her business, of course, but the two of them had come to a delicate arrangement, built partly on Solomon's willful ignorance and partly on the precision of Esther's arrangements.

Both, therefore, were caught off guard when someone knocked a few minutes after eight o'clock one morning. Augusta's father was usually gone by then, but Mrs. Diamond had arrived just as he was leaving. Augusta followed him to the foyer and stood behind him as he opened the door.

"May I help you?" he asked when confronted with the sable-clad woman standing unapologetically in his hallway.

"I'm here to see Esther," Mrs. Diamond said, without offering her name. Even with her father standing between them, Augusta could smell the cloying sweetness of Mrs. Diamond's French perfume.

Given both the hour and the extravagance of the woman's appearance, Mr. Stern assumed that this customer was new. He had never seen Mrs. Diamond before.

"There's been a misunderstanding," he said politely. "Esther doesn't see customers for another hour yet."

"This is the only time that is convenient for me today," said Mrs. Diamond. "She will have to see me now."

Decades of running a retail establishment had trained Solomon Stern in the art of customer service. Over the years he'd been cried to, screamed at, and even threatened on occasion. Customers had been thoughtless and rude. He'd been awakened in the night for a single stamp and told he should be grateful for the business. But nothing had prepared him for this stranger's unequivocal sense of entitlement. Augusta watched as his pupils darkened with a palpable disgust.

"Ah," he said, frowning. "Time for me to go. Augusta, I'll leave this to you and your aunt." He stepped around Mrs. Diamond without looking back. Augusta knew he would have questions later, but for now she put that out of her mind.

She led Mrs. Diamond to the kitchen, where Esther was still sitting with one hand wrapped around the handle of her teacup. She had not bothered to tidy up the table but had left everything exactly as it was. Augusta could see from the tightness of Esther's features that her aunt was annoyed.

When Esther did not stand or say hello, Mrs. Diamond stood awkwardly beside the table and waited for Esther to acknowledge her presence. When this did not happen, she cleared her throat. "Good morning, Esther," she said.

But Esther still did not respond. She took a few bites of her toast and washed it down with a sip of tea. When she finished, she addressed her niece. "Augusta," she said, "I'm going to wash. Please clean the breakfast dishes before you leave for school."

Mrs. Diamond blinked in surprise and crossed her fur-covered arms over her chest. "I have a very busy morning," she snapped.

Unmoved, Esther drained the last bit of tea from her cup. Only then did she turn to Mrs. Diamond. "You can wait here, in the kitchen," she said. "I'll see you at nine o'clock."

After Esther left the room, Mrs. Diamond shook off her coat and threw it over the back of a chair. She smoothed the folds of her skirt and tucked a hair behind her ear. An awkward silence filled the space, but Augusta did not trust herself to break it. Would Esther want her to offer Mrs. Diamond tea and make her comfortable while she waited? Or was the whole point to leave her ill at ease as retribution for her disrespect?

It was Mrs. Diamond who spoke first. "Is Esther your grandmother?" she asked.

Augusta shook her head. "My grandmother's sister," she explained. "She came to live with us after my mother died."

Usually when Augusta mentioned her mother's passing, she was met with sympathetic smiles. But Mrs. Diamond's expression did not soften. A dead mother *was* unfortunate, but Mitzi Diamond had witnessed many unfortunate things.

"You're lucky to have her," Mrs. Diamond said sharply. "I've met a lot of foolish women in my life, but that aunt of yours? She's no fool."

At dinner, Augusta's father had questions. "Esther, why was that woman at our door so early?"

"I apologize for the disturbance, Solomon. It won't happen again."

"She didn't look like your typical customer. Not many of them arrive in fur coats."

Esther shrugged. "All kinds of women come to me for assistance. I'm sure it is the same for you. A rich man buys aspirin the same as a poor one. Their headaches may strike for different reasons, but they both come to you for the same pill."

Augusta's father nodded in agreement. "Who was she anyway?" he asked. "I haven't seen her in my store."

"Her name is Mitzi Diamond," said Esther.

Solomon Stern almost spat out his food. "Diamond? As in Zip Diamond's *wife*?"

"I don't know anything about her husband," said Esther. "Why should her husband matter to me?"

"Because he's probably the most powerful and dangerous man in all of Brownsville! Augusta, why didn't you warn your aunt? Why didn't you tell me this was going on?"

Augusta sank down in her seat. "I didn't . . . I didn't think it was important . . ."

"Dammit, Augusta! Of course it's important! What's going to happen if Esther can't help? Or if Mrs. Diamond isn't satisfied with her treatment?"

"All of my customers are satisfied," said Esther.

"That isn't the point," Augusta's father insisted. "I saw what she was like this morning—demanding that she be attended to immediately. Do either of you honestly think she won't do something like that again? She's used to people falling all over themselves to give her whatever she asks. She's used to getting everything she wants."

"She knows she will get no special treatment from me," Esther said. "I made sure she understands this."

"Papa," Augusta interjected, "she's so grateful to Aunt Esther for helping her. You should have seen how weak she was at first."

Solomon Stern shook his head sadly. "There's nothing *weak* about a woman like that. Mitzi Diamond has all her husband's power behind her. To have lasted this long as that man's wife means she's more ruthless than any of us could possibly imagine."

THIRTY-THREE

OCTOBER 1987

After sandwiches by the pool, Jackie wanted to go back to Augusta's apartment.

"I want to show you the dress I brought," said Jackie. "You should probably try it on."

From the larger of her two suitcases, Jackie pulled a tissue-wrapped square, unwrapped it carefully on her bed, and held up the dress in front of her aunt. The afternoon sun poured through the guest-room window, illuminating the silk so that the fabric sparkled.

"What do you think?" Jackie asked.

Augusta stared. Unlike the pink dress she'd seen with Shirley, the deep and vibrant blue of Jackie's selection made her think of Aunt Esther. In an instant, she was back in the moonlit kitchen of her youth; back to the midnight lessons; back to the piles of fragrant herbs.

As close as she'd always been to her niece, she'd never told her about such things.

"My aunt Esther had a robe that same color."

Jackie's eyes twinkled. "I know," she said. "My mom saved it after Esther died. She kept it hanging in her bedroom closet until it got so moth-eaten she had to throw it away. I used to play dress-up with it sometimes. When I saw *this* dress, I thought of the robe, too." Jackie sat on the edge of the guest-room bed and beckoned for Augusta to sit beside her. "You never talk about Esther."

Hearing the name on her niece's lips filled Augusta with indescribable longing. "She came to live with us after my mother died—arrived with a trunk full of the ugliest dresses you've ever seen in your life. Nothing but shapeless black and gray sacks, a couple of white aprons, some plain black boots. She wore her hair wrapped up in a babushka like some ancient crone from the middle of the forest.

"The first time I saw her in that beautiful robe, I swear I thought I was hallucinating. The way it shimmered, that gorgeous blue silk. It was like seeing a moth that had turned into a butterfly. When she let down her hair, she looked twenty years younger. It was late at night, in our kitchen. Esther wore that robe only when no one else was around to see."

"You mean when she was mixing up her powders?"

Augusta sucked in a quiet breath and took a seat beside her niece. She wondered what else Bess had revealed to Jackie. "Your mother told you about that?" said Augusta.

"In the last few weeks before she died, yes. My mother said Esther was a remarkable woman."

"She was," said Augusta. "She was the most confident person I ever met—so sure of her gifts, so certain of her talents. She and my father didn't see eye to eye. He thought Esther was a quack and I thought ... well, I thought she was magical."

"My mother said Esther made a potion for her once—to help her decide whether she should marry my father."

"She told you about that?"

Jackie nodded. "Mom was on so many drugs at that point that I thought she might be imagining things. But she was perfectly lucid when she described it. She told me Esther made a powder for her that she stirred into a cup of wine. Mom said the love potion made her appreciate how much my father meant to her. She knew immediately after drinking it that she wanted to spend the rest of her life with him. You must have been there. Is that how you remember it?"

Augusta nodded. "Except Esther never would have called it a love potion. She was adamant that such a thing didn't exist. She said there was no way to force love on people. That trying was like committing some sort of sin. She was very clear that she wanted no part in playing with people's emotions."

"But what about the drink she made for my mom?"

"Esther would have said that the elixir could only give your mother clarity about her feelings. It couldn't change the feelings themselves." Augusta shrugged. "I know it sounds crazy to modern ears, but when I was young, I believed Esther could do anything. Your mother used to think it was crazy, too—that is, until the night your father proposed."

"And after that, she believed?"

Augusta nodded. "After that evening, yes, she did."

"Clarity can be a wonderful gift. To see something so unambiguously, to be free of all doubt—who wouldn't want that?"

"You'll get no argument from me," said Augusta. "But sometimes clarity reveals difficult truths. Not everyone is as lucky as your mother was." Augusta stood from her seat and tried to shake off the sorrow that threatened to overtake her. She would not allow her niece's visit to be ruined by the intrusion of those painful memories. "Let's see that dress now, shall we?" she said.

"Are you ready to try it on? I think we'd better check the fit and see if you like the way it looks. We can't have the guest of honor looking shabby at her own party!"

"It's not a party," said Augusta, scooping up the dress and taking it across the hall to her bedroom. She stepped out of her clothes and left them where they fell, in a careless pile on the carpet. Then she slipped the silk over her head and pushed her arms through the three-quarter sleeves. A lifetime of being single had made her skilled at zipping herself up on her own.

Before turning to her full-length mirror, Augusta braced herself for disappointment. She was almost eighty years old. Her breasts were deflated, her stomach was slack, her skin was like a wrinkled sheet of tinfoil that some penny-pinching housewife had used more than once. It was too much to hope for loveliness now, ridiculous to aspire to something akin to beauty. She closed her eyes, stepped sideways toward the mirror, and counted silently to three.

Jackie called out from the hallway. "How's it going in there? Do you like it?"

"I don't know," said Augusta. "I haven't looked yet."

When Jackie entered the room, Augusta's eyes were still shut.

Jackie's voice swelled with admiration. "Oh my," she said. "Oh, Aunt Augusta . . . *look*."

When Augusta finally opened her eyes, the woman in the mirror reminded her of someone she'd forgotten long ago. Someone spirited, girlish, and spry. As for the dress, the cut enhanced her waist and the flounce of the skirt elongated her legs. The neckline was wide—a modified boatneck that displayed her collarbones to their fullest advantage. And the way the sapphire silk showed off her coloring! Even without a stitch of makeup, the dress brought out the gray in her eyes.

"You look magnificent!" Jackie gushed. "What do you think? Do you like it?"

"I do," said Augusta. "It's . . . yes, of course I do."

She was so flustered by the woman in the mirror that she could not put her feelings into words. Her reflection was a kaleidoscope of buried memories. The sapphire fabric was the evening sky outside her half-open Brooklyn window, it was Esther's silk robe in the kitchen at midnight, and the bottles of Higgins inks on her father's store shelves. The trim at the edges of her skirt and sleeves was the silver in Esther's graying hair, the giant stockpot on the kitchen stove, and the band of her sister's wedding ring. In the mirror, Augusta's pewter eyes were the same as her mother's before she got sick: filled with uncomplicated delight.

Past and present, joy and sorrow mingled together in the shining glass. Augusta wasn't merely her eighty-year-old self—she was fourteen and sixteen, two and twelve. She was a child swimming in the ocean with her mother and a young woman watching her aunt make soup. She was a curious girl who asked too many questions. She was a grieving daughter at her mother's funeral and a maid of honor at her sister's wedding.

As Jackie embraced her, Augusta murmured her thanks, but she could not look away from the image in the mirror she saw over her niece's sloping shoulder. Oh, how she wanted to be that woman again—a woman who, yes, had suffered losses, but whose heart had not yet been broken beyond repair. A woman who was curious and hopeful and who still believed in the glimmers of magic that made their way quietly into the world.

THIRTY-FOUR

FEBRUARY 1925

The day before Bess and George's wedding, Augusta decided to bob her hair. Smooth chin-length walnut waves framed her heart-shaped face. The haircut had been slightly impetuous, but when Irving first saw her from across the sanctuary, she knew from his smile that she had made the right decision.

She wanted to spend more time with him at the reception, but there were out-of-town cousins and family friends to attend to. For the rest of the afternoon, she had to satisfy herself with distant smiles and admiring glances.

The newspaper forecast called for sunshine, but by the time all the guests were gathered, the February air smelled like snow. After the toasts were made and the cake was eaten, the flakes began coming down in earnest. Wind rattled the thick glass synagogue windows as guests began scrambling to depart.

George had hired a taxi to drive him and his bride the one mile east to their new apartment. After their goodbyes to relatives and friends, Augusta's father escorted Esther home. Only Irving and Augusta lingered to tidy up the reception room and move the gifts to the rabbi's study until the newlyweds returned to claim them.

By the time they tugged open the heavy doors of the drafty stone building, there were at least six inches of snow on the ground. The freezing wind quickened and howled, stirring the snow like a broom raises dust. Irving pulled Augusta back inside.

"I can't let you go out in that," he said. "You're going to get blown away."

"It's only six blocks," said Augusta. "If I don't go home, my father will worry."

But when they opened the doors a second time, instead of rushing into the snow, Augusta stared down at her feet—at the new satin shoes that Harriet Dornbush had given her for the wedding—and wondered whether a walk through the snow would ruin them beyond repair.

"I'll carry you," Irving told her, sensing her hesitation.

"Absolutely not! There's no way you can carry me that far!"

Irving flashed her a confident smile. "I'm a lot stronger than you think," he said. "Come on—at least let me try."

She clung to his back for the next twenty minutes while he stumbled blindly through the swirling snow. Even in the bitter air, Augusta could feel the heat of his fingers traveling through her stockings and up her legs. When she tightened her grip and said, "Don't drop me!" he promised her he wouldn't let go.

Finally they reached the door of her building, where he carried her inside and lowered her gently onto the marble floor. She felt a palpable ache when he released her—a shiver of sadness when she realized that their journey had come to an end.

"Thank you," she said. "That was more fun than it should have been."

"Anytime," Irving answered, his gaze fixed on hers.

He brushed the powdery layer of snow from her shoulders, her back, and her hair. When she reached out to do the same for him, he wrapped his arms around her waist. As she pressed her frozen lips to his, there was a sense that everything had changed between the two of them. Together, they had kept each other warm. Together, they had turned something dark into light.

The next few months were filled with stolen kisses—between the shelves of the local library when no one else was around to see, and in the stillness of the prescription room when her father was taking care of customers. These were the places she was most at ease. These were the places, Irving told her, where her beauty most overwhelmed him.

"What do you mean?" Augusta said. "I'm not looking for a compliment, Irving, I'm just trying to understand." They were in her father's prescription room then, surrounded by shelves of bottles and vials. She gestured toward the locked cabinet of poisons. "This isn't exactly a romantic place."

"Maybe not for other people," said Irving. "But whenever you're here or at the library, I can feel your brain at work. And when your brain is churning away, I swear it makes your whole face light up. There's nothing more beautiful than that."

Augusta laughed. "You think my brain is *beautiful*?"

Irving refused to be embarrassed. "I think you're happiest when you're using it—when you're doing your homework or studying your formulas or learning whatever is in your books. That's when you're the most yourself. And that's when you're the most beautiful to me."

The tears filled her eyes before she could stop them. She pressed her body into his and kissed him with a longing that nearly knocked them both over. She could not imagine that any other man would ever be able to see her so clearly.

But aside from Evie and Bess, Augusta told no one about her romance. She did not discuss Irving with Aunt Esther and she did not mention him to her father. The words Lois Diamond had spoken to her at Evie's party rang in her ears. *He's probably just being nice to you because he works for your father.*

When Bess questioned her about keeping Irving a secret, Augusta said it was because he worked at the store.

"Why should that matter?" Bess insisted. "George worked at the store for years."

"Yes, but George is in law school now. The store was always temporary for him. With Irving, it's different. He may not want to be a pharmacist, but he doesn't want to work anywhere else. He's hoping to be promoted one day, for Papa to make him a manager. He wouldn't want to get that job just because he's dating me. That's why we're keeping things between us quiet."

Bess raised an eyebrow. "Is that so? Because Irving told George that *he* wants to tell Papa, but *you're* the one who keeps refusing."

"Fine," Augusta admitted. "The secrecy is my idea. I just . . . I want to be sure that Irving isn't dating me because I'm the boss's daughter."

"Why would you ever think that?"

"I don't know. Someone said something to me once." Augusta neglected to mention that the someone was the daughter of the most powerful gangster in their neighborhood.

Bess put one arm around her sister. "That boy has loved you since the day he met you. Trust me, what Irving feels for you has nothing to do with our father or the store."

Irving invited Augusta to his senior banquet that spring. Though it had taken him a few extra years to finish high school, he had kept his promise to his mother to earn his diploma.

Augusta wanted to accept the invitation, but the public nature of the event meant that she would have to tell her father the truth. She knew that her father thought well of Irving, but she imagined that he might be angry when he learned she had lied. She decided to tell him on an evening when Bess and George were over for dinner. She wanted to have her sister's support, and she knew George's presence would keep her father calm.

She'd originally intended to break the news toward the end of the meal. But before they had even finished the soup, Augusta found herself blurting it out. "Irving asked me to his senior banquet," she said. "And I think you should know that we are dating."

Bess pretended to be surprised. "Augusta, that's wonderful," she said. "Irving is a sweetheart, isn't he, George?" George, who had already been warned by his wife, nodded amiably and said, "Of course. You know I love Irving." No one had bothered to tell Esther, but it was clear that she'd already suspected and approved.

Only Augusta's father was silent.

"Papa?" Augusta whispered. "What do you think?"

Her father looked up from his bowl, his soup spoon frozen in midair. Augusta was relieved that he did not seem angry, but the look on his face was full of grief.

"I think . . ." he began softly. "I think I've known about the two of you since Bess's wedding, or even before. I think . . ." He stopped and stared into his soup, as if he might find an answer in the bottom of his bowl. When he lifted his eyes to meet Augusta's, she saw that his cheeks were wet with tears. "Well, I just wish your mother were here to advise you about all of this. But I think . . . I think the way you look at Irving reminds me of the way your mother used to look at me."

THIRTY-FIVE

OCTOBER 1987

Augusta desperately needed some air. While Jackie phoned her husband and children in New York, Augusta decided to walk to the clubhouse and return the book she'd borrowed from the library.

"I'll be back in half an hour," she told Jackie, grabbing the paperback from her bedroom nightstand. "Tell the kids I said hello."

Inside the library, she was surprised to find Irving, so engrossed in the book he was holding that he didn't even look up when she entered.

"What are you doing here?" she said. "I thought you had cards on Friday afternoons."

He blinked at her from behind his glasses. "Sorry, Augusta, I didn't hear you come in."

"Don't you have your poker game now?"

"I gave up my game for a couple of months. I've got too much else to do."

"Like what?" she asked, narrowing her eyes, a hint of suspicion in her tone.

Irving tapped at the pages of his book and held it up so she could see: *The Norton Anthology of Modern Poetry*. "This, mostly. I have a lot of reading for my FAU class."

Augusta knew that Florida Atlantic University offered continuing education classes. But she never would have guessed that her old beau—the boy who swore that he'd never go to college—would have signed up for any of them.

"What are you taking?" she asked carefully, trying not to sound too shocked.

"I almost took 'The Tragedies of Shakespeare, Part Two'—I did 'Part One' in the spring, and it was terrific. But I signed up for 'Modern Poetry' instead."

She had expected him to say something practical—like a computer class or a lecture series on the history of the Cold War. But Shakespeare plays? Modern poetry? Augusta was positively speechless.

He smiled at her then, the fluorescent lighting reflecting off his slate-blue eyes. "You're the reason for the class, you know. I'm writing my paper on Robert Frost."

The mention of the venerable poet stirred a long-buried spark in the back of her mind.

"*New Hampshire*," she whispered. "The poetry collection I gave you for graduation."

"I didn't think you'd remember."

"I didn't think you'd ever read it."

Irving chuckled. "To be honest, I didn't—not for a few years, anyway. But I took it with me to Chicago, and I read from it every night to my boys. I still have the book—it's in my apartment."

"You kept it? After all this time?" It was almost too much for her to take in, the way the echoes of her past were increasingly finding their way into her present. The air in the library felt thick with wonder; dizziness made her sway to one side.

Irving leapt from his chair and steadied her by placing both hands on her shoulders. "Whoa, there, Gold—*Augusta*. You okay?"

His face was so close to hers that she could count the wrinkles on his forehead. She could see the silver hairs in his eyebrows. She could feel his breath on her lips.

There was so much she could have said in that moment, so much that she wanted to tell him. *I still have the gift you gave me, too—the silver necklace with the rhinestone that broke the first time I wore it.* But instead, she pulled away. "I'm fine," she said. "Of course I'm fine. It's stuffy in here, that's all."

When she remembered the paperback book in her hands, she scanned the crowded shelves behind him. She couldn't find any room, so she shoved the book into the narrow space between the tops of three Jackie Collins hardcovers and the shelf above it.

"One day," she said determinedly, "I'm going to organize all these shelves so that the books are properly arranged. It's impossible to find anything now. If I put everything in order, people will be able to find what they're looking for."

Irving shrugged. "I dunno. I think people like it how it is. This way, there's always a surprise on the shelves, a book you've never heard of before." He patted his small patch of thinning hair. "In my experience," he continued, "people come into this room thinking they know what kind of story they want to leave with. But at the end of the day, most of them have no idea. The book they first start flipping through isn't usually the book they end up choosing."

To Augusta, his words sounded like an excuse. "You don't need to remind *me* how easily people change their minds," she snapped. "You know what, Irving? I have to go. Jackie is waiting for me at home. Good luck with your paper."

As Augusta scurried into the hallway, Irving's smile flattened like a cake when the oven door gets opened too soon.

"Augusta, wait. Please don't leave. What did I say? Augusta! Wait!"

Despite his near-pitiful distress, Augusta didn't turn around. She fled down the carpeted clubhouse hallway, through the glass-edged double front doors, and out into the afternoon sunshine.

"You're studying *poetry*, aren't you?" she shouted over her shoulder.

"They should have taught you about *metaphors!*" She didn't care that pass-ersby were staring. She didn't care about the scene they might be causing.

"That wasn't a metaphor!" Irving shouted back. "I'm not smart enough for metaphors! Please, Augusta, stop for a minute. Jesus Christ, you're giving me a heart attack!"

She could hear the heaviness of his breathing as he struggled to catch up. "Do you know . . ." he wheezed, calling to her from behind. "Do you know the last time I was this winded? It was after I carried you home from Bess's wedding. In the snowstorm! Do you remember *that?*"

The mention of that afternoon stopped her cold. Despite the heat, Augusta swore she could feel phantom snowflakes on her arms.

Slowly she turned around to face him.

Even after he reached her, it took a few moments before he caught his breath. "Thank you for stopping," he said. He coughed a few times, straightened his shoulders, and clasped both of his hands in front of him. "Augusta. I hope you know that the last thing I want—the *very last thing*—is to upset you. Arrange the library shelves however you want. Hell, I'll help you, if you'll let me. I swear I'll learn the whole Dewey Decimal System if that's what it takes for you to forgive me."

Faced with this absurd apology, Augusta could not maintain her anger. This was a man who had carried her home for six long blocks in the middle of a blizzard. This was a man who had kept the book she had given him for over sixty years.

"All right," she said, trying not to smile. "But alphabetical order will be just fine."

THIRTY-SIX

AUGUST 1925

The next time Esther was moved to make her *not*-love potion, it was for her first customer, Fanny Lowenstein. Mrs. Lowenstein's twins had long since grown out of their picky eating phase. However, not everything in the Lowenstein household was running as smoothly as the boys' digestive tracts.

Fanny's husband, Sid, had been having an affair with a female sales assistant at the furniture store where he worked. Apparently, he and the woman in question had been unable to resist assessing the comfort of a new line of beds the store had stocked. They were caught one evening by the owner, who promptly fired them both. Soon the story was all over the neighborhood, and Sid had no choice but to confess.

As is so often the case when such secrets come to light, Sid's pattern of missed dinners, late evenings, and mood swings suddenly made sense to his wife. Still, Fanny was inclined to forgive, especially after Sid swore on his life that he would never do something so foolish again.

The second time Sid Lowenstein transgressed, it was at a different furniture store with a different assistant—this time on desks instead of beds. Despite the change in venue and surface, the culprits were once again discovered, and Sid was forced to confess a second time.

The humiliation and the stress had caused Fanny's skin to blister so badly that it looked as if she'd been burned. After a slew of doctors offered no relief, Mrs. Lowenstein found herself once again in Esther's cozy, hopeful kitchen, where her tale of woe poured forth in a torrent. After two weeks of Esther's remedies, the blisters vanished, and the flaking disappeared. Still, Mrs. Lowenstein's worries were far from over.

"Sid was staying with his cousin, but now he's asked me to reconcile," she told Esther. "This time he seems sincere."

"Oh?" said Esther. "Augusta, will you leave us, please? I need to speak privately with Mrs. Lowenstein." Augusta nodded and left the kitchen, but she could easily hear them from the living room.

"What do you think?" Mrs. Lowenstein asked.

"My opinion doesn't matter," said Esther. "What matters is what *you* think."

"He wants us to move to Massachusetts," said Mrs. Lowenstein. "He says everything will be different once we're out of New York. But, Esther, I don't know what to do. After all he's put me through, I don't know whether I trust him. And even more important," she whispered, "I don't know whether I still love him."

Augusta could almost hear her aunt thinking. Although Bess's situation had been different, the doubt Mrs. Lowenstein described sounded remarkably similar to Bess's dilemma when she was deciding whether to marry George. Augusta wondered how far her aunt would go to help Mrs. Lowenstein find peace. For the next few minutes, she held her breath waiting, but the women must have lowered their voices because no matter how much Augusta strained her ears, she could not hear the end of their conversation.

That night, Augusta was wide awake when Esther slipped silently out of bed. After following her aunt to the kitchen, Augusta watched as Esther collected ingredients from her apothecary case. From the tiny tins and stoppered bottles, Esther gathered what she needed: fenugreek seeds, mandrake root, sage leaves, dried rose hips, and chamomile. Before grinding them all together, Esther pulled a small glass bottle from a hidden drawer in the back of the case. From the bottle, she shook one final object, which she placed on the open palm of her hand: an emerald clover, no bigger than a thumbnail, a plant Augusta did not recognize.

"What is that?" Augusta whispered.

"They call it *raskovnik*," said Esther. "It's more common in my country than here. They say the leaves can unlock emotions. This is the most important ingredient. It helps to open a closed mind."

Augusta watched while Esther worked, swaying and humming as she ground her ingredients. The room smelled of maple and apples and roses—a scent that was green and impossibly fresh. The kitchen windows were lined with frost; the winter sky was an impenetrable black. But somehow, inside Esther's kitchen, the air felt as bright and hopeful as spring.

Esther's voice was lively and clear, and as Augusta listened, she felt her spirit lighten. This time, she felt the words within her, like the beat of her heart as it moved in her chest.

To ease the pain of those who suffer
To repair the bodies of those who are ill
To restore the minds of those in need

A week later, when Augusta came home from school, Mrs. Lowenstein was in the kitchen with Esther.

"I did what you told me," Fanny said. "I put the powder in a cup of wine and drank it before Sid came to see me. He showed me the papers for the house in Massachusetts and he described exactly how it would be. He made it sound so perfect, Esther; he said what a happy family we would be." She paused and took a deep breath. "Normally, when Sid talks like that, I get so terribly confused. But this time, I wasn't confused at all. It was like a sort of stillness came over me and I knew exactly what I wanted. I knew I didn't love Sid anymore. That I could never love that man again. And so . . . and so I told him no. The boys and I are going to move in with my sister in Queens."

That evening, when Augusta questioned Esther about the powder she'd given Mrs. Lowenstein, her aunt confirmed it was the same concoction she'd made for Bess the year before. "It is the most powerful of my recipes," said Esther. "Perhaps the most dangerous as well. In my life, I have prepared it only five times. Once for the rabbi of my village, once for my dearest childhood friend, once for your sister, and now for Mrs. Lowenstein."

Augusta could hear the exhaustion in her voice. The two of them were in their beds, speaking softly in the dark. "That's only four," Augusta said. "Who did you make it for the fifth time?"

Esther's reply was full of sorrow. "For a man I loved, a long time ago."

"What happened?"

"I'll tell you another time. It's late, and I'm very tired."

Augusta thought the conversation was over, but as her eyelids were growing heavy, Esther's voice pierced the darkness again. "Do you remember what I told you, Goldie, before we first visited Harriet Dornbush? When you asked why I couldn't slip some of my herbs into her soup?"

Augusta buried her body deeper under the weight of her woolen blanket. "Never treat anyone without permission?"

"Exactly. That is correct. We must never be careless with our knowledge. We must be thoughtful. We must be patient. My impatience once cost me someone I loved. I don't want you to make the same mistake."

THIRTY-SEVEN

OCTOBER 1987

After he patched things up with Augusta, Irving headed for the pool. It was the day before Augusta's birthday, and he still hadn't decided on a gift. Ever since she'd invited him to dinner, Irving had been racking his brain. Now that he was almost out of time, he decided to ask Shirley for help.

"I can't figure out what she'd like," he said.

Shirley was in her usual spot at the pool, reading about celebrity skin care routines, when Irving started questioning her. She lowered her *People* magazine a few inches and peered at Irving from over the top. "What she'd *like*? Well, for one thing, she'd *like* for you and Nathaniel to cut the crap."

"Excuse me?"

"Haven't you been at each other's throats long enough? It makes it stressful for the rest of us, you know. If you want Augusta to have a nice birthday, you can start by patching things up with Nathaniel."

"It's not a bad idea. But it's not exactly a *gift*, is it? Isn't there something you think she needs?"

"She's turning eighty years old, Irving. If there was something she *needed,* she'd have it by now." Shirley gave him a disappointed look. "I don't have time for this conversation and frankly, at your age, neither do you. You're obviously crazy about her. So why don't you *do* something about it?"

Irving scratched the place on his head where his hair used to be. "What's that supposed to mean?"

Shirley went back to her magazine. "You're a grown man," she said. "Figure it out."

It wasn't easy for him, but Irving pulled out his Rallentando Springs directory and called Nathaniel Birnbaum on the phone.

"Hello?"

"Nathaniel? It's Irving Rivkin. Do me a favor and don't hang up."

"Irving? This is . . . unexpected."

"You don't have to tell me. I'm as surprised as you are. Look, I'm sorry about the barbecue. I didn't mean to push you into the cheesecake. I'm not making excuses. I know I lost my temper. But I never intended for you to get hurt."

"Don't worry about me. I'm perfectly fine. Although getting the Jell-O out of my ears was a lot harder than you might think."

"Tell me about it," Irving said. "Vera and I are over, by the way. Whatever we were to begin with . . . anyway, it's all for the best."

Nathaniel cleared his throat. "Since we're on the subject of romance, I'd like to make it clear that I have absolutely no romantic feelings for Augusta. She and I are friends—nothing more. I don't want you getting the wrong idea. In fact, I'm beginning to think I'm developing real feelings for someone else entirely."

Irving smiled. "Let me guess. Shirley, right?"

Nathaniel sounded genuinely surprised. "I thought I was being discreet. Have I done something to give myself away?"

"You're forgetting I knew you back when you were courting Evie. You had that same dreamy look in your eyes when you were talking to Shirley the other day."

Nathaniel began to chuckle softly. "You really think so?"

"I do."

"Irving, can I ask you a question? You've hated me from the very first day I moved here. I'd love to know why."

Now it was Irving's turn to laugh. "Come on, Nathaniel. Don't tell me you don't remember."

"Remember what?"

At the start of the phone call, Irving had been pacing the floor. But now he came to an abrupt stop. "The night that you proposed to Evie? You don't remember what I told you at the restaurant?"

"I swear to you, Irving, I have no idea. I remember stopping at a little speakeasy before dinner, and you somehow getting us a bottle of champagne. That was the first time I tasted champagne, and I must have gone a little overboard. To this day, I rarely drink it. Anyway, everything that happened after that has always been a bit of a blur."

Irving could not believe what he was hearing. He'd been angry about that evening for so long that the rage had become a part of him. He could feel it sometimes, just below his skin, like a stinger from a bee that would not be drawn out. The poison had become a permanent reminder of the punishing twists and turns life could take. "I told you I was going to propose to Augusta. I told you I had the ring in my pocket. And then, before I had the chance to ask her, you led Evie out onto the dance floor and got down on one knee yourself! The whole place went crazy—everyone cheered. I couldn't ask Augusta to marry me after that. After all that planning, I knew I had to wait."

Irving swore he could hear Nathaniel thinking, trying to reconstruct the evening. "My god, I don't remember *any* of that. I have no recollection of that conversation, I *swear*. If I had known ... well, of course you must have been *livid*. As I said, I had too much to drink that night. It's no excuse, but I must have been so drunk that I didn't register whatever you told me."

"I never took you for such a big drinker."

"It's funny—Augusta said the same thing."

"What's the last thing you remember? About that night, I mean."

"Honestly? That flask you gave me. I thought it was filled with whiskey, but it must have been some kind of bootleg brew. Whatever was in it, I downed the whole thing. It went straight to my head."

"You don't remember leading Evie out on the dance floor? Or asking her to marry you?"

Nathaniel's voice grew wistful. "I have memories, but sometimes I think they're only the images Evie put in my head later. She described that moment to so many people—her parents, her brother, all our friends. After a while, her descriptions got lodged in my brain. But if I'm being completely honest, I'm not sure I have any real memories of my own."

"Jesus."

"Irving, I'm so sorry that I ruined your proposal. I had no intention of doing any such thing. You must have thought I was a terrible friend. It's no wonder you've been angry with me."

Irving sighed into the receiver. "You weren't a terrible friend. I should have handled it better. I should have talked to you about it afterward. Hell, I should have talked to Augusta. Instead, I gave up and left the building."

"You know, Evie always talked about that later. How you just up and left the three of us. The next day, she was awfully annoyed with you. Of course, that was nothing compared to how ticked off she was later, after we all heard about Lois."

Irving considered telling Nathaniel the full story then, considered confessing every detail of that awful night. But there had already been too many revelations, too many surprises for a single phone call. In the wake of his abandoned anger, Irving was suddenly exhausted.

"If you don't mind my asking," Nathaniel continued, "what *did* happen after that night? I mean, now that I know you were planning on proposing to Augusta, I guess I have a lot of questions."

But Irving couldn't open that wound just yet. "You know what, Nathaniel? I'm glad we had this talk, but let's save that story for another day."

"Of course," said Nathaniel. "We've got plenty of time. Hey—how about we go together to the dinner? No sense in both of us driving alone."

"That'd be great," Irving said. "I'm sure that would make Augusta happy. Actually, I was thinking maybe I could drop off some flowers with a card from both of us tomorrow. Just so she knows you and I are on good terms."

"That sounds like a wonderful idea. And Irving, thank you for the call. I really appreciate you taking the initiative."

"Sure thing," said Irving. "It's been too many years. We're both better off letting go of all that crap from the past. We don't want to keep making the same mistakes, right?"

THIRTY-EIGHT

OCTOBER 1925

Irving wished he had the money to buy Goldie something special for her eighteenth birthday, but the only present he could afford was from a pushcart on Belmont Avenue—a thin silver chain with a rhinestone drop dangling precariously from the end. By the time he got it home, half of the "silver" had rubbed off on his handkerchief. But by that point, it was too late to go shopping for anything else.

Although Mr. Stern had given Irving a raise, there never seemed to be enough money for everything he and his family needed. Irving's mother had been ill that past summer, and new hospital bills kept arriving. His brother was still going to school in Albany, still asking for money to cover room and board. The landlord who owned the four-story building where Irving and his mother lived had just informed them that the rent would be going up next month.

All of this made Irving incredibly tired. He was tired of the rumbling in his stomach, tired of the fraying cuffs on his shirts, and tired of the way his mother pretended that her morning coffee wasn't half chicory. Still, he could have held on a bit longer—could have continued to swallow his dignity—if only the rhinestone on Goldie's necklace hadn't fallen off of the chain less than ten minutes after he'd fastened the flimsy clasp around her neck.

"I'm so sorry." Irving grimaced. "I'll take it back. I'll get you something else."

"You'll do no such thing," she said. "I love this necklace. I'm keeping it."

"Come on, Goldie," Irving said. "Admit it. It's a piece of junk."

She cupped his cheeks in both of her hands and kissed him gently on the lips. "I will cherish this always," she said. "Because it came from *you*."

"Fine," he said. "But the next gift I give you will be special. I promise."

For the next few months, until December, Irving tried harder than ever to save. He stopped buying pretzels from the cart on the street, he stopped buying the newspaper for his mother in the mornings. But there wasn't much more that he could give up, and while his mother finally had a new winter coat, he desperately needed one of his own.

On top of that, he was all too aware of the special moments the new year would bring. Goldie would graduate from high school in the spring and begin pharmacy college in the fall. Sometime between those two milestones, Irving was hoping to ask her to marry him. He certainly didn't want to propose with a ring that fell apart on her finger.

In the hours before he fell asleep each night, Irving sorted through the problem. He didn't want to tell Mr. Stern about the hospital bills or ask for another raise, but he desperately needed to earn more cash. What kind of extra work could he do? Who would hire him part-time and make the payment worth his while? Zip Diamond's words played on repeat in the back of Irving's mind. *If you ever need anything, you let me know.*

Irving knew there would be risks getting involved with a man like Zip. He had not forgotten Mr. Stern's warning the day his bicycle was delivered. *Don't offer to do him any favors . . . If he gets his hooks into you, he won't want to let go.* But when Irving walked through the December cold, shivering in his shoddy coat, he felt as if he had no choice. When he thought about Goldie and their future together, his heart swelled with anticipatory joy. There was so much that he wanted to give her. There was so much that she deserved. He had six months to turn things around, to improve his situation. And if that meant asking Zip Diamond for a favor, well, that was what he would have to do.

More than two years had passed since the last time Irving had visited the brownstone on Glenmore Avenue. The brass handle of the paneled door was as shiny as ever, but this time, instead of Mrs. Diamond, Sammy's sister opened the door.

Irving had heard plenty of rumors about Lois Diamond. Her dresses were short, her hair was dyed, she cursed, she smoked, and she was constantly seen flirting with men all over Brooklyn. Although she was the same age as Goldie, she had a hardened, haunted look about her.

"Who are you?" she said to Irving, without so much as a hello.

"Irving Rivkin," he said. "I was wondering if your father was home."

Lois's eyes widened in delight. "Irving Rivkin? I remember that name. Well, well, well. Are you still working at Stern's Pharmacy?"

"Yes."

"And you're dating the pharmacist's daughter, Alice?"

"Augusta. But how do you know—"

"Really, Irving?" Lois interrupted. "Either you're incredibly stupid, or you've forgotten who my family is. We know everything about everyone who lives in this crummy neighborhood."

He held up both hands in mock surrender. "Sure," he said. "My mistake. Anyway, as I said, I was wondering if your father was home."

Lois pointed toward the living room. "He's in there," she said. "With my mother. What do you want from him, anyway?"

"How do you know I want something from him?"

Lois took a step closer to Irving and appraised him with fierce, narrowed eyes. "Everyone wants something from my father, Irving. The question is, what are you willing to do to get it?"

THIRTY-NINE

OCTOBER 1987

On the morning of Augusta's eightieth birthday, she woke to the smell of chicken soup.

At first she thought that she was dreaming. Augusta hadn't made soup for sixty-two years. She rolled over and read her alarm clock— how was it already ten in the morning? She'd told Irving she wouldn't be at the pool—she was going to sleep in during Jackie's visit. But sleeping in meant waking at eight, not ten. And either way, the hour didn't explain the scents of chicken stock, onion, and dill that had roused her from her slumber.

Slowly Augusta pulled back the covers, lifted her head, and sniffed the air. No, she definitely wasn't dreaming. Someone was making chicken soup in her apartment.

The galley-style kitchen had a table at one end and a pass-through countertop that opened into the living room. Augusta took a seat on one of the counter stools and watched her niece sprinkling salt and pepper into a pot she'd forgotten she owned.

"Good morning," Augusta said. "What's all this?"

The kitchen looked as if Jackie had been puttering around for hours.

In addition to the soup on the stove, there were scrambled eggs warming in a pan and a pot of fresh coffee in the machine. A small square carton of fresh blueberries waited by the sink to be rinsed, and two sesame bagels were on a plate by the toaster.

"Happy birthday, sleepyhead!" said Jackie, blowing her aunt a kiss across the counter. "I woke up early and borrowed the car—I didn't think you'd mind. Let's see . . . I stopped at the bakery for some bagels and then I picked up groceries at Publix." Jackie pulled a mug from the cabinet, filled it with coffee, and set it down in front of Augusta. Then she spooned some scrambled eggs onto a plate and pushed that in Augusta's direction.

"It's sweet of you to make me breakfast," said Augusta. "But what possessed you to make *soup*? It's going to be ninety degrees today."

Jackie sliced one of the bagels and popped both halves into the toaster. "It felt appropriate," she said, doing her best to avoid eye contact.

"You're on a long weekend away from your kids, and the first thing you want to do is cook? At ten in the morning? In the Florida heat?"

Jackie shrugged. "We can have it for lunch."

"*You* can have it—I'm saving my appetite for dinner tonight."

"It smells good, though, doesn't it? Bring back any memories?"

Augusta lifted the coffee cup to her lips. "I suppose it does," she admitted. "I take it your mother told you about Esther's chicken soup? Because I can't think of any other reason for you to go to all this trouble." She waved her hand in the direction of the stove. "Did your mother give you a recipe to follow? Bess was never much of a cook, as I recall . . ."

"The recipe is Esther's," said Jackie. "She dictated it to my mother before she died. Mom wrote down the basic ingredients, but Esther told her—"

"That she never made her soup the same way twice."

Jackie nodded. "Exactly. Mom said Esther liked to add a lot of extra ingredients and that she never really specified how much to use—dill, parsley, onion . . . Mom thought the dill gave the soup a nice kick."

"People don't cook like that anymore, making everything from scratch.

You know, Esther used to grind all her herbs with a mortar and pestle she brought over from Russia."

"I know," said Jackie. "With Hebrew letters carved inside."

"Your mother told you about that, too?"

Jackie was silent for a beat too long. "Aunt Augusta, I think we need to talk."

A heaviness pressed on Augusta's heart. She didn't want to talk about Esther. Didn't want to talk about her great-aunt's illness or her own futile attempts at healing. She pointed to the toaster. "The bagel is done."

Before Jackie had a chance to pull the two halves from the toaster, there was a knock at Augusta's front door.

"I'll get it," Augusta said, happy for an excuse to delay the conversation. She pulled the front of her bathrobe closed and marched down the hall to open the door. There, on her doormat, someone had left a bouquet of long-stemmed yellow roses. But whoever delivered it had not lingered long enough to make himself known.

As Augusta bent down to examine the bouquet, curiosity took over. Why would a person drop off a gift without waiting to greet the recipient? Immediately, Augusta thought of Irving. It would be just like him to behave this way—to send mixed signals, to run away. Would that man *ever* stop playing games with her? As she stared down at the yellow petals, Augusta's hands turned to fists. Between Jackie's soup and this bouquet, her birthday was growing more complicated by the minute.

Augusta did not know what possessed her then, but instead of picking up the flowers, she stepped over them and began to run down the shrubbery-lined walkway. When she reached the end and rounded the corner, she spotted the unmistakable backside of none other than Irving Rivkin. It wasn't even ten-thirty in the morning, but the sun was so strong that it felt like noon.

She shouted his name once, then twice. Slowly—very slowly—he turned around.

"Irving! Did you leave me flowers?"

"Good morning!" he said, walking toward her. When he got closer, he pointed to her bare feet. "Augusta, what happened to your shoes?"

"Don't change the subject," she snapped. "Did you leave me flowers or not?"

"They're for your birthday," he said brightly. "I know your niece is here, so I didn't want to bother you."

Augusta scowled. "What kind of person leaves a gift on a doorstep and then skulks away? Why do you have to be so mysterious?"

Irving stared at her, confused. "I didn't skulk away," he said. "I thought you'd be happy to have flowers on your birthday. And it wasn't my intention to be mysterious. Didn't you see the card we left?"

Now it was Augusta's turn to stare. "What do you mean, *we?*" she said.

"Me and Nathaniel," Irving said. "The flowers are from both of us."

Augusta shoved her fists into the pockets of her robe.

"We're burying the hatchet," he continued. "And we wanted you to be the first to know. We don't want you to worry about us tonight. We want your birthday to be perfect. It's all in the card that we wrote."

"Oh," said Augusta, suddenly deflated. All the anger that had been building inside her left her body in one lamentable sigh. "I see. Well then . . . thank you."

Irving tilted his head. "Do you want me to walk you back to your apartment?" He looked at her bathrobe and her bare feet again. "You seem a little confused this morning."

"For heaven's sake," said Augusta gruffly, "I'm not the least bit confused. I wanted to know who left the flowers, that's all."

"I didn't want them to wilt in the heat. That's why I knocked on the door."

Augusta nodded. "Of course," she said. "Thank you, Irving. I'll see you and Nathaniel tonight."

As she turned around, Augusta scolded herself for assuming the flowers were some kind of grand gesture. She told herself that her disappointment was absurd. *Be happy the two of them are getting along. Now maybe you can celebrate your birthday in peace.*

But when she carried the bouquet into her apartment, the smell of soup assaulted her again. Jackie was sitting at the kitchen counter, waiting for them to have their "talk." There would be no peace for her yet.

"What happened to you out there?" Jackie chided. "You disappeared on me."

Augusta held up the bouquet. "Irving dropped off flowers for my birthday. But I had to chase him down the sidewalk. You know what? Don't ask. It was silly, that's all."

Jackie waggled her eyebrows. "A bouquet of roses on your birthday, hmm? Sounds awfully romantic to me."

"It isn't. The roses are from Irving *and* Nathaniel. Apparently they're best friends now." Augusta laid the flowers on the kitchen counter and removed the cellophane with a pair of scissors. There, tucked between stalks of snowy baby's breath, was a card with her name printed neatly on the front. "'Dear Augusta,'" she read out loud. "'Happy eightieth birthday. We want you to know that your special milestone has inspired us to put past hostilities behind us. We look forward to celebrating with you tonight and we wish you many more happy returns. Your friends, Nathaniel and Irving.'" The note was as unromantic as possible. Not a trace of tenderness, not a hint of passion.

"Well, that's nice, isn't it?" said Jackie. "I mean, that was a very thoughtful gesture."

"Thoughtful, sure," said Augusta through gritted teeth. "What a *thoughtful* gesture from my *friends*."

"Why do you sound so angry?"

Augusta threw up her hands. She couldn't keep herself from shouting. "Because I *swore* I would never let another man hurt me, and now here I am, allowing it to happen! And not just some random man, mind you, but the *very same one* who hurt me the last time! Sixty-two years later, I'm feeling the same foolish feelings. Falling for the same dumb tricks. Misreading the same old signals. I may have turned eighty years old today, Jackie, but I'm still as stupid as I was at eighteen!" Augusta flung the card onto the counter and lowered her head into her hands. She took a slow, calming breath. "I'm sorry, sweetheart," she said. "Becoming eighty is turning out to be much more emotional than I anticipated."

Jackie slipped one arm around her aunt. "For what it's worth, I think it's good. It's healthy that you're finally admitting your feelings."

"Then why am I so miserable?"

"Because you can't have the highs without the lows. That's how love works."

"This isn't love," Augusta scoffed.

"I wouldn't be so sure about that. From everything my mother told me, you and Irving were in love once. Why can't you be in love again?"

"Because even though I was in love with *him*, Irving never felt the same about me. He liked me, sure, but at the end of the day, he chose someone else to be his wife. He loved Lois, not me."

"I'm not sure I believe that," said Jackie. "Just because he married *her* doesn't mean he didn't love *you*. Life gets complicated sometimes. Maybe there was a misunderstanding."

"I'm telling you, Jackie, I *know* he loved her." As she spoke, Augusta's lower lip trembled. "I did something back then—something I shouldn't have. *That's* how I know that Irving loved Lois." Augusta barely got out the last few words before her eyes began to tear.

"Tell me about it," Jackie said.

Augusta nodded. It was finally time to tell the truth.

FORTY

JUNE 1926

Augusta had a terrible feeling that Irving wasn't telling her the truth.

He'd been acting strange all that spring—bolting from the pharmacy when his shift ended, skipping invitations for Esther's dinners. When Augusta pressed him, he finally confessed that he'd gotten a second job. But when she asked where, he wouldn't say.

"It's only temporary," he told her. "It's nothing for you to worry about."

"When you say things like that, it makes me worried."

Augusta's sister was worried, too. Augusta was glad Bess was still working at the store—at least until the baby arrived. Bess placed one hand on her growing belly as she stood behind the makeup counter. "Irving won't tell George about his job, either," she said. "George thinks the whole thing sounds suspicious."

"Suspicious how?" Augusta said.

Bess frowned. "George was on his way to the library last week when he saw Irving outside Lois Diamond's house. Apparently, Lois opened the door and Irving went straight inside."

Augusta felt as if all the air had been sucked out of her lungs. Evie's birthday party had been almost two years ago, but Augusta was certain that Lois Diamond knew how to hold a grudge. *If I decide that he's worth meeting, I'll be sure to let you know.*

Was Irving dating Lois Diamond? There was only one way to find out.

When she confronted Irving that afternoon, he threw back his head and laughed. "That's the craziest thing I've ever heard!"

"Don't you *dare* call me crazy. You've been behaving oddly for *months*—skulking around, keeping secrets. What exactly am I supposed to believe?"

Irving took her by the hand and led her into the empty stock room. "I'll tell you," he said. "But you have to promise that you won't get upset."

"I'm already upset!"

"All right, all right. I understand, and I'm sorry. I've been doing some part-time work for Zip Diamond, that's all. Nothing risky—I promise."

Augusta's concern turned to fear, but she kept her voice low so her father wouldn't hear. "What the *hell* are you thinking?" she hissed. "You know what kind of man he is. He's a gangster, Irving! He's dangerous! You shouldn't be getting involved with him!"

"I had no choice, Goldie," Irving told her. "I need the extra cash. The fact is, working for Zip pays more than anything else I could think of. And I swear, he's been really decent to me. Mrs. Diamond says he likes having me around."

Irving seemed so sincere that it only made Augusta more confused. Irving sounded just like *she* had back when she'd tried to reassure her father that Esther treating Mitzi Diamond was the correct thing to do. Augusta had insisted that Mrs. Diamond meant no harm, that she posed no threat to any of them. And now here was Irving, saying the same. Her father had told her that she sounded foolish, that she was being naive. He'd maintained that the threat the Diamonds posed was not to be treated lightly. That any kind of association with them could lead to potential disaster.

But as she stared at the young man she loved, begging her to trust his decision, all that Augusta could do now was hope that her father had been wrong.

"I promise, it's just for a little while longer," said Irving. "Trust me, Goldie. Please, just trust me. I swear, I'm doing this for our future."

For the next few weeks, she felt more hopeful. Although Irving was still extremely busy, at least now he was being honest with her. He was more attentive, more communicative, and seemed to be back to his old self.

As further proof of his devotion, he'd planned a special date for the day after her high school graduation. "We have a lot to celebrate," he said. "And soon we'll have even more." His face lit up with a joyful glow. "I reserved a table at Arcadia Gardens—it's the fanciest place I could think of. I invited Evie and Nathaniel, too. I want everything to be special."

In the days leading up to the graduation, Augusta tried not to get her hopes up. Evie was sure that Irving was going to propose, but Augusta didn't want to make any assumptions. She told herself that there was absolutely no need to rush their future together. If Irving did not propose at Arcadia Gardens, it would happen soon enough. She loved Irving and he loved her—Augusta had no doubts about that.

Until suddenly she did.

The morning of her commencement dawned full of sunshine. The temperature was perfect, the breeze was gentle, and the skies were a cloudless cobalt blue. In an uncharacteristically affectionate moment, Esther kissed Augusta on the cheek while setting a plate of toast in front of her. "I am proud of you, Goldie," she said.

But later, Augusta didn't feel proud at all. After all the diplomas were handed out and the ceremony had come to a close, she scoured the crowded lawn in front of the school, searching for Irving. No sooner had she spotted him than she also spotted Mitzi Diamond making her way over to greet him. A moment later, Lois Diamond was giving Irving a peck on the cheek. Why was Lois kissing Irving? What was he doing talking to the Diamonds when he should be looking for her? And why was Zip Diamond nowhere in sight on the morning of his daughter's graduation?

A moment later, Bess was beside her, whispering a warning into Augusta's ear. "What is Irving doing with *them*?" Augusta's father was silent, but it was clear from the look on his face that he was wondering the same thing.

The encounter lasted only a moment. Soon Irving was in front of her, pressing an enormous bouquet of red and white roses into her arms. But no matter the flowers or his smile, Augusta could not surrender the vision of Irving with the Diamond family—Mitzi Diamond shaking Irving's hand and Lois Diamond with her lips on Irving's cleanly shaven cheek. *If I decide that he's worth meeting, I'll be sure to let you know.*

Bess pulled Augusta off to the side. "Lois keeps looking over at us— over at *Irving*, I mean. I don't like this, Augusta. You need to do something," Bess whispered.

"What am I supposed to do?"

"I don't know—but what if Irving is having doubts about the two of you? When I had doubts about George, Esther mixed up that powder for me." Bess tilted her head in Irving's direction and gave her sister a pointed stare. "Maybe Irving needs a push like the one Esther gave me."

There was no sleep for Augusta that night, no rest for her body or mind. Finally, sometime after midnight, she forced herself to make a decision.

She waited until Esther was asleep and crept into the dark kitchen alone, carrying her aunt's apothecary case. By the light of a few candles, she gathered the ingredients into a pile: fenugreek, mandrake, and sage. Rose hips and chamomile. She found the smallest drawer in the back of Esther's case and chose a single *raskovnik* clover just as the waxing moon outside emerged from behind a passing cloud. Next, Augusta closed her eyes and tried to summon the words she needed.

She thought back to what Esther had told her. *The words are not like the formulas in your books or the bottles on your father's shelves. You cannot memorize and repeat them. You must feel them in your bones.*

Would she be able to feel them now? Would she be able to succeed on her own? Augusta did not know the answer. The only thing she knew for sure was how much she loved Irving Rivkin and how much she wanted to be his wife. In her mind, she could see their wedding day. She could hear the crack of the glass beneath the heel of Irving's shoe, the clapping guests, and the cheers. Those imagined sounds formed a rhythm in her mind and then, from somewhere, a melody surfaced. As she ground the pestle against the brass bowl, she heard herself singing before her lips even parted.

> *To ease the pain of those who suffer*
> *To repair the bodies of those who are ill*
> *To restore the minds of those in need*

She sang for the years she would have with her husband, for the love she would shower on her children. She sang for every joyful day, for every warm and tender night. She sang for the brilliant future she wanted and for the life she hoped to make.

Over and over, Augusta sang the words, until the powder in the mortar was as lustrous and fine as the snow Irving had carried her through after Bess's wedding; the snow he had brushed so tenderly from her hair before kissing her for the very first time.

The next morning, she opened her eyes with a start. Last night's kitchen machinations already felt like a faraway dream. Augusta pushed her hand under her pillow and felt clumsily for the pouch she had hidden. It was waiting there, where she'd left it. Last night had been real after all.

She ate breakfast quickly, scouring the kitchen for any trace of what she had done. Had Esther heard the song Augusta had sung? Did she suspect what her niece was planning? Augusta did not linger long enough in the apartment to find out. As soon as she finished her coffee, she hurried down the steps to the store and put herself diligently to work.

All morning long, she made change for customers, dusted shelves, answered questions. She waited until her father left to get a sandwich at the deli next door before scurrying into the stock room for a pint bottle of his best whiskey. Augusta tucked the bottle into her purse and stored them both in the cabinet under the cash register, far away from curious eyes.

In the afternoon, she left the store early and went straight to her parents' bedroom. There, in the shallow bottom drawer of the bureau, she found a monogrammed silver flask. It was a gift her father had never used—a present from a wealthy cousin that he'd always claimed was too extravagant. He would never know it was gone.

She could hear Esther in the kitchen consulting with one of her most neurotic clients—one who would not be leaving anytime soon. Augusta shut the door to the bedroom, poured half the whiskey into the flask, and carefully sprinkled in the powder. Later she hid the half-empty bottle under her bed and tucked the flask into the purse she was planning on using that evening.

Once she had calmed her racing pulse, Augusta put on the pale pink dress she'd been saving for a special occasion. The dress was one of half a dozen that Harriet Dornbush had recently given Augusta after learning she was expecting again. "It was time to clean out my closet," said Harriet, happily patting her expanding middle.

Of all the dresses, Augusta liked the pink one the best. It was a dreamy, lacy, ruffled confection, complete with a drop waist and a wide satin sash. The color brought out the rosiness in her cheeks, the gold in her hair, and the hope in her heart. Never had she been more excited for her future; never had her mood been more buoyant.

Which was why it was so painful when everything she hoped for fell apart. Not only did Irving fail to propose that night, but he simply disappeared after Nathaniel got down on one knee. Augusta scoured every inch of Arcadia Gardens, but Irving was nowhere to be found. The next day, for the first time in years, he didn't show up for work. The rest of the week brought a slew of fresh horrors: Irving's refusal to see her, the news of his engagement to Lois, and his move to Chicago with her family. Then the final agonizing blow: Lois Diamond was pregnant.

Esther's response to her niece's confession only made Augusta feel worse. "I told you how powerful that recipe was. How powerful and how dangerous."

"You did," said Augusta, lowering her gaze. "But I made it anyway." She choked back the sob that rose in her throat.

"Did you tell Irving what it was for?"

A wave of shame washed over Augusta. When she shook her head, Esther's voice grew soft.

"I tried to warn you," Esther said, clucking her tongue against the back of her teeth.

"I'm sorry," said Augusta. "I wish I had listened. If I could take it back, I would."

Esther's expression was solemn. "I am sorry for you, Goldie. But some things cannot be undone."

FORTY-ONE

OCTOBER 1987

Augusta's hands trembled as she relayed the story. "I made Aunt Esther's elixir that night. The same one she gave to your mother to help her decide whether to marry your father."

"You thought it might make Irving want to propose?"

Augusta nodded. "It backfired terribly, of course." Her voice shrank to a whisper. "Or maybe the elixir did exactly what it was supposed to do. Maybe that's the real truth of what happened that evening. When Irving drank it, he realized that he loved Lois instead of me. Why else would he have left the restaurant so abruptly or proposed to Lois only days later?"

Jackie frowned. "Something about it doesn't make sense. From everything my mother told me, Irving was clearly in love with *you.*"

"Your mother wasn't exactly objective—she was my sister, after all. Bess loved me far too much to believe that Irving could choose anyone over me. But Esther knew the elixir was dangerous. I should have followed her advice more closely. I should have been more patient. If I hadn't been so reckless, maybe things would have turned out differently."

"But, Aunt Augusta, you had no way of knowing. My god, you were only eighteen years old!"

"And now I'm eighty and none the wiser." Augusta released a gloomy sigh. "History keeps repeating itself. I'm back in love with Irving Rivkin, and I still have no idea whether he feels the same."

Jackie flashed a mischievous smile. "What if the two of us try to find out? Why don't you finish your bagel? I'll be back in a minute."

The toasted bagel was hard and cold, so Augusta threw it in the trash. She was thinking about reheating her coffee in the microwave when Jackie returned carrying something so shocking that Augusta almost dropped her cup.

"Oh my god," Augusta murmured. "Is that what I think it is?"

Jackie nodded. "It barely fit into my carry-on," she said. "But there was no way I was going to check it. That's why I had to bring two suitcases." Jackie set Esther's wooden apothecary case on top of Augusta's kitchen counter.

Augusta forgot all about her breakfast. She forgot about the flowers and the cold coffee. "How long have you had this?"

"Mom gave it to me when she first got sick. She told me that Esther wanted you to have it, but after Esther died, you refused to take it. Mom couldn't bear to throw it away, so she kept it for you, all these years."

Augusta felt as if she'd traveled back in time. She was afraid to touch the polished wood, afraid that doing so would bring back all the anguish of that excruciating day. "Please," she said to Jackie. "I don't want it. Take it back home."

Jackie looked as if she'd been slapped. "I don't understand. I thought you'd be excited." Jackie unfastened the latch and swung open the doors of the case so that Augusta could see inside. "The bottles and tins are the same," she said. "But the herbs inside all of them are new. A friend of mine gave me the name of a homeopath in Chinatown. She went through the entire case and replaced every ingredient."

"I appreciate all the trouble you went to, but I can't keep this."

"Before you make up your mind—I have something else to show you," said Jackie. After a quick retreat to her bedroom, she returned with a compact bundle carefully wrapped in tissue paper.

Augusta didn't need to unwrap the paper to know what was inside. She had dreamt of the objects for decades—the brass mortar, scattered with faded letters that rose upward in a spiral to the edge. The sturdy pestle, worn smooth with use, which had fit so perfectly between her aunt's gnarled fingers. How many nights had Augusta watched Esther wield it, as if it were an extension of her own hand? When she pulled the paper off to reveal the set, they looked and felt just as she remembered.

"Come on, Aunt Augusta," Jackie pleaded. "You admit that you're in love with Irving. You want to know whether he's in love with you, too." Jackie gestured to the mortar and pestle. "Now you have the tools to find out."

FORTY-TWO

JUNE 1926

Irving hadn't been entirely honest when he told Augusta he was working for Zip Diamond. The truth was, *no one* worked for Zip anymore—not since his wife Mitzi had taken over. Zip Diamond's health was going downhill fast, and in the wake of his steady decline, now his wife was giving the orders.

Of course, no one was allowed to know. The number one rule of working for Mitzi was that Zip's illness was never to be revealed to anyone. That was why Mitzi hired Irving. He had no stake in the organization; he didn't know anyone in her business. Irving Rivkin was a complete outsider, and because he had no interest in rising up through the ranks, Mitzi knew he would never squeal about Zip to any of his competitors.

On the day Irving went to the Glenmore Avenue brownstone to ask for a part-time job, Lois Diamond brought him into their living room. This time Mrs. Diamond shook Irving's hand while Mr. Diamond stared at him blankly, as if he couldn't remember who Irving was. Instead of his usual suit and tie, Zip was wearing a cardigan sweater. Something about the man's changed appearance made Irving's heart sink.

"What can we do for you?" Mitzi asked brightly. When Irving

mentioned the possibility of part-time work, he was sure he could see the wheels in her head turning. "You know what, Irving?" she said. "You might just be the answer to all of my prayers."

After that, it became Irving's job to keep Zip company while Mitzi went out. Usually, their housekeeper stayed with Zip when no one from the family could be home, but even the loyal and long-suffering maid needed a few evenings off. That was when Irving could be of help.

Irving was incredulous. "You want to pay me to sit with him?"

"I need someone here to make sure that he doesn't get confused and leave the house. I can't have anyone he knows running into him on the street—Zip wouldn't want people to see him like this. His father had the same disease—it progresses quickly, Irving. In another year, he may not even remember the names of our children." Mrs. Diamond bit her lip, but she did not cry.

"In any event," she continued, "you're the perfect person to help. You don't know anyone who works for Zip. No one will try to get information from you."

"What would you like me to do with him?"

"Sit with him, chat, listen to the radio. Zip loves baseball, you know. You can always talk about that. Of course he'll need more help in the future. But he doesn't need any real nursing care yet. Your job will be to keep him occupied. If anyone comes to see him, tell them he's busy. The most important thing is that no one can know."

"I promise I won't tell a soul."

"Of course you won't," Mrs. Diamond said in a voice that bordered on menacing. "Because if you do, you'll be *very* sorry."

All that spring, several evenings per week, Irving reported to the house on Glenmore Avenue. Most of the time, he and Zip listened to the radio, talked about baseball, or played checkers. Sammy and Lois were usually out with friends and Mrs. Diamond was either on the telephone or taking meetings with "business associates" in other parts of Brooklyn.

After five months of working for the Diamonds, Irving had saved enough money to purchase an engagement ring for Augusta.

A week before Augusta's high school graduation, Irving knocked on the door of Solomon Stern's prescription room. It was too early for Augusta or Bess to be working. With the two of them gone, Irving was planning to ask for permission to propose. Instead of finding Mr. Stern alone, however, he found Mitzi Diamond sitting with him.

"I'm with a customer," said the druggist brusquely, pushing the door shut in Irving's face. Meanwhile, Irving lingered nearby to see what information he could overhear: Lois hadn't been feeling well lately. Dr. Birnbaum had prescribed some pills, but Mr. Stern was suggesting a different kind.

When he finally emerged from his consultation, Solomon Stern was in no mood for a private talk with Irving. "It'll have to wait," Mr. Stern said glumly.

An hour later, Mrs. Diamond returned, this time with Lois in tow. She deposited her daughter at the soda counter and demanded a banana split with whipped cream.

The Lois who sat at the counter that day was vastly changed from the haughty young woman Irving had been seeing at Zip's house for months. When Irving looked at Lois now, he saw that her once-rounded face had grown thin. She wore a loose, unflattering dress, and her arms looked like sticks poking out on the sides.

Lois took two bites of the ice cream and let the rest melt to a puddle in its dish. Her mother grew increasingly livid with every minute that passed. "You need to eat, Lois!" she barked. And then, moments later, "Please, darling. I thought chocolate ice cream was your favorite." But no matter what her mother said or did, Lois Diamond would not eat. It was clear that no matter how much influence Mrs. Diamond may have held over her husband, when it came to her daughter, her threats meant nothing. With Lois, it seemed that Mitzi Diamond had finally met her match.

The next day, Mrs. Diamond and Lois returned. This time Lois was wearing a fashionable summer dress—loose and drop-waisted, with a yellow sash. Aside from her too-thin cheeks and arms, she looked healthy enough to Irving.

As Lois browsed lipsticks at the makeup counter, Mrs. Diamond caught Irving's attention. "I need a few minutes to speak with Sol," she said. "But I want my daughter to see Esther, upstairs. Will you show her where to go? I'll be along in a few minutes."

"Of course, Mrs. Diamond."

Irving welcomed the break, especially since he was gathering his courage to speak to Solomon Stern about Goldie again. A combination of nerves and bad timing had delayed this endeavor for too long, so that what should have been a straightforward conversation now seemed to require tremendous effort. Stepping out to show Lois the way upstairs gave Irving a much-appreciated excuse to delay speaking to the pharmacist.

Irving led Lois around the side of the building. He tried to engage her in polite conversation, but she pursed her lips and refused to answer. When Esther ushered them inside, the apartment smelled of apples and cinnamon, as if she had spent the morning baking.

"This is Lois Diamond," said Irving. "Her mother will be up in a few minutes."

Esther nodded as if she'd been expecting them. "Come into the kitchen, Lois," she said. "My apple cake just came out of the oven." And then, to Irving, she added, "Augusta will be home any minute. You can wait for her in the living room if you like."

Though Irving left Esther and Lois alone, the walls in the apartment were so thin that their voices cut through them as if they were paper. As a result, Irving found himself listening to a conversation he did not want to hear.

"Your mother told me you would come," said Esther. "She is worried because you refuse to eat."

Lois did not sound moved by Esther's explanation of her mother's concerns. "I haven't been hungry," she snapped.

"Then why do you stare at my apple cake as if you would give your eye for a slice?"

"I was just looking at it, that's all. It's not a crime to look, is it?"

"No," said Esther. "To look is no crime. But I would be happy to cut a piece for you."

"I already told you, I'm not hungry!"

Esther's voice grew low and soft. "Starving yourself will not change your dilemma. Babies are resilient, even in the womb."

What is Esther talking about?

"I take it you've told no one, then?" Esther continued. "Not even the baby's father?"

Before Irving could grasp the meaning of what he'd heard, Mitzi Diamond breezed straight through the unlocked door of the apartment. She'd been there so many times to see Esther that she hadn't even bothered to knock. Irving jumped up from his seat and murmured a hasty goodbye. He did not want to be around when Mrs. Diamond learned of her daughter's condition.

The pregnancy of Lois Diamond was a dangerous piece of information—even more dangerous, perhaps, than Zip's debilitating illness. A prickle of worry nagged at Irving now, a gloomy feeling that this new knowledge was going to result in terrible trouble.

As he bolted out of the building, he almost slammed into Augusta, who was making her way down the sidewalk. Normally, he would have been thrilled to see her—he'd been waiting for her, after all. But now all he could think about was the Diamond family's secrets. He told himself that keeping those secrets from Augusta was the only way to keep her safe.

Decades later, he would wonder whether those first secrets were the beginning of the end.

FORTY-THREE

OCTOBER 1987

Augusta stared at the mortar and pestle in her hands.

The brass smelled faintly of all it had absorbed—every herb and leaf, every stick and root, every entreaty and supplication. How many powders and potions had Esther and her ancestors concocted with these instruments? How many illnesses had been squelched, how many men and women aided by the teas and tinctures these tools had wrought?

And yet, Augusta knew all too well that the tools were not a guarantee of success. That much had been proven on the night Irving abandoned her and cut her out of his life forever. It had not mattered that Augusta had followed the recipe exactly as Esther had once demonstrated, nor that she had spoken the words with all the faith and certainty she could muster. It had not mattered that she had worked her fingers to numbness, pressing the ingredients into a powder so fine and shimmering that its potency had filled the kitchen like a promise. None of it had mattered in the slightest.

"You don't understand," Augusta said. "Just because I have Esther's tools, it doesn't mean I can re-create her elixir."

"Why not?" asked Jackie. "You have the ingredients. Don't you at least want to *try*?"

"Sweetheart, I appreciate everything you've done—refurbishing the case, hauling everything down here. But this isn't some kind of geriatric fairy tale where everything gets magically fixed in the end. Trust me, it isn't going to work."

"How can you be so sure?" Jackie's question was thick with disappointment; her eyes were cloudy with frustration.

"When Irving first left me, I was desperate for answers—desperate for some kind of explanation as to why the potion had failed. At first I blamed the recipe—Esther had warned me of its dangers. After that, I blamed myself. I was greedy, impatient, self-centered. Then I began to wonder whether I had broken some kind of unspoken rule. By making a potion for my own benefit, had I violated the mortar's purpose? Of course I never learned the answer. And, like I told you before, maybe the answer simply was that Irving loved Lois more than me."

"You weren't greedy," Jackie insisted. "You were confused and in love, that's all. I know you were heartbroken when the potion didn't work in the way you wanted it to. But that doesn't mean you can't try again. Not to point out the obvious, but you're older now, and Irving is, too. You're both different people. You both have wisdom and experience that you didn't have before." Jackie gestured to the mortar and pestle that her aunt was still holding. "I really think you owe it to yourself to see what happens."

"I can't," said Augusta, her voice soft and trembling. She set the heirlooms down on the counter and took a careful step backward—as if standing too close to Esther's tools was causing her physical pain.

"Aunt Augusta, is there something you haven't told me? Why do you look so upset?"

Augusta released a heavy breath. A terrible ache settled deep in the center of her chest. She wrapped her arms around herself in an effort to get warm. Then she pointed a shaky finger at the ancient brass objects. "Because the last time I used those—the *very last* time—it wasn't to make the powder for Irving. The very last time, what happened was worse— much, much worse than a lost romance. The very last time I used that mortar, it was a matter of life and death."

"What happened?" Jackie whispered.

Augusta lowered her gaze. "I tried to make Esther well," she said. "I was convinced that I could help her. I thought that I knew everything, Jackie. But I didn't. And I failed."

FORTY-FOUR

SEPTEMBER 1926

For the first two weeks after Irving left for Chicago, Augusta spent most of her time in bed with her face turned toward the wall. She barely moved when Esther came into the room to leave her plates of toast and tea. It was Bess who finally forced her outside, Bess who made her put on a bathing suit and dragged her to the swimming pool at Betsy Head Park. In the water, Augusta was able to shut out the questions that ran on a constant loop in her head. How could Irving have done this to her? Who was the man she thought she knew? Had he ever truly loved her, or had he only been playing a part? She began going to the pool every day, swimming laps with a feral intensity. By the end of the summer, her arms were so strong that she was able to lift the heaviest boxes onto the highest shelves of her father's stock room.

In September, Augusta began taking classes for her degree at the Fordham College of Pharmacy. On Mondays, Wednesdays, and Fridays, she traveled via the elevated train to the corner of Bathgate Avenue and East Fordham Road in the Bronx. Tuesdays and Thursdays were for "Practical Pharmacy," which meant she earned credit working at her father's store. The deluge of homework, papers, and exams filled the space where her hopes for a life with Irving had been. For the next few months, she was so tired that although she and Esther still shared a bedroom, she fell asleep without hearing Esther's cough.

Her great-aunt's sickness began with a winter flu. Initially, Esther recovered, but even after the cough disappeared, the color did not return to her cheeks. Dr. Birnbaum was consulted, and various stimulants were prescribed. Esther accepted the doctor's medicine graciously, but it never seemed to do much good. Augusta's father made a tonic, but the liquid only gave Esther a headache. By December, Esther stopped seeing clients.

That was when Augusta started making soup.

Once a week, she visited the butcher to choose the chickens for the broth. In between reading her books, she chopped mountains of carrots, onions, and celery. When she asked Esther what else to add, Esther shrugged her bony shoulders. "Add whatever feels right," she said. "Parsley today, garlic next week. I never made mine the same way twice."

In the evenings, after they were both in bed, Augusta would tell Esther about school. One evening she described her botany class. "You would love it," she said. "The Botanical Garden is right next to campus, and our professor likes to take us for visits. Physiology is definitely the most difficult—we're learning all about digestion and the way our bodies absorb different medicines."

"Are there many other women?" Esther wanted to know.

"Five of us in my grade. Two hundred men and five women."

"At least you aren't alone," said Esther. "It's good to have other female colleagues."

"Were there any other women in your village who did the same work as you?"

"No," said Esther. "Only one man. We did the same work, we healed the same illnesses, but they called him the apothecary and they called me the witch." Her voice grew melancholy as she continued. "He was the man I fell in love with, the one I made the elixir for. I didn't tell him what it was—I was young and impatient."

Augusta sat up against her pillow. This was the story she'd been waiting to hear. This was the lesson Esther wanted her to learn. "What happened after he drank it?"

"He told me that he loved me deeply, but he didn't want to marry me. He was adamant that he would never marry a woman with a talent that rivaled his own. I told him about the elixir then, and he was furious that I had given it to him without asking. He refused to speak to me ever again."

"Oh, Aunt Esther, I'm so sorry." Augusta pulled the blankets up to her chin, her heart aching from the tragic implications of her great-aunt's revelation. After a long silence, she forced herself to ask the question that had been haunting her ever since Irving left Brooklyn. "Do you think women like us can ever have both? Can we have our work *and* have love? Or will we always have to choose?"

Esther's voice grew tired and faraway. "I do not know the answer," she said. "I can only hope that this new world is kinder to women like us than the old one."

As the weeks wore on, Esther's health grew worse. Her ninety-two-year-old heart was failing, and Dr. Birnbaum insisted there was nothing he could do. Meanwhile, Augusta, refusing to give up, consulted her books, looking for remedies. She described her great-aunt's symptoms to her professors. She searched the school library for answers. Esther tried to tell her the truth—that Dr. Birnbaum was right.

"Goldie, please. There is no medicine on this earth that will be able to fix my heart."

"You can't give up yet, Aunt Esther! Remember what Dr. Birnbaum said about Irving? Or what the doctors said about Mrs. Dornbush?"

Esther forced her lips into a smile. "This time the doctors are correct."

"No," said Augusta, her composure unraveling. "I don't believe that. Let me try—tell me what herbs I should use. There must be a recipe I don't know yet. Tell me the ingredients for a new powder. Let me try to make it for you."

"Goldie, do you remember what I told you when you asked whether I could have healed your mother? Sometimes, no matter what we do, a person's time on this earth must end. I have lived for ninety-two years, and that will have to be enough for me."

"But it isn't enough for *me*," said Augusta, trying to hold back her tears.

That night, after Esther was asleep, Augusta carried the apothecary case into the darkened kitchen. She lit the candles, she summoned the moonlight, she pulled every heart-healing herb she could think of from Esther's bottles and tiny vials: hawthorn berries, turmeric, juniper, red sage root, hibiscus. As she ground the ingredients in Esther's mortar, she sang the now-familiar words.

To ease the pain of those who suffer
To repair the bodies of those who are ill
To restore the minds of those in need

The scents grew stronger, swirling around her like a benevolent tornado. Augusta shut her eyes to sing. To pray. To plead. To beg of the moonlight. But when she opened her eyes, the scents fell flat, the candles sputtered, and the room turned cold.

She emptied the contents of the mortar onto a square of Esther's muslin. The powder was wholly unremarkable, but she saved it anyway.

The next day, before Augusta served Esther her soup, she sprinkled the powder into the broth. Esther ate the entire bowl, but the soup seemed to have no healing effect. As the afternoon wore on, Esther grew increasingly weak. "I've taught you well, Goldie," she whispered. "When I am gone, you will take my case. You will take my mortar, my pestle, my robe. You will learn everything you can at school and be the best of both your father and me."

Augusta gripped her great-aunt's hands, as if trying to pull her back into this world. "Please, Aunt Esther, please don't leave. Let me try again with another recipe. I'll do a better job tonight. I'll bring you a fresh bowl of soup tomorrow."

Aunt Esther's smile was full of love, but the old woman was resigned.

"You have brought me more comfort than you can imagine, more than an old woman deserves. But there is no magic any of us have that can make someone live forever."

The condolence card from Chicago came only one week after Esther's funeral. Augusta wondered how Irving heard the news so quickly, but she supposed that his in-laws still had contacts in town. The stationery was gilt-edged and gaudy—selected by Lois, without a doubt. *Mr. and Mrs. Irving Rivkin* was engraved in gold lettering at the top. Augusta felt sick from the sight of it—when she traced the gold letters, her fingers burned.

Dear Augusta, it said. *I am so sorry for your loss. Yours truly, Irving Rivkin.*

The words were so simple but so burdened with meaning that Augusta wanted to scream. Which loss was he referring to? She had lost him—the love of her life. She had lost the life that was supposed to be hers. She had lost her greatest mentor and champion. Since Esther had first come into their lives, Augusta had aspired to be the best of both her father and her aunt: to pair Solomon's wisdom with Esther's insight so that she might treat every customer in the most holistic and thorough fashion. But now her confidence had waned.

By the time Augusta received Irving's note, she was no longer the golden girl he remembered. When she'd first met him, she had barely wanted to look up from her books. But when she did, Irving had seen her. He'd seen her intelligence and her ambition. He'd recognized the light that glowed inside her. It was no wonder that Irving had liked her nickname. But she could not be Goldie anymore. She'd lost her belief that she was worthy of Aunt Esther's teachings. She'd lost her faith in the last scraps of magic that might be left in their dreary world.

As she tore Irving's note into bits, Augusta made a silent vow. She might have failed to heal Esther, but she would not fail another patient again. She would study and earn the highest marks in her classes. She would learn as much as she could to make her great-aunt and her father proud.

She would never eat another bowl of chicken soup again.

FORTY-FIVE

OCTOBER 1987

Jackie made her aunt a fresh cup of coffee and insisted she sit down to drink it.

"Aunt Augusta, you must know by now that Esther's death wasn't your fault. My mother told me how sick she was. She was ninety-two years old, with congestive heart failure. There was nothing anyone could do."

"Thank you, sweetheart," Augusta said. "Part of me knows that now, of course, but sometimes it's still hard for me to believe." She took a few sips from her mug until the ache in her chest faded and she was ready to talk. "When Irving left, I was devastated. But when Esther died . . . I felt as if all the magic in my life died with her. I felt like I wasn't worthy of her tools—the apothecary case, the mortar, the pestle. I felt like they weren't meant for me. That was why I couldn't accept them. I didn't realize that your mother had saved them for all these years."

"Aren't you even the least bit tempted to use them? Aren't you curious about what might happen?"

"Why would I want to take that risk? Remember, the last time I made that elixir, the man I loved married someone else."

But Jackie would not be discouraged. "As I see it, the worst has already happened. What more is left for there to go wrong? You and Irving stay apart for sixty *more* years? You've already been burned, Aunt Augusta. This time, you don't have anything to lose."

"I don't know," Augusta objected. But even as she protested, she was also curious. "Is that why you made the soup today? To try to convince me?"

"I thought it might put you in the right frame of mind," Jackie said. "You know, bring you back to Esther's kitchen in Brooklyn."

Augusta looked back at the mortar and pestle. This time, her expression softened. "The last time I used those, I wasn't honest with Irving. I didn't tell him what I put in the flask. If I do this again, it would have to be different. This time, I would have to tell him everything."

Jackie grinned. "Does that mean we can get started?"

For the rest of the morning, they were busy preparing. Augusta sent Jackie back to the store for candles and a package of egg noodles. In the meantime, she cut up an old cloth napkin to make something resembling Esther's muslin squares. When Shirley stopped by with some cherry Danish, Augusta took the string from the bakery box, cut a piece, and put it aside.

Once Jackie was back, Augusta added carrots and parsley to the pot. When something about the soup still didn't seem right, she added dried rosemary from Esther's apothecary case. Ten minutes later, her apartment smelled exactly like Esther's kitchen. At last, Augusta turned down the flame on the soup pot and smiled.

She had neither the time nor the skill to make Esther's famous kreplach, but she added egg noodles to the pot and let them simmer in the broth. By the time the soup was finished, her mouth was watering.

The taste was everything she remembered—rich and salty and full of flavor. One spoonful, and she was back in Brooklyn, listening to the sounds of the crowded avenue wafting in through their open windows: children playing stickball, men selling peanuts, babies crying for their mothers. She could see her father reading his morning paper across from her at the breakfast table; she could smell Bess's lavender perfume. She could hear Esther humming as she worked.

For a moment, Augusta could remember what it felt like to believe—not in the magic of witches or fairies, but in the magic of women who knew how to heal; the magic of women in the quiet of their kitchens, who could sweeten a bitter woman's heart or soothe a man's temper with a cup of tea. The ones who knew how to bring down a fever, assuage a toothache, or quiet a child with nothing more than a spoonful of honey, a gentle hand, and a few whispered words.

After they'd eaten, Augusta was resigned. She did not know whether she would remember Esther's recipe or whether the proper melody would find its way to her lips. She did not know how she would explain the strange elixir or its purpose to Irving. Even if she did manage to explain it, she did not know whether he would agree to drink it. She had no way of knowing whether her eightieth birthday would mark a joyful and fresh beginning or whether the sorrows of her past would be repeated a second time.

There was only one way to find out.

Esther had always worked after midnight in order to avoid attracting the attention of Augusta's father. But Augusta's work would now be done in the broadest light of day.

She drew her curtains shut against the sunshine, but light escaped around the edges, filling the apartment with an uneven glow. Though the candles weren't necessary, she lit them for old times' sake. The smell of soup lingered in the air; the atmosphere was almost dreamlike. Augusta's eighty-year-old bones felt as if they were eighteen again.

From inside the apothecary case, Augusta chose her ingredients and formed a small pile of what she required. She whispered the names the way Esther had done. Fenugreek seeds, mandrake root, sage leaves, dried rose hips, and chamomile. From the depths of the case, Augusta searched for the final ingredient—the tiny *raskovnik* that Esther had showed her all those years ago.

What was it that Esther had said of the plant? *They say the leaves can unlock emotions.* Augusta turned the case around and opened the fitted back panel. Her finger found a tiny groove in the wood revealing an almost invisible drawer. Inside was a tiny stoppered bottle with a single green clover preserved inside. She did not know whether it had been left by her aunt or replaced by the diligent homeopath, but she supposed it did not matter.

As she ground the ingredients in the mortar, her thoughts turned to a long-buried memory—a day on Coney Island, after her mother took ill—the one time her father had joined them at the beach. In her mind, Augusta heard her mother's laugh as the water lapped at her feet. Augusta focused on those two sounds—the laughter in the air and the waves on the sand. A tune came to her then from a place beyond words, from a place filled with all the love she had lost.

> To ease the pain of those who suffer
> To repair the bodies of those who are ill
> To restore the minds of those in need

Augusta sang for all the years she had wasted, for all the love she had wanted to give. She sang for the past and for the present, for all the mistakes she had made.

When she was done, Augusta knew the powder was perfect. She knew it would do what she had asked. Irving's answer, of course, would depend on him—it was something she could not control. But as she tied up the pouch with the bakery string, she decided that, for the first time in years, she felt as if there might just be a bit of magic left in the world.

A few hours later, Augusta put on her new dress and a pair of heels she hadn't worn since New York. After she applied her makeup, the only thing left to deal with was her purse—a silver clutch that she filled with everything she needed for the evening: Altoids, aspirin, lipstick, keys. And of course the small fabric pouch tied with cotton string . . .

They were a few minutes early pulling into Shirley's driveway, but Shirley was already waiting outside. The sky was a mélange of blues, pinks, and a ripe, vibrant orange. *Soon,* Augusta thought, *the sun will set, and my birthday will be over.* She wondered whether she would be brave enough to carry out the task she had set for herself.

"Augusta!" Shirley practically shouted. "You look absolutely stunning!" Before she slid into the car's back seat, Shirley opened the passenger-side door to get a better look at Augusta's dress. "Jackie, you can shop for me anytime."

"I don't think you need my help. That's a great dress you've got on."

"I picked this one up when I took Augusta shopping. I brought it into the dressing room for *her,* but she insisted that the neckline was too low."

Augusta tried not to roll her eyes. "Not all of us are blessed with your confidence, Shirley."

"Or my décolletage."

As Jackie drove, Augusta told Shirley about the bouquet of flowers from Irving and Nathaniel. "They called a truce," Augusta said. "Can you believe it?"

"Oh, I believe it all right. Irving was having a conniption over what to get you for your birthday. I told him that the best gift would be to call off his war with Nathaniel. Thank goodness I finally convinced him."

"Did you convince Nathaniel, too?" asked Jackie.

"I'm sure Nathaniel didn't need convincing." Shirley's voice grew wistful. "Though it sure would have been fun to try."

Augusta sat up straighter in her seat. "Shirley! Do you have feelings for Nathaniel? I thought there might be something going on! Why didn't you say anything before?"

"I wanted to," said Shirley, "but I was too nervous. When you first moved here, I thought for sure that Nathaniel had his eye on *you.* I didn't want to interfere. But now that you and Irving are together—"

"We're *not* together," Augusta clarified.

"Not *yet,*" Jackie added.

"So much intrigue," Shirley chuckled. "See, Jackie? I told you Augusta spices up this place. Anyway, now that Irving and Nathaniel are friends, we can all have a nice, peaceful evening. Augusta can celebrate her birthday dinner without any unnecessary drama."

Augusta thought about the pouch of powder in her purse. "We'll have to see about that," she said.

❖

FORTY-SIX

OCTOBER 1927

Augusta spent her twentieth birthday taking a toxicology exam. Bess and George came for dinner with the baby, but the roast Augusta made was barely edible, and the cake Bess had baked wasn't much better. In the year since Esther passed away, Augusta and her father had gone back to sandwiches for most of their meals. Dinners had become forgettable again, and the layer of dust on the mantel grew thicker every day. Gone were the days of Esther's brisket, Esther's kugels, Esther's apple cake. Augusta missed the kugels and cakes, but she did not miss the chicken soup—she did not even miss Esther's famous kreplach.

At the end of dinner, Solomon Stern presented Augusta with a gift—a white cotton coat similar to his own. "I thought you might wear it at the store," he said. "I know you have two more years until you graduate, but I think it will make you look more official." The next day, he welcomed her back to his prescription room. "There's a lot here to keep you busy," he said. "The work will help you the way it's always helped me."

After that, he let her listen in on all his consultations. If a customer objected, he explained that Augusta was getting college credit for the time she spent working at the store.

Most of the customers were accepting, but a few of them were less than kind. One day, after she stepped out of the prescription room with a box of pills she'd compounded, the customer who'd ordered them—Murray Fishman—told Augusta's father to make them again.

"I assure you that your prescription was simple enough for any pharmacy student to make," said Mr. Stern.

"It's not because she's a student," said Murray. "I won't trust any girl with my medication. Women are supposed to be wives and mothers. They aren't supposed to be pharmacists!"

Solomon Stern's face turned red with anger. "Listen here, Murray, you can't talk that way. Not in my store, at least."

"What do you mean, I can't talk that way? Girls shouldn't be messing around with people's health! Augusta may be your daughter, Sol, but you can't honestly tell me she can do the job as well as a man."

"Not only can she do the job as well as any man, I guarantee you she can do it *better*. Augusta's not even done with school, and she already knows as much as I do. If you don't like her making up your pills, you can damn well get them somewhere else!"

Murray Fishman left his box of pills on the counter. They could hear him grumbling as he left the store. "I've been coming here for twenty-five years, but never again—do you hear me, Sol?"

Once Mr. Fishman was finally gone, Augusta's father tried to reassure her. "Don't pay attention to him, understand? Murray Fishman is a buffoon. You're going to be a terrific pharmacist. You love the work, and that's all that matters."

Augusta tried to put the incident out of her mind, but it wasn't easy to forget. She was grateful that her father had stood up for her, but she wasn't sure she agreed with him. Was loving her work *really* all that mattered? What about loving another person? Murray Fishman's rant made her think of the story her aunt Esther had told her about the man she'd been in love with. *He told me that he loved me deeply, but he didn't want to marry me. He was adamant that he would never marry a woman with a talent that rivaled his own.*

Was *that* why Irving hadn't wanted to marry her? Because she'd wanted a career? She'd always thought Irving was so supportive of her ambition, so admiring of the work she wanted to do. But what if she had been wrong? What if all men were like Murray Fishman or Aunt Esther's village rival? What if romantic love was as elusive and as far-off as the medicine that might have saved her mother?

What if Augusta didn't find it until it was too late?

FORTY-SEVEN

OCTOBER 1987

La Vieille Maison on East Palmetto Park Road offered fine French dining in a fanciful setting. The restaurant was a southern Florida institution—an eclectic 1920s Mediterranean mansion complete with soothing fountains, charming gardens, and a mix of interior and exterior dining spaces filled with hand-painted tiles, wrought-iron stairways, and whimsical country French decor. The wine list was extensive, and the service—from the accommodating valet to the charismatic maître d' to the army of tuxedoed career waiters—was flawless. Augusta had heard that the food was fantastic.

"You didn't need to go to all this trouble," she said as they followed the waiter up the stairs to a private room with one round table perfectly set for their party of five. Augusta lost count of all the cutlery—fish knives and soup spoons and forks of all kinds. There were more plates than any one person needed and glasses for every conceivable beverage. The heady scent of lavender and roses filled the intimate space.

"Of course I did," Jackie said. "You don't turn eighty every day. Now, where do you want everyone to sit?"

Augusta chose a seat facing the door and pointed to the chair on her left. "You sit beside me on this side, Jackie. Shirley, you take the seat on my right." Each of the women placed their purses on the floor beside their chairs. They were looking over the menu when they heard Irving's voice from out in the hallway.

"You weren't kidding about this place, Nate. Thank god I wore my good suit."

A moment later, one of the waiters led the two men into the room, where each of them wished Augusta a happy birthday. "Time for introductions," she said. She pointed to the taller man first, who stepped forward to shake Jackie's hand. "Jackie, this is Nathaniel Birnbaum."

"I'm sure your aunt has told you," he said, "but I was lucky enough to know both of your parents. They were wonderful people."

"What a lovely thing to say. Thank you." Jackie turned to the shorter, squatter man. "And you must be Irving."

"Guilty as charged. I was your grandfather's delivery boy. What a stand-up guy he was. And your mother, Bess—she was a sweetheart. A terrific saleswoman, too. She used to stand behind the cosmetics counter and give all the neighborhood women advice—tell them which color lipsticks looked best and which perfume their boyfriends would like. There wasn't a girl on our block over the age of fifteen who didn't buy makeup from your mother." Irving shook his head and sighed. "Jeez, what I wouldn't give to be with her and George tonight."

Augusta could see Jackie's eyes tearing up. "I'm sure they would have loved being with everyone." She blinked a few times. "Now then," she said, "shall we take our seats? Irving, you sit next to me, and Nathaniel— you're between Irving and Shirley. Oh, good, they're bringing in the champagne."

Before Augusta had the chance to protest, a bottle of Perrier-Jouët was popped and Jackie was raising her glass. "Aunt Augusta, I'm so happy to be here tonight to celebrate with you and your friends. You are the strongest, most brilliant, and most remarkable woman I know. Happy eightieth birthday!"

"Hear, hear," said Nathaniel.

"Happy birthday, darling," said Shirley.

"You forgot the most beautiful," Irving said, raising his glass in Augusta's direction.

"You're all very sweet," said Augusta, blushing slightly. "But there will be no more birthday talk until I've had a chance to look at the menu. I've barely eaten anything all day and I'm starving."

"You should have had more of my soup," teased Jackie. She turned to Nathaniel and Irving. "I made chicken soup this morning—a family recipe from the old days in Brooklyn. Do either of you remember Augusta's great-aunt Esther?"

"Who could forget her?" said Irving. "Everyone in the neighborhood knew Esther. And everyone loved her chicken soup. I was just talking to Gold—to *Augusta* about it a few weeks ago. Esther used to make homemade kreplach—you never tasted anything so delicious in your life." He lowered his voice to a mock whisper as the waiter returned to take their orders. "Don't tell the chef, but I doubt he could make anything as good as Esther's soup."

Shirley laughed. "I don't see kreplach on this menu."

"They do have consommé," said Augusta. She turned her attention to the waiter. "I'd like the Bibb lettuce salad and the sole for my main course." When it was Nathaniel's turn, he asked for the pâté en croûte and the suprême de volaille.

"Listen to this guy," Irving said, clearly impressed with Nathaniel's accent. "What did you order anyway?"

"Chopped liver and chicken."

"Perfect!" said Irving. "I'll have the same."

"They're keeping champagne on ice for us," said Jackie. "But if you want wine or a cocktail, please order whatever you'd like."

Augusta asked for a vodka martini, and both men ordered a glass of Scotch. After the drinks arrived, Jackie excused herself to go to the ladies' room. "Aunt Augusta, why don't you come with me? We can touch up our lipstick."

Once they were out of earshot, Jackie wanted an update on the plan.

"Should I distract him? Spill something, maybe? And then you can put the powder in his Scotch?"

"Absolutely not!" said Augusta. "I told you, I have to be honest with him. I'm going to stand up and say a few words and then I'll tell him how I feel. But I need more time to sort it out."

"Don't take too long," Jackie warned.

While Augusta waited for Jackie, she sat down at the vanity table and glanced at herself in a gilt-edged mirror that took up most of the powder-room wall. There she was again—the girl in the glass: the girl who believed that a bowl of chicken soup was enough, perhaps, to save a boy's life; the girl who believed that a pair of worn-out shoes could help a melancholy woman become pregnant; the girl who believed that the powder in her purse might be able to help her finally learn whether the man she had loved for over six decades felt the same way about her.

Augusta opened her clutch and stared at the white cloth pouch. What could she possibly say to Irving that wouldn't make her sound like she'd lost her mind? Could she confess her feelings for him in front of Shirley and Nathaniel? How could she explain Aunt Esther's recipe and what she believed it could accomplish? How much would she have to say if she hoped to make him understand?

After they finished their appetizers, Jackie kicked Augusta gently under the table. She tilted her head toward Irving's half-empty glass and raised her eyebrows conspiratorially. Augusta gave her head a tiny shake and went back to buttering her bread. When the waiters returned with their entrées, Jackie asked them to bring the men more Scotch.

"I really shouldn't," Nathaniel said, but Jackie insisted. "If you don't feel well enough to drive home later," she said, "you can ride with us in Augusta's car." She kicked Augusta under the table again, this time with a little too much force.

"Ow!" said Augusta, wincing slightly.

"What's wrong?" said Irving. "Are you all right?"

"My shoe is pinching," Augusta lied.

Jackie bent over and poked her head beneath the tablecloth. "Let me take a look," she said. "Is the strap sticking into your ankle?"

Augusta bent her head down, too, so they were both out of sight of the other guests. "Knock it off with all the kicking," she whispered. "I'm getting black and blue already."

"You need to *do* something," Jackie whispered back. "Are you going to use the powder or not?"

"I don't know yet, Jackie," Augusta hissed. "First I need to know how clear Irving is about his feelings."

"The man is eighty-two years old! He isn't *clear* about anything!"

Augusta felt Shirley patting her on the shoulder. "Is everything all right down there? What are you two whispering about?"

"Did you drop your fork?" Irving asked. "I've got an extra if you need it."

"No, no," said Augusta. "Jackie is just fixing the strap on my shoe." To Jackie, she whispered, "I've been waiting sixty-two years for answers. *You* can wait until I finish my entrée."

"Fine. If you need me, give me a signal."

"What is this? *Mission Impossible?*"

When Jackie and Augusta emerged from under the table, Shirley was raving about her lobster medallions.

"Evie loved lobster," Nathaniel said. "That was part of why she always wanted to get a house in Maine. Funny, but I haven't been able to touch the stuff since she passed twelve years ago."

"My Bernie loved hot dogs," said Shirley. "But only the ones you get on the street, from the carts, in New York. I'm not such a fan of them myself, but whenever I visit my kids in the city, I always have one, in Bernie's honor." She scooped a piece of lobster up from her plate and held her fork out to Nathaniel. "Go ahead," she said. "I'm sure Evie would have wanted you to enjoy it."

Augusta watched Nathaniel lean forward and take the bite that Shirley offered. He closed his eyes as he chewed, and when he opened them again, he was smiling. "If Evie were here, she would have ordered that, too. Thank you, Shirley. That was very kind."

Augusta was happy to see Shirley and Nathaniel getting along so nicely, but the intimacy of their encounter seemed misplaced at a dinner that was supposed to be a celebration for her. The memory of that night at Arcadia Gardens came back in an excruciating rush: Nathaniel leading Evie onto the dance floor, the look on his face when he sank to one knee, the way the crowd erupted in applause—all the moments she imagined were going to belong to her and Irving.

She didn't want that to happen again. She didn't know if she could bear it.

Filled suddenly with fresh resolve, Augusta stood up to begin her speech. She felt her arms and legs grow taut as she tapped her spoon against her untouched glass of water. Her hand was shaking so fiercely, however, that instead of a single gentle tap, the force of her spoon against the glass propelled it across the cloth-covered table, where it bounced off Irving's ample stomach and landed directly in his lap.

"Oh no!" she said. "Irving, are you all right?"

The shock of being struck in the gut with a full glass of water rendered Irving temporarily mute. He put the empty glass on the table, looked down at his soaking wet shirt and trousers, and began to shake with laughter.

Soon everyone else was laughing too. Nathaniel and Jackie pushed their napkins toward him to mop up some of the liquid. Augusta ran out of the room to summon some waiters to tidy up, and Irving excused himself to go to the men's room. "I'm going to see if there's a hand dryer in there. I'll only be a couple of minutes."

"I'll come, too," said Nathaniel, and Shirley rose from her seat as well. "It's as good a time as any for a trip to the ladies' room. Jackie, do you want to come?"

"No," said Jackie. "I'll stay here. Someone has to hold down the fort."

FORTY-EIGHT

JUNE 1926

Solomon Stern looked concerned. "Irving, I need you to hold down the fort. Augusta has the day off to study for finals and Bess's doctor wants her to take it easy until the baby comes. It's just you and me in the store today and I have a customer coming at four. I need to speak with her privately when she arrives. I'll meet with her in the prescription room, but I'll need you to handle the register."

"Of course, Mr. Stern. No problem," said Irving. Though Mr. Stern did not name the customer, Irving was all but certain the meeting was with Mitzi Diamond. She'd been at the store two days in a row—at first to discuss Lois's appetite, and now, Irving assumed, the pregnancy. At four on the dot, Mrs. Diamond appeared, dressed more for dancing or dinner out than for visiting a drugstore. This time, Lois was nowhere in sight—in her place was a mountainous man named Hank whom Irving recognized from the Diamonds' home. Lately, Hank had been accompanying Mrs. Diamond on most of her "business" errands. Irving did not think his presence at the pharmacy was a particularly good sign. What kind of business could Mrs. Diamond possibly have with Mr. Stern?

Luckily, there was a lull in customers, which allowed Irving to position himself near the door of the prescription room. Irving couldn't make out every word that was said, but he heard more than enough.

Mrs. Diamond began the conversation. "You heard about the fire, I assume? At Finkel's Drugstore in Williamsburg?"

Irving heard Mr. Stern gasp in alarm. "No! When did it happen? Was anyone hurt?"

"It happened last night. Mr. Finkel is fine, but his wife and son are in the hospital, recovering. They lived over their store, like you. The firefighters got them out just in time, but the store is burned to bits."

"My god, that's terrible! Do they know what caused it?"

"At this point, there are only rumors. In any event, the loss of Finkel's has left me with a problem I'm hoping you can solve. Before the unfortunate conflagration, Mr. Finkel had been filling prescriptions for me."

Irving could hear Mr. Stern's fitful cough. "What kind of prescriptions?"

"Whiskey—for medicinal purposes, of course. He filled one hundred prescriptions each week. I had asked for an increase to one hundred and fifty, but unfortunately, Mr. Finkel refused. I'm hoping you can be more accommodating."

Mr. Stern coughed again. "One hundred and fifty does seem excessive. Those prescriptions are being carefully monitored. I could lose my license—or the store."

"I don't need an answer now," cooed Mrs. Diamond. "Why don't you take some time to think it over? I like you, Sol. You're an excellent pharmacist. I would hate for you to face the same problems as poor Mr. Finkel."

Irving couldn't hear Mr. Stern's reply.

"Decisions like this require focus," said Mrs. Diamond. "And I know what a busy time this is. In a few days, both of our daughters are graduating from high school. I think we should talk next week, once the festivities are behind us. I'm sure that once you think it over, you'll see how beneficial our arrangement can be."

As the conversation came to a close, Irving scooted away from the door and pretended to rearrange the Sloan's Liniment bottles on the other side of the cash register. By the time Mrs. Diamond and Hank left the prescription room, Irving was busy helping a customer. Mrs. Diamond nodded at him and made her way out of the store.

Mr. Stern emerged ten minutes later, his eyes bleak, his face ashen. Irving would not bring up the marriage proposal today. Once again, that discussion would have to wait.

FORTY-NINE

OCTOBER 1987

After everyone was settled back in their seats, Augusta tried again to give her speech.

But this time, she was thwarted by the arrival of her birthday cake. The cake, covered with fondant roses and candles, was so enormous that it took two waiters to carry it properly. Its placement in the center of the table necessitated the hasty rearrangement of all the remaining silverware, plates, and collection of half-filled glasses.

"That cake is big enough for an army," said Irving.

"There goes my diet," Shirley said.

As Augusta did her best to blow out the candles, everyone in the room joined together in singing a chorus of "Happy Birthday." The cake was removed and carried to a sideboard, where the waiters cut and plated the slices.

Jackie lifted her glass and winked at Augusta. "May all of Augusta's birthday wishes come true." As the others raised their glasses, Irving eyed his suspiciously. Nathaniel threw back the rest of his drink and murmured something about taking Jackie up on her offer to give him a ride home.

"The cake is delicious," Augusta told her niece.

"Decadent," Shirley chimed in.

"This cake," said Nathaniel, his voice groggy and slurred, "is almost as sweet as Shirley."

Irving put a hand on Nathaniel's arm. "You all right there, Nathaniel? Hey—did you pick up my drink by mistake? I thought I had most of my Scotch left ..."

"Uh-oh," Jackie mumbled not so quietly. Augusta gave her a worried glance.

"Sorry about that," said Nathaniel.

"No problem," said Irving. "I need my wits about me. I'd actually like to say a few words."

Augusta felt her face turn hot. "I wanted to say something, too."

"You go first then. You're the guest of honor."

"No, no. That's silly. You can go first."

Suddenly Nathaniel stood from his seat. "I also have something to say." He turned to Shirley and put one hand on his heart. "Shirley, you're a wonderful woman. For weeks now, I've wanted to tell you so, but I've been struggling with my feelings. In all the years since Evie has been gone, I have never once looked at another woman, but now, with you—"

"NO!" Irving shouted, pounding his fist on the table with such force that the olive at the bottom of Augusta's martini glass quivered. "Are you *kidding* me with this crap, Nathaniel? After we had that whole talk? You're going to do this to me AGAIN?"

Nathaniel sank back into his chair, looking utterly confused. "What did I say? What did I do?"

"The same thing you did sixty-two years ago when I told you I was going to ask Augusta to marry me!"

Jackie's mouth fell wide open. Shirley placed one hand over her heart.

Augusta was the first to break the silence. "You were going to ask me to marry you?"

"Of course I was!" Irving shouted. "Until this ..." He pointed at

Nathaniel. "Until this *schmuck* stole my moment! And now, he's trying to do it again!"

Nathaniel lowered his head into his hands. "My god, Irving, I'm so sorry. I never dreamt . . . I had no idea. I never should have had that second glass of Scotch. Or the third, actually, if we're being technical. In fact, I really shouldn't drink at all, considering that the first time I caused all these problems, I downed everything in that flask . . ."

Shirley patted Nathaniel's hand. "Don't worry, everything will be fine. Let's get you a cup of coffee."

Augusta gripped the sides of her chair. "What flask was that, Nathaniel?" she demanded.

"A flask of whiskey—at least I think that's what it was. I swiped it from Irving on the night Evie and I got engaged."

Augusta crossed her arms over her chest. "Irving Rivkin, that was my father's best whiskey! I was very clear that it was for *you alone*."

"I *know*," said Irving. "But Nathaniel drank the whole damn thing before I could even get a sip."

"Wait a minute," Jackie said, a smile forming on the edges of her lips. "Irving, are you saying that you never drank what was in the flask Augusta gave you?"

"That's right."

"And now, tonight, you're telling us that Nathaniel took your glass of Scotch by mistake?"

"Yeah, and—"

Augusta let out a soft groan. She reached for the clutch beside her chair and opened it up to check the contents. It was just as she suspected—the pouch of powder was gone. "Jacqueline Esther Rosenthal, *what did you do?*"

Jackie shrugged. "When you spilled the water on Irving, I thought that was the signal."

"For goodness' sake, there *was no signal!*"

Jackie was the first to laugh. Next Augusta started giggling. Eventually the giggle turned into a howl until Augusta was doubled over in her seat. Her entire body began to shake. Despite their elegant surroundings, they were behaving like children at a circus.

Meanwhile, Irving was fuming. He frowned at Augusta and shook his head. "You know, I was finally going to tell you the truth tonight. I was going to tell you I *loved* you!"

The confession made Augusta laugh even harder, so that a trickle of tears ran down her cheeks—until the laughter subsided and her tears fell in earnest. A terrible clarity dawned on her as she grasped, perhaps for the very first time, exactly how much she did not know.

At the sight of her tears, Irving's face softened, and he walked around the table to embrace her. He took a handkerchief from his suit pocket and carefully dabbed the tears from her face. In his eyes, Augusta could finally see all the hurt he had suffered in all the years they'd been apart. "Why are you crying?" he whispered.

"Because, you *schmuck,* I love you, too."

Irving could feel his heart singing in his chest. He could smell Goldie's eucalyptus shampoo; he could taste the chocolate cake on her tongue. For about forty-five seconds while she was kissing him, he was the happiest man in the world.

He should have known it wouldn't last.

When she pulled away to catch her breath, he saw the white-hot flash of anger building in her still-wet eyes.

"Wait a second," she said as she struggled to catch her breath. "If you wanted to ask me to marry you, why did you walk away that night? Why did you cheat on me with Lois? How could you leave for Chicago without even saying goodbye?" She crossed her arms over her chest and took a step backward, away from him.

Irving had never told a soul the truth of what had happened—not his mother, not his brother, and especially not Augusta. For decades, fear had paralyzed him. Even after Zip and Mitzi died, he couldn't bring himself to recount the tale.

"It's a long story," Irving told her.

"So?" Augusta said, her arms still crossed. "I've got plenty of time."

"We have all the time in the world," said Shirley, waving over a passing waiter. "Excuse me, can you take away these glasses?" She nodded at a still-wobbly Nathaniel. "And please, bring everyone some coffee."

FIFTY

JUNE 1926

After starving herself for months, Lois Diamond must have been ravenous. Irving did not know the extent of her hunger or what she had eaten to break her fast. All he knew was that first thing in the morning, he was told to make an emergency delivery of Pepto-Bismol, Papoid Digestive Tablets, and aspirin to the house on Glenmore Avenue.

Sammy Diamond answered the door.

"Hey there, Sammy," Irving said, holding out the white paper bag. "I brought these for your sister."

"Thanks," Sammy said. "Are you coming over tonight to sit with my dad?"

"I've got tonight off," Irving said. "I've got a big evening planned, actually."

He did not mention the ring he'd been carrying in his jacket pocket every day that week—a slim gold band with a pearl at the center. It was a modest ring, nowhere near as splendid as the woman who would wear it. But at least the pearl and the gold were real, and nothing would fall off or tarnish. Irving promised himself that one day, he would buy Augusta a jewel that was worthy of her.

Back at the store, Solomon Stern was a wreck. Irving had been planning to tell him about the proposal and to ask him for his blessing. But Hank was sitting at the soda counter—supposedly nursing a chocolate malted, but really to serve as a reminder of Mitzi Diamond's quiet omnipotence. Irving wanted to reassure Mr. Stern and offer some words of support, but he did not want to confess that he'd eavesdropped on the conversation with Mitzi.

Irving didn't like keeping secrets—not from Mr. Stern and not from Goldie. He promised himself that once they were engaged, he would tell her everything—Lois's pregnancy, Mrs. Diamond's threats, everything she deserved to know. Meanwhile, Mr. Stern was in no state to hear about their plans for the future. They would have to secure his blessing after they were engaged.

The rest of the day sped by in a blur. Every so often, Irving's fingers would grip the pearl in his pocket. He ran his thumb along the rounded edges and tried to imagine how Augusta would react when he asked her to marry him. Would she whisper her answer or shout it loudly for everyone at Arcadia Gardens to hear? He did not care—all he wanted was for Augusta to say yes.

Before the restaurant, he and Nathaniel brought the girls to a popular speakeasy where the four of them shared a bottle of champagne. Irving was glad to leave the place—it was darker and grittier than he expected, and he had the feeling that nothing good would come of staying there for too long. Nathaniel didn't notice the danger—after his first glass of champagne, he became oblivious to the seedy men lurking in the darkened corners and the hard, overly rouged faces of the women sitting near them.

"It's time to go," Irving said when one of the men stared at Augusta for too long.

"But why?" said Nathaniel. "We're having fun."

"It's time for dinner," Irving told him. "The girls are hungry, and we need to go." He took Augusta by the hand, guiding the four of them up the steps and out of the subterranean room, and leading them all out to the street in search of a cab. Nathaniel was still protesting their departure, but after Irving pulled him aside and told him his proposal plans, he promised to be more cooperative.

Dinner and dancing at the restaurant followed. Everyone in Brooklyn knew Arcadia Gardens. For twenty years it had been the most elegant establishment in the borough. The dance floor was sunken in the center of the room so that diners could watch their fellow patrons gliding across the parquet. Brass table lamps added a golden glow and Tiffany-style windows in blues and greens adorned the wall behind the orchestra, dappling the room with rainbows of light.

Arcadia Gardens, like all its competitors, had suffered during Prohibition. Because it was not allowed to sell wine and cocktails, profits declined, and crowds fell off. At the time of Augusta and Irving's visit, the restaurant had lost some of its former glory. The table linens were threadbare in places; the once-polished floors were scuffed and dull. Still, to Augusta's and Irving's eyes, it was as lavish and sophisticated as a restaurant could be.

Although alcohol was not officially served, several of the patrons were under its influence. Everywhere Irving turned, he saw men pulling flasks out of their jackets and passing them under the table to their friends. Irving hadn't thought to bring any, so he was surprised when Augusta opened her purse and showed him the silver monogrammed flask. She handed it to him on the dance floor, where he tucked it into his pocket. "I brought you some of my father's best whiskey," she said. "It's only for you, though, not for sharing. I couldn't take much without him noticing."

"You didn't have to do that," said Irving.

"But you went to so much trouble to arrange tonight," she said. "I wanted to do something nice for you. Why don't you wait for me at our table—Evie is waving at me, and I think she wants company in the ladies' room."

At the table, when Irving showed Nathaniel the flask, the latter plucked it from his hands. Irving couldn't understand how two glasses of champagne had had such an effect on his friend, but Nathaniel definitely wasn't himself. He unscrewed the tiny cap on the flask and swallowed down every last drop. As he handed the flask back to Irving, he offered a sheepish apology. "Don't say anything to Augusta," Irving said. "She brought that whiskey for me."

When Evie and Augusta returned, the four of them ordered their dinner. Tuxedoed waiters served oysters, lamb chops, and lyonnaise potatoes from silver platters. They were in the middle of their meal when Nathaniel suddenly put down his napkin and asked Evie to dance with him.

Irving didn't think anything of it at first—in fact, he was glad to see them go. He was happy to be alone with Augusta, happy to have her undivided attention. He contemplated whether he should propose right then, while they had the table to themselves.

His thoughts were interrupted, however, when the entire restaurant began to applaud. There, in the center of the dance floor, was Nathaniel Birnbaum, down on one knee, asking Evie to marry him. She was wrapping her arms around his waist, and he was kissing her in front of everyone. The applause swelled and all the dancers cheered. The maître d' presented Evie with a single red rose.

Irving felt a crush of anger beating at him from inside his chest. *I told him* I *was going to propose. How could Nathaniel do this to me?*

Augusta sat up in her chair to see what all the fuss was about. "Is that . . . is that Nathaniel and Evie in the middle of the dance floor? Did he . . . did Nathaniel *propose?*"

Augusta flung her napkin on the table and ran down the steps to congratulate her friend. Irving watched the girls embrace, but he could not bring himself to join them. He could not congratulate Nathaniel in the wake of such betrayal. There was no way he could ask Augusta to marry him tonight. All his planning had been for nothing. His proposal would have to wait.

I need some air, Irving thought. *I need to calm myself down before I punch Birnbaum in the face.* He tried to push through the crowd of diners, all straining to see the couple on the dance floor, all trying to inhale some of the joy that filled the space like expensive perfume. The main entrance was blocked by the crowd, so Irving ducked out a side door that led directly into the alley.

When he got outside, the first breath he took was one of palpable relief. The air was warm, the sky was clear, and the June moon was as round and lustrous as the pearl waiting inside his pocket. It was a perfect summer evening.

Except for the body on the pavement.

There in the alley, lying faceup, was a man with a knife stuck into his throat. The man did not move, but his eyes were open, and his head rested in a pool of blood that expanded even as Irving watched. Irving's initial reaction was disbelief—he could not process what he was seeing. He bent down to get a closer look and felt the sharp barrel of a gun being pressed into the small of his back. Slowly he lifted both hands in the air.

"Irving?" said a smooth, familiar voice coming somewhere from his left. "Irving Rivkin, is that *you*?"

He was too stunned to answer out loud, but the voice continued. "It *is* you! Hank, put the gun away."

"Mrs. Diamond?" said Irving, afraid to move. He felt the bulky presence of the massive bodyguard behind him.

"Hank, I told you. Put the gun *away*."

Mitzi Diamond emerged from the shadows into Irving's line of vision. The streetlamp lit her up from above as if she were a Broadway star and the alley was the sordid stage that had been built for her alone. Despite the temperature, a black fur stole was wrapped loosely around her shoulders. She was still holding the white lace handkerchief she'd been using to wipe the blood from her manicured fingers. *Blood has never bothered me, young man.*

"You can put your hands down now, Irving," she said. "Tell me, what brings you here tonight? This is quite a swanky place—it must have been a special occasion."

"I was . . ." He tried not to stare at the body, but the face of the dead man was strangely familiar. "I was having dinner with my girlfriend. I was going to propose."

"Charming," said Mrs. Diamond gruffly. "But you didn't manage to ask her?"

"Excuse me?"

"You said that you were *going* to propose, implying that you hadn't yet. So what prevented you? What happened?"

"Oh that . . . there was another proposal. Another couple got engaged. Everyone in the restaurant was clapping for *them* and I felt like the timing wasn't right."

Mitzi Diamond began to pace back and forth in the narrow alley. "So much of life really *is* timing, isn't it? For instance, take a beautiful girl like my Lois. She goes to a party and meets this fellow, here." She pointed to the man on the ground by her feet. "*This* is Freddie Schechter, by the way. You might not recognize him, Irving, but he was also the boy who took your bicycle when you stood up for my Sammy all those years ago. That was the day I met you, remember?"

Irving nodded, but he did not speak. He couldn't believe that Freddie was *dead*. That Freddie would never speak again. Would never laugh. Would never breathe. Irving felt his legs weaken beneath him. He choked back the bile rising up in his throat.

"Now," Mitzi continued, "if Lois's timing had been different—if she'd gone to her friend's party a little bit later or skipped the gathering altogether—she might not have met Freddie Schechter and none of us might be here right now. *But* Lois *did* go to the party and she *did* meet Freddie, and they dated in secret because she *knew* how her father and I felt about him."

Mitzi Diamond's voice was low and hypnotic, the kind of voice that could keep a man frozen in place for as long as she wanted. "And then poor Lois's timing got worse. You're old enough to know about such things, Irving—women's cycles and all of that. My point is that if Lois's *timing* had been different, if she had been a tiny bit luckier, perhaps, Freddie might never have gotten her pregnant. Do you understand what I'm saying?"

Irving nodded again and Mrs. Diamond resumed her pacing.

"You know, that's something you and Lois have in common. You both have *terrible* timing. Look at what happened with your proposal. And then?" She gestured toward the ground. "Then you walked straight into all of *this*. Out of the frying pan and into the fire." She chuckled. "Honestly, your timing couldn't be worse."

As she rambled, Irving's thoughts were racing. A trickle of sweat slid down his neck. What was Mrs. Diamond going to do now? Was she going to kill him, too? Rough him up so he wouldn't talk? All of Solomon Stern's past warnings echoed like gunfire in his head.

Meanwhile Mrs. Diamond was mumbling under her breath, talking herself through her next move. Hank looked as if he were growing restless. He shifted his weight from side to side, stared up at the moon, and sighed.

"Am I *boring* you, Hank?" Mrs. Diamond growled.

Hank straightened his shoulders and planted his feet like a soldier at attention. "No, Mrs. Diamond. Absolutely not."

"Good," she said. "Because I'm *thinking*." The pacing continued for a few minutes more until finally Mrs. Diamond stood at ease. "How perfect," she said, sounding pleased with herself. "Honestly, I couldn't have come up with a better solution if I'd planned it this way from the beginning." She moved closer to Irving and patted his shoulder. Her smile sent a chill through his entire body.

"I take back everything I said about you, Irving. As it turns out, your timing is absolutely impeccable. What's more, you're one hell of a *mensch*. I knew it from the day I met you. I always told Zip you were one of the good ones."

"Thank you, ma'am. That's very nice, but—"

"We've known each other a long time, Irving. Zip and I have always been good to you, haven't we? Zip got you that bicycle. I helped you pick a new coat for your mother. And since you've started acting as Zip's companion, we've all become thick as *thieves*, haven't we?"

"I'm very grateful to you both for everything you've done—"

"In fact," said Mrs. Diamond, "it's almost like fate, the way that all of this worked out. Zip is going to be so pleased."

"I'm sorry, Mrs. Diamond, but I'm not following."

"No? Then let me try to explain. Lois is four months pregnant, Irving. Four months pregnant and unmarried." Mrs. Diamond kicked absent-mindedly at the tip of Freddie's shoe. "The father is in no position to marry her now—not since I got a bit *carried away* when he refused my suggestion. It was lucky I had my knife on me—Hank's gun would have caused too much of a ruckus in a neighborhood like this. In any event, my beautiful girl is now in need of a husband. And who better than you for the job? You're practically one of the family already."

Irving's arms and legs went numb. When he blinked, all he could see was darkness. He bit his lip until he tasted blood. "And what if . . . what if I say no?"

Mitzi Diamond's laugh was as lifeless as Freddie Schechter's open eyes. When she spoke, she used the same matter-of-fact tone most people used to discuss the weather. She counted off the gruesome possibilities on her still slightly bloodstained fingers. "Someone might break into your mother's apartment. Or your girlfriend might have some sort of accident—drivers these days never look where they're going, and people get run over all the time. Of course, there's always your boss's store. I know how much you love Stern's Pharmacy. It would be such a shame if it burned down—did you hear about Finkel's, by the way?"

FIFTY-ONE

OCTOBER 1987

As Irving described Mrs. Diamond's threats, Augusta reached for Jackie's hand. Nathaniel's face turned white as a sheet.

"What a monster!" Shirley said.

"Horrible!" Nathaniel agreed.

Jackie seemed less surprised than the others. And as always, she had questions. "So that explains why you married Lois. But why did the whole family leave for Chicago?"

"When Freddie Schechter's body was found, they found Mitzi's handkerchief in the alley. She'd thrown it into one of the garbage cans, but some overeager cop fished it out. She wasn't worried about going to jail—the Diamonds had too many judges on the payroll for that. But the handkerchief was monogrammed with her initials, and she worried that if they mentioned it in the papers, Lois would figure out who killed her boyfriend. To this day, Lois doesn't know it was her mother. Plus, Mitzi never liked Brooklyn anyway. She always wanted an excuse to go back to Chicago."

"My mother told me that after you moved, they left my grandfather alone," said Jackie. "None of the other racketeers in the neighborhood came within a block of the store."

"I struck a deal with Mitzi," Irving said. "In addition to marrying Lois, I promised never to tell her that her mother killed her boyfriend. Mitzi promised to leave Stern's Pharmacy alone. She told me she would spread the word that Solomon Stern and his family were off-limits."

While Irving talked, Augusta paced. She walked to the sideboard where the cake had been cut, then to the windows overlooking the courtyard. She lifted the champagne from the ice bucket and took a swig straight from the bottle. "You weren't in love with Lois," she murmured, trying to make sense of it all. "You weren't the father of those babies." She poured another swig of champagne down her throat before she turned to face him. "So why didn't you tell me the truth?"

Irving frowned. "I wanted to, but I couldn't risk it. Mitzi Diamond was a piece of work, but you were no shrinking violet, either. I knew that if you got wind of the truth, I wouldn't be able to stop you from confronting her. And that was too dangerous to think about. I could make my peace with your hating me. But not with Mitzi hurting you. You have no idea how brutal she could be."

"And the boys?" said Augusta. "You raised them as your own. Did you ever tell them?"

"Only after they were grown. Honestly, the boys were the easiest part. We had no idea Lois was having twins—there were no sonograms back then. But after they were born, Lois and I were both too busy and too tired to find enough energy to keep hating each other. My life didn't turn out the way I wanted, but Bill and Michael have always been the best part. I promised to keep working as Zip's companion, and Mitzi promised to keep the kids out of the family business. Like I told you, Michael became a doctor, and Bill teaches geometry."

Augusta's voice grew whisper soft. "But after Lois left you and the boys, why didn't you try to get in touch with me then?"

He hung his head. "I tried to see you, Goldie. I swear, I tried. I came back to New York for the Victory Parade back in 1946. Both of my boys were drafted in '45, but they never made it overseas. By that point, the war was almost over. It was their idea to meet in New York and go to the ticker-tape parade together. We spent that day in Washington Square, and then the next day, I took the subway to Brooklyn alone."

Irving looked up, his eyes finding Augusta's. "Brownsville was different from what I remembered. The stores were new, the sidewalks were filthy. I didn't recognize anyone. It didn't feel like home anymore. Still, I was determined to find you. I figured—what the hell—I'll try the store. For all I knew, you were still there."

Augusta's lips parted in surprise. "In '46? I *was* there then."

"I know," he said. "I saw both of you through the window."

"Both of who?"

"You and Jackie. At least, that's who I know it was now. But then, all I saw was you holding a little girl who had your dimples and your father's eyes. You were hugging her close to your chest and laughing. I knew—I was convinced—that the girl was yours."

"I used to go to the store all the time," said Jackie.

Augusta nodded. "She did." It dawned on her then—Irving's comment on the day they first met by the pool. "That's why you said you heard I had a daughter. You didn't *hear* it from anyone. You *saw* it with your own eyes."

Irving smiled sadly. "I figured you were a mother and a wife. I didn't want to blow up your life again. Not after everything that had happened and all the pain I'd already caused."

"Well, you were *wrong*," Augusta snapped. "Jesus, Irving. You were *so, so* wrong. We could have had so much more time. Think of all those years we wasted."

"I know," he said softly. "That was the first thing I thought of when you showed up here and said that you'd never married. I should have gone into the store that day. I don't know how to apologize for that." He took a tentative step toward her. "I wish I could go back and change the past, but we both know I can't do that, Goldie. All I can do is promise to love you for all the years that we have left." He reached out his arm and took her hand in his.

"It isn't too late for us," he promised.

Augusta could feel her heartbeat slowing. She could feel her breathing even out. This was the man who had always seen her, the one who had always encouraged her career. This was the man who'd said she was at her most beautiful when she was thinking. This was the man who'd saved her father's reputation from people who'd wanted to burn his store to the ground. The man who had carried her home in the snow, who had saved her book, who had put himself at risk just to save for a ring to make her his wife.

It isn't too late.

"I have to believe we were meant to find each other," said Irving. "I mean, of all the places you could have moved to, somehow you chose Rallentando Springs. If that isn't fate, I don't know what is."

"It wasn't fate, it was Jackie," Augusta said. "She's the one who sent me the brochure. If it hadn't been for her . . ." Augusta stopped in the middle of her sentence. She glanced at her niece, who looked away. "Jackie?" she said. "Jackie, did you . . . No. *No.* It isn't possible. You couldn't have known . . . there's absolutely no way."

"Surprise?" Jackie said with a sheepish smile. "Promise me you won't be angry."

Shirley clapped her hands together in a show of obvious delight. "Jackie, you are absolutely *marvelous!*"

"I don't understand," said Augusta. "How did you know where Irving lived?"

"I found out through Harold Glantz."

"Harold Glantz?"

Jackie nodded. "He's from Brooklyn, too, you know—Flatbush, though, not Brownsville. Anyway, you remember the second night of Passover, when Philip and I took the kids to his cousins? Harold and his wife were there. Harold's wife is related to Philip's cousin. Harold said he was from Flatbush, and when I told him that my parents grew up in Brownsville, he said his tennis partner did, too. Irving's name was in my head from everything Mom had told me, and the idea of *two* Irving

Rivkins seemed like too much of a coincidence. Harold said he lived in Rallentando Springs, so I called and asked for some brochures."

"What if Irving and I had ended up *hating* each other?"

Jackie shrugged. "I was willing to risk it." She turned to Irving and Nathaniel. "Since this seems to be the time for confessing secrets, it's probably best if I tell you *now* that I'm the one who spiked Nathaniel's drink. I meant to spike Irving's drink, of course, but we all saw how *that* turned out." Jackie released another bubble of laughter. "History keeps repeating itself with you two!"

"You spiked my drink?" Irving said. "What did you spike it *with*, exactly?"

"It's a long story," Augusta said.

"So?" said Irving. "I've got time."

FIFTY-TWO

OCTOBER 1987

For breakfast the next morning, Augusta and Jackie picked at Shirley's cherry Danish. Afterward, Augusta drove Jackie to the airport. While they were stuck in traffic on the turnpike, they went over the events of the previous evening in excruciating and hilarious detail.

"It was a birthday I'll never forget," said Augusta. "I can't believe that Nathaniel managed to drink Esther's elixir *twice*."

"I shouldn't have put the powder in Irving's drink," Jackie said. "Though, in my defense, when you spilled the water, I really did think you were giving me a signal."

"Maybe it was a good thing, in the end. Nathaniel confessing his feelings certainly made Shirley happy. And Irving seemed to understand when I explained about the elixir. I'm happy that he finally knows what I did all those years ago."

"You're not mad at me for tricking you into moving to Rallentando Springs?"

"How could I be mad? Besides, your scheme did a lot of good. It helped to solve a sixty-year-old mystery. It forced me to come to terms with my feelings. It gave me back the love of my life."

"When you put it like that, it sounds like I gave you the best birthday gift ever."

"That's exactly what you did."

"What do you think will happen now? With you and Irving, I mean?"

"We'll see," said Augusta. "God knows we're not young anymore, but hopefully we both have some good years left. Years we hope to spend together."

After saying goodbye to her niece, Augusta was in the mood for a swim. After all that had happened, she should have been tired, but the truth was, she felt more energetic than ever. She hadn't been in the water all weekend and her muscles were taut and restless. She put on her bright red bathing suit and headed over to the pool.

Irving was waiting for her. "I ordered you a turkey club," he said. "No mayo, chips on the side."

"Perfect," she said. "But I think I'll have a quick swim first. I could use some exercise."

"About that. I asked for the sandwiches to go. I thought we might try something different today—you know, in honor of your birthday."

"My birthday was yesterday."

"Yeah, well, when you hit the big eight-oh, I hear you get an extra day to celebrate. Anyway, I never got you a present, so I thought I'd take you for a little outing. When was the last time you went to the beach?"

Augusta felt the blood rushing to her cheeks. After all these years, did he still remember the conversation they'd once had?

With my mother gone, I don't feel as brave as I used to . . . I don't go to the beach anymore.

He gave her some time to let the question sink in, and while she pondered, a dozen more emerged. Was this what it felt like to be with someone who truly knew you? Who knew both the best and bleakest parts of your past? Was this what it meant to have someone support you, to have a companion who pushed you to be better and braver than you ever thought you could be? *Was this the magic her life had been missing?*

"Not since my mother died," she whispered.

"They got beautiful beaches down here," said Irving, holding out a wrinkled hand. "What do you say you and I go and have ourselves a little picnic? We'll eat our lunch and look at the water, and then if we're feeling brave, we'll jump in."

The water was warmer than Coney Island; the sand was softer between her toes. It shifted a bit beneath her feet, but it didn't feel as unsteady as she remembered. Above them, the sky was a clear cobalt blue. The clouds were as light and as fluffy as the kreplach in Aunt Esther's soup.

The two of them floated on their backs together, side by side, holding hands. The waves were gentle, lazy rollers, lapping sweetly at their ears. When they'd had enough of staring skyward, she pointed to the nearest marker—a red-and-white buoy about fifty feet away. "Do you want to race me?" she said.

"Nah. Let's just swim over. You go first and I'll be right behind you." Before she set off, Irving reached for her hand. "It looks like there might be a couple of waves out there, Goldie. Are you sure you want to swim out that far?"

Augusta Stern nodded her head and smiled. "I'm positive," she said. "If there are waves, we'll swim around them together."

OCTOBER 1988

Augusta Stern eased out of bed a few minutes after midnight.

Irving opened a single eye. "Are you working tonight?"

"Yes," said Augusta. "Dora Shapiro is coming over in the morning. You should go back to sleep."

"Happy eighty-first birthday, Goldie," he murmured before blowing her a kiss and rolling over.

From the hook on her bedroom door, Augusta removed a short silk robe and slipped it over her nightgown. Although it was blue, it was different from Esther's—lighter, less structured, unembellished.

On her way to the kitchen, Augusta passed a credenza where Esther's brass mortar and pestle were displayed along with her father's *U.S. Pharmacopeia* and a framed photograph of her and Irving on the porch of Nathaniel's house in Maine. Augusta lit a few candles and placed the brass mortar in the center of her kitchen table. Although it was late, she wasn't tired.

A few months after her eightieth birthday, Harold Glantz had pulled her aside after Book Club. Gail, his wife, suffered from arthritis, and was in the middle of a painful flare-up. She'd seen her rheumatologist twice, but the medicine was no longer working. When Harold mentioned it to Irving, Irving had said that Augusta might be able to help.

"What did you tell Harold about me?" she'd asked Irving later that evening.

"I said that you were the best pharmacist in New York City. And I may have mentioned that you have a special talent for unconventional treatments."

"That's what you said? *Unconventional treatments?*"

Irving shrugged. "I thought you might want to take the old mortar and pestle out for a spin. Was I wrong?"

"It's too late to start all that up again."

But Irving had pulled her into his arms and kissed her with the fervor of a man half his age. "How many times do I have to tell you? It isn't too late for *anything*, Goldie."

"Do you really think it's a good idea?"

He'd winked at her then, those roguish blue eyes twinkling. "Remember how I loved watching you do your homework? You don't want to deprive an old man of that pleasure, do you?"

After Augusta's success with Gail, Rose Hoffman called about her psoriasis and Brenda Martin cornered Augusta at the pool to ask about her palpitations. "I've seen three cardiologists," said Brenda, "but every single one of them says that it's nothing."

There were so many women who wanted her help, so many women who felt overlooked by their doctors. *They see an old woman with gray hair,* said Brenda, *and they assume we're all exaggerating. Meanwhile, when my husband goes for his appointment, they treat his cold like it's the bubonic plague!*

Augusta couldn't disagree. And so, when the requests grew too numerous to ignore, she found herself in business once again. Most often, she compounded her mixtures during the day, but sometimes, like the evening of her eighty-first birthday, she chose to work in the hours after midnight, just as her great-aunt had once done. On those nights, Augusta immersed herself in her memories until she felt like a young girl in Brooklyn again.

Now, outside the windows of Augusta's apartment, a sprinkling of stars shone in the southern sky. She made a pile of dried valerian, chamomile, dogwood, lavender, and peppermint. Dora Shapiro had acute insomnia, and Augusta was hopeful that she could offer some relief. After checking her ingredients, Augusta placed them in the mortar, ground them carefully with Esther's pestle, and chanted the familiar words.

To ease the pain of those who suffer
To repair the bodies of those who are ill
To restore the minds of those in need

How good it felt to hold the mortar; how reassuring it was to feel the weight of that familiar object in her hands. As Augusta pressed the pestle into the sides of the bowl, she thought about the women who had come before her and all the good they had done.

The melody came to her easily then, and she sang the words in a soft, clear voice. She sang for the second chance she'd been given and for the confidence she had regained. She sang for the work she had always loved and for the man who appreciated her as she truly was. She sang for the present and the future, for all the bright days that lay ahead.

When she was done, Augusta could feel the potency of the powder lingering in the evening air. She emptied it into a muslin square, tied the pouch with cotton string, and left it near the toaster oven. In the morning, she would give it to Dora and tell her to drink it in a cup of warm water. Later, she and Irving would telephone Jackie, and after that, they'd have dinner with Shirley and Nathaniel. They would celebrate not only Augusta's birthday, but her anniversary with Irving.

After eighty-one years and two failed love elixirs, Augusta Stern knew exactly who she was—a woman of science like her father, an old-world healer like her aunt. She believed in medicine and in miracles. She believed in family and in love. She believed in the power of moonlight in kitchens, in the power of women, in the power of words. She believed that even on life's darkest days, a bowl of chicken soup could offer comfort.

She believed that the world still held a bit of magic for those who were patient and wise enough to wait.

AUTHOR'S NOTE

I first heard about my husband's great-grandmother over thirty years ago. Married to a pharmacist who died unexpectedly when she was only in her twenties, Goldie Litvin decided to get a pharmacy degree so she could run the store she inherited. In 1921, she was one of just a few women to graduate from Fordham's School of Pharmacy. My husband's mother, Carol Loigman, spoke often of her grandmother's razor-sharp mind, her wondrous diagnostic skills, and her devotion to both her family and career. Goldie ran her Bronx store for decades, and when she gave it up, she worked decades more as a hospital pharmacist in Manhattan. Because she didn't want to retire, she doctored the date on her pharmacy license so no one would know her real age. Her given name, I learned only recently, was not Goldie but Augusta.

The idea of a book about Goldie was in the back of my mind for years. But to be honest, it wasn't Goldie herself that I felt the urge to explore on the page. As impressed as I was with what I knew of the woman, it was her drugstore—the 1920s pharmacy setting—that captivated my imagination. I liked to picture the store's prescription room, with shelf after shelf of neatly labeled bottles, shining brass scales, and compounding tools. When

I closed my eyes, I saw girls in long skirts sitting at the soda counter, sipping egg creams.

I tucked this idea for a setting away and drew it out again only after I had completed my third novel, *The Matchmaker's Gift*. In that novel, I fulfilled a long-held wish to add some magical realism to my writing. What better place than a pharmacy, I thought—with all of its powders, potions, and tinctures—to serve as a backdrop for another such story? My problem, of course, was that atmosphere alone isn't enough to create a novel. Who were the characters populating the world that I wanted to create? I only hoped that as I began my research, the inspiration for them would find me.

In the meantime, I had plenty keeping me busy. My eighty-four-year-old father, who lived in southern Florida, had recently been hospitalized. Following his release, it became clear that he could no longer live on his own. After touring half a dozen assisted-living facilities, we finally chose one in Boca Raton. The entire process—from convincing him to move, to cleaning out his condominium, to leaving him alone in an unfamiliar place—was both heartbreaking and stressful. Ultimately, what got us all through the transition was the kindness and the humor of his fellow residents.

My father was an incredibly social person. He loved good gossip—romantic or otherwise. The fact that he couldn't cross a room without a walker in no way diminished this part of his personality. After my mother died in 2007, my father had several long-term girlfriends. His last relationship ended before his move, but from the way he threw himself into the social affairs of his new community, I knew he was hoping to find someone else, to find the companionship we all desire.

During my periodic visits to Florida, I would sit with my father in his favorite place—the first-floor lobby of his building—where groups of men and women (mostly women) would gather to talk and tell stories. This was where the dirt was spilled, and this was where my father wanted to be. Sometimes I participated in the conversation, but most of the time, I sat and listened.

It was there, in the carpeted lobby of a Boca Raton assisted-living facility, that the voices of my characters, Augusta Stern and Irving Rivkin, found me. It was there that I realized who they would be, the history they would share, and the mistakes they would make. I remember thinking how funny it would be if one of my father's former girlfriends ended up living in his building. How much aggravation would that cause and how much drama would ensue? What if it wasn't a recent girlfriend who arrived, but someone he had loved decades earlier? What if he had never married my mother, but carried the anguish of an enigmatic lost love from his twenties into his eighties ... until the mystery woman showed up again when he least expected it?

My editor, Sarah Cantin, is not only brilliant but has the patience of a saint. She waited—first as I wrote one hundred lackluster pages about assisted-living residents, and then as I droned on about 1920s pharmacies, the discovery of insulin, and the curative powers of chicken soup. She encouraged me as I overexplained my title idea, inspired by O. Henry's marvelous short story "The Love-Philtre of Ikey Schoenstein"—the tale of a jealous night-shift pharmacist and a false love potion comically administered. Then, she continued to wait and to encourage me until I finally found a way to combine my hodgepodge of ideas into what eventually became *The Love Elixir of Augusta Stern*. I will be forever grateful.

My research began with the book *Corner Druggist* written by Robert B. Nixon, Jr., in 1941 about his father's career. It was here that I came to understand the early pharmacist's role as advisor, therapist, and confessor. The patient anecdotes in this memoir helped me portray Solomon Stern's role accurately. I then turned to *Drugstore Memories: American Pharmacists Recall Life Behind the Counter, 1824–1933*, edited by Glenn Sonnedecker, David L. Cowen, and Gregory J. Higby, and *A Pharmacist's Memoirs: Fifty Years of Ukrainczyk's Brighton Pharmacy* by Julius Lichtenfeld. I found *Magic in a Bottle*, by Milton Silverman, Ph.D., to be incredibly helpful in understanding the way that various categories of popular early drugs were viewed by those in the medical profession.

I am lucky to have a wonderful local pharmacy of my own—Drug

Mart in Millwood, New York, where the owner, Richard Glotzer, was kind enough to connect me with his father, pharmacist Ira Glotzer. Born in 1937, Ira told me about his early days as a stock boy and delivery boy at a drugstore in Brooklyn. He explained his fascination with the field and gave me some insight into the kinds of tasks Solomon Stern would have given his young daughter. Richard also put me in touch with his cousin, Ira Rabinowitz, who spoke to me at length about the kinds of work hospital pharmacists do. Dr. Steve Covey was also an invaluable resource regarding doctor and patient interactions with hospital pharmacists.

In order to better set the scene for Stern's Pharmacy, I scoured eBay for early editions of *American Druggist* magazine and found several editions close to the time period I wrote about. In the pages of this magazine I found advertisements for all of the products Stern's Pharmacy might have carried on its shelves, as well as all of the equipment Solomon Stern might have used. I was also able to procure a copy of *Eventide: The American Druggists' Syndicate Home Monthly* from August to July 1908, the 1938 *American Druggist Pharmacy Handbook*, and an 1897 copy of *The Standard Formulary* published by G. P. Engelhard & Co. Together, these sources helped me bring the world of Stern's Pharmacy to life.

To amplify the details of living in Brownsville, I turned to the following sources: *Brooklyn in the 1920s (Images of America)* by Eric J. Ierardi; *Brownsville: The Birth, Development and Passing of a Jewish Community in New York* by Alter F. Landesman; and *Brownsville, Brooklyn: Blacks, Jews, and the Changing Face of the Ghetto* by Wendell Pritchett.

Anyone who knows me knows how much I love a good gangster story. In order to flesh out Zip and Mitzi Diamond, I read both *The Rise and Fall of the Jewish Gangster in America* by Albert Fried and *Our Gang: Jewish Crime and the New York Jewish Community, 1900–1940* by Jenna Weissman Joselit. I also found a 1922 article from *The Saturday Evening Post* called "Inside the Bootleg," which was helpful in understanding how a bootlegger might start his or her business.

In order to build Esther's role in the story, I wanted to learn more about Jewish folklore and mysticism. For this I turned to *A Time to Be*

Born: Customs and Folklore of Jewish Birth by Michele Klein. I also found great inspiration in the following additional sources: "Some Observations on Jewish Love Magic: The Importance of Cultural Specificity" by Ortal-Paz Saar in *Societas Magica*; "Magic Bowls of Antiquity" by Samuel Thrope in *Aeon Psyche*; and "Who Wrote the Incantation Bowls?" by Dorit Kedar, submitted in partial fulfillment of the requirements for the degree of philosophy to the Department of History and Culture Studies at Freie Universität Berlin. These works helped me create Esther's mortar as a modern-day incantation bowl—a kind of magical amulet with a formula written along its inner walls.

The Love Elixir of Augusta Stern is a reminder that age doesn't change who we are, that second chances are always possible, and that it is never too late to try to recapture the lost magic of our youth. It is a story that explores whether ambition and love can ever truly co-exist, and whether a woman can have both a profession and a partnership (I hope Augusta shows that she can). It is a story of inexplicable talent, of a gift handed down through generations, the kind of gift that makes the women who wield it seem problematic—and even dangerous—to the insecure men around them.

In the end, I owe the heart of this novel to my husband's parents and to my father. The manuscript was written between two immense losses—the death of my father-in-law, Barry Loigman, in June 2022 and the death of my own father, Harris Cohen, in June 2023. Regardless of whether you knew either man, I'd like to think you'll find the spirit of both of them within the pages of this story.

ACKNOWLEDGMENTS

Thank you to my readers for their support and for welcoming my words into their hearts.

Thank you to my agent, Marly Rusoff, for her kindness and her confidence. Thank you to Mihail Radulescu. Your sweetness and humor will always be remembered.

Thank you to my brilliant editor, Sarah Cantin, for all of the time and attention she lavished on this manuscript. Sarah's generosity and gift for storytelling is unmatched. A thousand thanks to the entire team at St. Martin's Press: Jennifer Enderlin, Lisa Senz, Anne Marie Tallberg, Drue VanDuker, Katie Bassel, Rivka Holler, Brant Janeway, Michelle McMillian, Michael Storrings, Ginny Perrin, Chris Leonowicz, Lizz Blaise, Nikolaas Eickelbeck, Nancy Inglis, Amelie Littell, and Susannah Noel.

Thank you to my mother-in-law, Carol Loigman, for answering my questions about the *real* Goldie and for sharing her memories with me. Thank you to Richard Glotzer, Ira Glotzer, Ira Rabinowitz, and Dr. Steve Covey for their assistance in navigating the details of this story. Thank you to Leslie Powell for all of your help.

Thank you to the early reviewers of this book for taking the time to read the manuscript and for their kindness in recommending it.

Endless gratitude to my Thursday Author sisters. You are not only the wind beneath my wings, but you are the ink in my printer, ladies.

I have so many author friends to thank, but I am honestly afraid to begin listing names for fear of leaving someone out. I am grateful to all of you, my creative family, for your camaraderie and encouragement.

Thank you to the Jewish Book Council for all it does to ensure that Jewish stories survive.

Thank you to the booksellers, the reading group leaders, the bloggers, the Instagrammers, and the TikTokers. Your support means the world.

Thank you to all of my friends and family, especially the ones who indulge me when I get that faraway look in my eye . . .

All of my love to Bob, Ellie, and Charlie, my favorite people in the world. I am so grateful for you.

ABOUT THE AUTHOR

Randi Childs

Lynda Cohen Loigman is the author of *The Matchmaker's Gift*, *The Wartime Sisters*, and *The Two-Family House*. She received a B.A. in English and American literature from Harvard College and a J.D. from Columbia Law School. She grew up in Longmeadow, Massachusetts, and now lives in New York.